Enjoy!
Frankye Craig

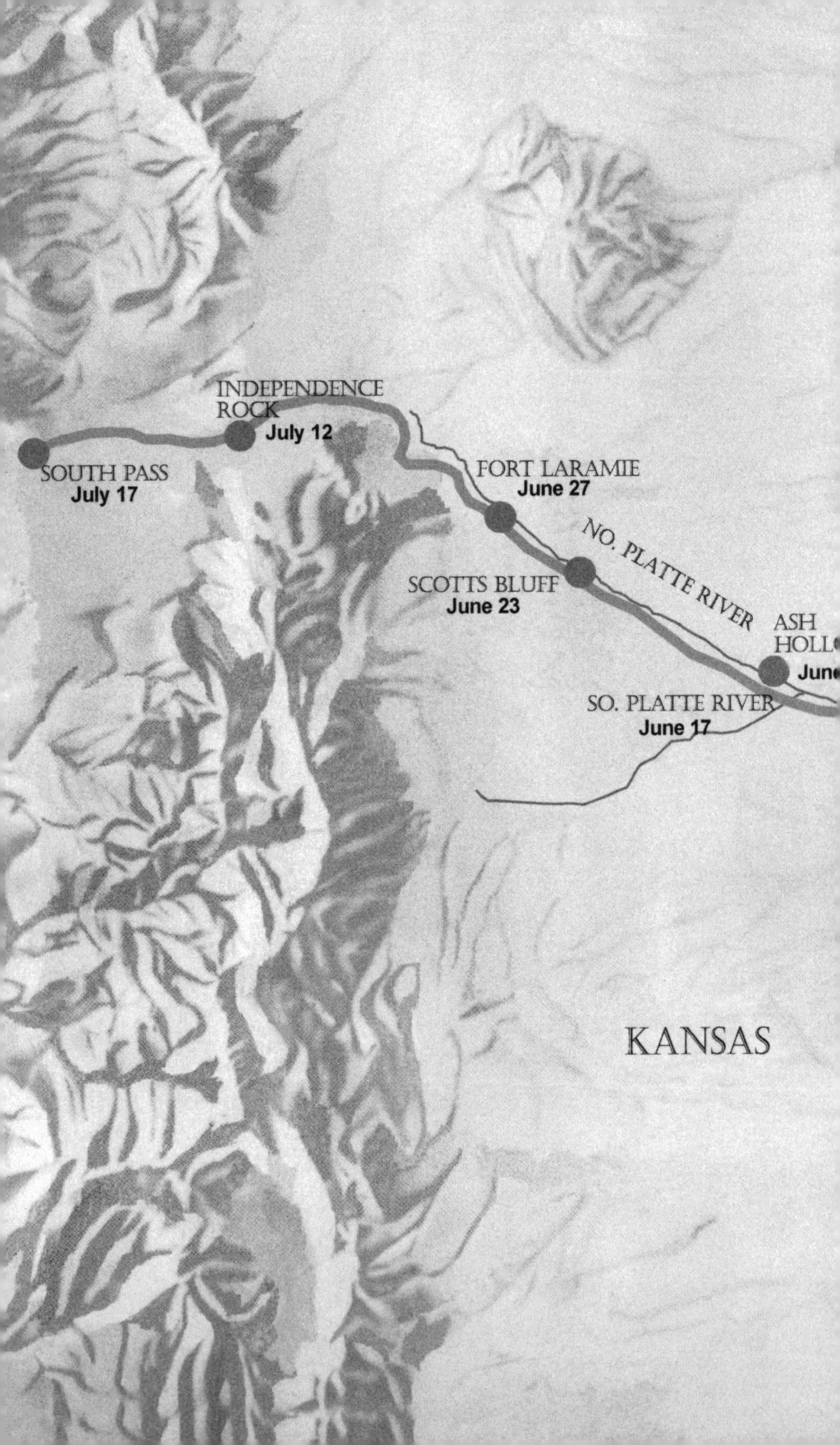
INDEPENDENCE ROCK
July 12
SOUTH PASS
July 17
FORT LARAMIE
June 27
NO. PLATTE RIVER
SCOTTS BLUFF
June 23
ASH
SO. PLATTE RIVER
June 17
KANSAS

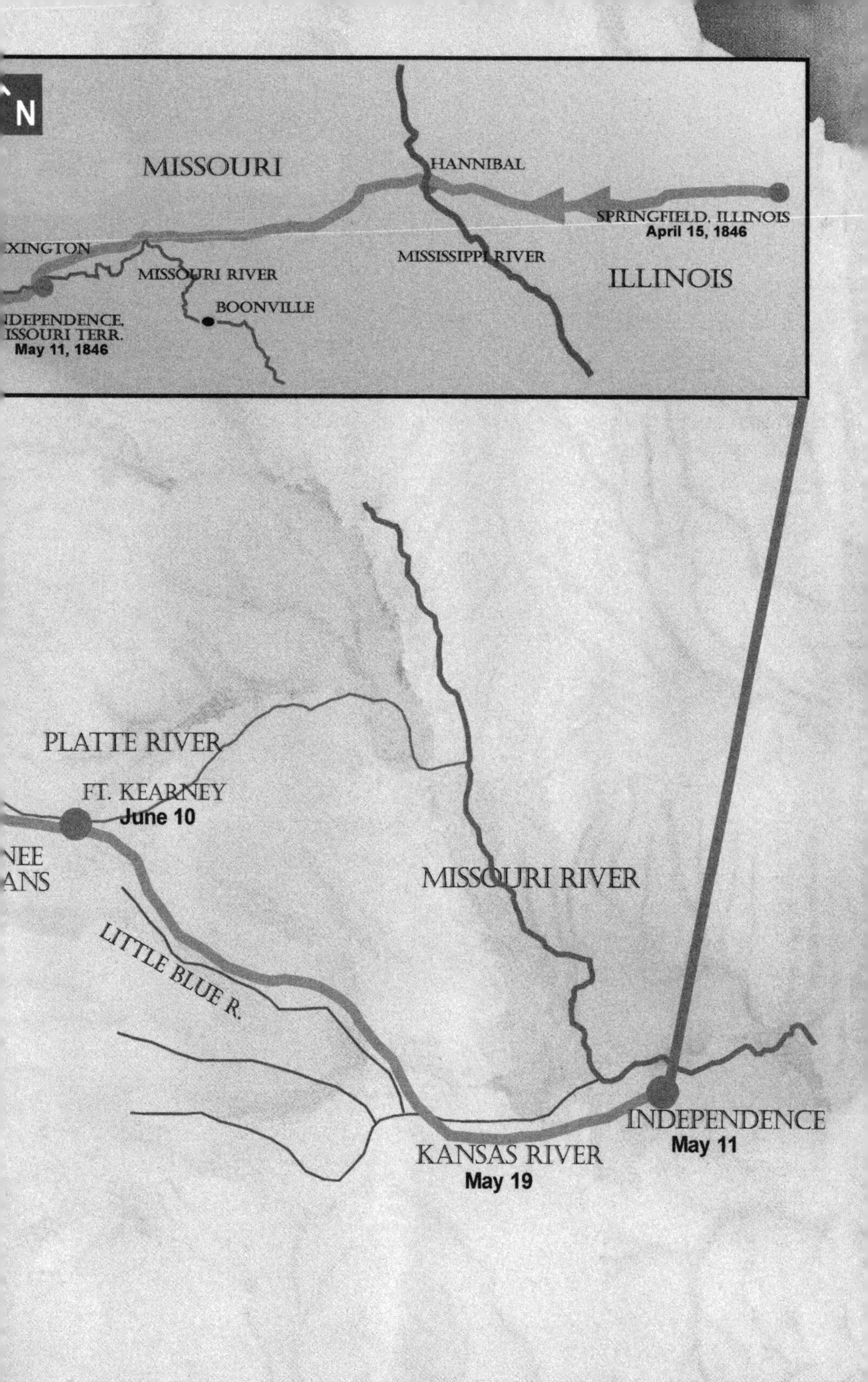
N
MISSOURI
HANNIBAL
SPRINGFIELD, ILLINOIS
April 15, 1846
XINGTON
MISSISSIPPI RIVER
MISSOURI RIVER
ILLINOIS
BOONVILLE
IDEPENDENCE,
ISSOURI TERR.
May 11, 1846
PLATTE RIVER
FT. KEARNEY
June 10
NEE
ANS
MISSOURI RIVER
LITTLE BLUE R.
INDEPENDENCE
May 11
KANSAS RIVER
May 19

The Fateful Journey Of Tamsen Donner

The Fateful Journey Of Tamsen Donner

Frankye Craig

21st-Century Publishing
Henderson, Nevada

The Fateful Journey Of Tamsen Donner

Published by 21st-Century Publishing

ISBN: 0-9722624-6-6

Cover Illustration: Diana Monfalcone
Interior Design and Production: R.L. Rivers

1st Printing: April 2006

This book is dedicated to the members of the Donner Party and their descendants.

Contents

Author's Note

I became interested in the saga of the Donner Party while putting together the Donner Party sesquicentennial event in 1996. Since then I have become acquainted with descendants and many Donner Party researchers, historians, and writers. I have experienced the usual frustrations; there is very little first-hand information on the details of the entrapment in the Sierra and even less about the happenings in the Donner Family camp.

During and after the rescues, the horror of the conditions and the loss of life in the camps became titillating news and these accounts painted a grotesque and unfair picture. Some of these accounts carried down through the years and became the basis for much of the literature. Those who recognize the name Donner will in the same instant think of cannibalism. That is an occurrence; not the story.

I have taken the basic facts from various accounts of that time for the historical framework and added deduction and logic to make the story whole in the mind of the reader. It is my hope that this book will give the reader a humane and empathetic perspective toward all the members of that unfortunate group.

I greatly credit the researchers and writers, both contemporary and past, who have done the deep research that has brought to light information not only on the Donner Party, but on the history and people of the great migration of 1846.

January 1, 2006
Alder Creek

The wind keens and moans, blasting snow and ice across the meadow, carving the tops of snow drifts into graceful undulating lines. A hawk banks and circles against the clear blue sky. Nothing else stirs except nature. It is cold and it is beautiful. Here, covered by the crisp sparkling dunes of snow and a century-and-a-half accumulation of dirt and forest debris, lie the bones of George Donner, Jacob Donner, Betsey Donner, and the others who perished here.

I am Tamsen Donner, the wife of George Donner. It has been a long time since I resided in that domain of existence, but the events are still seared upon my soul. By your count, it was the year of 1846. Most of the souls from that time and place have gone on, but I could not; I have stayed close. My energies and thoughts went out to my daughters—alone, bewildered, bereaved of their loving parents. With them I suffered from the cruelty and the meanness of the horrible things that were said about those who escaped from the prison in the mountains.

Some people, in their safety and smugness, have criticized

us. But what do they really know of our story? Do they know that we were, for months, trapped in deep snow? That we huddled in miserable huts that never allowed us the comfort of being warm or dry, our food supplies dwindling day by day and then totally gone? Could they know the anguish we felt as we watched our families, our children, and our friends slowly sicken and die? From this non-earthly plane it is of nothing, but in that existence it was torment and excruciating pain.

The hands that have written our history have not been good or kind and much of our story has been taken from fantastic, lurid accounts in the newspapers of the time. Later writers took parts from these accounts and made of them what they wanted. I assure you, the plain facts were sufficiently horrible that they needed no embroidery.

Yes, it is true that some of us had food and did not share. It is true that some of us did eat the flesh of our dead. We had hard choices to make and we made them in order that we, and ours, might survive.

When Mr. McGlashan, a newspaperman and writer, became interested in our story some thirty years after the terrible ordeal, the pain my daughters felt when they were asked to talk of that horrible winter in the mountains called me once again to the earthly abode. They did not want to relive the most painful part of their lives, but eventually they, and most of the others, came to trust Mr. McGlashan and the stories came out. Not all of them told the true story. Some who talked of the ordeal had forgotten how it really was or they wanted the story to be told in a different way. Several felt that some things were best left up there in the mountains. Mr. McGlashan took it all down and began to understand the deep complexities of the events and the people. He had compassion and decided he would not tell everything he had been told.

Now, in these later years, once again the seekers come, researching, debating, excavating. They walk the trail where we walked. They search the ground where we camped. They try to find us, seeking to learn what they do not know, looking for clues that will bring us closer. They want to pull aside the misty curtains of time that drape our story, but I want to close those curtains for all time. I am a guide, a teacher, and I want to get back to my work here in this realm, a realm that most in the earthly form cannot comprehend.

I will tell you of the fateful journey. I will write it down and then I will go on. I will not come back again. The story happened within a realm of consciousness that was Tamsen Eustis Donner's: wife of George Donner, mother of Eliza, Georgeanna, and Frances, and step-mother to Elitha and Leanna. One member of a company of people on their way to California.

April, 1846
Springfield, Illinois

The day was cold and dreary and my mood was somber as I watched our young hired man, Noah, stride to the front of the wagon and shout the command to start. The wagon lurched and began to move, creaking as the wheels rolled over the uneven ground. The oxen murmured and rolled their heads, trying to get comfortable in their yokes. Sitting beside me on the wagon seat was our youngest, Eliza, who was just three, and peering over our shoulders were her sisters, Georgeanna, four, and Frances, six.

The older girls, George's daughters by a previous marriage, Leanna and Elitha, twelve and fourteen, had gone on ahead with our other two wagons earlier in the day.

An hour before, I walked for the last time over the grounds and then through the Illinois home in which I'd lived since I'd married George Donner seven years before. I'd sat down in my rocking chair beside the big fireplace and poked at the cold ashes, trying to get my emotions under control. *These ashes are almost as cold as my heart,* I thought. The tears that I'd been holding back now streamed down my face. I hated crying but could not stop. *There's no turning back now. The homestead is sold, the wagons are loaded, and all is in readiness to leave. Except for me.*

As I rocked I could hear the men outside catching up and yoking the six oxen that would pull our family wagon. The wagon was loaded and ready to go, but I could tell from the sounds coming from the yard that the oxen were not too anxious to start their work. I could hear George yelling at them.

"Damn it, get in there. Noah, head 'em off! Godamighty, that ox is a blockhead!" *How I wish George would stop using swear words!*

The commotion continued for several minutes, but finally subsided. George came into the house knocking his hat against his leg and stomping his feet to get the dust off. He pulled a handkerchief out of his pocket and wiped his face.

"I'm gonna kill that dumb ox if'n he don't stop balking like that. I'm out'a patience. I'd lay him out right now 'cept I ain't got no replacement."

"Except I do not have a replacement," I corrected.

George ran his hands through his thick black hair. "The children are in the wagon. We're ready to go."

"Let me get some clean clothes for you out of the wagon. Don't you want to change?"

"No. I want to get on the road. We're late gettin' started as it is," he growled.

"George, what if this doesn't turn out the way we hope? What if you or I should sicken or have an accident? What would happen to our children with no family to take them? We'll be so far away."

"Tamsen, stop frettin'. We've done everythin' we can to prepare. We have the best wagons, good men to drive an' plenty of supplies. What do you think could go wrong?"

"I don't know. I just have a terrible apprehension. I wish I hadn't given in ..."

George looked at me, hands on his hips and exasperation on his face. "This is one hell of a time to start that."

I was forming a reply in my mind, but gave it up. *Why is it that I am balking now, like Buster the ox? Is it because there's no good reason to leave? Oh, yes, the salubrious climate. What were the other reasons?* I shook my head, trying to get my thoughts gathered, wrapped up, and tucked away again in some far recess of my mind, not to be released to whittle away at my resolve.

"I'm sorry, George. I guess I'm just having some last-minute jitters." I sighed and stood up, pointing to the chair. "I've had to leave so much that is dear to me. This was my mother's chair and I've rocked all my babies in it. It has to go."

"Tamsen, there's no room for it. I've gone along with all the stuff you piled up to take. All those heavy books!"

"George—"

He held up his hands. "I'm sorry, honey. But how do you think we can get it in?"

"This chair has to go with us or I'm going to sit down in it and wave good-bye as you go through the gate."

"Godamighty!" George picked up the chair and walked out to the wagon. "Noah, move that there beddin' an' see if you can get this in there. We'll have to take the damn thing out ever' time we need to get in the wagon."

"George! Please stop using swear words!"

As the wagon rolled through the gate, sadness clutched at my heart. I looked at the farm as we turned into the road and passed along our fence line. The sturdy log and stone house, anchored by its two chimneys, would not have our family to warm and protect ever again. The children would never laugh and play in the big barn and we would never again taste of the bounty from our orchard. The field where George had raised many fine horses would never again hear him whistling for them to come to him. My throat constricted and I fought a new onslaught of tears.

George was walking beside the wagon and I saw that he also was looking at the homestead. He looked up at me.

"It's hard to leave, but we need to think ahead to the new life in California."

Yes, the new life in California. I did agree to go, and truly, I am excited about it. But something is depressing my spirit. I cannot deny it.

Eliza snuggled closer, holding my hand tightly. I smiled at her as I wiped my tears away. George seemed melancholy too, but he would quickly shrug it off; the anticipation of new places, new experiences, and new opportunities would quickly overcome his sadness. Not so for me.

I was shocked when George had come home one day and talked of removing to the Pacific lands. I was against it, and why not? We were well established and had friends and family all around us. But George had a penchant for moving on. He'd already moved several times from place to place. Born in North Carolina, he and his family had moved west in stages. Kentucky, Indiana, Illinois. A year in Texas, but Texas didn't suit him. Now, it seemed that the rhythms of maturity were primed for another change. George, at sixty-two, wanted to yonder again.

It was a frightening thing to contemplate, this journey to California. The route was a new one and there was no road, just a trace here and there. We would travel across two thousand miles of mostly unknown wilderness, through the territory of the wild and savage Indians where so many dangers might await us. After leaving the Missouri Territory, we would find rare vestige of civilization for hundreds and hundreds of miles, and those would only be crude fur traders' forts, peopled by a few white men who were half-savage themselves.

Joining us for the long journey were four young men: Noah James, who was now driving our family wagon, Samuel Shoemaker, Hiram Miller, and John Denton. The three men had left earlier with our other two wagons and would be waiting for us at the meeting place in Springfield, two-and-a-half miles away. The young teamsters would be working for us to earn their passage to California. They were looking forward to the adventure, to seeing the new land that was being so romantically touted. The two older girls had gone ahead with the teamsters and their half-brother William, George's son by his first wife. William would go as far as the last settlements to help herd our extra livestock.

After we'd gone about a mile, we could see the white-topped wagons belonging to Jacob, George's brother, turning into the road up ahead.

Although Jacob, at fifty-nine, was younger than George, he seemed older. Jacob didn't have the physical strength and size that George had. George was more than six feet and strongly built, while Jacob was four inches shorter and spare in frame. He was different from George in his appearance too, with light sandy-colored hair and blue eyes, while George was dark-haired with brown eyes. George usually had a mild and pleasant manner, but Jacob was oft-times nervous and grouchy. He suffered from some sort of weakness, perhaps of the heart. His wife Elizabeth, whom we always called Betsey, was several years younger than Jacob. Betsey was tall and thin, with reddish hair and pale freckled skin. They had seven children. Their two oldest, Solomon and William Hook, in their teen years, were Betsey's sons by a previous marriage. The five younger were George Jr., Mary, Isaac, Samuel, and Lewis.

When we stopped to greet them, the girls jumped down from the wagon and ran off to see their cousins. Betsey approached our wagon with Lewis in tow.

"Betsey," I said, "I have lunch for everyone. If George will stop long enough, we can spread some quilts on the ground."

George was checking the wagons and heard my suggestion. "No, we ain't stopping. Just hand the food out and we can eat as we're movin'. I've got a lot to do before night."

Betsey shaded her eyes with her hand and looked up at me. "You been cryin', Tamsen?" she asked. "I thought of all of us, you'd be the last one to cry. I done got mine over with. I'm plumb tuckered out. I worked half the night tryin' to get everythin' done. The new owner came in yesterday, wantin' us to tell him all this stuff, like how to do this an' that. I told him if'n he didn't know more'n that, he shouldn't be buyin' a farm. Then he starts fussin' that we was carrying off stuff he thought he'd bought with the farm. We left so much as it was. Half our stuff didn't sell, with nobody havin' any cash money." She looked at me alarmed. "I've got to head to the bushes. I think all the goin's on has affected my insides."

"Betsey," I called to her as she dashed for the woods, "put your bonnet on. You'll burn after being indoors all winter."

The men palavered awhile and decided to move Jacob's loose stock along in front of the wagons instead of behind. As they rounded up the stock, I opened my picnic basket and handed out food to everyone.

"Frances, find the girls and bring them. We'll eat in the wagon. Father is ready to move along."

We had agreed to meet up with the James Reed family just outside of Springfield. James and his wife Margaret had four children: Virginia, Margaret's daughter from a previous marriage, Martha, James Jr., and Thomas. Also with them was Margaret's elderly mother, Sarah Keyes. They had two servants, Eliza and Baylis Williams, a brother and sister, and three drivers: Milford Elliott, Walter Herron, and James Smith. When we arrived at the meeting place, the girls ran off to join the other children. I took my toilet articles from one of the calico pockets hanging from the wagon bows and stared in the mirror. What I saw was a small round face, framed by dark braids wound around my head. My usually clear blue eyes were red and swollen. I dashed some cold water on my face and dried it off. *Brace up, Tamsen, and get on with it.*

The girls returned in a few minutes much excited. Frances climbed into the wagon and pulled on my hand. "Mother, Mother, come look! Patty and Thomas's wagon has a door like a house."

"Yes, in a few minutes. First I must change my dress and comb my hair and you must also."

Frances's curly blond hair had escaped from its ribbon and her apron was no longer the crisp white it had been this morning. I looked out at the other two girls standing by the wagon. They were even more bedraggled than Frances. I had carefully braided their long dark hair that morning, but I saw that the ties had come loose and both girls would need their hair braided again.

"We must wash up and change our dresses, girls. Please come in the wagon. Look, Georgeanna, set up the ladder. I think it was knocked over when Frances got in."

"Mother, we ain't dirty," said Frances.

"Frances, we do not say 'ain't.' It is not proper English."

"Everybody does, Mother."

"We do not. Come, Georgeanne, Eliza, you must change your dresses. Then we'll go see the wagon."

The girls were awed by the big Reed wagon. Well, we all were. As we approached I noticed Baylis, the Reed hired man, sitting in the shade made by the wagon, whittling on a stick.

"Hello, Baylis. How are you?"

"Ma'am, I'm all right, but I wish the sun would hurry up and go down."

I wondered how Baylis would fare on the journey, as he was afflicted with a condition we called albino; he had white, almost translucent, skin. The poor man suffered greatly from sunlight and usually he slept in the day and moved about at night. He'd been with the Reed family for years and they were so used to his condition that they scarcely thought of it.

The Reed family wagon was like a home on wheels. The entrance was on the side, similar to a coach in this respect, and the wagon bed was built up along the sides over the wheels to provide a base for beds, front and rear. Margaret and James joined us as we looked at the wagon.

"Tamsen," said Margaret, "I want to show you the inside of our wagon. James has done marvelous work to make the wagon nice for us."

James fingered his neatly trimmed mustache. "It's the most comfortable wagon that's ever headed west," said James. "I see George unyoking. I'll go over and see if I can help."

I don't know why I disliked James Reed. Perhaps it was because he always seemed cold and aloof and had an arrogance that annoyed me. James would have been considered by most to be a handsome man with his regular features, slightly curly dark hair, and even teeth. He wasn't tall, but was sturdily built. Margaret was also strongly built, but acted frail. Her features were too strong to be considered pretty, but she was always well groomed and beautifully dressed. I admired the clothes she wore, but I could not be comfortable following the latest trend. My tailored clothing suited my small size and personality better than the layers of skirts and big sleeves currently the fashion. James was the same age as I, forty-five, but Margaret was considerably younger at thirty-two.

Margaret beckoned to me. "Tamsen, come in and say hello to Mother." She held her hand up in front of the girls, who were more eager than I to see the inside of the wagon.

"Children, perhaps you can see the wagon another time."

Eliza's lower lip was trembling in disappointment. I quickly decided to do something special for the girls to make up for their disappointment. "Children, go find your cousins. I have planned a special treat for all of you. I'll be along shortly." They skipped off, always eager for a special treat.

We stepped up into a tiny room with two leather-covered spring seats facing each other. Margaret lifted one of the seats. "We have every convenience. Under here we have storage compartments. And in here, I have all my sewing things and the children's books and toys. We even have a stove to keep Mother warm."

She pointed to a tiny wood stove, its pipe extending through the canvas of the wagon. My first thought was that it would start the canvas afire, but then I noticed that a ring of metal had been installed to keep the hot pipe from the canvas. I agreed that James had thought of everything. I turned to the bed where Margaret's mother reclined.

"Mrs. Keyes, you look as snug as can be," I said. I patted the soft featherbed on which she lay. "Is this the featherbed we worked on last winter?"

"Oh, yes, it's the best one I've ever had. James has made everything so nice for me. And I can hardly believe it, but I feel just wonderful today. Perhaps the journey will be better for my illness."

"Mother has perked up quite a bit and we think that the drier climate later in the journey will ease the consumption."

"My son Cadden will be returning from the Pacific lands this year," said Mrs. Keyes. "We hope to meet him on the journey."

"Mother is very anxious to see him again before ..." Margaret's voice trailed off and an expression of pain came on her face. She put her hand to her temple and blinked back tears. I felt a rush of sympathy for her. Margaret's mother was in the last stages of consumption. In later times it was termed tuberculosis. I bade good-bye to Mrs. Keyes and we left the wagon.

"How are you holding up under the strain of leaving?" I asked Margaret.

"I've had one of my sick headaches all yesterday and today. This morning I was so overcome with grief that I had to be helped to the wagon. The parting has been very sad for all of us. Even James had tears in his eyes."

"It's very sad for us also. The children hate to leave their cousins and their friends, but they're excited about the journey." *And I have this presentiment that we should not go. It tightens my throat and quickens my heart so at night I can't sleep. I try to shut it out, but it won't leave me.*

"I have the greatest confidence in James," said Margaret. "He always knows what he is about, never fails at anything. So I have no worries regarding a safe journey. I just wish I didn't have to put Mother through it."

I strolled back to our wagons thinking about Margaret's mother. The doctor had told them she had but a few months to live. *How could James do this to Margaret? How could she have been so pliant as to accept his demand to pick up and move this very year, as if no other would do? James treats women with respect, but I think he expects them to be docile and subservient, not disposed to questioning the "authority" of men. George is different and I am so thankful for that.*

I thought back to the time that I first met George. He was so handsome, a fine figure standing there in the church yard asking to be introduced to me. I liked that he was tall, although I was just a whiffet, under five feet tall and less than a hundred pounds. I was taken by his kindliness, his generous nature, and his willingness to always give others the benefit of a doubt before he formed an opinion or made a decision. I could not bear to be married to a man who didn't treat me, and others, for that matter, as independent persons with knowledge, beliefs, and opinions, and as an equal in society and in marriage.

That evening in the campground, many people joined us for one last get-together before we became nomads. There were several there from my reading group, including our dear friend Mr. Francis, owner of the *Springfield Journal.* We gathered around the fire, our hearts sad, knowing that we would probably never see each other again. I stood beside George and murmured the platitudes and good-byes, my mind whirling, my head buzzing, as if something, some *thing,* was trying to get into my consciousness. I had the feeling that my mind was searching, trying to focus on a scene, but it was all fragmented and dark, a cold wall of icy fear standing between the dark in my mind and the picture. I could hear the people near me talking, but as from a great distance.

"I sure hate to see you all go off. You'll probably be attacked an' killed by Indians. An' poor Miz Keyes a dyin', why on earth you would want—"

"Mother, stop yammering. By God, Reed, if I were a younger man, I'd go along with you. They say that in California there's no winter, don't need fire but to cook. It would sure help my rheumatism."

The old preacher took Jacob's boys aside for a talk. He leaned both hands on his cane, his voice quavering with the excitement and the effort to stand up. "Boys, remember your old home, the place where the bones of your grandparents are buried. Keep the faith of your fathers and live honestly before man and God."

"Reverend Culpepper, our grandparents ain't buried here. They's back in Kentucky," said Solomon.

"Tamsen," George was nudging my shoulder, waving his hand in front of my face. "Honey, are you asleep on your feet? Is somethin' wrong?"

Yes! Yes, something is very wrong ... but what? My mind traveled a great distance, it seemed, before I realized that Mr. Francis was standing before me.

"I'm sorry. I was ... I felt dizzy for a moment."

"Tamsen," said Mr. Francis, "be sure and write often. I'll publish all your letters in the paper so the home folks can follow the journey." He turned to George. "What did you do about your paper money?"

"Come with me, I'll show you," said George. George put his arm around my shoulders and we walked to our wagon. I leaned into George, glad for his strong body. At the wagon we showed Mr. Francis the quilt that I had stitched over the winter.

"Tamsen sewed it inside this quilt. I hated to pay fifteen percent to convert it to metal and ten thousand dollars in coin would have considerable weight. We've heard that with all the American trading ships coming in to California, we'd be able to exchange or barter American dollars there without too much trouble."

"How very ingeniuous and talented you are, Mrs. Donner." Mr. Francis turned to George, shook his hand, and then took my hand in his.

"I'm sorry that you're leaving Springfield. We need more gentry here, not less, but I wish for you abundant health and the greatest of prosperity in the new land."

We retired soon after seeing the last friend off, but I could not sleep. I tossed and turned, uneasy and nervous from things that were running through my mind. *I have this feeling that something terrible is going to happen to us. What can it be? What can I do to prevent it?*

I got up and stepped outside the tent, a damp, chill breeze fluttering against me. The flame in the lantern hanging on our tent pole guttered and danced, making eerie shadows on our wagon next to the tent. The dogs came over to me from their place under the wagon, wagging their tails and whining softly as they tilted their heads up at me with questioning looks. They were also feeling uneasy in this new and strange situation. One was a little spaniel that the girls could not bear to leave behind and the other a large mixed breed that had shown up at our door one day. He became an excellent watch-dog and snake and rabbit chaser. I petted them a little and then pointed back to the wagon and they returned to their beds. I filled my lungs with the cold night air and breathed it slowly out. *Tamsen Eustis Donner, there is no good reason for you to be nervous and mopey. It's a good move for us, for the children. We have everything we need to make it so ... our health, our family, money. We will have a wonderful new life in California.* I returned to my bed, the unease, once again, pushed into the back of my mind.

• • •

The morning was chilly, the sky leaden with the threat of rain. Mists were still clinging to the hollows and streams as we began our journey. It took some time to get everything in order. Several oxen had strayed off in the night and had to be found, returned to camp, and yoked up.

It was a cacophony of noise and a hubbub of activity. Oxen, horses, dogs, and children all moving in different directions, the women darting around putting their gear away, the men shouting and cursing as the recalcitrant oxen were put in the yokes. The horses were side-stepping and tossing their heads up and down in nervousness. At last the lead wagon jerked forward, its white canvas top swaying as the wheels rolled over deep ruts in the road. The other eight wagons soon fell in behind, with the loose cattle bringing up the rear. It was quite a caravan.

• • •

There were several places where overland travelers could gather before "jumping off" into the wilderness and we'd decided on the village of Independence. We would travel southwest for about a month through Illinois and the Missouri Territory to reach Independence. Here we would leave civilized country and enter the country of the savage Indians.

By the time of our mid-day rest, the clouds had cleared away and the sun began to warm the earth and we mortals traveling over it. I thought over the preparations we had made for the trip. I noticed that Georgeanna was coughing and I wondered if I had remembered to put elm bark in my box of medicines. The slightest sign of illness in my children would fret me. I had lost my first husband, Mr. Dozier, and first child, a boy, to illness, and then shortly before my husband's death I had lost another child, a daughter, born prematurely. After their deaths I returned to my childhood home in Newburyport, Massachusetts, to recover from my grief. During that time I studied the healing arts, determined that in the future I would apply all I learned to aid others.

Two years before we began our journey, in addition to the usual bilious fevers, we'd had an outbreak of erysipelas, a horrible skin disease that covered the body with lesions, and influenza. The next year it was cholera. Removing to a place where there was little sickness was a powerful incentive for me to go. George had another arrow in his arsenal of argument for the move. He'd suggested that I could start a school for girls. This was a dream I had harbored in my heart for a long time and this prospect was what finally won me over.

◆ ◆ ◆

The journey to Independence was pleasant. Our only problems were deep mud and the crossing of rivers and streams. Sometimes a wagon would get so bogged down that the men had to double or triple the teams to extricate it. The children and I would ride in the wagon if the weather was unpleasant, but when it was nice we would walk. Several of the children would ride on our horses and found it exciting to scare up the wolves, deer, and wild game as we moved through the countryside.

The men worked with the oxen, training them to the yoke and to respond to commands. They were unmanageable at first, their antics causing a lot of trouble, especially in the morning chain-ups. They weren't always agreeable to being yoked up to face a day of hard pulling. They would leap and run about trying to avoid the yoke, causing great confusion and bellowing amongst the other stock.

We soon settled into a routine, the women unloading and loading the items needed to make camp and prepare food. Each morning the bedding would have to be shaken out, rolled up, and replaced in the wagons; the tents had to be taken down; cooking utensils cleaned and stowed away; and then the process was repeated in reverse that evening.

Each family prepared and ate breakfast in their camp, but in the evening we usually had a communal picnic. We would prepare food for the next day's noon stop the night before. Betsey and I had several disasters before we learned how to cook over a fire in the ground. Many times the food was ruined through one mishap or another, usually by being burned. One time a swarm of gnats got into our bread dough, turning it black, and we had to discard it and start over. The most common accident was catching the bottom of our dresses on fire. It wasn't long before I cut my dresses off shorter and re-sewed the bottoms and Betsey decided to do the same. Margaret Reed was appalled at the idea.

"Perhaps that would be acceptable for a domestic, but my husband wouldn't countenance a dress that short for me," she declared.

I didn't care a fig about what people thought. To me, it was more important not to be set on fire and to be comfortable than to worry about showing a little of my ankles to the assemblage. Margaret's attitude irritated me. *Of course, she doesn't need to worry about scorching her dresses. She never does any cooking or washing. Her servant girl does it all.*

We traveled through the timber and over the prairies where it was the most convenient and crossed the sloughs and streams where they could best be forded. Hannibal, on the bank of the Mississippi, was a bustling village where we bought provisions and George had some blacksmithing done before we ferried over the river on a flat boat. At Lexington we crossed over the Missouri River and then followed the well-worn trace of the Santa Fe Trail to Independence.

We encountered snow, sleet, rain, and fog, but also many clear days when we gloried in the warm sun and breathed in the wonderful smell of the earth awakening from the hibernation of winter. We met many people along the road and we would stop to talk and visit. We were on an adventure and everything encountered was new to us. The excitement built as the memory of our previous homes began to fade in our thoughts.

• • •

May 11, 1846
Independence, Missouri Territory

It was the second week in May when we arrived in the vicinity of Independence. The crabapple trees along the road were a mass of white blossoms that wafted a wonderful fragrance on the breeze. The town was situated about six miles from the Missouri River on the southern side.

The first thing we did was to buy all the newspapers, as we were eager to learn more about the different wagon companies that were forming up in campgrounds outside the city. Independence was the principal outfitting place for traders who engaged in the Santa Fe market and the caravans of traders' wagons presented a most fantastic and interesting sight. They were pulled by as many as ten or twelve yoke of oxen that were herded through the streets by drivers constantly cracking their whips over their heads.

We visited the mercantile district and marveled at a community that was half-civilized and half-savage, an exotic blend of all manner of mankind streaming through the streets. In a few days one might observe more variety of language, culture, and

Missouri Republican,
ST. LOUIS, APRIL 14, 1846

EMIGRANTS TO CALIFORNIA.–

There are now in this city a number of gentlemen on their way to Independence or Weston, to join a company which is going out this spring to California. They will leave the city during the week, and it is expected, if the grass on the plains is sufficient for the subsistence of their horses and stock, that they will commence their march between the 1st and 15th of May. The cold and wet weather of the spring has delayed them some weeks. It is expected that this company, which is composed entirely of men, will consist of from one hundred and fifty to two hundred—some say three hundred. A number go out merely to see the country and enjoy the sport of the trip, now a fashionable excursion with many of our western young men. Of those going for this purpose there are several English gentlemen. A few take this trip to improve their health, but the largest number go with the purpose of remaining in the country.

So far as we have been able to acquire information on the subject, we are led to believe that the larger number of the emigrants, going out this year, will make California the place of their destination. It is decidedly in the ascendant in popular favor, as compared with Oregon.

Nevertheless, there will be a large number of emigrants for Oregon; and, counting the women and children few of whom go to California, it is probable that the difference will be small.

The companies for California will follow the Oregon route until they reach Fort Hall, when they will diverge in the direction of the Great Salt Lake, and thence to the place of their destination. We wish them every success in their enterprise.

endeavor than in the total of one's lifetime to that date.

That afternoon it commenced to rain, making movement about the town impossible because of the deep mud, so we returned to camp. The men made the rounds, inspecting and appraising the various wagons, teams, and equipment and endlessly discussing the business of journeying across the country. The Reed wagon drew a lot of attention and comment, as did James's gray horse, the purebred Glaucus.

"Suh, that seems a heavy wagon not t' have a jointed tongue. When y'all get into rough country, the strain might break the axletree."

"No, this wagon was built to stand bad conditions. I daresay there's no finer anywhere on this road now or in the future."

"I agree you've a fine wagon. I'm a carriage maker by trade, so I've some experience. I'd hate to see y'all get in a tight spot an' have trouble. Most likely you could have it changed out here quickly."

"What is your name?" James asked the man.

"Suh, I'm William Eddy."

James's tone was curt. "Well, you may be right, Eddy, but I don't believe I'll have any problem with this wagon."

"I told him he should have it jointed, but he didn't agree with me either," remarked George.

James stiffened and his face began to flush. I took George's arm in mine. "George, the girls have been alone all afternoon. It's time we headed back."

"Huh? Oh. All right, James, we'll see you at the campfire tonight."

James grunted an assent and we moved off.

"George, it is of no use to disagree with James. He is inflexible. He seems to have a tension inside, a coiled spring he holds down."

George looked at me and chuckled. "He may be a little stiff-necked."

"Oh, George, look!" I exclaimed. "It's Zeb, that old mountain man that came to Springfield two years ago."

Zeb was dressed in the same greasy buckskins with the same dirty, faded, red handkerchief tied around his head that he'd worn when he was in Springfield. He was hunkered down against the wheel of a wagon, regaling a group of men and boys with stories of his exploits. We stood listening. His flappy lips caused a spattering of spittle to fly as he talked.

"Most a' my life I been in the mount'ins trappin' an' huntin' beaver," he said. "I done fit Injuns dozens a' times, still got an arrer head or two whar they got me. I done lost my outfit two, three times from bein' attacked by the varmints. The Blackfeet are the worst, by damn. I hate them Blackfeet, an' the Crows are bad, too. I been starved 'most to death, froze 'most to death, fallen down cliffs, chased by bees an' hornets. I been chawed and clawed by grizzly b'ars an' other critters an' even my damn horse."

Zeb stood up and opened his shirt to the crowd and showed some terrible-looking scars. Then he pulled up his trouser leg and showed even more. There were gasps from the boys in the crowd. Zeb wiped his mouth with his sleeve and squatted down again. He took his hunting knife out of its sheath and began to stab the ground with it.

"The beaver business, it don't shine no more," he said. "It's through. Gone. Now the thing is Oregon an' California. That's whar the opportunities be. The fur-men are lookin' fer new prospects. Some are guidin' greenhorns out to the new lands. Ol' Bill Sublette an' Black Harris, they're doin' it. I'm headin' west m'self." He jerked his thumb toward the wagon behind him. "I'm guidin' this here wagon party out to the Oregon Territory."

"Do you know much of California?" someone asked.

Zeb stood up and put one foot on a stump, crossing his arms over his upraised leg. He used his tongue to gather up his chaw and spit it out.

"I think it be a good land. Thar's no winter an' anythin' kin grow all year round." Zeb took a plug of tobacco out of a pocket and bit off a hunk, his jaws working it as he squinted up his eyes and considered the question. "Th'ar ain't many people, mostly Mexicans. Thar's no more'n five or six hundred whites in the whole damned country. The Mexicans don't like work. They spend thar time doin' fandangos an' such like. The men w'ar outfits all fancied up with embroid'ry an' silver an' thar saddles 'er the same way, they are. But as horsemen, they shine, let me tell you. Yes, it be a good land and thar's land a'plenty fer the takin'. An' soon she'll be United States territory."

"How's the best way to get there? To California?"

"I'm of a mind that the Oregon Territory is the best place, but if'n yer needle's set on California, I allow it's the next best. How to get thar?" Zeb squeezed his eyes into little slits and slowly scratched his beard while he contemplated the question.

"If'n yer wantin' to take a wagon, ye foller the Santa Fe trace to the Kansas River. Good-sized river, ye'll have to ferry a'crost this time a' year." He paused to spit. For Zeb spitting was not a neat affair and as a result his beard and the front of his buckskin shirt had a dirty brown stain down the center.

"Then yer gonna head north to the Platte River an' foller it west to the Shining Mountains. Then ye go along the Sweetwater to Bridger's Tradin' Post. 'Course, you could take Sublette's cutoff just shy of Bridger's if'n ye wanted to an' didn't need supplies. It'll take ye to Fort Hall a little shorter. From both it's north to Fort Hall an' then west, then south down to Ogden's River. Foller on 'til the river ends in a sink an' then keep on west 'til ye gits to high mountains, higher than anythin' ye seen so far. After the last mount'ins ye'll find the holdin's of John Sutter. New Helvetia, he calls it. I've heard he's mighty fine to 'mericans."

"Who's he?"

"He's some kind o' furriner. He owns most 'a the valley o' the Sacramento terr'tory, got hisself a land grant cozyin' up to the Mexican governor, Alvarado. He's got Injun slaves, e'en made some into soldiers, fancy uniforms an' such like. He's got a fort an' does ranchin' an' farmin'. He has a sight of mills, e'en a tannery. I heered tell he has nigh on to six hundred workin' fer him, most a 'em Injuns. He's wantin' more 'mericans in the country."

Zeb cleaned one of his fingernails with his knife and then

put the knife in his belt. As the crowd began to move away, Zeb called out.

"Mind ye now, ye don't want ter git to the high mountains late in the season, 'cause the passes close with snow. Ye could be trapped fer the winter."

Trapped for the winter? That sounded a little farfetched to us at that stage of the journey, but which route to take was the topic of our conversation that evening as several of our group sat around the campfire. I saw Betsey's fourteen-year-old boy, Solomon, squatting down by the fire, stabbing the ground with a huge knife. He was wearing a new buckskin shirt. I noticed a big lump in his cheek which he was awkwardly moving around in his mouth. *Is that a chaw of tobacco?*

"Solly," I said, "that's a nice shirt."

"I traded fer it at the store with some stuff I had an' I traded fer this knife too, Auntie Tamsen." Solomon looked over to George. "Hey, Uncle George, I asked Zeb 'bout a way to get to the Salt Lake without havin' to go by Fort Hall an' he said he'd never heard of a way to go with wagons. An' he should know, bein' a famous mountain man an' all."

"Didn't Hastings say in his book there was a road?" asked Jacob. "An' didn't Frémont come through that way?"

"I haven't read anything of Fremont's journey, but I've heard about it. We have Hastings's book," replied James Reed. "Virginia, would you go to the wagon and get my valise, please?"

When Virginia returned with the valise, James took the Hastings book out and thumbed through it until he found the page he wanted.

"I can find only one reference. It says the most direct route, for the California emigrants, would be to leave the Oregon route about two hundred miles east from Fort Hall and thence bear west-southwest to the Salt Lake and continue down to the Bay of Francisco."

"That doesn't say there *is* a route," I remarked.

James looked at me and held his hand up to stop me from saying anything more. "Hastings speaks well of the route. I'll quote," said James. "'All streams are easily forded, buffalo herds are plentiful beyond the Rocky Mountains and the California Indians are inoffensive.'"

"Well, we'll find out more as we get farther along," said George.

"Which Injuns you speaking of?" said Jacob. "Warn't there a story of Joe Walker havin' trouble with Injuns when he was crossin'?"

"Zeb's fit Injuns fer years an' he says—"

James frowned and spoke before Solomon could finish what he was intending to say.

"I don't think you can put much stock in what that old has-been says. I've been told the Kansas Indians are peaceable and there's no reason the other tribes will be hostile. They'll mostly just try to pilfer whatever they can. I'm more concerned about the Mormons than I am about Indians."

"I 'eard that the buggers are five thousand strong and heavily armed," said John Denton, "and loikly to kill every non-Mormon emigrant they moit come across."

"The Mormons just want to get away from bein' persecuted 'cause of their religion," said George. "Missouri was supposed to be their promised land an' now they're bein' driven from there. I think if you leave them alone, they'll leave you alone. I just hope they ain't goin' to California. They need to find a place to themselves."

Many in the camps were quite alarmed and such anxiety was manifested about the matter that Colonel Russell, a renowned leader amongst the wagon camps, sent out an express to Colonel Kearney at Fort Leavenworth to ascertain the truth. Kearney reported that some two thousand Mormons had crossed the river, but were peaceably disposed. Another rumor had it that a party of Englishmen, supposedly sponsored by their government, was on the trail ahead of us bound for Oregon. Their aim was to stir up the Indian tribes along the route, inciting them to acts of hostility against the American emigrants. It wasn't quite settled yet whether the Oregon country was a possession of the

United States or of Britain and some people suspected the British wanted to discourage American emigration. Most sensible people were not excited by these rumors, but interminable meetings were held to assess the situation.

None of this dampened the enthusiasm of the gathering emigrants. The children ran about and played, taking in the general excitement and multiplying it by double. The young people gathered in the evenings around the campfires and there was much merriment, with talking, singing, and playing of instruments. We had many musicians in the company. Especially talented were the Fowler girls, Ann and Minerva, who played the violin. I took advantage of the lull in the journey to write a letter to my sister.

May 11, 1846

My dear sister, I commenced writing to you some months ago, but the letter was laid aside to be finished the next day & was never touched. A nice sheet of pink letter paper was taken out & has got so much soiled that it cannot be written upon & now in the midst of preparation for starting across the mountains I am seated on the grass in the midst of the tent to say a few words to my dearest only sister. One would suppose that I loved her but little or I should have not neglected her so long, but I have heard from you by Mr. Greenleaf & every month have intended to write. My three daughters are round me one at my side trying to sew. Georgeanna fixing herself up in an old India rubber cap & Eliza Poor knocking on my paper asking me ever so many questions. They often talk to me of Aunty Poor. I can give you no idea of the hurry of this place at this time. It is supposed there be 7000 waggons start from this place, this season. We go to California, to the bay of Francisco. It is a four months trip. We have three wagons furnished with food & clothing etc. drawn by three yoke of oxen each. We take cows along & milk them

& have some butter though not as much as we would like. I am willing to go & have no doubt it will be an advantage to our children & to us. I came here last evening & start tomorrow morning on the long journey. Wm's family was well when I left Springfield a month ago. He will write to you soon as he finds another home. He says he has received no answer to his two last letters, is about to start to Wisconsin as he considers Illinois unhealthy.

Farewell my sister, you shall hear from me as soon as I have an opportunity, Love to Mr. Poor, the children & all friends. Farewell. T. E. Donner

May 13, 1846
Independence, Missouri Territory

We arose the next morning and beheld a brilliant rainbow arching in the sky. It was a magnificent gate for us to enter the Kingdom of the West. I stood transfixed, glorying in the sight. But suddenly I felt cold air surround me and everything around me became a gray haze.

"Honey, what's the matter?" George was talking to me, standing beside me. I grabbed his arm.

"Oh, George, I'm frightened. This is a mistake. We shouldn't go."

"Honey, it looks likely to rain any moment. We need to get under cover."

Soon clouds closed in and the sky became overcast and very gray. Thinking back on that day, now I know it was an omen of things to come. I felt it, but I couldn't accept it.

That afternoon rain fell heavily, accompanied with loud peals of thunder and flashes of lightning. I crawled into the wagon where my rocking chair was lying on top of some kegs. My nose tickled at the wet, musty smell of the wagon. Rain drummed against the canvas and the lantern swung crazily as gusts of wind rocked the wagon as if it were a boat on the high seas. I managed to position the chair so I could sit down in it and began to write the first entry in my journal.

May 13, 1846

The morning began beautifully with a rainbow beckoning us to enter the promised land. It was late morning when we got started and it was slow going because of the deep mud. Twice wagons were mired and could only be extricated by double teaming. This was followed by a terrible storm with rain and incessant flashes of lightning. The rain fell heavily all morning and then it cleared and the sun shone out warm and bright.

We came upon a man and son plowing a most fertile field. The man, a Mr. Milliron, is an emigrant from Virginia from four years previous. He had a large family of wife, sons, and daughters. We made camp a half-mile from the log cabin belonging to this family.

The glories of spring are now unfolding. The green leaves and flowers of all colors make a brilliant display along the road, and thousands of birds made music for us.

In the morning we moved on in more rain. Later the skies cleared and the sun appeared. We decided to go no farther that day as we wanted to dry out the baggage that had suffered from the rain. The smaller girls and I took a stroll away from camp and gathered a large number of prairie peas in our aprons. I made it a practice to find wild produce to include in our meals and to preserve for later use. I was very interested to discover what new plants and fruits we would find in this new country. Whenever I encountered an interesting plant, I would take a leaf or a flower and press it in my notebook along with a description.

May 14, 1846

We approach what is known as the Blue Prairie, the road becoming drier and easier going. The vast prairie opens before us and we behold a magnificent landscape of green undulations and flowered slopes, an ocean of vegetation stretching away as far as one can see. Truly a grand sight, one that we have never before experienced, as it is with each unfolding day. Today I collected pink verbena and wild indigo.

We're hampered a good deal by rain & mud. Today the sky cleared & I strung up lines in the wagons so I could hang some of our wet things to dry while we moved along. This evening I made griddle cakes and two loaves of bread, stewed berries and apples, and prepared meat for breakfast. Then I mended a pair of pants for George. It's hard to find time to write.

Clean water was an absolute necessity for me. George would sometimes become very impatient with my "foolishness" as he called it. When we had a choice, I would ask him to get the cleanest water he could find. We sometimes had words about it.

"George, please send Noah and Samuel farther up the stream to get our water."

"That's too much trouble. They've got more important things to do to make camp. Here, I've brought you one bucket to start the meal with. We'll get more later."

"George, I will not use this water. It has been fouled by previous camps and the animals have already gotten into it. I'll wait to start the evening meal until I have clean water."

"Godamighty! With all we have to do, we have to humor you too!"

George called to Noah, who was unyoking the oxen.

"Noah, take Samuel an' some buckets to get water. Tamsen,

you go with them an' show them where to dip. I don't want to be blamed for not getting you the *right* goddamned water!"

I frowned at George. *After eight years of my nagging him, he still uses swear words.*

George was not alone in his disregard of matters of sanitation and of health. Sometimes I felt that I was considered something of a "witch" when I talked of my ideas of preventatives and remedies for ailments with which people were so often afflicted. This bothered George.

"Tamsen, don't try to help other people. They're likely to blame you if'n they don't get well. Let them do the way they've always done."

"George, I don't try to impress my beliefs on them. When I see sickness, I want to help as best I can."

He threw his hands up in exasperation. "I don't know why I open my mouth. You always do what you want anyway!"

"No, I don't. You're exaggerating."

The rain continued. We set up the canvas fly off our wagon and tried to stay out of the wet.

"George, it's impossible to cook. Our meal is going to be a cold one."

"Can we get enough fire to make coffee? If I just had coffee I could tolerate ever'thin' else."

I managed to make a kettle of coffee and several in our company gathered around under the canvas hoping to get some of the strong brew. The rain was a steady fine mist, the air so wet we coughed as we breathed it into our lungs. The rain ran steadily off our cover, wetting the backs of the men trying to crowd under the tent.

George squeezed the water from his mustache with the knuckle of his forefinger. "The road is gonna be knee deep tomorrow. I wonder if we shouldn't just lie by until things dry out. It's hard on the animals."

"I think that's a good idea, George," said James. "We need to do some repairs anyway. I think I will ride ahead and visit with other groups to get a feel for the people and which group we might want to join."

James turned to me. "Mrs. Donner, would you visit with my wife? She's not feeling well. Her mother is having a lot of problems these last few days and Margaret is taking it hard. Perhaps in your medicines you have some laudanum or something that will help?"

I walked in the mud and rain to the Reed wagon carrying a packet of remedies. I found Eliza and Baylis sitting on stools under the fly tent, looking bedraggled and limp. I leaned over and took off my shoes, which were heavy with mud.

"Poor Miz Reed," said Eliza. "She's jes' not feelin' good at all."

I knocked on the side of the door before entering. Virginia was sitting on the bench seat beside her mother's bed. Margaret raised up on one elbow and then fell back on her pillows. "Oh, Tamsen, this is the worst headache I've ever had."

"I have a tea for you that might help, Margaret. I see that you have no fire to warm it, but you can drink it as it is." I looked over to Mrs. Keyes. Patty was sitting on the edge of her Grandmother's bed.

"Poor Grammy, she's been coughing a lot." said Patty.

"I've brought medicines that may relieve the coughing and help her sleep. I will need a cup and a spoon."

"I'll get it," said Patty.

We propped Mrs. Keyes up and I gave her the medicines, one of which was laudanum.

"I don't think anything is going to help, but you are so sweet to bring me medicine, Tamsen."

"It should make you more comfortable, Mrs. Keyes."

I poured some of the tea I'd brought into the cup that Patty gave me and kneeled on the bench seat next to where Margaret lay in her bed.

"Mother has been suffering terribly with the headaches," said Virginia.

"I've brought some medicines. Margaret, can you sit up and drink this tea?"

"The laudanum helps my headaches, but I've used it all. I thought you would bring some. James said—"

"I have brought a medicine tea. Drink it until you fall asleep."

"You don't have any laudanum?"

"Margaret, laudanum is not good for a healthy person. It makes you feel better for only a short time and then you feel worse than before, requiring even more laudanum. Try the tea. I believe it will help you."

"But Tamsen, I need laudanum. I need to sleep. James told me you would bring me some." Margaret began to cry.

"Why won't you give it to her?" asked Virginia. "You can see she's suffering. Why be so cruel?"

I looked at Virginia. *I must have patience. After all, she is very concerned for her mother.* "Let us see if the tea doesn't help first, all right?"

Jacob was late joining us at the cooking fire the next morning for breakfast. He stretched and then sat down on a log close to the fire, scratching his beard.

"I didn't sleep hardly a wink with the goddamned dogs barking all night," he complained.

The night had been a particularly bad one with a group of wagons coming in next to us in the night and, seemingly, they had a hundred dogs. The barking ranged from an annoying shrill high-pitched treble all the way down in tone to deep baying, answered, of course, by the dogs in our group.

"George," said Jacob, "I don't cotton to Reed thinking he's gonna be the leader an' tellin' us what to do. He always has to be the biggest frog in the pond."

"Well, he's had experience in leading in the war an' all an' he's an intelligent man. We don't have to go along if we don't want to. Just sit back an' see what happens. No point in gettin' riled up when there's nothin' to get riled up about."

We were in the middle of preparing breakfast when the wind commenced to blow, followed by heavy rain. Our fire was extinguished by the onslaught and we took cover in the wagons.

"Our bread ain't gonna cook through with the fire out, ain't been goin' long enough," said Betsey. "Ever'thin we have is wet through an' I cain't hardly walk with the mud stickin' to my feet in a ball. I don't think I can endure another day of mud and wet. Our men're crazy to put us through this."

May 15, 1846

This evening we camped in the curve of a stream, which I understand is the Wakarusa. It is a very pretty site with a grove composed of oaks, hickorys, dogwoods & willows circling our camp.

We've had rain and more rain. The wet and muddy conditions are hard to contend with. It's difficult to prepare meals, difficult to make a fire & moving the wagons almost impossible.

Ex-Governor Boggs, of Missouri, & Colonel Thornton and his wife, Nancy, who are from Illinois, stopped to visit at our camp. Colonel Thornton is a well educated man, very refined, as is his wife. Both have problems of health. Mr. Thornton is asthmatic and suffers greatly from the blowing dust on their journey. They are traveling through, desiring to catch up with the wagons headed by Mr. Russell. They expressed their reason for making the journey to the Pacific as a search for a more healthful environment.

All of our clothing & bedding materials are wet. The men have had to chop trees & brush to make a roadbed through the worst sections of road. The strains of travel are beginning to claim us & even the sunniest amongst us have grown a little surly. When the wagons are stopped I hold school for the children.

We passed what was called "Lone Elm," a solitary tree serving as a marker on the prairie. Young John Breen told us later that it was here his family encountered a group of hunters returning with furs. They gave his family some dried buffalo meat and told them that they had no idea what they would suffer before they reached California. They didn't believe them.

Each evening the discussions around our fire centered on our anticipation of joining up with other groups of wagons as we would soon enter Indian country. James Reed had been riding ahead visiting and talking with various companies, getting an idea of what manner of company they were and whether they were for Oregon or California. He reported his findings to our group as we sat around the campfire.

"Colonel Russell's company appeals to me the most. It seems it is an unwieldy business, this forming of companies, but Russell's company seems serious about organizing properly. I'm going to make petition to them."

James stood up and brushed his pants off with his hands. He followed me as I carried some things to put away in my camp kitchen on the back of our supply wagon.

"Mrs. Reed seems to be well today, Mrs. Donner, and her mother rests more easily. I appreciate your attentions to them."

"You are welcome, James. I have been so busy I forgot that Mrs. Keyes will need more of the medicine. I will make some up now. Could you have someone bring me the bottle so I can refill it?"

"Of course. I will bring it myself and carry it back too."

As we proceeded, the country rose into a high rolling prairie almost entirely destitute of timber. We noticed many grouse, but not very many other birds. The barren terrain caused a little consternation amongst the ladies and girls in our camp. Elitha and Leanna were concerned about privacy.

"Mother, there's no place that's private, you know, to go. We're afraid to walk away very far from the wagons. What can we do?" asked Elitha. "I'm going to embarrass myself any minute."

"Well, you could walk a short distance away and take turns holding your skirts out as a screen."

"Mother! There are wagons everywhere."

"Well then, climb into the sleeping wagon and use the night jar."

Matters of privacy were a little ticklish on the trail. The older women in the group adjusted to this fairly well, but for the young women, whose sensitivities were very easily bruised, it was a more difficult matter. As a rule, we found our privacy in the sleeping wagon. We washed and dressed ourselves there where we stored our necessities and clothing. Other matters requiring privacy were usually undertaken when darkness covered all. It would be ridiculous to assume that the moment the wagons rolled all urges and passions were suspended for the six months of the journey. Even with darkness, however, privacy was hard to come by. The sleeping arrangements in the Jacob Donner family were causing a problem for Betsey.

"Tamsen, I don't know what to do with Jacob! We're crowded in the tent sleepin' with three children beside us an' he's pullin' up my night dress. And for sure I don' need to get with child on this journey. You know how sick I get in the mornin's. You got a preventer that I kin take in yer witch's brews?"

"Witch's brews?"

"Jacob says you must be a witch cause you're always brewing up one concoction or nother. I didn't mean to make you mad."

"My witch's brews, as you call it, have helped you and your family and a lot of others, Betsey."

"Oh, Tamsen, I'm sorry. I didn' say it mean like."

"I know, don't fret. I've heard of different remedies but I don't have one. If you could keep nursing Lewis, maybe that would—"

"Oh, I quit him from it last winter. I jes' got tired of five years of kids hanging on me, sometimes two at a time. I had to paint my teats with the bitters to make him give it up. Poor little feller was bawling fer days like one a' the calves shut off from its mother."

In the afternoon we met three returning Santa Fe traders who were driving a herd of very poor-looking mules that they had obtained in Chihuahua, Mexico, to sell in Missouri. The gentleman in charge seemed to be intelligent and honest in his statements.

"Suppose that feller knows what he's talkin' about? He said

that the journey he'd just been on was a hard one, but that our journey will be even harder and would shorten our lives by at least ten years."

George laughed. "You think it's been that hard? Seems like we been on a continual picnic."

"I don't figure I have ten years anyhow, so I guess it don't matter," said Jacob.

We diverged from the Santa Fe Trace following the wagon road to the right. It continued to rain steadily during the day and night, saturating the ground even more. The next day we reached a small creek with steep banks that gave us a great deal of trouble, as we had to use ropes to lower the wagons into the defile and then pull them up the other side. It took several hours and fatigued the oxen even more than had the struggle to pull through the deep mud earlier in the day.

In the afternoon, we crossed a creek called the Wakarusa and camped in a grove of large timber. In the evening we were visited by several Potawattomie Indians, none of whom could speak English, but they could pronounce the word "whiskey." They did this as they exhibited small pieces of silver. I believed spirits to be one of the banes of civilization. Now this depravity of the white man was being made available to the redskin, who seemingly had as little resistance to its effects as he had to the virulent diseases that marched along with "civilization."

• • •

The rain finally ceased as our march continued, the landscape becoming a high rolling prairie. The wagon caravan wound slowly over hill and hollow and we could hear only the mutter of the wind and the creaking of the wagons, occasionally interspersed with a snippet of conversation or the "gee-haw" and "whoa-haw" of a teamster carried on the breeze. The sun beamed down, burning our skin. Leanna and Elitha, walking with me, pointed to a rise ahead.

"Look, Mother, are those Indians?"

"Yes, but don't be alarmed. They mean us no harm."

Some of the men in the group who were on horseback gathered at the front of the train as we neared the Indians. There were two men and two squaws with their children. George and Jacob came up to where we were walking beside the wagons.

"They appear to be Kansas Indians, a sorry lot," remarked George.

I took some bread and meat to them. The Indian mothers carried their babies on their backs in a wrapped blanket arrangement. Only their little round faces showed, their black eyes staring out in wonderment at these strange white people and their huge conveyances. My heart melted whenever I would see the little Indian children.

May 18, 1846

My Dear Friend,

In compliance with my promise, I proceed to give you a hasty & brief account of our journey with the California emigration to this point.

We crossed the Kansas River yesterday by placing the wagons on flat boats & swimming our horses and oxen. These boats are operated by French Indians who charge one dollar for each wagon. The boats are poled across the river two wagons at a time. The river was in a low state & if we had chosen to go six miles out of our course, we could have forded it without difficulty. Our normal rate of travel is between twelve and twenty miles a day.

We expect to join the company headed by Colonel Russell by tomorrow at the latest, as they are waiting for us to come up with them at a place called Soldier Creek.

We heard the war news some twenty miles back from here, but the particulars we did not receive until last evening when Mr. Webb, of the "Expositor" newspaper, came through with mail. It has created no alarm in our camp nor in any other as far as can be ascertained, with most seeming to anticipate pleasure rather than otherwise in the conflict with the Mexicans when we arrive in California.

We are followed & accosted almost every hour by numbers of the prairie denizens, most gaudily dressed & mounted on their wild ponies. They pass & re-pass our column, bantering constantly for trades or gifts.

It is a great mistake in supposing that the Indian is devoid of curiosity. I think we are chiefly indebted to that quality of nature for their frequent visits. As yet I do not think they have stolen anything from us, but perhaps we have been saved by our vigilance.

Our party continues to enjoy the most robust health.

Mrs. George Donner

The Russell party took a vote on our petition to join them and our nine wagons were accepted. We felt good about joining an organized wagon party, but also worried that it was much too large a company to be efficient. Our group brought the number of wagons in this company to 55 wagons and well over 350 cattle.

News was brought to the train by a Mr. Webb, editor of the *Independence Expositor*, and Mr. Hay, the great-grandson of Daniel Boone. They reported the existence of hostilities on the Rio Grande between Mexico and the United States. We all wondered how this state of affairs would affect us upon our arrival in California. Most of us felt that California would soon become a territory of the United States either by war or by purchase. Many in our company, mostly the young men, were excited by the prospects of a revolution and hoped that the hostilities would wait for them to arrive so they could participate.

George was of a different opinion. "We ain't goin' to California to create a revolution nor do anythin' that would be a discredit or a dishonor to ourselves or our country. I'm afraid that ambitious men will cause a spirit of war amongst the emigrants an' those folks there who already favor comin' under the domain of the United States. I'm hopin' that it can be done in a peaceable fashion an' in good order."

Church services were held by the Reverend Dunleavy and all of us attended. After the service we had a potluck dinner.

"Seems like that preacher," said George, "all he knows is fire and brimstone. I don't see how a lovin' God could ever be mean enough to create a place like Hell. There's enough Hell on earth without there bein' any call for it elsewhere."

George looked at me after I nudged his leg under the table with my foot. Questioning the common view on religion did not set well with some people. Mrs. Thornton placed her handkerchief over her mouth and coughed delicately.

"You folks are from Illinois?" she asked.

"Yes, we are. Springfield."

"Oh, we're from Illinois also. Quincy. Did you attend a church in Springfield?"

"The Germany Prairie Christian Church," I answered. "It was George's church from long before we were married, Mrs. Thornton."

"Well, that meal was spectacular!" exclaimed Mr. West. "It is amazin' how you women can put on such a spread out here in the wilderness. Have any of you ever experienced buffalo meat?"

"Actually, you are using the incorrect terminology, Mr. West," said Mr. Thornton. "They are correctly called *bison.*"

"Is that right? I always heard them called buffalo—"

"Yes, but strictly speaking, they are *bison.*"

Mr. Thornton always seemed a bit peevish.

That evening, Colonel Russell, obviously stimulated by the illustrious visitors and the arrival of our group, and also by a liberal dose of spirits, climbed on a stump and treated all to his oratory. I remember him as a large, portly man, his gray hair always covered by a Panama hat. He began by welcoming us to the "Russell" train, acknowledging that we were the finest of citizens and introducing us to the assemblage. Then he addressed the group and told us that we were the vanguard of "Manifest Destiny."

"Y'all are history," he said. "Do not think of history as somethin' remote that concerns only kings, queens, an' generals. It concerns *you.*" He brought a jug up to his mouth and drank from it, wiping his mouth with the back of his hand. "Yes, you an' your families march across the pages of history. Often it is that he who plows a furrow is of more importance than he who leads an army. The army can destroy, the furrow can feed."

It was an interesting thought, being the vanguard of the great migration that was sure to follow and helping to civilize and build a whole new territory.

The next morning thirteen wagons separated themselves from the train, giving as a reason that the company was too large and too slow. It seemed to be a common occurrence that groups would form together, only to separate and form again with another group. Other than the usual amount of confusion and bickering that would take place in a large group of disparate people, we enjoyed a smoothness of travel that surprised us.

We next traveled through a high, undulating country. As it was dry for a change, it was easy going for our teams. We camped for the night on a tributary of the Kansas River, which had oak trees lining its banks.

It was not long after we camped that we were visited by a large contingent of Kansas Indians numbering perhaps four or five hundred. One young man, very handsome, seemed to be a leader over the young men of the delegation. He had suspended from his neck a medal with a likeness of the United States President, John Tyler.

Everyone was amazed at the dress and demeanor of the Indians, as these were the first we had seen in any number. The three youngest girls clung to my skirts and we backed up to the wagon to observe, but not be in close proximity to this colorful but dirty assemblage.

"Mother, what makes that noise when they walk?" asked one of the girls.

"They have some metal pieces attached to their garments that jingle when they move. It's quite musical, isn't it?"

"Yes. I think I would like to have some jingles," said Frances.

That evening we placed a strong guard around our encampment, fearful that if we didn't, the morning would find us short of many items, including our animals.

May 22, 1846

Our camp is filled & surrounded by Indians of the Kansas tribe, numbering perhaps four or five hundred. They are mostly in a wretched condition, their clothing in tatters & exceedingly dirty and foul. Some have long hair, very unkempt, but others, probably warriors, have shorn their heads close to the skin except for a tuft extending from the forehead over the crown of the head down to the neck, resembling the comb of a rooster.

In spite of their ragged demeanor, many have an intelligent countenance. They are well-proportioned & almost handsome in appearance. One of the men was Ke-he-ga-wa-chuck-ee, meaning "the rashly brave" or "fool-hardy." He was a commanding figure, supposedly a chief, about fifty-five years of age. An arrangement of trade was made & Ke-he-ga-wa-chuck-ee pledged that none of his people would steal or molest our encampment in any way. However, later in the night two Indians were taken prisoner. As it turned out they were there by appointment with a member of the train who wanted to trade whiskey for a horse. They (the Indians) had concealed their visit from the chief because they did not want to share the whiskey with other Indians. The trade fell through & the Indians were discharged, much to their relief, and they returned to their camp.

With the dawn the Indians were back begging for food. A collection was made of flour, bacon, and other things, and was given to the chief to be shared amongst his villagers. This seemed to content the Indians and we left them.

We moved on through a fertile valley. On the one side was a chain of mound-shaped hills and on the other a creek, which had been given the name "Hurricane Creek." We observed the wild rose and the tulip in full bloom.

We had been followed by several of the Indians and one of them gave us a root, which I prepared. It was as good as the finest Irish potato. I wanted to find where we could dig them, but wasn't able to communicate with the Indians on this matter. It was frustrating not to be able to converse with these people. George remarked how fertile the ground seemed to be and marveled at the agricultural possibilities of the land.

"The few who populate this land, these poor wretched Indians, don't have the least sense of the natural wealth of the country. If they would just learn to use the hoe an' some seed, they wouldn't have to scrounge the countryside searchin' for the little game there is."

I thought about George's remark for a moment.

"George, you're just looking at a small part of the picture. They are a Neolithic culture, hunter gatherers like the earlier people in Europe. I'm not sure they aren't perfectly happy spending their days in the freedom of these wild spaces rather than tied to the plow."

"There's Indians who farm an' grow their sustenance or most of it, anyways. Like the Mandans, the Indians who live on the upper Missouri."

"Yes. But I don't think these nomadic people will adapt to our ways anytime soon. Someday they will be forced into a more civilized manner of living, but it seems a shame. Their wild country will be forever shrinking away in the face of an onslaught of westering white people."

"Hmmph." George didn't agree. "It's a waste of good resources to have only a handful of Indians holdin' sway over so much good land."

"But they have, I should say *had,* immense freedom. Can you imagine? They roam this glorious land and take from it everything they need to maintain themselves. At least they could before their contact with the white man. It's like, if you cage a wild animal, it will die. The same holds true for these wild people. Why can't we, I mean the white people as a whole, be content with what we have? Why do we have to take their land from them? Every one of us crossing this land had enough where we were but we want more. But in order to get it, someone else—the Indians, the Mexicans—have to move over and let us in."

"We ain't takin' their land, Tamsen."

"Are not taking, George. No, not us. But someday it will be taken by others just as it has been from the Atlantic to the Missouri. But as we travel through their land we take the grass, foul the water, hunt and kill the animals. We take these things from them. George, can't you understand what I'm saying?"

"I ain't—I'm not hankerin' to have anythin' to do with the Indians or their country. We have to cross their land. They're gettin' their price by all their beggin' an' stealin'."

May 25, 1846

We crossed a stream known as Vermilion Creek. It is the largest stream we've had to cross since leaving Kansas. The eastern bank was very steep & the crossing so difficult that it took several hours. The current of this stream is stronger than the streams we have crossed on the prairie so far. We are on a gradual incline that will eventually take us to a much greater elevation in the Rocky Mountains. Perhaps that is the reason for the faster flow.

We are told that between this stream & the Big Blue River

there is neither wood nor water. We have filled our water casks & stocked up with wood.

This evening we camped on a high elevation of the prairie about five miles west of the Vermilion. As we were making camp a violent storm struck with thunder, lightning & a torrential downpour that wet everything. Our wagons were in danger of being overturned, the wind was so strong.

It soon passed over & we were rewarded with a most beautiful rainbow. It is almost worth the violent attack as the air is cleansed & we are free of the choking dust that has been plaguing us. Our travel 15 miles this day, only 10 yesterday.

Mr. Bryant came to our camp to talk with George.

"I am beginning to feel alarmed at the slowness of the company," he said. "Many of the party appear to be desirous of shortening each day's march as much as possible and once encamped are reluctant to move. Would you back me up in a resolution aimed at getting the board to impose a better discipline?"

"I feel it's hopeless, but let's see if we can get the board of governors to beat on people a little bit," replied George.

The following morning came dark and gloomy and rainy, with a howling wind piercing us through our soaked clothing to our very bones. We were delayed starting off, because one of our drivers was wretchedly sick from the affects of a drunken spree the night before. He was put in one of the wagons where he lay moaning most of the morning.

"It's always somethin' that keeps us from gettin' started early," complained George.

"It's disgusting!" I told George. "Where do they get this stuff?"

"I think that several in the company still have whiskey to sell to the Indians."

"I hope the supply runs out soon," I said.

May 27, 1846

I feel sorrow for these poor wretched Indians, but over time immemorial people have conquered other people & imposed their culture & their law on them. Is this as God intended? It doesn't seem reasonable, but every time a nation conquers another, they invoke a God-given right.

Today we reached bluffs that overlook the Big Blue River. A most terrific thunderstorm raged throughout most of the night with deafening crashes of thunder, torrents of water & fantastic meteoric displays. As a result of the storm, the river rose several feet & we have been unable to ford it since. This delay, added to our already slow pace, has affected the mood of the company quite negatively. As the Indians would say, "Their hearts have become bad."

A meeting of the company was held yesterday morning at eight o'clock to draw up additional regulations for the governance of the wagon train during the journey. In these assemblies some of the men become very combative & the use of violent language is common. (Women do not usually attend, but they would most likely make a better job of it.) A motion was made to appoint a standing committee to try the officers when charged with tyranny or neglect of duty by any individual of the party & it was carried, whereupon all the officers resigned.

Mr. Bryant was dismayed at the course of events & asked the company to reconsider this vote. The company then voted to the opposite effect & reelected the officers. Mr. Bryant says that this illustrates the dilemma of emigrant life where no law prevails except the will of the people. He thinks that most people want order and organization & to do what the majority considers right, but unfortunately, there are men & women in the emigrating parties who perpetually endeavor to produce discord & this causes much dissension & waste of time with innumerable meetings.

The country was still rolling hills, but now we noticed that it was broken up somewhat. We began an ascent over elevated ridges and reached the bluffs that overlooked the Big Blue River. Cottonwoods grew out of dense undergrowth on the tongues of land where the river made a bend. It was impossible to cross, as the stream was much swollen from the recent rain, and it appeared that we would be unable to cross for a day or two. Most of the women, myself included, brought out the kettles and tubs and began the work of washing the Kansas dust and mud from our clothes and bedding.

"If childbirth don't get'cha in yer twenties an' thirties, the hard work a' washing the damned clothes will surely do ya' in by yer forties," griped Betsey as we bent over the washtubs.

"I told our men that I would wash their clothes if they would bathe. They look like pigs and smell worse. But George told them to wash their own clothes and bathe too. I'm relieved. It's hard enough doing ours."

"Yeah, but our teamster, Jim Smith, he's smarter than the rest. He's sparkin' that daughter of old man Brunell an' gettin' her to do his wash. The other boys are looking to do the same. The old man's wonderin' why his old maid daughter is all a'sudden so popular."

That evening I rearranged part of our wagon in order to sit inside in my rocking chair, shaded and away from the confusion. The canvas was tied up to allow the breeze to come through. On the other side of the wagon a group of our men were squatted down talking, cleaning guns, and doing other small work that was a constant thing on the journey. I was exhausted from the day's work, but I was determined to write one of the letters I had promised to Mr. Francis. The girls were in Jacob's camp with their cousins and George was attending one of the interminable meetings.

I relaxed, gazing out at the view of the countryside. We were camped in a delightful grove of large trees whose leaves rustled and twinkled in the breeze. I picked up my pencil and was ruminating on how to begin, when I noticed a woman walking alone along the little stream bordering our camp. She was a fleshy woman with very light hair. I guessed that her intention was to bathe, as she was headed into some thick bushes. As I watched her I became aware that the talk of the men, which had been low, sporadic, and mumbling, had suddenly enlivened, with laughter. My ears perked up, but I was not even conscious of it until I got a grasp of the conversation. They were talking about the woman.

"Too fat for my taste, but you know Bunzel? That big oaf in with Harlan? He's been throwing his leg over that mound regular like, but pretends he don't even know her come daytime."

"She's been chasing after Noah here. You done give in yet, Noah?"

"I'm so damn horny I'd take up with most anythin' but not that one. I heard she almost kilt ol' Zins, almost squashed and smothered him an' he deflated like a stuck rubber mattress. He only lasted part of a night."

They all laughed uproariously.

"Well, pretty soon it don't matter what it is, it starts lookin' good after dark. When we gets into the real Injun country a man might find a willin' squaw. I done heard tell these Injun women like it. You gives 'em a few beads or ribbons an' they spread wide an' their men make the arrangements."

I could feel my face turn hot and anger flooded through me. *What trash!* I stuck my head out through a side opening overlooking the men, who evidently had no idea I was nearby.

"If you men even think of dallying with any woman in our camp or any Indian woman, your employment will be immediately terminated. Do you understand me?"

The men gawked up at me in consternation.

"No ma'am, no ma'am. We's just talkin', didn't mean anythin' by it."

"I did not mean to eavesdrop, but I could not help overhearing. Nevertheless, I mean what I say."

"Yes'm. We sure won't—"

"You won't what?" asked George, who had just walked up. The men all scattered like quail, disappearing into the camp. After I had explained to George what had transpired, he remonstrated with me.

"Tamsen, that's nothin' a lady should have gotten involved in. You should have just pretended you never heard. Now the men'll be all embarrassed an' not actin' natural. It was just men talk."

"Don't give me that nonsense, George. I will not have our men involved in such dirtiness. Think about our girls. Things like that just get around."

"It's life, it's human nature. It's a side of men—" He looked balefully at me, embarrassed. "You can't expect—look, Tamsen, what they do on their own an' out of our camp is their own business."

"George, just let me hear one snippet about any of our men and I will keep my word. The guilty party will be banned from our camp."

"Don't you think you're overreactin' on this?"

"I am not going to back down, George."

"Why did I think you would?"

May 28, 1846

Another terrible rainstorm during the night with deafening crashes of thunder & crackling of lightning. Two of Mr. Grayson's oxen were found dead this morning, struck by lightning. The torrential rain soaked through our covers & wetted down what we had so laboriously washed & dried yesterday. Few could sleep last night during the storm & most of us are "dragging" today. Incessant meetings are held to review, adjust, & reaffirm the rules & regulations, but most of the time they are ignored or not enforced. The party operates as a democracy & all laws have been proposed to a general assembly to be passed by a majority. Disputes are arbitrated, but the court of arbiters hasn't much authority & most of the time the condemned party is acquitted after taking the decision to the assembly of the whole. George is disgusted.

The river had risen several feet during the night and it was evident we would not be able to cross for several days. Dissension was reaching a breaking point. A meeting was held and after much abusive language and talk was thrown about, all the officers resigned. Mr. Bryant stepped into the fray and reasoned with the group, whereby the officers were re-elected. The incessant quarreling and dissension caused the breaking off of groups and families from trains, only to join or be joined by another group just as unsatisfactory or as unhappy as in the previous situation.

As we lay by in camp waiting for the waters to recede, we had an opportunity for some exploring. About three-fourths of a mile from our camp we found a beautiful spring of water, very cold and pure. It flowed from a ledge of rocks, falling about ten feet into a pool. We named it "Alcove Springs."

The water continued very high, so a call was made for workers to construct a raft that we might ferry our wagons over without waiting for the waters to recede. A number of men assembled with their axes and other tools. They felled two large cottonwood trees, from which canoes were hollowed out and a cross-frame made to fit the wheels of the wagons. When the craft was finished it was christened "Blue River Rover" and all commenced to cheer as she floated down the river to the embarkation point.

May 31, 1846
Alcove Springs, Big Blue River

Mrs. Keyes died two days ago. I attended to her as best I could, but could do nothing for the eye that pained her or her blindness. I feel that my medicines helped relieve her suffering somewhat, but death could not be forestalled. Everyone is gloomy, but we do all we can to comfort the family. I feel badly for Patty & Virginia who were very close to their grandmother. A coffin was made from a cottonwood tree & a stone fashioned and engraved. A Presbyterian minister, Reverend Cornwall, gave the service. Margaret is a Methodist, but there is not a Methodist minister within reach, if at all. It is a beautiful spot, which has been named "Alcove Springs" by Mr. Bryant. Several, including James Reed, have carved their names upon the rocks from which the spring flows. James promised Margaret that someday they would return & take her mother back to Illinois.

We commenced to cross the wagons over the Big Blue yesterday afternoon and the last wagons were ferried over about nine o'clock *this evening. The day was very cold, 48 degrees at 4:00 this afternoon, then it commenced to rain with a fierce wind. The cold & rain & the extreme physical demands have taken a toll on everyone.*

A fight in which fists & knives were weapons of choice broke out near the river bank between two drivers who were normally peaceable men. They were separated quickly & no damage was done to either. This is an example of how perpetual irritations experienced on the journey can come to a boiling point.

We have now covered one mile since we were brought up short by the Big Blue.

The weather took a chill turn, the kind of raw chill that creeps through the clothes and draws up the skin. Soon masses of black clouds rolled in and it commenced to rain. The fall in temperature and the rain made the night extremely uncomfortable. With the ferocious wind it seemed like we were in the middle of winter rather than early summer. In the morning we moved from the bottom land of the Blue to a high rolling prairie. We noticed that timber was becoming scarce.

June 1, 1846

Today we passed the graves of two children buried within the past few days. At the head of one was a stone with the inscription, May 28, 1846, & the other was dressed with a small wooden cross.

How sad! These poor little children, left in this desolate wilderness with no one to care for their graves. I weep for their mothers, how they must suffer!

Epidemics of diarrhea are raging. We believe it is the water that is giving us this physicking. I mix our drinking water with corn meal and let it settle out, hoping some of the minerals & alkali will be absorbed.

Again we had to cross a stream, a tributary of the Blue, another vexing task. After crossing, we camped in a bottom a distance off the road. It is obvious that a large company with a great many livestock is in front of us. It is becoming difficult to find an area that has not been grazed.

It seems with each passing day we have more & more altercations and disagreements. Today a dissension that had simmered from the first boiled over. Two men of the company, Oregon emigrants who were partners, have been engaged in a heated dispute for several days. One owned the wagon & the other the oxen that were pulling the wagon. Today on the road, the owner of the oxen wanted to exercise his right of ownership by taking them from the wagon. The wagon owner refused and the matter was brought to a meeting of arbitration, but before any justice could be applied an angry confrontation broke out between the two men & threatened to become bloody. The camp was aroused by the noise & intervention took place, but the dispute was not settled. As a consequence, the two groups, those bound for California & those for Oregon, agreed, in an amiable way, to separate. This relieved us of the burden of the quarrelsome men, but many of us were saddened because we had developed friendships & attachments to these people over the course of the journey.

People were not the only creatures to have developed attachments. In our company there was a man who owned a small mule named Willy. Ridden mostly by the man's daughter, a girl of about ten, they would often join one of our girls riding our mare, Margaret. Within a few days the mule developed an attachment for the mare. The sentiment, however, was not reciprocated on Margaret's part and she intimated as much by using her feet and her teeth to inform Willy that she would have no part in the "affair." These signals of displeasure had no affect on the little mule except to increase his devotion and whenever at liberty he sought to get near to her and when restrained he became much distressed.

When the wagon party bound for Oregon left us, Willy left with his master, but soon appeared on our march happily trotting alongside our mare. Willy's owner, Mr. Tibbets, a small, weasel-faced man who had the annoying habit of constantly sucking on his teeth, was very unhappy as he had to travel many miles to collect him. His displeasure came to a boiling point on his second trip to collect Willy and he began to beat the wayward mule with a heavy stick. He held Willy's head tight with his rope and hit his flank hard with the stick, the mule braying and dancing his rear feet away as each blow descended. George saw this and came up. "Sir, lay off that animal. I don't think beating on him is goin' to get him to change. He's plumb fixiated."

"I'm flat wore out chasin' this stupid mule."

"Mr. Tibbets," I said, "why don't you sell Willy to us and put you both out of this misery? Our girls can ride him."

George started shaking his head and frowning and began to say something, but I gave him a look and he stopped. Mr. Tibbets paused as he was preparing to give Willy another whack. He slanted his eyes over at me and lowered his arm, sucking on his teeth for a moment. "How much you plan on paying fer this exceptional mule?" Avarice had replaced the anger in his voice.

"What do you think is a fair price?" I asked.

"This mule is the best natured critter I ever seen, not contrary at all like most mules. I wouldn't take less than thirty dollars." He patted Willy affectionately.

"Mr. Tibbets, I need to talk this over with my husband."

George and I walked off a short distance, putting a wagon between us and Mr. Tibbets.

"That's robbery, Tamsen. We don't need no mule to be a bother to us."

"Willy's not a bother at all and the little girls can ride him. He won't stray away from Margaret. We don't want Mr. Tibbet's telling people we stole his mule and we don't want him mistreating him either. Give him thirty dollars," I said. "Consider it ransom."

George took the money from his money belt and we walked back to Mr. Tibbets and Willy, now surrounded by all five of our girls.

"Here's thirty dollars, Tibbets. My wife will write up a bill of sale for you to sign."

Leanna and Frances held Willy's rope while George lifted Georgeanna and Eliza onto Willy's back. Leanna started giggling. "He reminds me of a beaver when he pulls back his lips and sucks on his teeth."

"Willy sucks on his teeth?" asked Frances.

"No, stupid. Mr. Tibbets."

So Willy became part of our family. Everybody was happy except our choosy equine, Margaret.

June 3, 1846

Our route takes us over an ever-ascending landscape. Timber is only to be found near streams or springs. The days are pleasant, the breeze enough to cool the skin. Our march has been over a high tableland dotted with small trees indicating the localities of a spring or a pool of stagnant water.

During today's travel we encountered a group of four Shawnee Indians returning from a hunting expedition. They were invited to overnight in Mr. Bryant's camp & they did so, having supper and breakfast with him. Our group made busy writing letters as the Indians agreed to take mail back with them.

We were moving on an inclined plane, but so gradual it was not readily detected. The vegetation seemed to be slower coming on than further back on the road. Trees were still bare of foliage and flowers were just beginning to come into bloom.

I was always looking for vegetables and fruits to include in our meals and plants that had curative potency. Earlier in the journey I had collected dandelion leaves, butterfly weed, and sassafras bark. The day before I'd found sweetflag roots. This day as I was walking out to the side of the wagons, I spied a patch of prickly pear. Someone had told me that eating the prickly pear could prevent scurvy and I determined I would harvest some, but the sharp needles defeated me. Later in the march I obtained the necessary weapons from the wagon and attacked a plant, managing to acquire several clumps of it, which I carried back to the wagon in a cloth bag. That evening I boiled the cacti so the needles would drop off. The soft interiors of the joints were delicious.

There were numerous accidents and breakdowns with the wagons within the company. One day it was Mr. Bryant's wagon, damaged so severely that several hours were needed for repairs. The train moved on, but several in the group stopped to help, including George and Jacob. While the men were working on the wagon, we women took advantage of the time to catch up on chores. I was leaning over our fire, keeping a close watch on some baking pies, when I heard one of the boys calling to me.

"Auntie Tamsen, look."

I looked up to see Solomon, trailed by the rest of the children, carrying a huge rattlesnake. The head of the snake was jammed in the fork of a large stick, the body curling and whipping as it tried to free itself. The terrible mouth gaped open, tongue flashing and curling between dripping fangs. I dropped the pan I was holding and shrieked for the girls to get away, then sprinted for the wagon. I picked up our rifle, but it wasn't charged. Throwing the gun down, I ran for the Bryant wagon and yelled at the men to come kill the snake. Solomon dropped the stick when he saw the men running up with guns and the released snake coiled itself up, but then decided a retreat was in order and made off, passing under one of the wagons and heading toward another with the men in hot pursuit. They shot at it, missing completely, but finally one of the men picked up a huge rock and threw it down on the snake's head. It lay twitching for a few moments and then was still.

I grabbed a branch off the firewood pile and took after Solomon, hitting at him as he held up his arms to ward off the blows. By that time Betsey, who'd been resting in her wagon, came on the scene wondering what was going on. She saw the men kill the snake and then looked around to see me thrashing at Solomon. She put her hand on my arm.

"What'd he do? Tamsen! What did he do?"

Panting and shaking, I dropped my stick and shouted at Solomon. "Don't you know what could have happened? One of you might have been bitten. How could you do such a stupid thing around the girls?"

Solomon slunk off and I collapsed on a chair, still shaking. George came and patted my back. "Honey, the snake's dead. The girls are all right. It was just a prank."

Mr. Bryant examined the dead snake. "If no one else wants it, I'll take it. I have heard they're quite edible." He rolled the rock off the snake's head and picked it up.

"I don' know, Bryant, my throat just kind of shuts up at the thought of snake meat," said Mr. Curry, who traveled in company with Mr. Bryant and usually prepared their meals. Solomon followed Mr. Bryant back to his wagon. "Mr. Bryant, I'd like some of the skin to make a hat band."

"Do you like snake meat, Solomon?"

"I never et any, but I'm willin' to try it."

• • •

The next day we came up to a stream that had steep banks and caused a delay in the forward movement of the train. Betsey and I and the children sat down under a cottonwood tree near the stream, watching the wagons skitter one by one down the side of the near bank and then slowly ascend the far bank, pulled by the oxen in front and pushed by sweating and cursing men in back.

As we watched we saw one of the wagons begin to tilt. Several people shouted a warning, but once started, the wagon could not be stopped from falling. The helping men jumped out of the way as the wagon fell over on its side, throwing a woman and small child into the water and mud. Fortunately, they escaped injury, but the contents of the wagon were muddy. Our forward wagon passed while the wagon was being pulled out of the stream. While our men were crossing the rest of our wagons and stock, Betsey and I helped the woman gather up the things that had spilled out and then we moved on.

"They'll have to lay by. The pole of the wagon was broken," said George. "The man's got help. He's travelin' with a bunch of other Germans."

That evening Betsey and I discussed the family while we were finishing up our chores.

"I feel sorry for her," said Betsey. "Such a pretty little woman, an' that man treats her terrible like. Miz Hoppe said she's seen him beatin' on her. And her so far along with child."

"Yes, I've seen it too. Something should be done about it."

"Done about what?" asked George, who was sitting nearby talking to James Reed.

"You know the man that had the turned-over wagon today?"

"Name's Keseberg."

"We cannot abide the way he treats his wife. He has a violent temper and takes out his anger on her and beats her."

"I don't know the man, but I've heard he's downright unsociable."

"I wish that you would speak to him."

"Tamsen, I ain't gonna interfere in another man's affairs."

"If you saw this man approach another with the intent to batter him or shoot or knife him, what would you do?"

"That's not the same thing."

"How can you say that? It's an assault no matter how you look at it."

"We ain't goin' to get involved in somethin' that's none of our affair."

"I disagree with you, George," said James. "Something should be done about it. A man who is brutal to women disgusts me. I'm going to talk to the man."

The next evening James went to the Keseberg wagons.

"What you want?" Mr. Keseberg asked him.

"You have been observed beating your wife and it will not be tolerated."

Mr. Keseberg looked around and then motioned James away from his wagon.

"What affair is it of yours?"

"I'm making it my affair. If such treatment happens again, I will see to it that you are expelled from the company."

"You have not the right to tell me what to do, Reed, and you cannot expel me from the company."

James's tone was short. "I advise you that you will be removed from this company if you mistreat your wife again. Good day, sir."

James was a difficult man to understand. I appreciated his concern about the treatment of Mrs. Keseberg and I thought his sympathy was genuine. Still, I wondered if he acted because of real feelings of sympathy and a desire to protect or from a compulsion to exert his will over others.

The Keseberg wagons fell farther back in the column and since we didn't meet them in our daily activities, I forgot about the family. Then one day while we were stopped for our noon break, Mr. Keseberg came to our camp. He looked worried and tense and he approached me with his hat in his hand.

"Please excuse this interruption in your meal, Mrs. Donner. I beg of you to come to my wife. It is her time and she needs a woman's help."

"Of course. Let me gather up some things."

"Mother," said Leanna, "I'll help."

I grabbed up my medicine bag, some clean cloths, and a sheet and followed Mr. Keseberg back to his wagon.

Mrs. Keseberg was lying on a narrow pallet that ran the long way of the wagon, her little girl sitting on the bed at her feet. The wagon was stifling in the mid-day heat. I placed my hands on Mrs. Keseberg's stomach. The baby was very low but did not feel right.

"How long has it been?" I asked her.

"Yesterday before we stop. I think something is wrong. My daughters came in only two hours."

I began setting out the things I had brought. Then I looked out the cover opening for Mr. Keseberg.

"Mr. Keseberg, would you wet down the cover on this wagon? And please, raise the side sheets. It is beastly in here. I will need a kettle of hot boiled water and a bucket of clean water."

"I don't have a fire."

"Build one immediately, Mr. Keseberg. Ask one of your company to drench the cover on this wagon. Leanna, try to swish the flies out of here."

Just then Mrs. Dunbar came to the cover opening.

"I saw you hurryin' here, Miz Donner, an' I figured you might need help. What can I do?"

"Oh, thank you. I will need hot water that has been boiled and Mr. Keseberg has no fire."

"I'll get it. The neighbor wagon has a fire."

"Wait, please." I searched for the herbs I wanted in my medicine bag. *Raspberry leaves ... to relax the muscles and ... yes, elderberry bark for pain and to help things along.*

"Mrs. Dunbar, would you make a tea from these? Use about a quart of boiling water."

I felt coolness as someone began wetting down the canvas of the wagon and a little breeze as the side curtains were tied up. A bucket of cool water was handed up. I wrung a sheet out in the water and hung it up in the back opening of the wagon so the breeze coming through the cloth might cool us a little. Then I wet a small cloth and sponged Mrs. Keseberg's face, arms, and chest.

"Thank you," she whispered.

Mrs. Dunbar appeared at the wagon opening and I motioned to Leanna. "Honey, step out. There's not enough room for all of us."

Mrs. Dunbar climbed up into the wagon and Mr. Keseberg handed up a kettle of hot water.

"Mrs. Donner, we must move out. The wagons are leaving," he said.

"Oh, *Gott*!" groaned Mrs. Keseberg.

"Mr. Keseberg, let them pull around. We can't be jostled to pieces in here. This is not going to be an easy birth."

"No! Make yourselves ready. We cannot be left behind."

"I brought a clean ground sheet," I told Mrs. Dunbar. "Let's prepare the bed for birthing."

Mrs. Keseberg raised up on an elbow and pointed to a bundle on top of a trunk. "The birthing things, they are there."

"Mrs. Keseberg, shall I send your little one with Leanna? My girls will take care of her."

"Oh, yes, please."

"What is her name?"

"Ada."

I called to Leanna and carefully handed the child down to her.

"Go to our wagon, Leanna, and take the child with you. Her name is Ada. Tell your father that I will be with Mrs. Keseberg for a time."

"Should I come back?" asked Leanna.

"No. You and Elitha look after the little ones."

The wagon jolted and then began moving. I looked at the laboring woman, exhausted and weak, every muscle sore, now to again be bumped around by the movement of the wagon.

"Your husband is an ass, Mrs. Keseberg."

"Yes."

The wagon rolled and jerked over the uneven ground. I frequently gave Mrs. Keseberg sips of the cooled tea. She moaned and cried as the pain of the labor increased. Twice the wagon stopped and Mr. Keseberg inquired about his wife.

"She is having a hard time and the jostling of the wagon is not helping any."

"I cannot stop. We must not be left behind. It is dangerous."

Mrs. Dunbar and I could not find a place to be comfortable. We perched here and there on the boxes and gear that were in the wagon, jerked back and forth and up and down as the wagon lurched and jolted over the rough road. I was worried. The birth was taking much too long and the breech birth posed a grave threat to the child. Death from childbirth was a frequent occurrence. A woman lived in fear that the birth would be difficult and she would die in childbirth or that she would come down with childbed fever a few days later and die from that.

Anger nettled me. *How could this man have been so thoughtless, so cruel, as to begin this journey with his wife far along in pregnancy? With all the hardship of taking care of a small child and the hard work of the journey?*

The contractions became very close together, but the baby was making no progress. Finally, the wagons stopped for the evening camp.

"Do you think we should try to turn the baby?" Mrs. Dunbar asked me.

"I think it's too late."

"Oh, *Gott.* I knew something was wrong," cried Mrs. Keseberg.

"Mrs. Keseberg, when you feel the next tightening, push."

"Oh, *Gott.* Oh, *Gott.*" Mrs. Keseberg cried out and groaned in each effort. Mr. Keseberg's face appeared in the cover opening. "It is taking so long."

"Please make hot water as soon as you can and stop bothering us!"

I immediately felt sorry for my irritation. The man was obviously very concerned. When he returned with the water, I apologized. "I'm sorry, Mr. Keseberg, for speaking harshly. I don't think it will be much longer."

Finally, the baby came out. He was a little blue in color but soon found his breath and managed a squeaky little cry.

"You have a beautiful baby boy, Mrs. Keseberg."

After we washed and oiled the baby, he pinked up nicely and we wrapped him up and handed him to his mother. She was too exhausted to do anything more than cuddle him next to her. She placed her hand on my arm. "I am very grateful."

We finished the work of cleaning up and left the wagon. Mr. Keseberg was hovering nearby.

"You have a fine son. The labor was hard, a feet-first birth. She is very weak and must have complete rest for several days. I will come back later to see her."

I attended Mrs. Keseberg for several days until she could resume her normal activities. I did not see the Keseberg family again until we were almost to Fort Bridger.

June 8, 1846
The Valley of the Platte

My Dear Friend:

We reached bluffs overlooking the valley of the Platte River yesterday & today we are on the Platte, the River of the West. The river is sluggish & not very deep, no more than four feet at the deepest. There are only a few trees & these are cottonwood. All around on the prairie we see flat white patches of alkali.

The course of the Platte River is generally from west to east & we will follow it for some distance. We are beginning to see the bones of buffalo, but the live creatures have not as yet appeared.

Our girls, who have been thoroughly briefed on what to expect on our journey, have been asking when we might see the buffalo. Every day someone thinks they have spotted one of the creatures, but it is always something else. Yesterday two of our men chased what they thought were buffalo, only to discover it was other men out hunting.

We have had a couple of Indian scares. A report came in that Pawnees ran off over a hundred head of livestock in a company about ten days ahead of us and two men were killed when they attempted to recover the stock. One of the men killed was Mr. Trimble. Another company about three miles ahead of us had a party of twenty or thirty Pawnees attempt to break into their camp, but they managed to keep them off. These events caused several families to turn back. Needless to say, this caused our company to double the guard.

Mrs. George Donner

Day after day, week after week, we went through the same weary routine. Breaking camp at day-break, yoking the oxen, cooking our rations over a fire of scrub-oak, buffalo chips, or sagebrush, packing up again the coffee pot and camp kettle, then rushing to pack everything away and gather up the children before the wagons would start rolling again, only to do everything in reverse when striking camp that evening. Often there wasn't water enough to wash clothes or to bathe. This was very vexing for me, as it was my habit to bathe often and I required everyone else in the family to do the same.

One particularly nice evening I had finished with my chores and the children were in bed. George was at a neighbor's fire talking with the men. The day had been very hot and the dust particularly thick and cloying and I was miserable being so dirty and caked with alkali dust. The caustic burned and itched terribly when trickles of sweat would activate the harsh chemicals.

I decided to take advantage of the solitude to go to the river to cleanse myself of the layers of dirt and dust that would not succumb to my ministrations with a bucket of water and cloth. Taking my toilet bag from the hook just inside the wagon opening, I went over to George and whispered to him that I was going to the river to bathe.

"I'll go with you. Might be Indians lurking around."

"I would rather go alone. It will be all right. There are camps all around. I feel perfectly safe."

I followed a narrow path through a thicket of willows to the river. As I approached the stream the sounds from the camp became muted—the growl of a dog contesting the ownership of a bone, a snatch of talk, the laugh of a woman. It was a beautiful evening, the dusk thick and soft. The chirping of the crickets and the sound of the river talking to itself was pleasant and calming. I sighed. *Moments of solitude are so rare on this journey.*

Moving along the river I found a small open space that led to an eddy in the stream surrounded by growth. I bent over to remove my shoes and suddenly I became aware that I wasn't alone in the thicket. There was a rustling and cracking sound, dry brush being disturbed. Fear shot through my body and my heart began pounding, my breath coming in ragged puffs. *What is it?* More rustling, low grunts. I straightened up, one shoe still in my hand. *A large animal?* I listened carefully as I slowly bent and placed the shoe back on my foot. I turned my head in the direction of the sound and at first could see nothing, but as the moon emerged from behind a cloud and illuminated the thicket I made out two forms on the ground a few feet from me. Moving, rising, pushing. *Oh! Good Lord!* I moved backwards and as I did my foot crushed a piece of dry brush over a hole in the ground. The noise as the wood broke and the shriek that I uttered as I fell caused dogs to begin barking and then I heard shouting.

"Over there. In the willows."

I was sprawled out on the ground, sharp sticks poking me, afraid that if I made a sound, someone would commence shooting. There was crashing and snapping and then a man knelt down beside me.

"It's a woman hurt," he called.

"No, no. I'm not hurt. I was just going to the river to bathe and fell. I'm all right."

"It's Mrs. Donner," he said to the other men. As they helped me up—I'd twisted my ankle when I fell and was gingerly testing it—one of the men discovered the couple in the weeds.

"Who's this?"

The man jumped up and began making a retreat, hopping along as he tried to pull up his pants and run at the same time. The woman had sat up, but was still on the ground, her fair hair gleaming in the moonlight. One of the men stepped through the brush and began to curse.

"Christ sakes! Lucinda, what the hell are you doin'?"

"None a' yer damned business!" Lucinda got to her feet and stalked away, shaking her skirt down and brushing it off with the palms of her hands. The man came back. "That woman is a caution."

The men helped me back to our wagons. George was coming to see what the stir was about and was upset to see me limping between the two men. My face was burning in embarrassment from my predicament and the scene that I had encountered.

"I'm sorry you had to see somethin' like that," said George later. "That woman should be thrown out of this company."

"What about the man?" I asked George.

He looked at me in surprise. "What for?"

The next day I was riding in our wagon nursing my sore ankle when Mrs. Hoppe, who had been waiting by the side of the road, signaled Noah to stop the wagon.

"Mrs. Donner, I'm Mrs. Hoppe. I will be so glad when we're out of this dust. I've heard you're a healer an' I wonder if you would have a treatment for my eyes. I cain't sleep at night they're so inflamed."

"I'm pleased to meet you. Will you come up and join me?"

"I'd be pleased."

Mrs. Hoppe was a large fleshy woman with a red sun-burned face. It was an effort for her to get up into the wagon, but she soon settled herself and Noah started up again.

"I have a wash for the eyes that has helped us," I told her. "In fact, I have two. I will give you both and you can see which works best for you."

"That's mighty nice of you, Mrs. Donner. Could you give me enough to treat my children too?"

"Of course. Are you for California or for Oregon?" I asked.

"We're goin' to California if'n my husband don't change his mind. You're for California, aren't you?"

"Yes, and I doubt we'll change our minds."

"Well, I never wanted to go. I was content, never suspectin' my life would be turned upside down like it's been. One day my husband comes in with a man I never seen before. He says meet Mr. Scanlon, he's buyin' our farm. I said we ain't needin' to sell the farm. My husband didn't say nothin', just took that man all over the place. When he came back he says we're goin' to California. My folks couldn't bear to see us go off, so they pulled up stakes an' come with us. I hope this journey don't kill 'em off."

We were quiet for a few minutes, then Mrs. Hoppe spoke again.

"Well, this is embarrassin' for me to talk about, but I'm at my wits end. You know of Lucinda?"

"Yes."

"I want her out of my camp. I'm askin' some of the women to get together to talk about what can be done with her. I thought she'd help with my chil'ren an' the cookin' an' she does some, but the help I get ain't worth the trouble. We're meetin' at the Dunleavy wagon after supper. Will you come?"

"Yes."

"Well, thank you kindly. If you'll ask your man to stop the wagon I'll get down. I want to talk to some more ladies."

I bade Noah to stop and Mrs. Hoppe lowered herself to the ground, grunting with the effort. That evening I told George where I was going and he was not happy.

"Tamsen, we don't need to get involved with Mrs. Hoppe's problems."

"George, I have already agreed to go."

"Godamighty! Don't agree to have anythin' to do with that Lucinda woman. I don't want her in our camp."

"George, will you stop your ranting? Give me some credit for having some sense. Elitha, you and Leanna look out for the little ones while I attend the meeting."

"Oh, Mother, we were just going to the evening music. Why do we have to watch them? We can't have any fun if they're in the way."

"Elitha, now you mind Mother," said George.

Elitha flounced around a little, but then gathered up the three girls and with Leanna and a group of young people started off. I could hear snatches of talk and giggling about Lucinda.

There were about seven ladies at the meeting. I knew Mrs. Dunleavy and Mrs. West, but was not acquainted with any of the others except Mrs. Hoppe. As we settled ourselves under the fly tent of the wagon, several boys drove livestock past the camp, raising a cloud of dust that slowly drifted over us.

"You'd think they'd have more sense than to drive them animals where the wind carries the dust right into camp," complained Mrs. Hoppe. "They ain't got no more sense than the critters they's drivin'."

A crow coasted overhead and let itself down next to the cooking pit, eyeing us as it pecked in the offal left from cooking. I stared at the crow and it stared back at me, its beady eyes never wavering. *How strange. There's something about that crow that disturbs me.* A chill went through me.

Mrs. Hoppe's voice broke into my thoughts and I forced my mind away from the eerie feeling I was experiencing. She introduced the ladies all around and then launched into the discussion.

"You all know why we're meetin'. Somethin' must be done with that Lucinda woman. I cain't tolerate her another day in my camp."

"You know," said one of the ladies, "I don't understand how she came to be with you in the first place."

"Well, she started out with us, but then went over with the Harlans—"

"Did you ask Mrs. Harlan to come to the meetin'? She ain't here."

"I did. She said she'd had enough of Lucinda an' wasn't goin' to get involved again. Anyways, I was tellin' you 'bout Lucinda.

After the first man run off, she got married again to Mr. Zins. Actually, I don't think a preacher spoke over them. That lasted only a night an' he run off. Then, what got the Harlans mad was she started on one of their drivers an' *he* run off to get away from her. I agreed to take her, thinkin' she'd help with the chil'ren an' we didn' have any single men in our camp. There's something wrong with her. She's dumb!"

"She cain't talk?" asked Mrs. Crabtree.

"No. She ain't got no brains. She's stupid. Last night she was out in the bushes, you know, with a man. I don't know who the man was. Miz Donner, you was out there. Did you see who the man was?"

"It was Mr. Bunzel."

"Bunzel! So he don't mind workin' if'n it's in the bushes. My husband says he cain't get him to do his share of the work. He's always sayin' he's tired an' he's one of the biggest an' strongest men in the company."

Mrs. Dunleavy waved her head scarf to get the attention of the group. She spoke in a queer little up and down squeaky voice.

"The Reverend thinks you should try praying with Lucinda. Get the Lord in her and then she'll give up her wicked ways."

"I tried that, I really did. I don't think Lucinda ever got the hang of what we was prayin' about," replied Mrs. Hoppe.

"What does Lucinda say when you talk to her?" squeaked Mrs. Dunleavy.

"She just keeps sayin' she wants to get married up. She says there wouldn't be no trouble if she just had a man. She likes the beddin' down, but the men just stop too soon. She wants a man that'll keep it up."

"Well, who doesn't?"

Mrs. Dunleavy gasped and pressed her handkerchief to her mouth. A shocked silence descended and everyone stared at the lady who'd just spoken. Her face turned red and she looked down.

"There is something not right about Lucinda," I said. "Her mind has not matured and her thinking is like that of a child.

How can I put this? It's like she has an itch and feels there is no good reason why she shouldn't scratch it. I don't think she understands that her deportment offends."

"I've pretty much come to the same conclusion," said Mrs. Hoppe. "But what if she gets with child from this? It's a wonder she hasn't already."

"Well, let her," said Mrs. Dunlap. "Why worry ourselves about it? It wouldn't be born before California anyways."

"Mrs. Hoppe," I said. "Perhaps there is someone who has a wagon and would allow Lucinda to stay in it alone. She's big and strong and I am sure she's capable of driving the team. If you would provide the necessities for her, she wouldn't need to bother you in your camp. You could close your eyes to what she does."

None of the other ladies had any other ideas to offer Mrs. Hoppe and we chatted about different things for a while and then the ladies got up to leave.

"I'll talk to my husband," said one of the women. "We've got three wagons and only one driver. My ten year old's been drivin' fer us. I'll see what my husband says 'bout gettin' her off in a wagon to herself."

Mr. Campbell reluctantly agreed, provided that Lucinda would take reasonable care of the goods that were in the wagon. At first it seemed to work well, but in a few days it all fell apart. After the company had formed camp for the evening, Lucinda's wagon was nowhere to be seen. Mr. Campbell became uneasy and decided to go back on the trail to find her, just when he saw her walking up to camp.

"What's the trouble?" he asked Lucinda.

"I'm tired of fussin' with those damned ox. I'm goin' back with Miz Hoppe. I ain't no ox driver."

"How far back you left 'em?"

"Where we stopped fer nooning."

"Goddamn it! That's at least six miles. The Injuns probably got the ox and the wagon goods too by now."

Mr. Campbell and his driver jumped on their horses and

pounded off in a flurry of dust, rifles across their saddles. They didn't return until late in the night. The next morning they brought the wagon up to the Hoppe camp. Mrs. Hoppe was just starting her breakfast fire.

"I don't know where Lucinda is. I wouldn't let her near my camp last night. Most likely she's out in the bushes."

"Could have lost my whole outfit and the oxen too. By damn, I'm through trying to help that woman," yelled Mr. Campbell.

He motioned to his driver and they began to throw Lucinda's things out on the ground. Just about that time Lucinda came out of a thicket, yelling and screaming at the men. A crowd formed and the commotion attracted Colonel Russell.

"We cannot leave a woman by the side of the trail. I do not believe we have sunk that low ... yet," he intoned. "This is a company of good Christians. Speak up. Will one of you obey God's law to succor the unfortunate?"

He looked sternly at each person, his faded blue eyes rheumy and bloodshot. One by one they kicked dirt with the toe of their shoes and looked away. Mr. Russell sighed deeply.

"Go on, go on, all a' you."

He was left alone with Lucinda, who was gathering up her things and wailing. Mr. Russell opened a small trunk that had been thrown out of the wagon and stuffed some of the things that were on the ground inside and picked it up.

"Come with me," he said to Lucinda. He led her to the Harlans' camp.

"I ain't gonna have that woman in my camp," yelled Mrs. Harlan when she saw them approaching. "You take her on out of here."

Mr. Harlan was hitching up his oxen and tried to ignore Mr. Russell, but he stepped in front of him.

"Mr. Harlan, there is nothin' to be done but you take her in. Zins married her and that makes her a part of your company. I have the full weight of the company board behind me."

Mr. Harlan threw the gear he had in his hand down on the ground. "Goddamnit!"

• • •

I botanized, wrote in my journal, and held school for my children and several other children when we had a cessation in our march. Occasionally, I wrote letters for the time when a way could be obtained to send them back to the States.

There was a paucity of firewood at this point in the journey and the dung of the buffalo was gathered and used as fuel for our cooking fires, burning hot and clear with virtually no flame. The ground was spotted all around with the disks and we would gather them as we walked, throwing them into a canvas we had stretched under a wagon. Collecting the fuel was one of the chores I assigned to the children. As we journeyed along we would find buffalo skulls, pieces of board, or paper stuck onto a stick with messages written on them. This was a form of communication between forward companies and those who would follow on the trail.

"Mother, one of those messages said that a six year old girl is lost. Do you think the Indians got her?"

"No, she was found and sent ahead to her company. I know how relieved her parents must be. Girls, you must always stay close to the wagons."

June 12, 1846

My Dear Friend:

We are now in the country of the Pawnee Indians, a tribe reported to be vicious savages skilled in thievery. So far we have had little trouble with Indians. Our most pressing problem at this point is the condition of our wagon wheels, which have contracted so much from the effects of the dry atmosphere in this area that the tires have become loose. We are in sagebrush & alkali country now. The atmosphere has changed. It is hard to tell distance; the whiteness glares & hurts our eyes. The sage gives a pungent perfume across the plains.

The temperature has been unseasonably cold & many in our company suffer from sickness as a consequence.

Our march has been over a high tableland of prairie, an expansive inclined plane occasionally dotted with clumps of trees, usually signaling a small stream or spring.

We are beginning now to look for buffalo & every dark object spotted upon the horizon causes a chase, only to be something else. On June 5th we crossed the Little Blue River, following it until diverging from it on the 7th, reaching the bluffs of the Platte on the 8th. The Platte here is about one-hundred fifty yards wide, very sluggish & in no place more than four feet deep. Mosquitoes have been very troublesome since entering the valley of the Platte. It would be a good practice for the future emigrant to put some netting in with the other necessities of travel.

Yesterday we met a party returning to the settlements by water with a quantity of buffalo skins. They had abandoned their boats because of the low level of the Platte & were desirous of trading with the emigrants to obtain horses or mules in order that they could continue their journey. The party consisted of Mr. Bordeau, Mr. Richard, & Mr. Branham, a half-breed Mexican, an Indian, and several Creole Frenchmen of Missouri. The Americans were all of a countenance that characterizes the trapper & traders of the mountains—hardy, resolute, ever ready to meet danger in its most threatening forms. We traded with them for some of their buffalo skins, giving in exchange flour, bacon, sugar, and coffee.

Mrs. George Donner

There were signs that many buffalo had been in the area, as their bleached white bones and dung littered the plains, but still the live creatures were not around. Numerous antelope were seen, but they were too fleet for our hunters mounted on even the fastest horses.

One evening we had just pitched camp when a man approached leading a horse with a dead antelope draped over the saddle. George spoke to him as he neared us.

"Your horse must be a fast one to bag an antelope."

"No, sir, I didn't use my horse. I used this here stick."

He held up a long stick with a handkerchief tied to it and explained to us how he had killed the antelope. "First, you make a stick like this one. You can use a handkerchief or any such white cloth. The antelope is a curious critter and when he sees you moving this handkerchief back an' forth, real slow like, he wants to know what it is. Some are more curious than others. You have to get the right one to see your flag an' after a time he'll come close an' you can get your shot in.

"How long a time did you lay out?" asked George.

"I had my wife to drive the wagon an' I went ahead this mornin' 'til I seen tracks where they go to water. So I went off from there a good distance an' waited. Toward evenin' they came along an' I got one curious about my flag. I jes' kept on movin' it a little an' this here buck he jes' couldn't resist seein' if there was somethin' he should know about an' I got him."

We kept looking for the buffalo herds, but it wasn't until mid-June that buffalo finally appeared on our menu. Messrs. Grayson and Boggs returned to camp after an overnight hunt with their horses loaded with the better pieces of a buffalo cow. They reported that they had seen large numbers of the creatures. This caused a stir among the men and boys in the camps and they began cleaning their rifles and sharpening their knives.

This activity very nearly caused a serious accident in our camp. Betsey's boy, Solomon, went out hunting with no result. When he returned to camp, he placed his fully charged weapon in the wagon amongst some bedding, planning to go out again after our noon stop. As we were eating we heard a rifle bellow very close by, but we didn't think much of it until Jacob came running toward us, yelling.

"Where's Solomon?"

"Why, he's over there," Betsey pointed. "What's the matter?"

"That stupid boy a' yourn left a charged gun in the wagon. It's lucky I wasn't kilt."

Jacob grabbed Solomon's arm and tried to pull him away to the outside of the wagons with one hand while still holding on to the rifle with the other. "A man was killed just recent this same fool way! He had no more sense than you do!"

"Pa! I'm sorry. I'm sorry," cried Solomon. "I won't do it again."

Betsey was hanging onto Jacob's arm. "Jacob, stop. It was an accident. He's sorry."

Jacob threw Betsey off and raised the gun over his head, preparing to bring it down on Solomon, when Betsey grabbed the gun with both hands and hung on, causing Jacob to fall down backwards. Solomon ran, disappearing in the crowded camp. Jacob stayed on the ground, bent over, sucking in air. "I'm goin' to kill that kid," he gasped, trying to rise.

"Let's get him over to the shade," said George. "Noah, give us a hand here."

With George on one side and Noah on the other, they got their shoulders under his arms and with Betsey lifting up his feet, they took him over to a sliver of shade by the wagon and laid him down.

"I just lost my breath, that's all," croaked Jacob. "Just let me rest fer a spell."

"I have medicine," I said. "If we can get him to take it, it might relieve his distress."

"He'll take it," said George. "Go get it."

I ran to our wagon and searched through the packets of folded papers in my medicine box until I found the one I wanted: *For weak heart, 1 tsp of each in qt of boiling water. Dose one cup frequently until symptoms abate. Goldenseal, Skullcap, Cayenne, Lily of the Valley.*

George took the tea to Jacob every two hours and stayed with him to make sure he drank it. "He's gettin' real feisty, so I know he's better," he reported back to me. He picked up the paper of herbs. "This ain't your writing."

"It *isn't* my writing. George, please stop saying ain't. It was given to me by a healer that I studied with back home in Massachusetts. She was a long-time friend of my mother."

Jacob resumed his normal duties, but many times we noticed him leaning against the wagon or sitting down when normally he would be active. After a week Betsey found Solomon staying with a family in one of the forward companies and brought him back.

• • •

One day three men from another train came to Mr. Bryant, begging him to assist a boy whose leg had been crushed under the wheels of a wagon. When he returned to camp the following day, he told me of the experience.

"The child's leg was already in a gangrenous state and he was near death. The injury occurred days ago and had been wrapped up, but that was the extent of the treatment. I felt there was no point in causing more pain by an amputation, but the mother insisted. A man stepped forward saying he would take off the leg, but the poor little fellow died before the procedure was completed." Mr. Bryant made a gesture of helplessness. "The father of the boy was suffering from inflammatory rheumatism. He could not move a limb and had violent pains in all of his bones, which, added to his mental anguish over the death of his child, overwhelmed him. It is a problem that those afflicted by disease will take medicines thinking that large quantities will more effectively cure and this was true with this man."

"What medicine had he been consuming?" I asked.

"Calomel."

"Oh, no. Then he was suffering from mercury poisoning."

"I'm afraid so. I left him some medicine and admonished him not to deviate from my directions. I was asked to see another man, suffering from a weakness of the heart, but I could do nothing for him. Perhaps the journey will effect a cure."

"But Mr. Bryant, surely you feel gratified that you have, to some degree, relieved those you could help."

"At least no one I've treated has died as a result of my ministrations. I believe the application of common sense along with a little knowledge of herbal remedies may work to relieve sickness and disease better than the practice and habit of bloodletting and strong cathartics. Personally, I think these methods are more likely to kill than cure."

He rose tiredly from his seat by our campfire and bid me good-night. I sighed. It felt so good just to sit and enjoy the coolness of the evening. *I should get out my journal,* I thought. The dust that was constantly in the air as the wagons moved along had settled and I could see the stars floating against the dark blue velvet of the heavens. The noise of the wagon encampment had softened and faded. It was a dreamy moment.

I reflected on the conversation I'd had with Mr. Bryant. It was stimulating to me to discuss medicine, botany, and science. I was educated—a teacher, writer, artist, and independent thinker. This was highly unusual for a woman in those times. Not to say that many women did not aspire to be more than a house drudge, they did. But the culture of the times wouldn't allow it. Those few who would break free were punished. Not physically, of course, but in other ways even by their own kind. Yes, other women could be worse than the men. I remembered how supercilious Mrs. Reed was when we discussed my reluctance for the journey.

"A woman does what her husband requests, Tamsen. I suppose some women of the lower class might deny a husband his right—"

"Right? Oh, please, Margaret, spare me."

I thought about Margaret and her headaches and constant illness and it occurred to me that Margaret was probably the cause of her own illness. *But why?* My reverie was broken by a voice booming into the quiet.

"Who is this sitting here enjoying the night air? Ahh, it is Mrs. Donner, the little medicine woman."

"Good evening, Mr. Russell. Are you feeling any better?"

"A small improvement and I thank you for your ministrations. I followed your instructions implicitly! What was that you said? This is to amuse the patient while nature cures the disease?"

"That was a quote from Voltaire, Mr. Russell."

"Voltaire. Mrs. Donner, you amaze me. Now if you could find in your medicine bag somethin' we could sprinkle in the food to make this company more agreeable, I would be most grateful."

"Mr. Russell, the task is a hopeless one."

"I believe you are right. Damnation!" He slapped at his face. "Mosquitoes are worse here than any place I've ever been."

Mosquitoes were a constant plague. We put smoldering buffalo chips in the wagon and our tent before retiring and the smoke would discourage the pests somewhat, but still we were exceedingly vexed with the insects. As one would observe people in camp or on the road, there was a constant motion of arms and hands waving and slapping. The whole night would be filled with the whining of their wings.

Mr. Russell moved away into the dark. "I must be off to check on the night guards. Last night we had sev'ral horses run off an' that delayed us this mornin'. Ever' mornin' there's somethin' that keeps us from leavin' promptly."

June 16, 1846
On the Platte River

My Old Friend:

We are now on the Platte, 200 miles from Fort Laramie. Our Journey, so far, has been pleasant. The roads have been good, & food plentiful. The water for a part of the way has been indifferent–but at no time have our cattle suffered for it. Wood is now very scarce, but "Buffalo chips" are excellent–they kindle quickly and retain heat surprisingly. We had this evening Buffalo steaks broiled upon them that had the same flavor they would have had upon hickory coals. We feel no fear of Indians. Our cattle graze quietly around our encampment unmolested. Two or three men will go hunting twenty miles from camp– & last night two of our men lay out in the wilderness rather than ride their horses after a hard chase. Indeed if I do not experience something far worse than I have yet done, I shall say the trouble is all in getting started.

Our wagons have not needed much repair, but I cannot yet tell in what respects they may be improved. Certain it is they cannot be too strong. Our preparations for the journey, in some respects, might have been bettered. Bread has been the principal article of food in our camp. We laid in 150 lbs. of flour & 75 lbs. of meat for each individual & I fear bread will be scarce. Meat is abundant. Rice and beans are good articles on the road–cornmeal, too, is very acceptable. Linsey dresses are the most suitable for children. Indeed if I had one it would be comfortable. There is so cool a breeze at all times in the prairie that the sun does not feel so hot as one would suppose.

We are now 450 miles from Independence. Our route at first was rough and through a timbered country that appeared to be fertile. After striking the prairie we found a first-rate road & the only difficulty we have had has been crossing creeks. In that, however, there has been no danger. I never could have believed we could have traveled so far with so little difficulty. The prairie between the Blue and Platte rivers is beautiful beyond description. Never have I seen so varied a country–so suitable for cultivation. Every thing was new and pleasing.

The Indians frequently come to see us, & the chiefs of a tribe breakfasted at our tent this morning. All are so friendly that I cannot help feeling sympathy & friendship for them. But on one sheet, what can I say?

Since we have been on the Platte we have had the river on one side & the ever varying mounds on the other–and have traveled through the Bottom lands from one to ten miles wide with little or no timber. The soil is sandy, & last year, on account of the dry season, the emigrants found grass here scarce. Our cattle are in good order & where proper care has been taken, none has been lost. Our milch cows have been of great service–indeed, they have been of more advantage than our meat. We have plenty of butter and milk.

We are commanded by Capt. Russell–an amiable man. George Donner is himself yet. He crows in the morning, & shouts out "Chain up, boys! Chain up!" with as much authority as though he was "something in particular".

John Denton is still with us–we find him a useful man in camp. Hiram Miller and Noah James are in good health & doing well. We have of the best of people in our company, & some, too, that are not so good.

Buffalo show themselves frequently. We have found the wild tulip, the primrose, the lupine, the ear-drop, the larkspur and creeping hollyhock, & a beautiful flower resembling the bloom of the beech tree but in bunches large as a small sugar-loaf & of every variety of shade, to red and green. I botanize & read some, but cook a "heap" more.

There are 420 wagons, as far as we have heard, on the road between here and Oregon and California.

Give our love to all enquiring friends, God bless them.

Mrs. George Donner

June 17, 1846

Two nights ago an Indian was discovered lurking in the bushes, no doubt intending to steal one of the horses. An alarm was given & he ran off with great speed.

Mr. Bryant returned today from a forward train where he ministered to several people. In this one camp, within a space of a few hours, there was a death of a boy & his funeral, a marriage, & the birth of a baby. Tomorrow, our wagons will pass by the place of these *events & soon it will be deserted & unmarked, except by the grave of the unfortunate boy. Such is the checkered map of human suffering & human enjoyment. Twenty three miles were covered today.*

We plodded on. The wind blew dust into us, kicked up by the wheels of the train. It entered our mouths, noses, eyes, and lungs, and covered us so thoroughly we matched the brown gray earth upon which we traveled. The alkali in the gritty dust inflamed our eyes. I treated my family with an eye wash and doctored the eyes of our oxen with it too. Each noon and evening George would help me wash the nose openings and eyes of our oxen and apply the treatment. Some oxen in the train were affected so severely by the dust that they became temporarily blinded. The poor faithful creatures were now so tame and gentle the girls could ride on their backs.

We had our usual family picnic for our supper that evening, and there was much to talk about.

"Colonel Russell has resigned his post," reported George. "That means the rest of us will resign also. I'm happy to give up my post. I'm tired of all the vexations."

"I heard Mr. Bryant is going to leave the group," said Jacob.

"Yes, it's true," replied George. "He doesn't like the progress of the company. He and some other men are planning to buy mules at Fort Laramie and continue on packing. Mr. Russell wants to go with them."

"Who else?"

"Miller, Buchanan, Nuttall, some others, 'bout ten in all."

"Well, they're single men," said Jacob. "I mind that it's a good thing to travel faster, but with families we cain't do it. If someone gets sick or injured, how could they be carried? Our wagons're slow, but it's the best way fer us. We couldn't pack all our goods anyways."

George got up and started kicking dirt over the last embers

of the fire. "I've heard that if we're at Independence Rock by the fourth of July, we're doing fine. I think we'll make it. I'm turnin' in. I'm some tired from fightin' the wind an' the dust all day. This is the damndest country for wind."

June 18, 1846

Mr. Russell has resigned his post & all the officers also. Mr. Boggs was elected in his place. The trail today has run along the north bank of the south fork of the Platte. We encamped at that point where the road diverges from the stream to cross over the prairie to the north fork. We have seen large herds of buffalo during our march today, some of which approached so close that there was danger of their mingling with our loose herds.

We met on the road today a party of men returning east from Oregon. They were traveling with their baggage on the backs of mules & horses rather than in wagons & were making between twenty-five & thirty miles a day. Their reports of the fertile portions of the Oregon country were favorable.

At last we have found the fabled buffalo. Every day our men engage in this sport. It's not much of a fair fight, as the creatures are quite dumb and slow. One can be felled & lie there moaning in his death throes & those around him will continue feeding or sleeping, not knowing something dangerous has entered the herd. But once alarmed, they are quite dangerous, lumbering to their feet in an instant to begin a stampede that will crush anything in its path to the dust of the prairie. One incorrect move on the part of the horsemen taking chase is often fatal.

The Indians have the art of killing buffalo while on the run, chasing them with their fleet-footed ponies, which are specially trained for the buffalo hunt.

Our hunters were astounded at the firepower that an animal can sustain without falling. They learned quickly that it is useless to shoot a buffalo in the head, as his thick skull simply flattens the bullet & it falls harmlessly to the ground.

I remember well the first time our group had an organized hunt for buffalo. There was a large area, extending several miles, where salt had accumulated on the ground and the buffalo herds came to lick the salt. James Reed and two of our teamsters participated in the hunt. When they returned with several of the choicer parts of a buffalo, James felt compelled to do a little crowing.

"I was very successful. My purpose was that the hunters might see that a *sucker* had the best horse in the company and the best and most daring horseman in the caravan. Well, I removed the stars from their brows."

We laughed amongst ourselves at James's desire to prove that he was as good or even better than the so-called professional hunters of the caravan. He had been smarting, because some of the hunters had critiqued him and pronounced him a greenhorn and a "sucker."

A day later James ran a wounded buffalo into the camp. The beast was crazy with fear, snorting and dashing here and there, spilling and breaking camp gear as it ran and jumped around camp with James trailing it on his horse trying to drive it away. When he came back, I called to him as he passed by me on his horse. He reined around and came close to me, shading his eyes from the sun.

"Do you realize the danger and harm to which you have exposed us with this unnecessary bravado? You very nearly caused injury to Mrs. Dunlap and her children."

"I'm sorry to have upset you, Mrs. Donner. Good day." He slapped his horse with the ends of the reins and the startled beast jumped, its hooves kicking up small stones and dust, and they galloped off. George was unhappy with me for saying what I did to James.

"Tamsen, most men don't take kindly to being chastised as if you were their school marm."

"Well, he needed chastising. That was a very stupid thing to do. Mrs. Dunlap is prostrate in her tent, hysterical from the experience."

"Well, tell her to get up and get on with her work. Nobody was hurt," George grumped. George was a kind and patient man, but he hated to get involved in any sort of dissension.

• • •

We crossed the ridge between the South and North Platte rivers, a distance of some twenty miles. It was through some of the roughest country we had seen, all ridges, mounds, deep hollows, and sand, with sparse vegetation and the only water a stagnant pond or two. The road struck directly up a bluff, rising quite rapidly at first, then very gradually for about twelve miles when we reached the summit and a most magnificent view. Before and below us the river wound its way through broken hills and green meadows.

Behind us was undulating prairie rising gently from the South Fork over which we had just passed. On our right was the gradual convergence of the two valleys and immediately at our feet was Ash Creek, which fell off suddenly into deep chasms, leaving only a high narrow ridge that gradually descended until falling off sharply into the bottom of the creek. The entry into the hollow was particularly difficult. Ahead of us a wagon overturned and two oxen were killed and several injured.

The men double-rough-locked the wagons, removing all but one yoke of oxen. We began the descent with trepidation, but we made it down with no serious problems. After reaching the hollow we found a pure cold spring and patches of currants and gooseberries. That evening we feasted on berry pies.

June 20, 1846

There has been a tragedy in the company ahead of us. A man, a Baptist minister, started out in the middle of the night to take his turn at guard duty. Feeling the night cold, he wrapped his blanket around his shoulders for warmth. His son thought the approaching figure was an Indian, took aim, and fired. They buried the man in the road and scattered the ashes of the campfire over his grave, hoping that the Indians would not find the grave and dig up the body. Today we traveled about 30 miles.

June 22, 1846

My Dear Friend:

We descended into the valley of Ash Hollow after winding our way down a steep ravine to the river bottom. There we found a weathered cabin constructed by trappers who'd been caught in snow last winter. No doubt it will collapse in the next winter's snow, but for now it serves the purpose of a prairie post office. Inside there was a niche where people had placed letters waiting for anyone passing east to carry them on to the settlements. Many Indians are in the area & we surmise that this place is a crossroads or trading spot for the different tribes.

For several miles after leaving our encampment, the wagon-trail passed over a sandy soil and the wheels sank eight or ten inches. The bluffs that wall in the river valley are rugged and sterile with barren sands & perpendicular ledges of rock. The country is parched looking with very little vegetation & the winds pick up loose sand, coloring everything a dusty gray. The width of the Platte here is narrower than below & the water most disagreeable.

Today we saw the edifice known as "Chimney Rock" from a distance of about forty miles. It is a small spire, standing out in bold relief. Two days more & we arrived to it about noon. I suppose it to be three hundred and fifty feet high. From there another great edifice resembling a building with wings and domes came into view.

The countryside here, this valley of the Platte, has a very rough and hilly nature, but a peculiarity we notice is that the knobs, or bluffs, are only to be found upon one side of the river at a time, sometimes on one side & then on the other. The wagons often wind along under these bluffs & in their broken appearance you can imagine houses, castles, towns & anything which the imagination can conceive. These suddenly disappear & then on the opposite side of the river the ragged bluffs begin again with their castles and towers.

We traveled on, coming up to a formation known as "Scott's Bluff." The story goes that the name derived from a man named Scott, who had been in the company of a group of trappers who were employed by the American Fur Company. They were returning to the settlements in boats when Scott became too ill to travel & he was left in the boat to die as his companions traveled on. Upon their return to their employers, they told that Scott had died & they had buried him next to the Platte. The next year a party of hunters discovered a skeleton, & ascertained that it was Scott from papers & clothing still there. He had managed to leave the boat & reach the bluffs where he had died.

Stories like these are oft told. One wonders about the frailties of man to leave a companion to die alone in the wilderness.

Mrs. George Donner

The trail left the river as we approached Scott's Bluff, crossing a level plain and ascending a ridge. As we reached the summit of the ridge, we had our first glimpse of the Rocky Mountains. We thought the peak we saw way off, a hundred or a hundred and fifty miles, was Laramie Peak and then in the far, far distance, the Wind River Mountains. The next day was pleasant and the girls and I walked a little to the side, wanting to remove ourselves far enough where the tortured shriek of the wheels wouldn't be as loud, nor the dust as bad. A soft breeze kept us cool.

"This country has such a magnificence," I said. "It's raw and untamed, but it's good to have open space, a freedom—"

"I think it's ugly," exclaimed Elitha. "No trees, no green grass. All broken up and jagged. I hope California is not like this or I will hate it."

"Will California be like this, Mother?" asked Frances.

"I believe, at least I've heard, that where we are going, to the northern part, there are gentle rolling hills covered with oak trees. We can expect that in the winter time, the land will be green, but in the summer there is hardly any rain, and everything dries up and turns a golden color. But there are many parts where there are rivers and streams and sloughs, with lots of trees. The summers are rather hot, but the air is dry, so the heat is not as bothersome as what we had in Illinois."

"And there is an ocean," said Georgeanna. "Isn't there, Mother?"

"Ah, yes, a big ocean. I grew up near the ocean, the Atlantic Ocean, and I miss it. I have heard that the Pacific is much nicer, more gentle, and warmer. More blue, too, I think. But I don't think we will have opportunity to visit the ocean any time soon, because it will take a while to get settled. We won't have time to sight-see. Look, I think the wagons are stopping to make camp. We'd better get back."

About eight miles east of Fort Laramie, we came across a small building of logs, which was known as Fort Bernard. A trading post of sorts, it was owned by a Mr. Richard who greeted us cordially when called upon. Since it had been many, many weeks since we had seen an inhabited house and although it was of the crudest construction, we felt somehow that we were once again touched by civilization.

There were many men there to trade with the Indians. They had flour and other goods that they had packed in by mule and horse four hundred miles from the headwaters of the Arkansas River. Encamped at this post was a party of Sioux Indians on their way to join the main body in their expedition against the Snake tribe. They had recently returned from a war against the Pawnees and had twenty-five scalps to brag about and many captured horses.

Our wagon group hosted a banquet for the traders and others of the fort. Not a banquet that you would expect in the east, but nevertheless it was adequate and especially appreciated by some of the traders who hadn't tasted the products of flour, sugar, and coffee for months.

I asked one of the traders if he could speak the Sioux language. "Yes'm, but mostly just enough to get my tradin' done. Now, New, he talks it good."

"Which man is Mr. New?" I asked.

He pointed to a man sitting cross-legged on the ground, a small pipe in one hand and a mug of coffee in the other. He was a bearded man, his tangle of pepper-gray hair tied back in a horse's tail. He arose from the ground as I approached him. His faded blue eyes squinted out at me from under brows as thick as a bird's nest.

"Mr. New?"

"Yes, ma'am. I'm New."

"I'm Mrs. George Donner. My husband and I are members of the wagon company."

"Right pleased to meet'cha, ma'am."

I looked around and spied a box I could sit on and bade Mr. New to seat himself again.

"I understand you speak the Sioux language, Mr. New."

"Yes ma'am. I been with and around the Injuns fer twenty years or more."

"I would like to visit one of their doctors, a healer."

"No, ma'am. That wouldn't be likely."

"Why not?"

"Well, they don't have doctors like you're a'thinkin'. Their doctors are called shamans. The shamans, they do, well, I guess you might call it hocus pocus. They shake rattles, spit stuff out'a their mouths, sing and dance around, such like."

"Do they effect cures?"

"Sometimes the patient gets well, dependin' on if the shaman knows his potions and cures. These here Injuns know a passel 'bout what plants and such can cure certain things."

"I have an interest in botany and plant cures. I would like to learn what plants they use."

Mr. New knocked the ashes from his pipe. "No, it ain't likely they'd allow it, you being a woman, an' a white woman to boot. The shamans, they're real touchy. You see, they depend on fear an' myst'ry to keep their power, their med'cine. They have to convince the Injun that comes to 'em fer a cure that they have the med'cine to drive off the bad spirits that's caused the sickness. That's why they do all their hocus pocus, to make the patient believe the shaman has somethin' special that'll make a cure. It be a tough job. Sometimes if the patient isn't cured, the family will kill the shaman or he loses his standin' an' he don't have a practice no more. Now, in any Injun camp thar's gonna be a woman or a man that knows how to use herbs and plants fer certain things."

"Would one of those people speak with me?"

"Ma'am, I wouldn't know who those people would be. There's thousands of Injuns here. I ain't lived in a Injun camp fer many years."

"You lived among them?"

"Yes ma'am."

"Perhaps you know some of their cures?"

Mr. New took out his tobacco pouch and refilled his pipe, tamping down the tobacco. I took a small stick out of the fire and held it for him while he puffed on the pipe to get it started. I sat back down and waited for him to collect his thoughts.

"Now, a partner a' mine, a long time back, had a broken leg. We was stayin' with the Sioux fer the winter. We sent fer the head shaman an' he came, but he said that broken bones warn't his line of work an' he sent in this old Injun who said he was a Bear Dreamer. It seems the Bear Dreamers specialize in broken bones an' such. He looked at the break, an' it was a bad one with the bone comin' through the skin. He said he could fix it, but we'd hav'ta give him a horse in payment before he'd start the work. 'Course we were in no position to dicker. After some prelim'aries an' hoopla the Injun mixed up a salve an' smeared it on my friend's leg."

"Do you know what the salve was made of?"

Mr. New looked down into his coffee cup and reflected for a moment. "It was bear grease an' som'thin' he called *hu-hwe-han-han pe-zu-la*. This here salve kind'a relaxed my partner, an' then the healer pulled the bone in place an' laced a rawhide 'round the break."

"And your partner didn't seem to have pain?"

"Well, no, but he'd drunk a pint'a whiskey 'fore the healer got there."

"Was the break cured?"

"He was up an' walkin' around not too long after that. Had to use a stick to walk with fer a while. He got hisself drowned not too long after that. I'll allow that if 'n we'd been in the white man's camp when he broke his leg, they'd a cut it off an' he'd a been a cripple or died from the gangrene."

"I would like to know what the, ah—" I looked at what I'd written down, "*—hu hwe han han pe zu la* was."

"Mebbe I can find out fer you."

He puffed on his pipe for a moment, then took it from his mouth. "Now, if'n you had gut pains, you'd look fer some horsemint an' drink a tea of it. Fer the trots some take a concoction with lambsquarters, an' fer stomach pain a tea made of verbena's good."

He put the pipe in his mouth again, but then removed it and

pointed it at me for emphasis as he thought of something else. "I mind that the root of calamus could help a toothache. Some claimed it, but it never helped me none."

"I'm familiar with the plants and cures that you've mentioned, except the calamus. Do you know what it looks like?"

"It's the root you use. The leaves are kind'a narrow like, yellowish an' green, has a yellow pod that comes out at a angle. It has kind'a a spicy smell."

I handed Mr. New an open page in my notebook and my pencil and asked him if he would sketch the plant for me.

"Wal, I ain't much hand at this, but I'll give it a try."

Mr. New made an excellent drawing.

"That's very good, Mr. New. I think I know it as sweetflag. The other one, *hu hwe*—"

"Missus, I'll ask around an' see if I can find out an' I'll come to you."

"Are you sure I can't arrange a visit?"

"Yes'm, it don't pay to get too close to them Injuns. They might just hold you fer ransom. The Sioux're not too bad right now, but you never know."

After dinner we all went to watch the shooting demonstration. The Indian archers showed much skill and proficiency with the bow and arrow, attaining great distance with accuracy. We didn't stay long, as it was hot and the children soon became bored, so we missed the excitement surrounding a shooting mishap. That evening at the community campfire, the men were all abuzz talking about it. An old mountaineer by the name of Bill Williams had his rifle burst as he fired at a target.

"See, this is how it happened," related one of the men. "Old Bill was wantin' a new rifle. He looks at ever' rifle in the camp 'til he found one he considered the best of the bunch. Someone tried to talk him out'a the purchase, tellin' him it was a unlucky gun an' that with it the owner had accidentally shot an' prit' near killed a man, an' had clipped a piece off the ear of another.

"Old Bill didn't cotton to this suggestion that he did'n know a good gun when he saw one, 'specially from a greenhorn all decked out in a brand new buckskin suit. So he says, 'See here, I've hunted an' trapped in these mountains fer sixty years an' you needn't think that you kin teach me anythin' 'bout a rifle. Just get back under your wagon an' mend your moccasins an' don't bother me.' So he paid fer the rifle an' marked off a hundred 'n fifty yards an' put up a mark. He loaded the gun heavy to see how she would carry fer the distance." The story teller raised his arm in demonstration, pulling an imaginary trigger. "He aimed at the mark an' fired. Blowie! The rifle burst the breech, a piece 'a the barrel split out, the stock blew to pieces, an' the lock flew fifty feet away. The blast knocked Ol' Williams flat on his back, full a' splinters. They thought he was dead an' was discussin' what to do with him when someone poured some whiskey down his throat an' he comes to an' staggers into the post proclaimin' that nothin' could kill him, much less a blankety-blank rifle."

• • •

It was only a half day's journey from Ft. Bernard to Fort Laramie, or Fort John, as it was also called. Laramie was situated on the Laramie River near its junction with the Platte, surrounded by an extensive plain. As we approached the fort all eyes turned to a great spectacle stretched out over the plain.

"Mother, Mother! Look! Look at all the Indians!"

The girls ran to me, pointing across the plain. We gazed in wonder at the hundreds of conical shaped tents spread out across the valley, resembling fields of hay gathered into stacks. The plain was alive with activity and horsemen galloping back and forth showing off their prowess and their exotic costumes. A constant stream of people walked to and from a large mud-walled stockade.

The fort was the principal trading post of the American Fur Company, a square shaped structure with outer walls of mud bricks around a center area of about one-half an acre. On three sides there were various rooms in which the living and working aspects of the fort were carried out. The fourth side was a main building of two stories with towers guarding the corners of the quadrangle. Although there was always the possibility of a war attack, the gates were closed more often against the constant carousing and stealing by the Indians.

The Sioux were preparing to go to battle with the Snake and Crow Indians and were holding war-dances, working themselves into frenzy. It appeared to us that some were helped to attain this state by the effects of whiskey.

At the fort we were able to purchase some supplies and take care of much needed repairs to our wagons. We had brought goods along for the purpose of trade and we bargained with the Indians for buffalo skins and moccasins. I was squeamish about trading for pemmican or meat, although some in the train did. I was fascinated by the Sioux. They were a handsome people in the main, more prosperous looking than the Indians that we had met earlier.

Mr. New found us at Fort Laramie. "Howdy, ma'am, Mr. Donner." He wiped perspiration off his face with a handkerchief. "Hot, ain't it? Miz Donner, I found a squaw that knows a lot about cures an' such an' she said she'd let you talk to her if you're still of a mind."

"Oh, Mr. New, that's wonderful."

George didn't like the idea. "Tamsen, are you intendin' goin' into that Indian camp? What are you thinkin'? That's no place for a cultured white lady, nor any white lady."

"George, I want to find out what I can of their use of plants to cure illness. I will probably never again have the opportunity. I want to go and Mr. New has already made the arrangements."

"You'd best bring along somethin' to give the squaw as a present," suggested Mr. New.

George would not permit me to go alone with Mr. New, so he and Charles Stanton, who had a keen interest in observing the Indians at close range, accompanied us. As we approached the camp several dogs rushed out at us, snarling and barking. Mr. New hit the more aggressive one with a big stick and kicked at the others and they decided to leave us be. As we walked through the camp I could see children and women peeking at us from behind the lodges and from the door openings. *We're just as strange to them as they are to us,* I thought. There was one lodge that was much larger than the others and was painted with brightly colored horses and other objects. The depictions were crude and stylized, but dramatic none the less. Some men were sitting in front of the lodge in a circle. I guessed it was the Indian version of the country store.

"These Injuns, now, are notional," said Mr. New. "They can be friendly one minute an' jump up an' cleave you with a battle axe the next. Did you remember to bring yer presents?"

"Yes."

"That's good. Now, ma'am, the Injuns think it's rude to look at another directly in the eyes. So remember that. I'm goin' to go in an' see how the wind is blowin', so to speak. You all stay here."

As we waited for Mr. New I looked around. A small, dirty, naked boy played about, tended by an older child, a girl of about twelve. I noticed that the boy's eyes were terribly infected and were swollen shut. The sight touched my heart. *Poor thing!* There was food stewing in a bag suspended from a tripod of poles, but it was not over the fire. I was curious to know how the food was being cooked and stepped closer to look. I turned as Mr. New spoke.

"The men have to stay out here, but we can go in."

"Mr. New, how is this food cooked?"

"Y'see the stones there in the fire? When they're hot enough, they're dropped in the food an' boils it. The cookin' pouch is made from a buffler stomach, lasts a few days, then they eat it too. This here squaw must be poor 'cause most of these Injuns have traded fer iron kettles. They prefers 'em."

"I can understand why."

George made a wave of his hand and he and Mr. Stanton squatted down in a little shade made by another lodge and prepared to wait, swatting away flies with their hats. I lifted my skirts and stepped carefully through the detritus scattered about in front of the lodge.

"You gits used to it, ma'am, livin' with 'em."

"I'm sure."

The lodge was dim inside and it took a moment for my eyes to adjust. Then I saw a woman sitting on the floor of the lodge. Her black hair was unkempt and straggled around her face. Although her skin was wrinkled and leathery, I sensed that she was younger than I. *Sunbonnets are unknown to these women,* I thought. She wore a plain skin tunic tied with a thong around her waist. Mr. New spoke to her and then he motioned for me to sit down and the two of us sat on a skin on the ground in front of her. A long conversation between Mr. New and the Indian woman took place.

"Her name's somethin' like Blue Whirlwind. I told her you're wantin' to know about the bone-break cure."

The woman rummaged through several baskets that were near her and brought out a whitish root about six inches in length and handed it to me. I turned the root over in my hands, trying to think of what it could be. She spoke directly to me, the sound of her speaking choppy and guttural.

"She says this is the root that is used to help with settin' bones. She says that you smash it up, then mix it with bear grease an' smear it on the break. She says you can have the root. Best you give her the present you brought now."

I smiled at the woman, caught myself looking directly at her, and dropped my gaze as I handed the package to her.

"Tell her that I am very grateful. I would like to know more. I am particularly interested in knowing if they have something that can ... prevent conception." I felt my face redden. It was hard for me to speak of this with Mr. New, but I had no choice. After a long discourse between Mr. New and the woman, she opened the parcel and I could see that she was pleased as she fingered the things inside. She smiled, her tongue lolling out between large gaps in her front teeth. *This woman's life must be very hard.* I wondered if the beautiful young Indian girls would look the same in only a few short years.

"Miz Donner, jes one o' those ribbons would have made her

happy. You'll be spoiling her for the next time a white wants somethin'."

Blue Whirlwind delved into her baskets and brought out a square of folded skin, unwrapping it to reveal a powdered substance. There followed a long harangue to Mr. New and then the woman fluttered her hand in front of her chest, hunched her shoulders forward, and gasped for breath.

"*Hua*," Mr. New nodded. "She says this here stuff is good fer breathing problems. I ain't fer sure, but I think she's tellin' me it's made from the roots of skunk cabbage. She says you can have it, she has more."

"What is the dose? How is it given?"

It was a little arduous, but we finally managed to get the information and the woman gave me a few more remedies. I carefully folded the medicines in papers and wrote the information down on each packet. Then Mr. New rose and said we should leave.

The woman raised her hand and spoke quickly to Mr. New.

"She's got somethin' else," he said.

The woman got up and went to the back of the lodge. When she returned, she unfolded a small leather packet and showed me a dark powder inside. She lowered her voice to a whisper as she turned and spoke to Mr. New. Then she stopped abruptly and looked piercingly at him and then at me.

"She says many Indian women use this stuff here to prevent gettin' with child, but it's sacred an' only known to a few women. She could be beaten, or worse, if the men found out she knows of such a thing an' used it. She's gonna give it to you because she thinks if you teach the white women to use it, there will be fewer whites an' she thinks it will be a good thing."

"Oh. Did she tell you what it is?"

"She says the powder is made from wild carrot seed."

"How is it taken?"

Mr. New spoke to Blue Whirlwind and she responded by shaking out a small amount of the powder in her palm and showing it to me. I quickly judged the amount, and then she poured the powder back into the container and handed it to me.

"She says you take that much of it every day," said Mr. New, "with lots of water. She says it works for some who use it without fail. Others who don't use it right can get with child easier."

I gathered up my things and stood up as did Mr. New.

"Please thank her again for me. Mr. New, I noticed the child outside, the little boy, has infected eyes. I have something that might help his condition. Is she his mother?"

Mr. New conversed with the woman.

"She's the grandmother. She wants to know what cure you have."

"I have two treatments. Both are an eye wash and the wash must be done many times. But if she will allow it, I will go back to camp and prepare the remedies and bring them back. I will instruct her in their use."

The grandmother called out and shortly the girl I had noticed before entered the lodge holding the boy by the elbow. The grandmother had him sit next to me so I could have a better look at his eyes. She spoke another long string of guttural words.

"She wants to know if you really think you have the power to cure his eyes."

"I can try. It has helped many of our people during this journey."

"She says she wants to see yer cure. I told her we'll come back."

We all traipsed back to camp. George was upset when he found out that I was going back to doctor the boy's eyes.

"Godamighty, Tamsen. Why do you want to get involved with the Indians? What if he screams or something when you doctor him and they think you're hurting him? They could kill you."

"I will explain everything to the woman. I think she'll understand."

The boy's eyes were so encrusted that it took several gentle washings before his eyes were open enough to apply the medicine wash. I gave her two curatives, one of zinc sulphate and one of elderberry flowers and told her to use one for a day and the other the next. I told her that she must first boil the water with which to bathe his eyes and make the healing solution. I had brought an iron kettle and I put it down in front of the woman.

"Mr. New, tell her that my power to cure comes from fire and if the water is not boiled in this kettle over fire the medicine will have no power."

When we left the lodge, Mr. New looked at me quizzically.

"Ma'am, why'd you tell her the water had to be boiled over fire? You don't believe in hocus pocus like they do, do you?"

"No, but I couldn't be sure the water she will use is clean water. When I use boiled water in healing, it seems to effect a better cure. Not only that, Mr. New, I have found that when water is questionable, a good boiling before use seems to keep one from getting sick as often."

"Well, don't that beat all."

When we returned to camp I made supper. We sat in a circle with several of our family group as we ate our food. Mr. New took his plate and sat down, but before he began eating I noticed that he cut off a small piece of meat, held it up to the sky and then buried it in the soft ground under his feet. He saw me looking at him and grinned sheepishly.

"Larned that from the Injuns, ma'am. That'll guarantee there'll always be meat. I've had some hungry times."

"I guess we kind of do the same thing, in our way," I replied.

The wind had picked up and a sudden gust blew dust into our circle as a grizzled old mountain man came by riding a mangy looking mule, leading another with a large pack on its back. The man nodded at Mr. New.

"That's Old Perrault. He works fer Bordeau. Seems he got mad 'bout somethin' or 'nother an' made insults an' now he's leavin' in a huff. He's off to Fort Union through all these Sioux fixin' to go on the warpath. He'll be lucky they don't lift his hair."

"Who is Mr. Bordeau?"

"You ain't met him? He's the factor here at the fort."

"Oh, yes. No, I haven't met him."

"Mr. New," asked George, "have you knowledge of the country south of Fort Bridger? Have you heard of a road whereby one can go south from there to the Salt Lake?"

"No sir, there ain't no road. I never been there, but I know it be powerful rough country. Nothin' but Injun trails. The only way I know fer wagon parties is to go up by Fort Hall. There's been wagons go that way these last few years. Yer people thinkin' of takin' that there route that Frémont was on?"

"We're leaning that way."

"Jim Clyman just came through there with that Hastings feller. He's here now headin' east after bein' on the Pacific Coast. If I was you, I'd find him an' ask him of the route. He knows more about headin' west than just about any man. He was with Jed Smith when they found the South Pass."

August 28, 1846
Ft. Laramie

It was quite an experience to visit the Sioux encampment. An Indian woman, Blue Whirlwind, gave me many interesting Indian remedies. I was very impressed with the art of these people, especially the beadwork. I traded some gew-gaws for a beautiful pair of moccasins and a parfleche. The parfleche (sounds like a French word) is a container made of stiff leather and decorated in various modes with beading and quillwork. The work is exquisite. I understand from Mr. New, the man who helped me visit the Indian woman, that they have specialists in their crafts. For instance, those who make their skin lodges are paid for this work and those who do the finest beading or quillwork always have an eager clientele for their products. These arts are done by the women, while the men specialize in the articles of war and special powers, their "medicine."

The next day George sought out Mr. Clyman and brought him to join us for our evening meal.

"James," said George, "Clyman here, he tells me he knows you from the Blackhawk War."

James waved a mosquito away from his face and squinted at Mr. Clyman. I got the impression he didn't like anything about him.

"When did you muster out?" James asked.

Mr. Clyman's voice was raspy and he cleared his throat several times before speaking. "I was with Early's comp'ny at Dixon's Ferry, where you were, then with Dodge's Battalion. I mustered out in Missoora in 1834."

Mr. Clyman was a tall man with a bearing and a dignity that impressed me. His light brown hair and clear blue eyes contrasted with a complexion that was brown and weathered. He had a little twist to his mouth as if he had lost some teeth on one side. I guessed his age at about sixty-five, but when someone asked him he said he was fifty-four. I dished up a plate of food for him and he sat down on the ground, cross-legged, to eat.

"Ya'll from Illinois, are you? What part?" he asked between mouthfuls of food.

"Sangamon."

"That right? I spent some time there doin' surveyin' work fer Colonel Hamilton. 1821 'er 22, it was."

"You've just come from California?"

"That's a fact."

"What do you make of it?"

"Well, some're goin' to like it an' some not. Personally, I think it's a little short of paradise. It depends on what you're lookin' for. We traveled in that territory for twenty-eight days, mostly through the Spanish settlements, an' there was only three places where we slept in a house an' those three were owned by foreigners. The usual ranch is from six to twelve square miles, some're real large. There's one I passed which belonged to a Mexican gent that was thirty-three leagues."

"What would that be in acres?"

"Lemme think now." Mr. Clyman squeezed his eyes shut

and concentrated. "That's close to one hundred forty thousand acres."

"The hell you say."

"Their ranchos are huge. Like nothin' you ever seen before. On this one they cultivate only four or five hundred acres, the rest is used for grazin'. There's twelve or fifteen thousand head of cattle an' seven or eight thousand head of horses. They don't feed their animals grain. You cain't find a single kernel to feed yer horse in California, but I seen the biggest field of wild oats on the globe, some two or three hundred thousand acres. It falls on the ground to seed the next crop." He hawked and spit, then wiped his mouth on his sleeve.

"There's opportunities in the territory, that's a fact. There's a man, Yount, has a flouring mill, the only one in the province. Has a saw mill too an' both are profitable. He's an American, been in the Mexican country thirteen, fourteen years."

"What be the situation now with the Mexican government?" someone asked him.

"Well, Frémont caused some alarm by raisin' the American flag at his camp near the Mission of St. John. Then the Mexican general, Castro, raised some four hundred men under arms at Monterey. You cain't tell what the truth is most times 'cause the reports are carried by hearsay by an ignorant an' superstitious people. But you might as well count on it, Frémont's bent on conquest an' the territory will fly the American flag. But it's been some time since I was there. I left Johnson's ranch mid-April."

"You came over the California mountains?"

"I did."

"There's a feller, Hastings. You heard a 'him? He says he knows of a route that's shorter than goin' by Fort Hall. Do you know anythin' of that shorter route?"

Mr. Clyman went through the procedure of knocking out ashes from his pipe and refilling it. "Yes, I came through there. I was *with* Hastings." Getting up, he took a stick from the fire and held it to the tobacco, sucking on the pipe until it was going. He filled his lungs and slowly breathed out the smoke.

"He's stayin' up by Fort Bridger waitin' on emigrants so's he can direct them back over this here route. You ask me, it's foolish. We came through packin' on mules. No wagons've ever gone there an' it will be difficult to do so. The country is rough, full of canyons an' choked with trees and brush."

"Mr. Clyman," said George, "we'd be obliged if you would give us as much information as you can about the country after Bridger's tradin' post."

Mr. Clyman picked up a stick, hunkered down, and began drawing some lines in the dirt. His bony shoulders hunched against the evening chill, his eyes squinting against his tobacco smoke.

"West a' Bridger the country is passable good. Here's Bridger," Clyman dug his stick in the ground, "an' here's that big butte west of there. You'll head west fer a spell an' at the Big Muddy River you'll take a southwesterly direction. You'll keep on thataway twenty miles an' you'll come to Sulphur Creek. A ways more, you'll cross the Bear. It's a fair-sized river. There's good trout in that river. Then another five, six miles you go off to the northwest, twelve, fourteen miles an' it's southwest fer twenty-five miles or so." He punched the stick in the ground and stood up. "Then yer troubles are gonna start. Yer gonna say, now why didn' we listen to Clyman?"

"What trouble?" someone asked.

"I been tellin' you. There's high mountains with a passel of canyons, real rough country. There's no road, mebbe a little Injun trail here an' there. The canyons are choked up with trees, brush, boulders, and such like. The streams're filled with rocks an' boulders an' there's places where there's cliffs on both sides.

"We understand what you're saying," said James, "but if there is a closer route, it is of no use to take a roundabout course. We trust that Mr. Hastings knows what he's about."

Mr. Clyman looked at James as a great bear might look at a squirrel. "Uh-huh? Well, each man floats his own stick."

He got up, his knees cracking as he straightened them out. "Been ridin' too damn long," he muttered. He placed his hat on his head, picked up his gun, and nodded at the men.

"Reed, Donner." He turned to me. "Thank ya' kindly for the supper, ma'am. I'd best be gettin' on."

I asked him if he would carry some postings on his return east and he said he would. Then he turned and walked off into the night. Jacob hadn't spoken during Mr. Clyman's discourse, but now he stood up and threw his cold coffee on the fire.

"Do you believe that? Fifteen thousand cattle on one ranch, an' that bein' one hundred and forty thousand acres? Thousands of acres of oats jes' growin' on their own? I think the man's a liar. We cain't put no stock in what he says."

June 27, 1846

My Dear Friend:

Two days ago we were at the outpost of Ft. Bernard, a trading post of very crude construction, situated seven or eight miles east of Fort Laramie. Here were encampments of two branches of the Sioux, one of the Ogallala led by Old Smoke, and two large villages of the Minneconjou Sioux.

At Fort Bernard the company hosted a banquet for the traders who are gathered at this place to trade with the Indians.

Fort Laramie has a commanding appearance, being situated in the bosom of a range of heights which form the commencement of the Black Snake Hills, near the junction of the Laramie & north fork of the Platte rivers. The plains surrounding the Fort are covered by the lodges of the Sioux who are preparing to send out a large war party against the Crows. There are perhaps two thousand in the vicinity.

The Sioux are a colorful and attractive people, one of the most powerful tribes in the country. Their standard of living is provided by the buffalo, as they use the skins and meat to trade for foodstuffs, blankets & other luxuries they desire. I am impressed by the beauty of some of the women & the clothing they wear with style and grace. Some wear costumes made of skin that has been worked to an amazing degree of softness & a pure white color.

The conical-shaped tents, which are their principal form of dwelling, are fashioned of buffalo skins & are very comfortable. I shall describe them for you, as I consider the lodges quite ingenious, & remarkably adapted to the life of the wandering savage.

The diameter of the lodge at the base is usually about ten feet. The hide covering is held in the conical shape by poles, held together at the top & spread in a circle at the bottom. A fire is kept in the center of the tent, which serves as warmth & for cooking in cold weather. The floor of the lodge is covered with buffalo skins. They arrange their sleeping robes around the center & many will sleep in one lodge. Around the perimeter of the lodge, perhaps two or three feet in height, is another wall of the skins of buffalo & this is designed to keep the air from coming directly into the lodge. In the heat of the day, they may raise the edges of the tent so that air may circulate & cool the interior.

When they break camp to travel, the tent is taken down, the hides folded, & the poles are fastened to pack-horses on each side with a framework supporting all their baggage. Sometimes the children are placed on top of the whole. They can travel fifty or sixty miles in a day, it is said, & all of the work to make this happen is done by the women. The men travel on horseback, ranging ahead & to the side, to protect the cavalcade.

Our caravan draws its slow length along. The road is lined with emigrants. A man returning east, a Mr. Wall, who stopped in our camp, has counted four hundred and ninety wagons.

The companies have got along remarkably well. They have lost but a few head of cattle. Some one hundred head strayed away from the advance company, but most were recovered.

A debate rages within our camp about the new route to the Salt Lake. I, for one, do not want to follow this new route. We have until Fort Bridger to make a decision. I shall report again when the opportunity to post letters presents itself.

We are now about 600 miles from Independence & about 1,400 miles from where we want to be.

Mrs. George Donner

The next morning Mr. Bryant, with nine other men including our former leader, Colonel Russell, visited our camp to say good-bye.

"Mr. Bryant, I hope you can help me solve a mystery," said I.

"I will certainly try."

I went to our wagon and brought back the root that the Indian woman had given me.

"Do you know what this might be? The Indians use it as a medicine for bone breaks."

Mr. Bryant turned the root several times as I had. Then he handed it back to me.

"This might be what is called umbrellawort. I would be most interested if the properties she speaks of are true."

I turned to Mr. Russell. "Mr. Russell, I hope we will see you again in California. Please keep drinking the teas that I have given you."

I sincerely hoped that Mr. Russell would achieve some benefit from the teas, but I also felt the spirits he was consuming would sooner or later overpower any benefit.

George shook hands all around. "Hiram, we'll see you in California. Colonel, we are appreciative of your service as Captain."

"Thank you, suh, thank you. I should not have agreed to take it again after I resigned the first time. I suppose my vanity was flattered an' I took the yoke once again, even though I knew it was problematical, my health bein' what it is. Take my advice, suh, an' never accept the leadership of a wagon party."

"That is good advice, George," I said.

"Yes, it is. You needn't be concerned. I won't become a captain of a company of emigrants. I value my good opinion of the human race far too much to lose it."

• • •

It was at Fort Laramie that the discussion of a shorter route to the Pacific became the topic of the day. We read Hastings's trail guide again and again, but could find only the one mention that there might be a more direct and therefore shorter route going south around the Salt Lake. The question hardly left our thoughts as we continued on our way.

After we left Fort Laramie our progress became much slower. Our animals were considerably weakened by the travel and lack of good water and forage. We traveled only thirty-two miles in the next three days. We chafed at the slow pace, knowing that we were falling behind the main emigration and the days of travel before the snow would close the Sierra were getting fewer.

On the third day, just after starting off after our noon stop, the girls and I were walking a distance away from the wagons when we noticed that the wagons had stopped. The air was so thick with dust we couldn't see what had stopped the train, but I felt uneasy. I looked around for Elitha and Leanna who had wandered away from us, and called to them.

"Girls, let's go back."

We stood waiting for Elitha and Leanna to come up when I saw George running toward us. He was shouting and pointing to our wagons.

"What is it?"

"Run!"

We could hear him now, and we started to run. As we got to him, he grabbed up Eliza and I pulled Georgeanna along. I looked back for Elitha and Leanna and yelled at them to help Frances.

George kept yelling. "Hurry! Get under the wagon!"

As we neared the wagons I could feel a throbbing in the air that turned into a vibration of the earth. People in the train were yelling and screaming. George pointed toward the north where a huge yellow brown cloud was bearing down on us. *Oh, my God. A buffalo stampede. They're going to come through the wagons.*

The noise was incredible as the mass of huge beasts pounded toward us. A wagon was knocked over and the oxen were swept under the mass of thundering bodies. We scrambled under our wagon and held the children between us. We were choking from the dust, almost unable to breathe, our hearts pounding heavily from the run and the fear. The ground shook violently. Our oxen were frantic, bucking and yanking in the bows, causing the wagon to jerk forward and sideways. We scrambled on all fours to stay underneath the wagon. One crazed buffalo ran between the wagon we were under and the next one, smashing against the pole of the wagon, splintering it. The huge beast collapsed on its front legs only a few feet from us, bellowing horribly as it struggled to get up, pushing itself forward with its hind legs. The oxen, now released, frantically pulled each other one way and then another, dragging part of the broken pole behind them. We were so stricken by fear and shock that it was a few minutes before we realized that the din was receding and the trembling of the ground had moved off. We heard gunshots very close and as we crawled out from underneath the wagon, we saw several of our company standing over the heaving and groaning buffalo that had run between the wagons.

"Broke his front legs on that pole, an' the pole's a goner, Mr. Donner," said Noah.

"Well, it could have been a lot worse. We saw a wagon break up right before they hit us. Let's go see if we can help."

The men came back with bad news. The owner of the wagon

had been killed while attempting to turn the beasts away. He left a wife who had given birth a few weeks before and was feeble in health, and several children, one of whom had been injured earlier from falling under the wheels of their wagon.

The man was hastily buried and the wife hired one of the single men in the company to drive her wagon. They struggled on, only to be abandoned by the faithless driver who, under the pretext of going to hunt, took their rifle and made off to another wagon group in the vanguard of the company. Shortly thereafter, the poor woman became sick with a fever and succumbed. The children were now orphans, the eldest fourteen and the youngest only a few weeks old. The woman was buried by the side of the road and her children were parceled out amongst the emigrants.

June 29, 1846

Seven children have been left alone in the wilderness, their lives in the hands of strangers. There are so many accidents and dangers on this journey. Each day that ends I am thankful that nothing has happened to us. I cannot bear the thought of something happening to the children and especially something happening to us that would leave our children alone with strangers. It is my greatest fear.

We celebrated Independence Day, meeting up with many friends, including Mr. and Mrs. Thornton. Once or twice on the journey I visited with Mrs. Thornton and found her very good company, as she was highly educated and genteel. We were quite surprised to find Mr. Bryant and Mr. Russell there. Mr. Bryant had stopped to await our party as he needed another man to fill out his company.

July 4, 1846

Today we feasted on buffalo meat, bread, beans, and greens at Beaver Creek. One of the ladies provided a pie made of sage hen and rabbit with a crust as light as a feather. Toasts were made, some with spirits, ours with lemonade, and songs and speeches were punctuated by blasts from muskets.

James Reed conducted a rite that was explained to us by Mrs. Reed. Some of James's friends in Springfield had given him a bottle of brandy, which he agreed to drink at a certain hour of this day looking to the east, while his friends in Illinois were to drink a toast to his success from a companion bottle with their faces turned west. The difference in time was carefully estimated. It was a wonderful day.

Mr. Bryant stopped by before starting out again.

"Good-bye again," I said. "I hope that we will have the pleasure of your company in California before you return to the East."

"I hope that will be so. Have you made your mind up on which route you will take?"

"George and I have been arguing about it. It seems that the company is inclined to follow Mr. Hastings. He's waiting at Fort Bridger to guide the wagons that wish to follow the shorter route."

"Well, that is the route that we intend to follow. We should have little trouble, because we are on mules," he said. "With wagons, I would be cautious."

Shortly, we saw the caravan of mules wending its way through the encampment joined by one of our drivers, Hiram Miller. One of the Bryant group, Mr. Kirkendall, had changed his mind and decided for Oregon, so Mr. Bryant persuaded Hiram to take Mr. Kirkendall's place. The mule train was much better handled now than it had been the first day they had set out from Fort Laramie.

They'd had only a short instruction in managing and packing the mules and they were barely away from the fort when they noticed that several of the packs were hanging under the bellies of the mules. We passed them on the road as they were struggling to re-pack and they suffered quite a bit of derision from some of our teamsters as we went by. We had talked of it as we sat around the campfire with Mr. Bryant and some of his companions.

"A Mexican pack-mule is one of the most sagacious and intelligent quadrupeds that I have ever met with," Bryant told us. "The mules, stupid though we regard them, know more about the business than we do. Several times I thought I could detect them giving a wise wink and a sly leer, as much as to say that we were novices and if they could speak they would give us the benefit of their advice and instruction."

We lay by for two days to rest and repair and then we set out again toward the setting sun. As we traveled, a steady stream of Sioux warriors, resplendent in war dress and paint, passed us. They were mounted on horses, which were also magnificent in war paint and decorations of various kinds. Several of the braves came very close to where I was walking alongside our family wagon, looking at me, talking and gesturing and making me very nervous. I stopped in stride and let the wagon go ahead and then crossed behind it to the side away from the Indians, but they continued along with the wagon, looking at me and shouting and waving their shields and spears.

George came running up. "Noah, stop the wagon. Let me get my gun."

The wagon stopped and George climbed in, muttering to himself, because he'd not put the gun on the outside rack that morning. I stopped him as he climbed out of the wagon.

"George, wait. Look—"

One of the fierce-looking braves had come close to us and in front of him on his horse was the young boy whose eyes I had treated. I walked to them and looked up. I could see that the boy's eyes were much improved.

"Little Elk, I am glad your eyes are better," I said.

He waved at me and grinned from ear to ear. The braves all yelled some more and then the group galloped off.

"I do believe that group was thanking you for fixin' the boy's eyes," said George.

"Yes, I think so too."

The caravan of Indians put the company on edge. Some of the warriors were very interested in Virginia Reed's pony and gathered around, pestering her until James came up and told Virginia to get in their wagon. He gave the pony to one of the teamsters. This annoyed Virginia very much, because she truly enjoyed riding her pony when the wagons were rolling. She was further annoyed when the Indians swarmed around the Reed wagon to get a peek in the looking glass that hung outside. As she was fretting about being confined to the wagon, she remembered how her father had startled some Indians with his field-glass by pulling it out with a loud click and pointing it in their direction. She took the glass off its rack and whenever Indians would approach the wagon, she took her revenge by scaring them with the field-glass.

This brings to my memory another story demonstrating the child-like nature of the Indians. A family in one of the companies was being annoyed and bothered by a group of Indian braves who crowded around them, most likely begging for something. The family was getting very vexed with these pests and the grandmother, for what reason I do not know, decided to remove her teeth, or by accident they fell out of her mouth. This resulted in a panic and the Indians fled in consternation, alternately jabbering and holding their hands to their mouths in awe. Shortly their curiosity got the better of them and they slunk back to observe her putting the teeth in and taking them out again, just to see the Indians falling over themselves trying to get away. But each time, they were compelled to return to observe this obviously powerful medicine woman.

• • •

We traveled on, through green country dotted with box elders, willows, and alders. We noticed a shrub new to us, which contained an oily substance which gave off a rather noxious odor. After leaving the Platte we ascended some bluffs and traveled an arid plain. Gritty billowing clouds of dust were raised by the wheels of the wagons and those in the rear suffered greatly from it. It was the practice of those who were in front of the caravan one day to drop to the rear the next so that no one wagon or group would enjoy a dustless journey. We noticed more and more rocky and fantastic terrain with deep ravines and chasms. As we topped a slightly higher point, we observed far away on our right high mountains covered with snow.

"Do you know what has caused the earth to be so torn up, so shook to its center?" Mrs. Dunleavy addressed the group of women who were sitting around fanning themselves, trying to rest a little after finishing the evening chores.

"No, what has done it?" asked Mrs. Dunbar.

"Sin! Sin has caused these rocks to reverberate, to be upheaved that they may be eternal monuments of the curse and fall of man. These fantastic formations are symbols of Divine Wrath."

"I allow they do make you feel a little humble, the castles and domes an' all," replied one of the ladies. "But you figger it's the Injuns that done the sin you're speaking of? I thought it was white people's sin that the Almighty cares about an' there ain't been no white people out here to speak of. That's like saying the animals sin, if'n you think it's the Injuns been doing it."

"Man's sin. All of mankind is sinners."

"I heard tell that missionaries have gone out to the Oregon country to bring the word to the poor savages there," said Mrs. Quincy.

"Seems like they should first finish the job with some of these white folks we been travelin' with. Not keepin' the Holy Sabbath like we been doin' just boils my blood," said Mrs. Dunleavy. "The Reverend is fit to be tied about it but nobody's listenin'."

Good water was hard to find as most springs and ponds were impregnated with salt, alkali, and sulphur. The water was toxic to people and animals if consumed in quantity. We were fortunate to find a small spring of good water after tasting of a terribly foul but beautiful stream in a little meadow. We noticed several dead oxen on the trail, and some alive but too exhausted to continue. As I walked past one dying cow, I stopped to read a note that was pinned to its head. The note stated that she had been left to die, but if anyone wanted her they might have her, and pleading that she not be abused as she had been one of the best of cows. She looked so pitiful I was brought to tears.

July 14, 1846
On the Sweetwater & South Pass

My Dear Friend:

We reached a well-known landmark of the mountains called Independence Rock. We were all disappointed as we expected to find a rock so high that you could hardly see its top, but seen from a distance and in comparison with some of the surrounding high peaks, it looked tame and uninteresting. It is about one hundred feet in height & a mile in circumference, shaped like a dome. This edifice was named after a Fourth of July celebration here by one of the first emigrant companies to Oregon. We explored this fabulous landmark, but decided not to join the legends of emigrants who have recorded their passing on this rock.

The following day we passed Dunleavy's company on the Sweetwater. Ahead of us a mile further up the river was Dunbar's, a mile further, West's. All of the people in these companies had started out together, but shortly after leaving Independence dissension & quarreling set in & the company was broken into fragments.

Now, we have met again and all is forgotten and forgiven and good feeling prevails.

Near Independence Rock we saw a large pond of water so strongly impregnated with the carbonate of potash that the water would no longer hold it in solution. Along the edges of the pond it was found in broad & perfectly white sheets from one to two inches thick. Many of the travelers collected the saleratus for use in leavening their bread.

This is where we joined the Sweetwater River. We followed it a distance when we came across a fissure in the mountain wall that ran parallel with the stream. The fissure is about thirty feet in width, with perpendicular walls on each side of the channel of the stream that flows through it. George estimates the walls are perhaps three hundred feet in height. It has the name of Devil's Gate.

Mrs. George Donner

"There is an Indian legend regarding this point of interest, the Devil's Gate," I told the group one night at the campfire.

"What is it?"

"A Great Bad Spirit haunted this valley of the Sweetwater. He drove the buffalo before him, gorging himself upon them and the smaller game and drinking the streams and springs dry. He was in the shape of an enormous beast with huge tusks. He pawed the mountainsides in fury."

"Mother, could it have been a mammoth?" asked Leanna.

"I think this would have had to be a very, very big creature, much larger than a mammoth. He was said to loosen huge rocks and send them flying into the valley with his hind feet. He caused earthquakes when he roared and terrible winds with his breath.

"A prophet called upon the tribes to cease their warfare and cooperate in driving the beast from the valley. They combined forces and made a crusade against the Evil Spirit. It was not long before they found him in this valley and the people attacked the beast with their arrows. The siege lasted many days until the body of the beast was full of arrows and he looked like a tremendous porcupine. The attack made him very mad and he stamped and snorted and then with his tusk he ripped a gap in the mountain. Through this gap the Great Evil One disappeared."

"He disappeared forever?"

"Yes, no one has seen him since."

"Well, I'm glad the beast is gone. That would be a big problem for us if it was still here," said George.

"I hope he doesn't come back while we are here," said Elitha. "It would scare these little girls." She made as if to leave and then crept back, shouting "boo" and making the little ones scream.

"Elitha, really! Girls, get everything picked up and put away and prepare yourselves for bed. We want to start on time tomorrow for a change!"

July 14

My Dear Friend:

No scenery has been more delightful than that seen in this day's drive. On our right the valley is bounded by the Sweetwater Mountains of from ten to fifteen hundred feet in height. A wild and romantic place. Today we passed through throngs of insects resembling the cricket. In places they covered the road and when the wagon wheels rolled over them the crunching sound reminded me of our buggy rolling over ice and snow back home. We gathered wild currants, a welcome addition to our meals, which has grown destitute of fresh produce.

Mrs. George Donner

The next night we were just leaving the campfire to make ready for the night's sleep when we heard a sound drifting toward us that was not part of the desert. At first it was soft and distant, then the sound grew louder and then the shape of a horse and rider could be seen. All heads turned when the horse and rider entered the campsite.

It was a young man by the name of Bonney, traveling east alone and bearing an open letter directed to all emigrants on the road. The letter was from Lansford Hastings, written at the headwaters of the Sweetwater. It invited those bound for California to concentrate their numbers and strength and to take a new route that had been explored by Mr. Hastings. He wrote that the distance to California would be materially shortened.

"George," said James Reed, "this is the most practicable route for us. Time is getting short. It makes no sense to take a roundabout route."

"Well, it might be. I'm going to reserve judgment until we meet up with Hastings and see how many wagons are going to take his lead."

"George," I said, "we know we can get there by Fort Hall. Why take a chance on an unproven short-cut?"

"I expect we'll have plenty of time to decide."

"My family is going on Hastings's route," said James. "I can see no advantage to going the longer way if there is a shorter route."

So we toiled on, not yet making the decision, but it was on our minds with each turn of the wagon wheels and with each step we took. We saw more and more dead cattle along the road and one of our own went down and none of my efforts could revive her. Then the little mule Willy became weak and sick and could not continue. We were delayed a whole morning as I tried every remedy to help Willy. The girls all clustered around him, putting wet cloths on his head and body, stroking him and begging him to get well, but it was all to no avail. He lifted his head and brayed, as if to say good-bye, and then he was gone.

We knew we were approaching the crest of the Rocky Mountains, the point where the waters of the continent divide. From that point on in our journey, streams would be running west to the Pacific. We reached a gap between the two ranges of granite mountains that were only a few hundred yards apart, and from this gap we had our first view of the Wind River Mountains.

A number of people in our camp were sickened by bad water. Our cattle suffered too and were forced to graze on herbage that had toxic qualities. This was imparted to some extent to the milk we were drinking, contributing to our sickness.

I felt that altitude may have had something to do with our illness. A body not used to exertion at high altitudes must suffer some consequences as it attempts to make an adjustment. The mountain men speak of this as mountain fever. They also say that once adjusted, sickness is rare. We'd discussed the hardiness of the mountain men one night at the campfire.

"They seem never to suffer from sickness an' a wound that would kill one'a us don't bother them."

"They's tough as hide leather, them boys. I mind that mountain man, Smith, was it? Cut his own leg off. He was shot by some Injun, breakin' the bones in his leg. There was nothing to do but cut 'er off, but nobody would do it, so he ups and does it hisself. An' lived to tell about it."

"You 'member that mountain man, the one that was clawed and mangled by a grizzly an' was left by his friends fer dead? He made it back to civilization after months of crawlin' through the wilderness, livin' off'n bugs and rotten carcasses."

"Yep. Yer thinkin' of Hugh Glass. I reckon they get tough from livin' as a savage. An' wasn't Jim Bridger one a' the ones that left him fer dead?"

"I allow you're right. I heard that."

"You know," said Charles Stanton, "I have observed some of these mountain men and I marvel at the ease with which they lapse into being an Indian, yet the Indian does not easily become a white man."

"I mind what Zeb said about Injuns," said Solomon. "He said the way they live is better'n our way, all cooped up inside a house an' never breathin' the natural air, wearin' clothes that itch you to death an' shoes that hurt yer feet."

"He might be right about shoes," said Noah. "I traded fer some moccasins an' they did feel right good, 'til I stepped on one of them prickly pear thorns. I put my shoes back on an' threw the moccasins away."

One of the ladies in our train became quite ill and I was asked to attend to her. I learned from her family that some two or three weeks previously, she had labored hard at washing during a hot, sunny day and then had bathed in very cold water. This caused her to come down with pneumonia. She had been administered very high doses of calomel and other medicines without experiencing any benefit and, I was sure, great harm.

"Mr. Leonard, you must stop these medicines you have been giving her. In quantity they are poisonous. I am giving you some teas."

"Tea? How's that gonna help her?"

"These are medicine teas, Mr. Leonard. Before I leave I will show you how to prepare them. Give her a cup every half-hour and you must allow her to rest for several days."

"Ma'am, how'm I gonna rest being jostled around in this wagon?" asked the woman.

"Perhaps you can stop for a day or two."

"No," said the husband, "we've got to stay with our group and they're moving out in the morning."

"I advise you that she should have perfect rest, but if you must move on, perhaps you could make a hammock of some kind for her in the wagon. It will be more comfortable. I cannot offer you much hope because she has been severely damaged, but at the least the teas should help her rest. I will come back this evening to see how she is doing."

The family moved along in the same company as we did and I watched over Mrs. Leonard the next few days. I feared that the family would not follow my instructions, because the habit of using the poisonous medicines in quantity was very strong. However, they followed my advice and in a few days she began to recover.

The next day, after we passed through the narrows at the Sweetwater, we encountered a group of four men returning to the States from California. They had been members of Captain Frémont's exploring party. I was always amazed to meet others of our race and language out here in this wilderness.

We saw more and more dead oxen along the road. The poor things dropped from exhaustion and then were made quick meals of by the wolves. There were a great many wolves in the area, and they were very bold. All night they kept up a wild chorus, the likes of which we had never heard.

"Mother, girls, look here," said George. "You can see where an ox has been pursued by wolves." He pointed to markings on the ground. "See, here he took a stand, only to struggle on a little further before he was brought down by the pack. I have noticed that the deer and the antelope go amongst the buffalo, hoping the wolves will not find them so easily."

The next day a man in the party related a story about an encounter with a wolf during the night.

"I was supervisin' the watch," he said, "an' waitin' for my time to go on duty. I lay down an' covered myself with my blanket, but felt uncomfortable without somethin' to put my head on. So I looks around an' I find a slab of bacon in a sack an' I use that fer my pillow. I lay there fer a time, everythin' still. I guess I dozed some, when all at once the bacon leaves from under my head. I jumps up an' I seen this big wolf backin' off, pullin' the sack of bacon, stoppin' every couple of inches an' growling. I was afeered a' shootin' at him bein' inside camp but I draws my knife an' swiped at him. I didn't get my knife in him, but he dropped the bacon an' run off."

July 19, 1846

My Dear Friend:

Yesterday we left the Sweetwater River & ascended the dividing ridge of South Pass. We hardly knew when we actually crossed the exact point where the waters began flowing west instead of east. There was a misconception amongst most of us that we would have a difficult passage through the South Pass of the Rocky Mountains, but this was not so. The gap in the mountains is many miles in breadth & the ascent very gradual.

After two or three miles of travel over a level surface, the trail descended to a spring known as "Pacific Spring." We are now into an arid undulating plain covered by wild sage. In front of us there are many buttes rising to some height above the plain. Some appear as castellated, others topped by domes. The company has lost several oxen from drinking bad water. We lost three, Jacob four & James Reed two. We have traveled about three hundred miles since Fort Laramie.

Mrs. George Donner

We encamped on the Little Sandy and it was here that we were joined by the Breen family. There were nine in the family, and with them was their friend Patrick Dolan. Patrick was a genial man, full of fun and laughter, just the opposite of Mr. Breen, who seemed taciturn and quiet. Mr. Breen was a thin man, rather small, and always a little bent or hunched as though he had a hurt inside. Oft times at the evening campfire he would play the violin and Patrick Dolan would dance a jig and they would talk of life in Ireland. We were amazed to learn that they had traveled all this distance alone. I asked Mrs. Breen about their travels.

"It must have been very hard with only two men and your sons to help."

"Aye, an' it was that. We had difficulties, but there was always someone comin' along that would help. We placed our faith in God an' the Virgin Mary."

The Breens were of the Catholic faith, I believe the only family in the train that were. Mrs. Breen had a brusque way about her, but underneath that stern exterior lay a soft heart. She always had a little clay pipe held in her teeth. There were many women who enjoyed tobacco, but I was never inclined to use it.

It became colder. During the night we were reaching for more blankets and in the mornings we had ice in our water buckets. Here, at the Little Sandy, it was decision time. Most of those going to Oregon turned off here at Greenwood's cut-off rather than continue on to Fort Bridger and then head north to Fort Hall on the old route. The emigrants to California had to decide whether to take this right hand road to Fort Hall or the left hand road to Fort Bridger. Many in the train left us here and the parting of new and old friends was sad. We proceeded on, still debating the merits of old versus new, tried and proven against the unknown.

As the wagons began to move the next morning, we pulled around a stopped wagon and our oxen almost walked into a woman on the side of the road. She was crying and wailing piteously. It seemed that the woman was distressed and angry and had refused to continue, trying to hold her children with her. Some men came up, picked up the children, and piled them in the wagon, then the husband drove off, leaving her sitting there. I tried to console her, but the woman's mind was deranged and I could do nothing for her. I was forced to leave as George would not hold our wagons.

"Tamsen, you can't do anythin' for that woman. Her husband's at the end of his rope dealin' with her craziness."

I worried about the woman all morning and mentioned it to Betsey.

"That poor soul!" exclaimed Betsey. "She came to my camp last night, talkin' crazy, walkin' around like she didn't know where she was. But I know what set her off. They was travelin' with her folks an' her daughter's family, an' they'd all decided fer Oregon an' turned off to Fort Hall this mornin', but the woman's husband said no, he was goin' to California. She couldn't bear to part with her daughter an' the little granddaughter an' the rest of her folks. She jes' went to pieces."

As we approached the evening camp we saw a wagon burning, the same family of the left-behind wife. There were several men helping to put out the blaze so we went on, looking for a good spot away from the crowd. That evening George reported the news about the unfortunate family.

"That woman got up, cut across the country, an' when her husband come up she tol' him she'd knocked her oldest child in the head with a rock when he'd come back to get a horse. The man believed her a'course, she'd been acting so strange, so he took off to go back an' find the boy. When he left she set fire to the wagon. Burned the cover and some store goods."

"Was the child hurt badly?" I asked.

"No, he hadn't even seen his Ma," replied George.

"She's likely goin' to come to her senses now or get another flogging," said Jacob.

"He *beat* her?"

"What else could he do?" said Jacob.

"You know what?" asked Betsey, "I know somethin' of how that woman feels. Her husband tol' her they'd be with her family so's she'd agree to go an' then he ups and takes off for California instead. Don't you men think he should keep his word?"

"If'n he decides a thing, it's the duty of his wife to go along with it without making a fuss an' causing trouble fer him. I'd do the same thing," said Jacob.

Betsey picked up a small piece of wood and tossed it at Jacob. "You just try an' not keep your word to me, Jacob Donner. I'd do more than burn your wagon."

◆ ◆ ◆

Charles Stanton came to talk to George.

"Sir, it's necessary that a captain be elected and most of us feel that you are the best qualified."

"Most venerable perhaps," replied George, "but qualified, no. That post requires a man that don't care about bein' nice to people, that can hold himself away from formin' friendships. You'll have no friends once you agree to take the job."

The company insisted that George should be their captain and he finally agreed.

"George," I began, "you said—"

"An' at the time I meant it. But who do you think could take the job an' carry it out? James would be a good leader because he feels superior anyway, but the people flat don't like him an' most likely wouldn't take direction from him. He knows it, we've talked about it. An' really, the position is in name only. James takes responsibility too."

That night as I lay beside George, the apprehension I had been feeling but had tried to ignore came back and I could not sleep. I shook George's shoulder. "Uhh? What's wrong?" he asked, groggy from sleep.

"George, I'm really concerned that we should not take this route."

"Route?"

"George. The supposed shorter route. I do not want to go that way. I feel—I have this feeling that it would be a terrible mistake."

"Godamighty, Tamsen!"

"Oh, I'm sorry I woke you, it's just—"

"No decision's been made. We'll have a meetin' to talk it over tomorrow night. It ain't nothin' to fret yourself about. Go to sleep."

July 28, 1846
Fort Bridger

We found Fort Bridger to be much more of a disappointment than Fort Laramie. It was just a small trading post established by Jim Bridger and his partner, Luis Vasquez, consisting of two or three crude log structures. It was redeemed somewhat by a beautiful setting in a fertile valley with clumps of cottonwood trees along the stream.

When we arrived we were surprised and disheartened to learn that Mr. Hastings had already departed with a train of more than sixty wagons, leaving word for late arrivals to follow in the wagon tracks of the group. We inquired of the people at the fort as to the feasibility of this route that Hastings was advocating and were told that we would find an abundant supply of wood, water, and pasturage along the whole line of road, with only one dry drive of thirty or forty miles.

The next afternoon I sat in my rocking chair by our wagon planning to write in my journal. A warm breeze rustled the leaves in the big cottonwood tree overhead, wafting a fragrance from the grasses and flowers that carpeted the meadow. I waved away a persistent fly, finally stunning it with a quick swipe of my fan. *At least I'm not besieged by gnats like we had at the camp last night,* I thought. I closed my eyes and leaned my head back in the chair. *I should get those berry pies started, but it's so pleasant, it's making me sleepy.* I started from my doze as I heard and felt the flap of wings and then I saw a crow alight directly in front of me. It side-stepped, first one way and then the other, all the while fixing me with its yellow eyes.

"Hello. You're a tame one," I said.

As I spoke, two more crows, smaller in size, flapped down before me, twisting their heads around as if questioning what was going on between the first crow and me. *Why is it that a crow somehow makes me think of death?* Then I remembered. *There were crows in the trees when we buried our little boy. They squawked so much we could hardly hear the preacher. And when I buried Tully too. I remember one of the men throwing stones at them.*

A chill ran through my body. I jumped up, shaking my apron at the crows. "Get away!" I yelled.

The crows startled and flew off into the top of the tree. Shakily, I picked up my journal that had fallen to the ground and sat back down. *This nervousness over taking the new route is affecting my senses.* I dusted off the journal and opened it, trying to get my thoughts back to writing. I noticed a man pass by and then turn back. His red hair was bright in the sunlight.

"We don't usually see crows around here," he said. "I 'spect they're lookin' for leavin's from the wagon train. Are ye writin' a journal?"

"Yes. I haven't been as faithful to it lately as I ought to be. I'm Mrs. George Donner. What is your name?"

"Goodyear, ma'am. I be Miles Goodyear."

"Do you live here at the fort?"

"Yes'm. I'm a trader."

"Oh, yes. I think my husband got an ox from you for one of our cows. She'll be a good milker again, I'm sure."

"Yes'm, he sure did. I wondered if 'n you might be interested in knowing, fer yer journal," he raised his arm and pointed to a patch of growth about a quarter mile away, "that there, in yonder willow thicket, a man by the name a' Black was killed by a band a' fifty Blackfoot Injuns. He defended hisself bravely for a long spell and e'en bein' wounded he killed a passel 'fore they overcame him."

"Poor man."

"Wal, that's how she is here in the mountains. Yer take yer chances."

"Mr. Goodyear, do you know anything of the route that Mr. Hastings has advocated?"

"Ma'am, it's mighty rough country. Hastings has been through there an' he led some fifty or sixty wagons out a few days ago. There ain't no road, but with all them wagons makin' a road it most likely won't be difficult for those who follow. There's some bad desert to cross, but if yer animals're in good condition, you might make it through without too many of 'em dyin' on you. Mr. Bridger's wantin' to have a road opened, trade's been mighty slow since most of the emigrants been takin' Greenwood's cut-off. I'd say that that feller Hastings an' Mr. Bridger are in cahoots. Bridger an' Vasquez want a road an' Hastings wants to get California filled up with men that'll fight to take the Mexican Territory."

"That is a reasonable conclusion," I said.

"Ma'am, there's a young man been staying with me. He's anxious to join up with a family goin' to California. He's got no means of goin' hisself. I been usin' him some, but he's wantin' to go on."

"Mr. Goodyear, he will have to talk with my husband. We have already agreed to allow a man who is sick to travel in our wagons. I don't know if Mr. Donner will want to take responsbibility for anyone else."

"You took in the consumptive man, Mr. Halloran?"

"Yes."

"That's mighty fine of you all. The family he was with left him here at the post. Truthfully, I can't see the man lastin' much more'n a few days."

"I'm afraid you are right."

• • •

The debate about the new route raged within our camp. That evening the children were put to bed and the group gathered around our fire. It was cold and I pulled a heavy shawl around my shoulders. A breeze was blowing and the fire glowed and died and glowed again as the wind played with it. The orange light of the fire flickered on the solemn faces of those assembled around it. George started the discussion.

"Y'all know there are sixty wagons ahead of us breakin' the trail, led by this Hastings fellow. Time is gettin' short an' this here route may cut many days off our travel. The men here at the fort say there's a forty-mile section without water, but with good plannin' we can overcome that."

"Do you remember what Mr. Clymer said?" asked Mr. Stanton. "He was against it in no uncertain terms."

John Denton spoke up. "That other bloke that came through, the one that had been with Mr. Frémont, he spoke unfavorably of the route."

"Sublette? I heard he tol' Cap'n Davis the southern way of goin' was the same miles as goin' north an' had sixty miles of desert."

"No. It warn't Sublette. This man was—"

"Jim, you must be speakin' of Joe Walker," interrupted Noah. "He's the man that's drivin' those horses through from California. It's said of him that he don't follow trails, he makes 'em. Walker thinks that Mr. Hastings wants to acquire men to fight in California for independence from Mexico. He says that independence will likely raise the value of the land, makin' Hastings a sight of money."

I remembered Mr. Walker very well. He was an impressive man, tall and well built. Handsome, I thought.

"Walker's a puke and a thief, stole those horses from the Mexicans. You can't trust what a man like that says," someone exclaimed.

"Walker's well thought of. Who are you to call him a puke anyway?" countered Noah.

"Well, ain't he?"

"Now, let's keep to the subject," said George. "Hastings *is* openin' this route an' we can follow him. It's already late in the season and we still have more'n a thousand miles to go."

I spoke up, ignoring the disapproving glance from James Reed. "If we go the old route we will still arrive at the peak of the Sierras in mid-October, in plenty of time before the snows. Everyone we ask about the new route is against it, except for these men at the fort, and of course, Mr. Hastings. And their motives are questionable. Why take a chance on the unproven?"

"No offense, Mrs. Donner, but these matters are best left up to the men," said James.

"No offense, Mr. Reed, but I have more common sense than most of you men and I feel we should not take the chance."

George shifted his feet nervously and cleared his throat, giving me a pleading look. *Oh, all right, George. But why don't you come to my defense?* I thought. I could see James tense and his lips thin. He stood up, took a few steps back and forth, and then put one foot on a log and leaned forward.

"I am going to follow the new route," he said. "There is said to be a savings of three to four hundred miles and a better route. On this new route we will not have dust since there are but sixty wagons ahead of us. And we are getting low on provisions."

"It would be good to get away from the dust," said Mr. Foster.

"We can stock up on provisions here at the post," I said. "And we're so far behind, even if we go north we'll be days behind the other wagons and their dust."

James made a gesture of exasperation. "The prices are exorbitant. These traders here will take your last penny in trade." James took his foot off the log and sat down again, continuing his discourse. "I grant you, there are some difficulties. According to Walker, who was with him, Mr. Frémont found a stretch of forty miles without water. Hastings will be out ahead looking for water and a route to avoid this stretch. Mr. Bridger and other gentlemen here who have trapped that country tell me that the route we design to take is a level road with plenty of water and grass, except for that one section of forty miles. I think we can make Sutter's fort in seven weeks from this day."

I sat listening. I would not embarrass George by arguing with the menfolk again. *How can James be so confident? So arrogantly sure of himself? Does he know more than Mr. Clyman, or Mr. Walker, or Mr. New? Hardly.*

"Whoopee! Only seven more weeks!" exclaimed Mr. Pike. "I'm all for that! No more sleepin' on the ground, eatin' dust, dyin' from thirst an' all the other things we been findin' so intolerable. It sounds good to me. Mother Murphy, what do you think?"

"I'm all fer cuttin' off some miles. Our animals are 'bout to give out an' we're running short on provisions."

"Aye, it hae the ring of reason," said Mr. Breen. "With yon party makin' the road, we'll not have the problem gettin' through the mountains that Mr. Clyman spoke of. I have provisions enough, but a shortnin' of the journey is welcome."

I sat listening as one and then another agreed that following the new route seemed a good decision. *But why take a chance? I know we should not go that way. Why can't they understand there's no good reason to take the risk?*

George stood up. "Y'all make your decision. The Donner an' Reed wagons are goin' to follow Hastings' party."

On the way back to our wagons, George hugged me. "My love, stop your mopin'. This seems like the best way for us to go."

"No, George, it is not."

Well, of course, I was right. I will digress from my story for a moment, because this is an important juncture in the journey. Picture yourself there that night, sitting around the campfire. Unease prickles and fear creeps into your mind. The group is lagging behind, probably the last company on the road. What if winter snows should come early and close the pass to California?

All the arguments have been put forth and picked apart, but there is one major point which negates all the arguments against taking the new route and that is that the party ahead, led by Mr. Hastings, is making the road. All the Donner Party has to do is point their wagons along the traces left by the wheels of the companies ahead. It was an incorrect decision, but it was not a *bad* decision. I was an advanced soul and thus could sense the impending disaster, but premonition, or intuition, was not, and still is not, given much consideration on the mortal plane.

July 30, 1846

My Dear Friend:

We arrived at Fort Bridger on the 28th & are laying by in order to recruit our stock & make repairs to our wagons. The decision has been made to take the short-cut advocated by Mr. Lansford Hastings.

When we arrived we found that Mr. Hastings had gone ahead leading sixty wagons. Mr. Bridger & Mr. Vasquez, the proprietors of the fort, have assured us the route is an agreeable one. We have been joined by several families and single men, some back at the Little Sandy, others at Fort Bridger.

Fort Bridger is sited in a bottom of a clear and bubbling stream about two miles south of the old wagon trail to Fort Hall. There are a number of traders here from the neighborhood of Taos. They have buckskins, buckskin shirts, pantaloons, and moccasins. Trade with the emigrants is an important commerce for them. Most likely this is the last chance I will have to send a letter back to the States until we should arrive in California.

Mrs. George Donner

Mr. Goodyear brought the young man that he had spoken to me about. He was dressed in ill-fitting mountaineer's clothing, used up moccasins, and a large Mexican-style hat. He carried a rolled-up Indian blanket. My first thought was that he was Mexican because of his way of speaking, but he looked very European, with a long narrow nose and a wide brow over deep-set eyes. He was small, but wiry. He told us his father had been a fur trapper, and was French.

"And your mother?" I asked.

"*Mi Mamá,* she was of the Pueblo of Taos, a Spanish woman who marry the *Anglo, Señora.* As a boy I live in Taos, where most of the people speak the *Español.* I know a little of the French, *tambien.* I know the language of the Indians who call themselves Utah and I have the sign language for others that live in the mountains and deserts that you must cross. I can be of much use to you."

"Do you know the country south and west of here?" asked George.

"No, *Señor,* I no travel that country. I no think it a good idea, but if that is the way you will go, I want to go with you. I will have trust in *Dios, Señor.*"

George chuckled. "And I guess we will too. What's your name, son?"

"I am called Juan Baptiste Trudeau."

"John, then."

"I say it the Spanish way, but you may say John. Is all the same."

"How old are you?" George asked.

"I have sixteen years, *quizas* seventeen. *Mi Abuela,* she lost the count. I am a man, *Señor.*

Juan told us that he had been with Kit Carson and Captain Frémont on their expedition to California but he left the group at the headwaters of the Green River. He had come to Fort Bridger determined to join one of the wagon parties.

At Fort Bridger we were also joined by two other single men: a young Mexican named Antonio: and an invalid, Luke Halloran. We had felt sorry for the man, all alone with no one to care for him. Charles Stanton, who had been traveling with us since the time we joined the Russell company, decided for California and remained in the company.

Several family groups became part of our company. Mr. William Eddy, his wife Eleanor, and two very small children were from Illinois. Also joining us was Lavina Murphy and her seven children including two married daughters, Sarah and her husband William Foster with one child, and Harriet and her husband, William Pike, and their two children. Mrs. Murphy's husband had died some years previous and she told me that she moved her family to Nauvoo, Illinois, after his death. We presumed she was of the Mormon faith.

"You sound to me like you are from somewhere in the South," I said.

"I was born in Tennesee. My pap was a poor dirt farmer, tryin' to farm on ground so steep we had to put stakes in the ground to keep from rollin' downhill. I run off from there an' I never want to go back."

Also with us was William McCutcheon from Missouri, his wife Amanda, and their infant daughter. There were several that our group labeled "the Dutchmen" because they were of German heritage: Lewis Keseberg and his wife Philippine and their two children; a man named Wolfinger and his wife Doris; Karl Burger, Augustus Spitzer, Joseph Reinhardt, and an older man, Mr. Hardcoop.

July 31, 1846
Hastings Long Trip

The fateful decision was made. The die was cast. The next day our wagons left Fort Bridger. The cattle lowed gently, the sun shone, and the breeze flittered through the leaves on the cottonwoods along the creeks. My thoughts could not escape from the fear and the prickling of all my senses. I walked along with apprehension dogging my footsteps.

We ascended from the valley in which Fort Bridger was situated, traveling to the left of a high and rather remarkable butte that overlooked the bottom from the west. Just out from the fort the road forked, the right-hand road the old trail to Fort Hall. I stood for a few minutes there as the wagons rolled past me, the gritty dust billowing in clouds, cold fear possessing me. *I know this is a terrible mistake. Why can't they see it?*

We followed the tracks of the party led by Mr. Hastings. There was no road, no trail, only the markings of the large company that preceded us. The country took on a more favorable aspect than that we had been passing through for several days. We crossed several plains which had good grass. The bordering hills had bright green patches of growth with clumps of aspens in the hollows. The route was favorable, but my fear did not abate.

Not too far from Fort Laramie, one of the Breen boys, Edward, suffered a broken leg. He and Patty Reed were running their ponies when his horse stepped into an animal burrow and took a hard fall. Edward was thrown from the pony, knocked senseless, his leg broken between the ankle and the knee. My girls came running to tell of Eddie's accident and I hurried over to the Breen wagons. Edward was lying on the grass beside the wagon, crying and moaning. Someone was sent back to the fort to bring aid and after a long time a bearded mountain man appeared riding a mule. He unrolled a bundle wrapped in canvas and proceeded to take out a meat saw and a long-bladed knife.

"How'ye. They call me Jim," he said.

Edward's mother didn't like the looks of the mountain man. "Mister," she asked in a shaky voice, "hae you experience in doctorin' a break like this? Hae you any surgical trainin'?"

"Har! Surgical trainin'? A'course I have." Jim spit a stream of tobacco juice that splatted on the dusty ground. "I've killed an' skinned out mebbe a hunnert buffler an' as many deer, to say nothin' of all t'other game. I've done more cuttin' on animals an' folks than nine out'a ten surgeons. I've cut arrows out'a people many times an' cleaned up bad wounds a'one kind or 'nother. I opine I've more experience than any ye so-called doctors. Let's git 'em up on a wagon gate. Do ye got any whiskey?"

Eddie commenced to pitch a fit as the man approached him with his tools. "No. Let me be! No, Ma, no!" He howled louder as they lifted him as carefully as they could to a table that was set up in the shade of his family's wagon. Someone brought a flask of spirits. Jim took the flask and put it to his mouth, draining most of the bottle. Then he put the flask to Eddie's mouth.

"Here, young'un, this'll hep ye stand the cuttin'."

"Get him away from me! Ma! No!" Eddie screamed.

Mrs. Breen was getting more and more nervous as Eddie begged not to have his leg taken off. Finally, not having any confidence in this dirty rough-looking fellow, she told him they would let Eddie have his way. They gave Jim five dollars and sent him back to the Fort, stiff with indignation that he wasn't allowed to demonstrate his skills.

"Margaret," I said, "clean his leg well with the whiskey. I have a medicine for broken bones. I'll be back in a few minutes."

By the time I returned with the salve I had made, Mr. Breen had made splints. I gave the boy some willow bark to chew and I spread the salve gently on his leg.

"Eddie, just relax now. In a few minutes we'll straighten your leg and bind it up. Keep chewing on that bark."

"Is it gonna hurt?" he asked.

"Yes, but perhaps not a lot. I've been told that this salve will relax your leg, that you might even become very sleepy and not feel much."

"What is that you're puttin' on?" asked Eddie's mother as she brought some rag strips for binding up his leg.

"This is made from a root that an Indian healer gave to me. A mountain man told me that his friend had been treated with it when he broke his leg. There's no harm in trying it."

I washed Eddie's face with cool water and placed a pillow under his head. "I think we'll wait awhile to give the salve a chance to work," I told his mother.

Soon Eddie began to relax and we began to straighten the bone. It was painful for him, but was much easier than I had expected. We bound the leg up in the splints and he was placed on a bed in his family's wagon. He suffered for a time with the jolting and jerking, but in a few days he could sit up and in a month he was riding his horse again.

We crossed a large Indian trail. Juan Baptiste was walking with me and the girls when we saw the first of several lodge poles lying on the ground.

"*Señora* Donner, you see? A company of Shoshone Indians, they go this way. They were in much hurry."

"How do you know?"

"You see, on the ground, poles for the lodges have been dropped, an' we pick up a buffalo skin that belong to them. The poles they no easy to find an' they have much value. The Indians they move fast, their soldiers no let them stop for the poles that drop off from the travois. You see the dung of their horses? It is much scattered an' that means the horses are moving fast. I think they try to get away from other Indians that want to make the war."

"Could it be a war party waiting to attack us?"

"I no think so. The people they move with all the village, the women an' children an' the old ones. They no make war when with all the people they travel."

"But how do you know they are Shoshone?"

"I see the tracks of moccasins. Each kind of Indian, they have ways of doing things. The way they make the moccasins, even so." Juan Baptiste turned to the girls. "You know the hand talk sign for the Snake Indians?"

"No."

Baptiste moved his right hand in an up and down waving motion. "See, like a snake moving. If I want to tell you that I saw a Snake Indian, I do this." Juan Baptiste placed two fingers outward from his eyes and then made the up and down waving motion.

"You see, *niñas*? This is what I say with the hand talk. I saw a person of the Snake tribe of Indians. I know something more. Soon we are going to have rain."

"Oh, Baptiste, we see the clouds. You aren't all that smart."

"I have much knowledge, but you have some too, little one. Why don't you get yourself in the wagon before you get wet?"

Frequently in the afternoons we were bothered by squalls of rain and when the clouds lifted, we could see snow on the tops of the mountains to the left of us.

August 5, 1846

It has been fairly easy going since Ft. Bridger. The first day we crossed a branch, some thought perhaps it was the Little Muddy, and camped in a little valley covered with fine grass and occasional clumps of cottonwood trees, willows, and other shrubbery along the stream.

We traveled over ridges where sometimes the western slopes would be abrupt and precipitous and the wagons were eased down, skittering and bumping over the rough terrain, rocks and dirt bouncing off down the slope.

Once we lost the road and descended into a narrow hollow enclosed by high yellow and red cliffs. At the end of the hollow we came to an almost impassable barrier of red sandstone and had to reverse our track to find the road again.

We ascended a high elevation on our left and passed over a plain with sage so thick it was difficult to force our way through. On the fourth day, yesterday, we crossed the Bear River, ascended a high ridge, and found a westward flowing river that led us down into a magnificent but fearsome canyon.

Towering red cliffs loomed over us. The wagons clattered and jolted over the rocks littering the floor of the canyon. Several times wheels would splinter or just roll off, necessitating a stop for repairs by the unfortunate owners. The sounds of people talking, the blows of hammers, the clatter of hooves would echo back and forth between the high rocky sides of the canyon. After making our way out of the defile, we followed the trail along the side of a stream for several miles and then the lead wagons stopped.

"What's the trouble?" asked George.

"No trouble. We found this paper stuck in that bush there. It's a letter," said William Eddy.

James Reed pushed his way through the group. "Here, let me have it." James read what was written and turned to the group.

"It's from Hastings. He's telling anyone that comes through here not to follow him."

"What? That can't be. We don't know any other way to go."

"He's saying that the canyon will be too difficult for us. He wants us to send a messenger ahead to find him. He'll return and point out a better route."

Jacob slumped down on a rock and began drawing lines in the dust with the toe of his shoe. I noticed that the sole was almost completely loose from the upper.

"He's been telling how good a road it is and now he's saying it's no good. The bastard," said Jacob.

"Let's make camp. We'll have to decide on a course of action," said James.

A meeting was held and James Reed, Mr. McCutcheon, and Mr. Stanton volunteered to go ahead on horseback to find Hastings. We expected that they would be back in a day, but the days dragged on with no sign of them. The opportunity to rest was welcome, but we were nervous, knowing we could not afford to lose this travel time. On the afternoon of the fifth day some of the children came running.

"There's a horseman coming!"

"Just one man?"

"Yeah, an' it's not one a' our horses, but the man's wearin' a hat like Mr. Reed wears."

It was James Reed. He looked very tired and dejected. We gathered around to hear what he had to say.

"Where're the other two men?" asked George.

"Their horses gave out. The country we went through was very rough. They'll meet up with us. Milt, see to my horse."

Margaret brought water for her husband and after he drank some, James poured the rest over his head and dried himself with his handkerchief. He found a stick, squatted down on his heels, and started to draw lines in the dust.

"This is about where we are and this is the Salt Lake. Between here and there is a maze of canyons that are steep, rocky, and filled with growth." James drew in several wavy lines and triangles to indicate mountains.

"The group ahead took a route other than the one Mr. Hastings wanted while he was ahead scouting," said James. He poked the stick into one of the lines. "This canyon here is the one they took." James tapped the stick on the second line. "This is the one Hastings pointed out to me—the one I followed back. When the other men and I left here, we followed their trail through the canyon and we could see where they had so much trouble. That canyon is extremely narrow, in places just barely wide enough to get by on the side of the river. Other places they were into the river. They had to move huge boulders and in some places had to fill in with rocks and brush."

"I don't understand why we can't follow 'em. The road's made now," questioned George.

"Well, what they could do and we cannot is pull up the steep cliffs," replied James. "They had to use a pulley and lift them up. We don't have enough men to do it. Even so, they lost one of their wagons and two oxen over a precipice. Look, if you men want to go on up by horseback and look it over—"

"It's my opinion we haven't the time. Already we've been sitting here for five days," said William Eddy.

"All Hastings would do was point out to me the way he thinks we should go. He couldn't come back all the way. I blazed the trail so we could find it again. We can go back and take the Fort Hall route or we can proceed and make a road. Either way it's going to delay our travel, but we still have time. I feel we have no choice but to go ahead."

Jacob made a bitter snort. "That goddamn Hastings. I knew we shouldn't've hitched our wagon to his."

"Well, I don't know what else we can do now," said George. "I reckon we don't have much choice but to proceed. If we go back to Bridger and then go to Fort Hall, how much time will we lose?

If we go on ahead, how much time will it take to get to Mary's River? We need to study on it. James, you get some supper and rest for a spell."

The group came to our camp just before dusk, the women sitting off to the side or behind their men. The meeting had a mournful feeling, reminding me of people gathered around a body waiting for the preacher to begin.

"I recommend that we proceed," said James. "It will be hard work, but with every man doing their part we can get through. I think, with direction and all our efforts, the work can be accomplished in a week or two, and we will then pick up the trail of Hastings's group."

The discussion went on into the night with hot arguments and purple recriminations circling the campfire. But finally, just about everybody agreed that we would proceed into the canyons.

The route pointed out to Reed by Hastings was a terrible, terrible choice. We had to make a road for wagons by a route that no wagon had ever taken before. It was heavily wooded and choked with brush. The men, aided by some of the women and children, hacked and chopped tunnels through the dense thickets, then heaved the wagons over gullies filled with the chopped brush, sometimes forced into riverbeds thick with boulders. It was a maze of canyons, leading to dead-ends. We would pull the wagons up inclines and over ridges, only to find more ridges on the other side. Everyone was exhausted and tempers were short.

James Reed came to our camp one evening to discuss our progress. "We've got to get everyone to do a fair share of this work," he said to George.

"Isn't everyone?"

"No. None of those Dutchmen, except Keseberg, are working a full day. Today Burger stayed behind after the noon break. Then Wolfinger left the work detail and then Reinhardt."

"Burger's hurting bad from blisters on his hands an' that big rock that rolled on him yesterday," replied George. "It's fortunate he didn't have a broken leg, but still he's mighty bruised up.

Hardcoop is old an' weak. He can't walk more'n a mile or two before he gives out. He's more of a hindrance than anythin'. Reinhardt now, I reckon he could do more. I'll talk to him."

"There's Spitzer," replied James. "He worked for a couple of hours yesterday and today he lay in camp. There are several others that are not pulling their weight, George. Everybody has got to pitch in. Jacob sits down more than he works."

"Jacob is a sick man, James," I said, "but still he works as much as he's able. He doesn't quit early." George frowned and put his hand on my arm, but I ignored him. "Betsey, her boys and I and our two girls have been working—I think we make up for any slack on Jacob's part. You could send Baylis and Eliza to help. They can do something."

"Baylis can't work in the daytime, afflicted like he is. He does his share standing guard at night," said James. "Eliza has to help my wife."

"Why?"

"Margaret can't be expected to do the cooking and chores for my workers."

"Perhaps Virginia could help Margaret with the chores. That would free Eliza to work."

James looked at me with irritation. "Women should not do this type of work."

George, as usual, tried to smooth things over. "Tamsen, the men'll get the work done. There's no call for the women to work." George got up. "I'll go talk to those men now."

"I'll go with you," said James. "It's about time they learn they have to do their share."

"James, I think it's best if you don't. There seems to be some hard feelin's between you an' them an' there's no point in rubbin' salt in the wound."

"What the hell are you saying? I have done nothing to—"

George wearily held up his hand. "James, let me do this. I'm too damned tired to do any arguin'."

"Have it your way, then." James turned on his heel and stalked off.

"George, I'll go with you," I said.

"Tamsen, this is men's business. I don't want you to get involved."

"I'll not say anything to embarrass you, George. I'll just visit with Mrs. Keseberg a little."

The German men were eating supper around their fire in company with Mrs. Keseberg.

"Greetings of the day, Donner, Mrs. Donner," said Mr. Keseberg. I sat down beside Mrs. Keseberg and cooed at the baby.

"He's growing so fast."

"Yes. He's a good baby."

"Sit yourself down, Donner," said Mr. Keseberg.

"Thank you," said George. He found a seat made from a stump. Nobody said anything. George cleared his throat.

"Well, it's been a back-breakin' job gettin' through these canyons an' we ain't there yet. There's a lot more work ahead of us. We're goin' to have to put in extra effort. Each one is goin' to have to work flat out."

"It iss nigger verk," said Reinhardt.

"I agree with that, Reinhardt, but we ain't got any niggers to do the work an' there's no way out of this other than to get the job done. Each one has to do his share the best that he's able. Now, Burger here's hurtin' from yesterday, needs to lay off a day or two. Mr. Hardcoop, we don't expect you to do heavy work, you're too weak. Wolfinger, I ain't complainin', you did what you could. Spitzer, you didn't work at all today. Reinhardt, you quit early."

Mr. Keseberg started to get up, but George held up his hands, palms out. "Keseberg, you been pullin' your weight. Nobody's sayin' you ain't."

"I will fight the man that does," said Keseberg. "You expect us to work harder than the others? Some of those whippersnappers, they're not working hard. And Reed—who gave him the job of boss-man? He can do some of the hard son-a-bitching work too."

"Aww, look, men, let's not get into petty bickerin'. I'll be talkin' to the rest of the men too. All we want is for everyone to do their share, best they can. What say?"

George looked around the group. A few nodded their heads, the rest looked sullen, but nobody said they wouldn't cooperate.

"Okay, here's what we're gonna do. We'll start at daylight an' work 'til noon an' then take a two-hour rest. We're in this together. We can't have anyone slackin' off while others work. Hardcoop, you can sharpen the tools. Burger, you can help the women who stay to camp with fixin' food. Reinhardt, you an' Spitzer turn out for a full day of work."

"Ve vill, but Reed and the others, they haf to do the same verk as us," said Reinhardt.

I went back to our camp and George went to visit the other camps. When he came back, he leaned against the wagon and watched me kneading bread for the next day's breakfast.

"I'll bake this tonight and share it around in the morning. How did it go in the other camps?"

"Oh, everybody's exhausted an' they're all mean as hell, but they'll do the best they can. I just wish we had more men."

"James's attitude bothers me, George. He acts like he's ordering his own workers around. People resent it. Did you see him put his hand to his knife when he and Keseberg got into it yesterday? He reminded me of a slave owner thinking about using his whip."

"No, I didn't. We're all on a short fuse. Tamsen, honey, don't you think you're a little hard on Margaret? She has those bad headaches an' all."

"It pays off for her, doesn't it? She can lie abed or read and crochet all day while her maid does her work. We need to have every able-bodied person pitch in and do whatever they can. George, I wonder if you couldn't use the oxen to pull some of the thick brush down. Wouldn't it be easier than chopping?"

"Uproot the stuff with chains? Might take more time than choppin', but we could try it."

"Well, some of that brush might be shallow rooted and pop right out."

"Yeah, mebbe so. I'll talk to the men, see what they think."

While I was finishing my bread baking, George gathered our teamsters and they worked out how they might use the oxen to pull out the brush and trees. The next morning the work group gathered in our camp.

"We're gonna try draggin' the big clumps out of the ground using a team," George announced. "We'll use our men to chain an' drive the team, an' the rest of you can work on clearin' what we can't pull out."

"George, do you have any more gloves?" asked Jacob. "My hands are plumb tore up."

"I got four pairs left, I think. Tamsen, where'd I put those gloves? We'll give 'em to the ones that need 'em the most."

"Vere iss Reed? He iss not verking?" asked Reinhardt.

"He's comin'," said Milt. "I see him saddlin' up over yonder now."

George turned to Noah. "Noah, you get the oxen started. Jim, bring along the chain. The rest of you pick up a tool and start on over. I'll be along," said George.

George walked over to the Reed camp to talk to James, who was already mounted on his horse. We straggled behind Noah and the oxen to the place where we'd stopped work the day before. In a few minutes George and James came up.

"Looks like George got Reed off'n his horse," murmured Jacob. "I wonder that the man can walk."

"All right," said George, "let's try it on that scrub there." He pointed to a clump of twisted and gnarled growth. Noah had brought three yoke of oxen and he coaxed them into position as the men drug chains to a clump George pointed out.

"Boys, get the chain around it close to the ground an' get it hooked in there real good." George squatted down to get a better view of the work. "Jim, couple more times, okay?" Then he straightened up and stepped back. "That might do 'er."

When everybody was standing clear, George whistled to get Noah's attention and signaled for him to start the oxen. The beasts, tired and poorly as they were, did their best. They strained and scrabbled around on the rocks for a minute or two and then the roots of the clump began tearing from the ground. The oxen bounded forward as the clump gave way, flinging a thick cloud of dust in the air.

"Whoa! Whoa there!" shouted Noah.

George waved his arm and James and his crew moved in and began to drag the big clump out of the way. While they were making ready to pull out a second clump, the rest of the work group began clearing rocks and smaller growth. The canyon was beastly hot and there was no cooling breeze. Sweat trickled down our bodies, stinging and itching under our clothes. Thorny, sharp limbs poked and lacerated our skin. The sun was almost directly overhead when Noah called to George.

"Mr. Donner, I think we need to get another team. These oxen have quit on us."

"Yeah," replied George, "it's about time to rest anyways."

We stopped the work and gathered around George. The black dirt of the canyon mingled with our perspiration to create a mud on our faces and arms. Our clothing was covered so thickly with it we could hardly see any color.

"We cleared more this morning than we did in the previous two days," said George. "Denton an' I looked over the next section. There's a place where there's big rocks, but not as much thicket. If we use the oxen to roll the rocks, I think it'll be faster than going through the brush. This afternoon we'll only need a few of the strongest men. We'll work on movin' those rocks. Everyone else can rest up."

"Oh, thank God," said Betsey. She held her hands out to me. "Look at these blisters on my hands. And my back is so sore I cain't hardly straighten up."

"And I also," I said. "But I think we've accomplished a lot this morning."

As we gathered up our tools and began to walk back to the camp, we heard angry voices. It was some of the German men, pushing their way through James's group, which had started to camp ahead of them.

"Iss goot you join the peasants to verk today, Reed," said one. "Oh, iss pity, you haf got your boots dirty."

James wheeled around, looking at the men, not sure which one had spoken. "Who's the sarcastic bastard?" he asked.

No one answered. James stood with his feet spread, hands tight in fists. "Speak up, you sorry son-of-a-bitch. Are you afraid to speak to my face?" James stood watching the men move off. He swung around as George and I approached. George tried to placate him.

"James. It ain't worth gettin' all upset over. We're all on edge. We'll all feel better after a rest an' some food."

"Mr. Reed," said Milt, "those Dutchmen ain't worth spit. They ain't worth gettin' riled up about."

James wiped the sweat and dirt off his face with a handkerchief and turned to walk away. "Bastards. I'll not be braced again," he growled.

• • •

That afternoon the children came running to tell us there were wagons coming. A tall, raw-boned man with a shambling walk and a face of leather came up ahead of three wagons.

"We didn't think we was gonna catch up with you people. We was told back at Bridger you were a week or more ahead. I'm Franklin Graves, from Marshall County, Illinois."

He shook hands with George and James. It was explained to him why he'd been able to catch up with us.

"Seems like those people at Bridger are a pack a' liars. They sure steered us wrong. Well, there ain't nothin' to be done but set to an' help get the job done."

In the Graves' party were Franklin Graves, his wife Elizabeth, and their nine children, including a married daughter, Sarah, and her husband, Jay Fosdick. Teamstering for them was John Snyder. They had originally intended to Oregon, but changed their minds at Fort Bridger. Oh, I am sure there were many times in the mountains that they asked themselves, why, why?

The men of the Graves family were all good workers and they joined in and the women helped too. The backbreaking task continued. A section of road would be made, a mile or two or three, and then the wagons would be brought up and we would camp again. The streams snaked along the canyons and we had to cross many times. In one canyon we crossed the stream nineteen times in five miles.

The land rose steadily, the trees becoming much larger. We ascended a high ridge where we could see far off, over lower mountains, the valley of the Great Salt Lake. At last! But there was still a lot of country to cross and it was rough country. We rattled and jerked down the other side of the ridge, bridging a steep ravine by filling it with trunks of trees and brush.

At the foot of the mountain we came to a stream and here James Reed's family wagon broke an axle. Mrs. Reed and little Tommy were tumbled around in the wagon, but they had only a little bruising for the experience. They were helped out and taken to our wagon as the men assessed the damage.

"I'm surprised it's held up this long, the country we been through," said William Eddy. "He's got no spare?"

"No, we're gonna have to find a good tree to make one," replied Milt. "I ain't seen any trees that'll do 'er around here."

"I'll help," said Eddy. "The quicker we get about it—"

"Why are we stopped?" James had just come up. He'd been riding out ahead on his horse scouting the area. With James was Charles Stanton and William McCutcheon, the men who, weeks ago, had gone with him to find Mr. Hastings.

"Sure am glad to see you men," said George. "You look pretty drug out."

"We were just about to kill my horse for food when Reed came on us," said Charles.

"Go on to my wagons an' Mrs. Donner will give you somethin' to eat. We'll be along after we figure out what to do with this broken axle. We sure want to hear what y'all have to tell us."

James dismounted and squatted down to look at the broken axle. "Damn it!" he exclaimed.

"I figure that if you'd had a jointed pole this would not have happened, Reed," said William Eddy. James straightened up and stared at him. George put his hand to James's shoulder, but James angrily jerked away.

"James," said George, "Eddy here's a coach maker an' has offered to help make a new one. Others will help, too."

James appeared dazed. "What?"

"These men will help with the repair. Send your men to scout for a tree an' bring it back. After supper we'll start on it."

James staggered to the door of his wagon, looked inside, and then back to George.

"Where is my wife? My children?"

"They're all right," I said. "They're in our wagon."

"Mr. Reed, me and Walter'll go fetch the tree," said Milt.

James stood a few moments gazing off into the distance. Then he seemed to collect himself. He walked back to his horse and began to take his saddle off.

"Milt, take care of my horse. Put my saddle on the dun. We'll leave after I've seen to my wife."

"Yes, sir. I'll do it. Are you all right? You know, we got plenty of help. There's no need for you to go."

"Damn it, Milt, do what I told you!" James yelled at him. Milt stood for a moment with a shocked look on his face, then started off leading Glaucus. After a moment James headed down the line of wagons.

"Seems he's swallowed a prickly pear," said George. "Mr. Eddy, would you commence to get that broken axle off? Let's see if we can't prop the wagon up secure enough so Mrs. Reed an' the children can use it tonight."

"Yes, suh, I'll commence." said Eddy. "But it won't be for that son-of-a-bitch. It will be for his wife an' children."

As we sat around the campfire that evening, Mr. Stanton and Mr. McCutcheon told us a harrowing tale of getting lost and almost giving up hope of finding us.

"We might never have come on to you. No telling where we were nor where you might be," said Stanton, "but we do know that we can't get to the Salt Lake by the direction you're heading now."

"The hell you say! We saw the valley from atop that mountain we just came over. We figured this here stream would take us to it."

"No. We have to backtrack on this stream and then cross over another ridge."

Everyone was disheartened. More thickets, streams, and boulders. More hacking and chopping. We were exhausted, at the limits of our endurance. But the pause to repair the Reed wagon gave us a little rest and on we struggled. More clearing, filling, rolling of boulders. Six long days, another ridge topped and descended. Then we came out into a meadow leading into a canyon and beyond was a plain. Finally, we would be through the nightmare of the Wasatch. We camped for the night and our scouts went out to survey this last canyon. When they came back, the news was not good.

"The canyon's choked with growth, thick as what we done come through, mebbe worse. It's gonna take several days of clearing to get through it, I'm thinkin'."

It was too much. We simply could not do it, could not face more hard labor. So we decided to go over the ridge and began the pull up the sheer north face of the canyon wall. It was risky, a chance that the oxen would slip and go over, that we would start up and not be able to pull the rest of the way, but we double- and triple-teamed and managed to get over. At last we descended to the valley of the Salt Lake.

• • •

The delay caused by waiting for Reed to return, the strenuous work, and the worry that provisions were going to run out had taken a toll on the group. Each day the cursing and bad talk increased and now quarreling was a daily constant.

"No difficult canyons?" said Mrs. Graves. "Those were the worst damn defiles I ever seen. Those people at Bridger, they want this road made. They want the wagons to travel past their place so they let us come on an' open the road. The bastards!"

Mr. Graves chuckled. "Why be so timid 'bout speakin' your mind?"

Mrs. Graves glanced around at the other ladies, a little embarrassed. Later that evening James came to our fire.

"Howdy, James. Set yourself down. Coffee?" said George.

"Yes, thank you."

"James, how do you keep your boots so clean and polished?" asked George.

James looked down at his feet and made a dismissive gesture. "Oh, Baylis takes care of my boots."

He took the cup of coffee I offered to him. "George, I don't want to travel with these people. My wife and children are not accustomed to associating with their kind."

"What kind do you mean? They seem like most of the people we were neighbors with back home."

"That's true, but we had a choice of whether to associate with them or not. These people are uneducated and vulgar."

"Well then, that means you don't want to associate with me either. I've had very little schoolin'. Tamsen keeps tryin' to refine me, but she hasn't scraped off all the rough edges yet."

"George—"

"James, I know what you're sayin'. But your attitude ain't gonna get you cooperation an' cooperation is what we need to get this company through. I ain't aimin' to tell you what to do, but for the good of all of us, we need to be together. If we spread out we're likely to look weak to the savages. We need to stay together an' work together to watch our stock, an' everythin'."

James frowned and pulled on his mustache. "We've not had any trouble with the Indians in this area."

"No. But that don't mean we won't."

August 18, 1846
The Dry Drive

Aug. 18

We all suffer from exhaustion, our livestock suffer more, and our wagons are racked almost to pieces. Yesterday a wheel fell off our family wagon. George is worn out from the work and having to deal with cross and cantankerous people. This afternoon harsh words were spoken, leading to a fight between one of the Reed drivers and one of the men in Graves's party. George intervened and with help from other men separated the combatants.

We see Indians that are called "Diggers," a term applied to them because the tribes that live in this area subsist mostly on roots, which they dig out of the ground with sharpened sticks. They refer to themselves as Sho-sha-nee. We had been told that these people would be treacherous and cunning.

We'd left the Wasatch Mountains, but we had no time for celebration. We made camp where there was good water and grass and then we hurried on the next day. At last we came across the trail of Hastings's wagons and camped that evening on the side of the Salt Lake.

Here it was that Mr. Halloran passed from that life into this life. James Reed conducted full Masonic rites for Mr. Halloran, as it was discovered that he was a Mason, and we buried him next to the grave of someone from a forward company. Luke wanted us to have his possessions and when we opened his trunk, we discovered among some personal things a sum of money in coin.

The road led along the base of the mountains in a northerly direction, then bent around the point of the mountain leaving the lake off to our right. We passed into an area where there were many natural wells filled with cold pure water. Some of our group tested the depth of several of the wells and found some more than seventy feet deep.

The next day we made a long hard drive and camped in a beautiful meadow where there were more wells and abundant grass. Then the trail swept off to the westward along what must have been a beach from some long-vanished lake high above the present. After a long drive through sagebrush plain, we came to a good meadow with excellent water. It was here we found shreds of a note that had been mounted on a board, but was torn apart, probably by birds. The scraps were gathered and I sat down with the board on my lap and pieced it together. The message was not completely clear, but what we could ascertain was that it had been written by Mr. Hastings and he was telling us that we had a desert crossing ahead of two days and two night's duration—without water.

Aug. 30

How much more can we stand? Our oxen are in terrible condition. How can we get them through without water? Somehow we must. We have no other choice. We have filled all our kegs with water and cut a supply of grass in preparation for the drive. We hope it will be enough. Food has been cooked to take care of meals for the next two days. Surely it will be easier going after this desert ordeal.

Before us lay a broad salt plain where grew only thorny, stunted bushes. Our direction was toward a mountain directly across and after a time we began to ascend a hill, nooning by the side of a spring high up on the mountain. After a rest, we journeyed on, descending onto the foothills of this mountain in a northerly direction, coming to a place where the road began to climb over very steep hills. We stopped and sent our riders out to assess the road. They returned to tell us we must double-team to get over. After much effort we crossed the mountain and camped on a ridge on the western side.

Early in the morning we began our crossing of the salt dunes, our wagon wheels sinking sometimes into soft sand and mud, other times rolling over a hard crust of salt that the hooves of the oxen broke through, the crust cutting and bruising their tender feet. Everyone who could walk did so to lighten the load on our oxen. The wagons were strung out over the desert with ours in the rear of the caravan. We were having a little more trouble than those whose wagons were lighter.

The desert was a blinding glare, like snowfields in the bright sun. A suffocating white dust hung in a cloud above the wagons, caking the nostrils of animals and men, blistering our skin, burning our eyes. The livestock snorted and sneezed continuously, trying to get the dust out of their nostrils. We saw strange mirages. At one time we thought we saw people coming, that

Hastings was coming back to help us; but, no, it was our own images reflecting back at us. We saw lakes, beautiful cool blue lakes shimmering in the distance. Then the lakes would disappear and in their place would be more glaring hot salt flats.

On the morning of the third day, several of the group reached a spring at the base of a mountain known later as Pilot Peak. We were still well behind and the Reed wagons were yet behind us. Then disaster struck the Reed family. James Reed had ridden forward in search of water and was returning to his wagons with buckets to help his oxen when he met up with his teamsters driving his unyoked oxen ahead. James told them where the water was, instructing them to continue on and when the oxen were watered and rested to come back and bring the wagons forward. He continued on and met his family walking toward him. All the next day they waited in the desert heat expecting their teamsters to return, but there was no sight of them. They used the last of their water. That night they huddled together with their dogs, shivering in the cold, and the next day they began to walk. The children cried for water. Mrs. Reed gave them each a piece of lump sugar to suck on, hoping to bring a little moisture to their parched tongues. Finally late that night they caught up with Jacob's family, already asleep. They lay down on the ground to await the dawn, again huddling together with their dogs, shivering in the piercing cold.

In the morning Betsey fed them a breakfast of bread and gravy, and when Jacob returned with his refreshed animals he took his family and the Reed family to water. Here they discovered that the Reed oxen had gotten away from the teamsters and stampeded off into the desert. The company had lost thirty-six oxen on the journey over the desert, and almost half were James Reed's.

We remained there at the spring for almost a week, searching for the missing livestock, but none were found. We began lightening our loads to spare the remaining oxen. Non-essential items were placed in wagon beds and buried. James cached most of his supplies and goods using two of his wagon beds. With his one cow and one ox and the loan of two more, he was able to proceed with his remaining wagon. The Reed family, formerly the wealthiest family in wagons, animals, and goods, was now almost the poorest in these things. The ordeal in the desert, the strain of losing all his livestock and having to leave two of his three wagons with most of his possessions behind, was beginning to tell on James Reed. Always imperious, now he was constantly irritable and short-tempered.

Sept. 4

Our little spaniel died in the night and we buried him on a grassy knoll close by the spring. The girls are grieving, Eliza has cried for hours.

The drive wasn't forty miles, but seventy-five or more. Our animals are in poor shape and one of our wagons was racked to pieces and we had to abandon it. Some in the company are worried they will not have enough provisions to see them through to California, but I feel we have enough and Jacob also.

It has been decided that men will be sent ahead to Mr. Sutter in California to obtain supplies and return to meet the company somewhere on the road. Charles Stanton and William McCutcheon volunteered to undertake the journey and left today.

We toiled on to the tortured shriek of the wheels accompanied by the curses and shouts of the drivers urging the teams forward. Several times we stopped and the men hammered wedges into the wheels to tighten them. After a day or two the country began to improve and we found water and grass on the eastern slopes of the valleys. We crossed still another pass and descended into a fine valley beyond. Two more days westward and then in the distance from our night's camp we saw a high range of mountains running north to south directly in our westward path. We could see no pass, no gap in this range.

We stood gazing into the desert, the range of mountains floating in the hazy distance.

"I expected," said James, "from what I learned from Hastings and others is that we would have come to a westward river, a shallow and muddy river by the accounts. But it looks like we'll have to cross another range of mountains before we find it. Some call it Mary's River, some Ogden's, but there's only one. We follow along that river for a good distance and then it drops into a sink. Then there's a desert to cross."

"Oh God, I thought we were out of the blamed deserts," cried Mrs. Murphy. She stabbed her finger at James. "It's your fault, Reed. You talked us into takin' that *Hastings' long trip!*" Her voice was a snarl. "Now you don't even know where the damned river is." She began sobbing.

James wheeled around to face her. "Madam, you, and everyone with you, made the decision for the route. I merely supplied information."

"You insisted on that route. You said the road would be made. You're a liar."

James turned his back to her. I could see the blood moving up his neck and his face flushing a deep red. Margaret began to walk away, but she saw the anger building in her husband and turned back to Mrs. Murphy. "How dare you call my husband a liar, you Mormon tramp!"

Mrs. Murphy raised her hand as if she intended to hit Margaret. "You snob! You think you're so high-falutin'—"

I stepped between them, pushing them apart.

"Please, Lavina, go back to your wagon," I begged. "It's hot and we're all tired. Please, go on. All of us are sorry we followed Hastings."

Mrs. Murphy's son-in-law, Mr. Foster, ran over from where he had been working on their wagon and pulled her away, still sobbing and shrieking. "Tramp! She called me a tramp."

I turned my attention from Mrs. Murphy when I heard Margaret begin to whimper and I felt her start to sway. James caught her as she was falling and we helped her back to their wagon and onto her bed.

"James, I have some medicines. I'll go get them. Wring a cloth out in cool water and bathe her face and chest."

When I returned, both Virginia and James were leaning over Margaret.

Virginia's voice was querulous. "Mother has a headache starting and now she'll be bedridden for days. My father told Mr. Donner he should not allow these people with us. This is all his fault."

I looked at Virginia for a moment, wanting to admonish her. No, I wanted to slap her, if truth be told. But I restrained myself. "Virginia, could you step away and let me in there, please? I want to give her some medicine."

Margaret was moaning and mumbling. "I never knew a woman could be so debased. How could she talk to me like that?"

"I think you gave as good as you got, Margaret," I said. "Can you sit up a little so you can take this?"

"No! No more of your goddamn tea!" cried Margaret. She grabbed James's arm, her face crumpling, tears squeezing out of her tightly closed eyes.

"James, tell her to give me some laudanum. Please, James."

"This *is* laudanum," I said.

Margaret's eyes flew open. She raised up on one elbow and with a shaky hand took the bottle, downing the liquid. Then she fell back on her pillows. "God, when is this nightmare going to end?" she moaned.

We waited a few minutes, not speaking, until Margaret's breathing became more even.

"Hopefully she won't develop a headache, but if she does and wants to take the teas that I have made for her headaches, I will bring them."

"The laudanum seems to help her more," said James.

"I felt it best to get her calmed down, but I won't give it to her again," I said. I took Margaret's hand. "Margaret, I sympathize with your feelings, but you have endured less hardship than any of us. It's time you stop wanting to be molly-coddled and kept in a cocoon of comfort. James needs all of his energy to help get this company to California. It's time you stopped this nonsense."

"You don't know how I suffer. You have no—"

Her voice trailed off and she fell into sleep. James made a supplicating gesture. "She can't help ..."

"I think she could if she wanted to." I stepped around James and left the wagon.

• • •

The next day we found the trail taking a turn to the south. The wagons all stopped and the men convened on a rise of ground.

"This just don't make no sense," said George.

James Reed pointed west. "There's nothing that looks like a pass. We could scout it out ..."

"No, Hastings would have already done that," said George. "I wonder how far ahead they are."

"Well," said James, "they were at the Salt Lake when I caught up with them. It took me three days to get back."

"And it was eighteen days getting through those sons-a-bitchin' canyons," said William Eddy disgustedly. "They're three weeks ahead at least. That bastard Hastings. When I get to California I'm goin' to find him an' beat the b'jesus out of him. I'll expose the lyin' son-of-a-bitch for what he is."

"Eddy, you're just whistling Dixie. Fellows like that there Hastings always get away with their doin's. It's the honest man that always seems to catch hell."

To get around this range of mountains, we were forced to take a long detour. We trailed south for three days until at last the road took a turn to the west and we ascended and then descended a gap in the mountains and camped for the night. We huddled around the fire, cold, tired, and unhappy.

"George," said William Foster, "I followed the road up a piece after we made camp and all I can see is a trail heading north. It follows this little river here, straight north. I hope it cuts to the west soon."

"Aw, it has to."

But it didn't. Not for three more days of traveling due north. We were only a mountain range away from where we had camped six days before to the east. The trail led off to the northwest into a canyon and there we camped for the night. The scouts came back to tell us that after this canyon we would be heading west again. This report relieved our gloom somewhat.

After two days more of travel, we found Mary's River. It was a pitiful excuse for a river—shallow, with warm unpleasant tasting water. But it was lined with willows and there was good grass in its meadows. We were done with wandering in the wilderness. But how far was it to California? And when would Stanton and McCutcheon make their way back with supplies? Each day as we followed the river we stretched our gaze west. Surely, any day now they'd be coming back.

• • •

There were Indians in the area. Sometimes one or two would come into camp. Most hung back, not sure how they would be treated. These Indians were much poorer looking than the Indians of the plains.

"George, did Baptiste find out anythin' from those savages?" asked Jacob.

"He doesn't know their language, but his hand talk seemed to work. They say it's two hundred miles yet to where this river goes into a sink."

"Two or three weeks to the sink. Then how much farther, do you reckon, to the mountains of California?"

"Must be four hundred miles yet, thirty more days of travel. It's the last of September, I think we're still all right. I'd be more comfortable if we had more provisions, but Stanton an' McCutcheon should be gettin' back soon."

It was at Mary's River that the Indians began to be a problem, wounding and running off livestock. Before we became wary of the Indians in the area, we allowed them to visit our camp. On one such visit came two men, one who could say a few words of English, such as "whoa" and "haw," that he'd picked up from some traveler. The Indians helped extinguish a grass fire that started from a campfire and threatened to destroy some wagons. This was much appreciated by the company, so they were treated especially well. After a good meal the Indians laid down by the fire for the night. When dawn came they were gone, along with a good shirt and two oxen belonging to Franklin Graves.

On another night Indians snuck around our camp and shot arrows into several of our oxen, wounding some enough that they had to be left behind. Our animals were in better shape than most of the others and as we moved on, our family group drew ahead of the others. Then, behind us on the trail, more trouble.

◆ ◆ ◆

We were a day or two ahead of the others when James Reed killed John Snyder. The group behind us had come to a place where there was a difficult sandy hill to ascend and at this place an altercation broke out between James Reed and John Snyder, who was driving one of the Graves's wagons. I tell the story as we heard it from James Reed, later from his family, and from the members of the company who were there.

Some of the wagons were being double-teamed to make the top of the hill. It was hot and arduous, and tempers were short. It seems that the Reed wagon, driven by Milt Elliot, was trying to pass the Graves wagon on the hill and became entangled with it. John Snyder was driving the Graves wagon and became very angry as Milt tried to pass with the Reed wagon. Snyder thrashed at his oxen, trying to get them to move faster. Reed then came up and admonished him not to beat his oxen or some such remark. The men got into it and the argument became more heated. At some point, John Snyder began hitting James Reed on the head and shoulders with his whip handle. Margaret became frantic and entered the fray. James, fearing for his wife's safety, drew his knife and plunged it into Snyder. The wound was mortal and the man died in a short time. James immediately regretted what had happened and threw his knife down in disgust and frustration. Then he tried to assist the dying man.

The company conducted a funeral for Snyder, after which angry sentiments flew about the camp. James told us that he and Margaret decided the best course of action would be for him to leave, go on ahead, and bring supplies back to the group. He hoped that by doing this he would ameliorate the tense situation. His version of the event was that he left on his own accord on a mission of mercy and not that he had been banished from the group. When James reached our camp, we saw that he had some nasty looking cuts on his scalp, which I cleaned and treated.

"The man hit me several times with his whip handle. Virginia did her best to help me," said James. "Margaret was so distraught she could not get up from her bed. Virginia and Milt will look out for her the best they can, but I am very concerned for my wife's welfare. I hate to leave her with those people. She's not strong like you are, Tamsen, even though you seem to think she is. The others promised me they would look after my family, but I have no confidence that they will do so with much charity."

"Young Snyder didn't seem to me like the sort to attack a man over a trifle like tangled wagons," George said when we were alone. "I can't believe James would pull a knife in an argument that could easily have been avoided. You don't know a man and he does not know himself, I reckon, until his true character is brought out."

"George, I told you there was something inside James that was held under tension."

"Did you see somethin' in Snyder too?"

"No, but I hardly knew him."

"Well, we don't know what really happened."

We heard more of this story when the group again came together. The Graves family was still very angry.

"It warn't no self defense like he tol' you," said Franklin Graves. "Reed knifed him up the Green River an' Snyder was a goner. It was murder pure and simple. If'n it was up to us we'd have hung him right there. Banishment is too good fer him."

Virginia Reed was adamant that her father had done nothing wrong and was furious at what the company had done.

"My father was sent out into an unknown country without provisions or arms and even his horse was at first denied him. When we learned of this decision, Milt and I took him his rifle, pistols, ammunition, and some food."

Oct. 7

My hand shakes so as I write this I fear it will not be legible. I cannot believe it is true, but there is no doubt. John Snyder is dead by the hand of James Reed. A moment of rage & a young life snuffed out. James goes ahead to California, Walter Herron with him. I gave them what few provisions we could spare & George sent along a letter to Mr. Sutter requesting supplies, promising to pay all expenses when we should arrive in California.

We struggled on, strung out along the route in separate knots of wagons, with no cohesion, no unity. Fear was on us, and panic. The disasters grew worse. Indians ran off Mr. Graves's horses. The next night they ran off eighteen oxen and a cow and the following night they shot arrows into a number of oxen and they had to be left behind. It was a measure of the degradation of the group that our men were too exhausted, too numb, to institute measures to protect our stock as had been the practice on the plains. It was a mistake to separate. If we had stayed together, it would have been easier to protect against the Indians.

We slowly made our way along the river, losing more cattle

from exhaustion and bad water. We reached the place where the river disappeared entirely into a sink and now we knew we faced another dry desert. Here the groups briefly came together. We crossed over a low ridge of sand hills, our oxen wading through the heaps of dry and ashy earth, sinking in many places nearly to their bellies. The plain was almost utterly devoid of vegetation, only an occasional strip of sage and a few clumps of brown grass. In the far distance a dim line of mountains could be seen fifteen or twenty miles in front of us. We made a dry camp, our animals exhausted from the work and the lack of food and water. George lifted my box of books out of the wagon.

"I'm sorry, honey, but we've got to lighten the load. This is the heaviest box left in there. I'm taking off some of the tools, my anvil and other things. That rocking chair of yours is heavy too—"

"No, George, I'll give up my books, but I will not part with that chair."

"Godamighty! It's only a chair, and an old one at that!"

We plodded on, crossing the ridge we had seen the day before. We stopped on the crest and surveyed the valley in front of us. There was no green to signal a source of water, nothing but dry, shimmering hot desert. Now our family group and the Murphy family group were in the lead, the rest falling behind.

In the group behind us, Mr. Hardcoop failed and could no longer stay on his feet. Mr. Keseberg, with whom Hardcoop had been traveling, put him out of his wagon to save his animals. Mr. Hardcoop then petitioned Mr. Eddy to allow him to ride in his wagon, but Eddy put him off also, saying that perhaps later, after getting through the deep sand, he could allow him to ride. All of us were walking to save the strength of our animals.

That day Mr. Hardcoop fell behind and didn't come up to the evening camp. Some wanted to go back to find him and bring him up, but the use of a horse was not offered. We were not with this part of the company when this occurred, so we were not put to the test. I cannot say what we might have done had we been there when Mr. Hardcoop was left on the trail.

Oct. 14

We are camped near a place of very sinister aspect—hundreds of holes that erupt with steam & boiling water. I believe this must be the place that Mr. Clyman told us about, where he lost his dog when the poor creature jumped into one of the boiling springs. When we arrived near this place, George took the dog to one of the springs & held him near it so that he was warned of the danger. We keep our stock gathered together. I remember George saying there was enough Hell on earth. This is certainly one of those places.

The company moved on, with disaster striking almost daily. The Indians killed or wounded more oxen, most of them Mr. Eddy's and Mr. Wolfinger's teams, and they had to abandon their wagons and gear. Mr. Eddy and his wife now were forced to walk and carry their two little children. They set out with nothing to eat, but a little lump sugar. All they had now were the clothes on their backs and no way to carry water. Mr. Eddy, desperate to provide water for his children, begged Mr. Breen for water and was at first refused. Mr. Eddy told it later that he took the water at gunpoint, but few of us believed that actually happened. Mr. Wolfinger stopped to make a cache and Mr. Spitzer and Mr. Reinhardt offered to stay behind to help him. Mrs. Wolfinger continued on, walking with some of the women.

As we rounded the point of a mountain we saw in the distance, glimmering behind a line of tall trees, at last, the Truckee River. Clear, flowing, pure water. The animals, crazed with thirst, set off toward the river at a pace we didn't know they could achieve in their weakened condition. The wagons bumped and lurched behind them as they went pell-mell down the riverbank to get to the water.

We camped at the river and the group behind came up. Later in the evening Reinhardt and Spitzer came in and told us that

Mr. Wolfinger had been killed by Indians. Three men went back to look for him, found the wagon and oxen, and brought it in. We joined the group that gathered around Mrs. Wolfinger.

"We found the oxen grazing along the river unyoked an' the wagon sitting there," reported William Graves, "but nary a sign of Mr. Wolfinger an' no sign of Injuns, Mr. Donner."

Mrs. Wolfinger was very agitated. *"Das Geld! Es ist nicht her. Haben Sil seinen Geld Beutel grefunden?"*

I turned to Mr. Reinhardt. "What is she saying?"

"I tell her that her husband wass kill by Indians and nossing can be done. She grieves that he won't haf a proper burial."

"We'll take her along with us," said George, "Tell her we can't go back to find his body, that we're very sorry for her loss."

The men brought her wagon to our camp. I tried to console her, but she remained very distraught, trying to tell us something that we could not understand.

George shook his head and made a gesture of helplessness. "*Nicht geld*—I think she's saying their money is gone."

The affair of Mr. Wolfinger bothered me and I could not let it go. I went to find Mrs. Keseberg.

"Please, would you come help us talk to Mrs. Wolfinger?"

"I feel sorry for her, Mrs. Donner, but I cannot help."

"Please, tell me why."

"Those men, Reinhardt and Spitzer, they tell my husband they are being blamed unfairly."

"I know of no one who is blaming them, but their actions are very suspicious. It doesn't appear likely that Mr. Wolfinger was killed by Indians."

Mrs. Keseberg made a supplicating gesture and her voice was pleading. "Mrs. Donner, I know nothing of what happened. Why don't you speak with my husband?"

I found him with his stock by the river.

"Mr. Keseberg, would you tell me what you know of this disappearance of Mr. Wolfinger?"

"I will have nothing to do with this matter. Some of them are accusing *me* of causing the man's disappearance."

"Mr. Keseberg, I cannot understand how you could refuse to help this poor woman."

"What you think I can do? Her husband was not found. Her money is missing. I had nothing to do with it."

"Those men—"

"*Ja*! Have you proof? No. You think what you will. And stay away from my wife. We don't want you meddling in our affairs. It was your doings that Reed threatened to force me from the company."

"You shouldn't be beating your wife. You deserved to be threatened. You didn't mind me meddling in your affairs when your wife was in childbirth and might have died without my help."

"I am grateful for your help, Mrs. Donner, but I will not be involved."

I saw George approaching. I knew from the look on his face that he was going to be unhappy with me, so I left Mr. Keseberg and walked toward him.

"Tamsen, sometimes you just have to let sleeping dogs lie."

"Sometimes the sleeping dog will awaken and bite the first person in his path, George. I tried to get Mrs. Keseberg to interpret, but she refused and he refused also. He told me I was meddlesome and to stay away from his wife. After all I did to help them. It makes me so angry."

"When we get to California we'll bring it up to the authorities there. What more can we do now?"

"We could have a tribunal of some kind."

"I don't see how. Our group is scattered out an' we're all fightin' just to get through. I don't think we could get the men together to discuss it. An' those German boys are stickin' together tight. They might not take it kindly were we to accuse them. We have only suspicions, no proof. We'll help Mrs. Wolfinger as best we can, but I don't see that anythin' can be done now. I'd like to get shut of all the problems these people have. It's hard enough to look after our own."

October 16, 1846
The Truckee River

We resumed our journey. Now we were into October with still a long way to go. We weren't concerned, as we had been told that usually the snows didn't close the passes until mid-December or later. We traveled up the valley of the river, which became narrow and walled in on both sides by high ranges of barren mountains. In the next two days we wound our way through the river canyon, crossing as the river lapped against one steep side and then the other. In places there was no level ground and we were forced to the hillsides, preferring that to braving the water which was fast, cold, and deep.

The nights were cold, but as the sun rose in the sky and lay on the land in a golden glow, we enjoyed the warmth. But as it finished its arc and fell in flames among the hills, a chill would fall again upon us. We saw numerous tracks of animals and also tracks of Indians. We caught glimpses to the west of high mountain peaks covered with snow. So early!

The Breen and Murphy wagons took the lead as we followed the river and we lost sight of them. After crossing the river for about the twentieth time, we observed that the trail left the river, winding up a canyon to the south. We stopped to rest and have our noon meal while the men talked over the trail's departure from the river.

"We should be gettin' close to that big valley we was told of, but why is the road leavin' the river? Don't make sense." George thought for a while and then turned to Noah.

"Noah, go on up the river an' explore a little. I'm gonna ride up this canyon to see what it looks like."

Noah returned first. "I seen why the trail had taken off up that canyon yonder. Up ahead the river narrows down an' goes between some cliff-like places an' there's big rocks. Where it does open up it's right soft an' marshy, full of water. That big valley's not too far past that. I don't think we can get our wagons through there. I hope that canyon's going to be easy like. George ain't back yet?"

"I see him coming yonder now."

George dismounted and William took his horse. We gathered around.

"Well, it's a steady uphill climb for three, four miles, a sight of gullies, but there's a road. The worst part is that after you get up to the top, there's a sharp decline. Does it look like we can follow the river, Noah?"

"It don't look likely, Mr. Donner. I think we'll have to take this here canyon."

We walked to save the oxen. The wagons creaked and groaned and the oxen murmured as they were goaded on. The wind came up, slicing us with its cold sharp edges. Jacob's wagons, which were in the lead, stopped part way up. George and I walked up to see what had caused them to stop.

"Just taking a rest, George," said Jacob. He was sitting on a large rock beside the trail. I looked at him and realized that he was sick. His skin was ashen.

"I just cain't get my breath. All'a sudden I just got weak an' I liked to pass out. My palpitator is banging against my ribs, seems like."

"Let's take a rest," said George. "I'm tuckered out myself."

After our meal we continued on. As we attained the top of the ridge, we looked down a very steep grade into a narrow canyon.

"It's past perpendicular, George," said Jacob.

"I reckon we're gonna have to lower 'em down with ropes or take a chance of breaking our wagons up. Look off yonder, you can see the valley."

"And yonder still, that must be the California Mountains. We're almost there."

"It's a mighty imposin' sight. Still, it's a hundred miles or more to the valley of the Sacramento. But once we get across the mountains, the travelin' won't be anythin' to worry over."

With ropes around a big tree, the wagons were eased down the steep slope, the men straining and cursing, but having real trouble only when the wheels would hit a ridge of stone or sink into a declivity and the wagons would threaten to tip over. At the bottom the teams were yoked up and we started again. We were in a narrow canyon, in one place so tight between high rocks that our wagon hubs scraped on each side.

It was late afternoon when we emerged from the canyon. We moved down a wide gentle slope, directed northward by a low line of brown hills on our left that ended with a flat pyramid-shaped hill. Directly ahead across the valley a range of high mountains dipped and bowed majestically in a march to the north. The sun perched at a dip between two peaks in a beautiful display of orange layered with lines of silver and blue clouds. The whole scene was washed with orange and pink as if brushed with a master stroke of a watercolor artist. The bowl of the valley was ringed all around with brown hills and as the sun sank behind the mountain, color flamed across the tops of the hills like molten gold, plunging the lower reaches into deep purple and gray shadows. Even as tired as I was, the scene captivated me. *I should like to paint this scene,* I thought. *What beautiful colors.*

"Look off there to the north, George, way to the other side. See those white tops? It's the rest of the company."

"Let's make camp," said George. "It'll be a day to get across the valley. We've got to go around those marshes."

Dawn came blustery and cold. We moved across the valley, fording several deep creeks flowing down from the granite peaks, our wheels crunching the thin ice that coated the shallow ponds. The wind whipped against us, flapping and snapping the wagon covers. The valley floor was sagebrush plain, endowed in places with luxuriant grass. It was devoid of timber except for clumps of willows fringing the streams and sloughs. As we moved to the north side of the valley, we saw herds of deer and antelope. In mid-afternoon we came up to the rest of the company camped in a grove of large trees. Milt Elliot, the Reed family's teamster, came to us soon after we situated our wagons and put the oxen to graze.

"Looks like you haven't lost any more stock. Have you had any more trouble with the savages?"

"No, but they're out there watchin' for a chance," said George.

Milt took off his hat and twisted it in his hands.

"Things aren't good between Miz Reed an' the others an' they don't have any food to speak of. Could I bring her an' the children to stay in your camp?"

"Of course, Milt. We'll help you all we can," I said.

"What came of her supplies?" asked George.

"They divided their provisions between several others back in the desert an' I think most of it's been used up."

"Well, Reed should be comin' back soon an' the other men too. I hope they didn't get into trouble."

The Indians continued to harass us, picking off our animals at night, shooting arrows into them so they couldn't go on. Then we were struck by more tragedy. Mrs. Murphy's son-in-law, William Pike, was killed by an accidental discharge of a gun in the hands of his brother-in-law, William Foster. One of the children came to report the terrible news and we rushed to the Murphy camp. The details were given us by John Denton who'd been in the camp at the time of the accident.

"The blokes were talking of going ahead to get supplies and sitting around making plans. They noticed the fire was getting low and one chap handed the gun to the other as he got up to get a piece of wood. It went off."

"Them pepperbox guns is risky," said Jacob.

Oct. 24

We buried Mr. Pike yesterday evening. As I stood by the gravesite I couldn't help thinking of how our company now cared for our dead. Early in the journey Mrs. Keyes was laid to rest in a wood coffin with full funeral rites & a carved memorial. Luke Halloran was given full Masonic rites & a coffin. Now young Mr. Pike, only an hour or two earlier full of life and vigor, is laid to rest in a shallow grave with only a blanket wrapped around him. No doubt in a few days an Indian will be parading the blanket in front of his miserable brush hut. It is a measure of the desperate condition of our company.

Our oxen slowly recover & ourselves also. Our wagons are in deplorable condition. The men have been making repairs as best they can. George thinks perhaps it will take two weeks to the settlements. This wearisome journey is almost over.

As I put my journal away, I had a feeling of contentment. Not much longer and our journey would be over. A new and exciting life was just over this last range of mountains. That night I was restless and with sleep came a terrible dream. There were crows, hundreds of crows. They were flying, over land, over mountains, over the land and mountains that we had crossed. I could see from afar that they followed us. I saw them come down, down, circling, circling a meadow where there were people. Children, women, men. Everything was white. The people were like skeletons. I saw this as from a high distance, a distance that I could not cross. I awoke with a start, my heart pounding with shock and fear. It had been our people, our company. My family, my children. They were begging for food! They had seen me and stretched their hands to me, but I could not help them! *Oh, God, what does this mean?*

The following day Indians crept up at dawn and shot more arrows into our cattle. William Eddy put a ball into one of the Indians and, flinging up his arms with a loud shriek he tumbled down a slope into some thick bushes. We were sure the Indian had been killed. Mr. Eddy waved his rifle in the air and shouted at the Indians who had run to a safe distance.

"I hope you burn in hell, goddamn you!" Eddy yelled after them. We all shared the same sentiment. They were taking what we needed to survive. These Indians were of the tribe called Paiute. They were much more troublesome than any we had previously encountered. We were weak and they knew it. As we traveled we would see them standing off, making derisive sounds and gestures at us, as though to say, "You fools, you'll not leave here until we get it all."

We had lost dozens of oxen since coming into the deserts, most from Indian depredations. Fortunately, on this occasion, none of the arrows maimed the animals badly enough that they couldn't continue.

• • •

The Breen family group left the next morning to begin the ascent of the mountains. We were anxious to continue, but George felt that our oxen must have rest.

"We've got a mighty big mountain to cross with a lot of steep rock face. Our oxen're bad off an' they've got to recruit. The deep snows don't usually happen here until way into December, at least that was what we've been told. Hastings, he came through here last December."

The following morning the Murphy family group moved off

and we were alone. In our group now were twenty-five people, about half children. The German men had stayed with us, as they had their gear in Mrs. Wolfinger's wagon. We now had two of our original three wagons. Jacob also had two and Mrs. Wolfinger had one.

That evening we gathered around the campfire for our evening meal, hunched in blankets around the fire. The leaves in the cottonwood and aspen trees rustled and shook in the wind that rose and fell like swells on a body of water. The canvas on the wagons and tents snapped and whumped in the wind, straining against the poles and tethers. A horse knickered and one of the men picked up his rifle and peered around a wagon into the dusk.

"Oh God," wailed Betsey, "not those damned Injuns."

"Hush! Listen."

Off in the distance we heard a faint clattering sound, a sound of hooves moving over rocks, and then a voice broke the stillness.

"Halloo, the camp."

"It's men a'comin', an' horses."

We all rushed over to the opening between the wagons and watched as shapes appeared out of the dusk. It was Mr. Stanton and with him two of Mr. Sutter's Indians mounted on mules and leading four that were heavily laden. Steam rose off the backs of the mules and they snorted and blew as they slumped wearily under their packs. The men dismounted and everyone gathered around, excited and happy, because now there would be food to get the company to California.

Margaret Reed and her children at first thought it must be Mr. Reed returning. They eagerly made their way to the front of the group that gathered around the visitors and were very disappointed to find it wasn't Mr. Reed.

"Mr. Stanton," asked Margaret, "have you any word of my husband? He was going to Sutter's to obtain supplies."

"Yes, ma'am. We met him four days back. He and Herron were in a poorly state, but they're all right."

"Oh, thank God! Children, did you hear? Papa's all right. He got through."

Margaret began to cry and the children jumped up and down, talking and laughing.

"They got fresh horses and went on to Sutter's for supplies," said Mr. Stanton. "They should be coming on, but it'll take them some time to get situated."

"We're sure glad to see you, Stanton. Why didn't Mr. McCutcheon come back with you?" asked George.

"He took sick. I didn't want to wait for him to recover and delay getting back."

He turned to George. "I met three groups of the others ahead of you. Is there anyone behind you?"

"Not alive," murmured one of the men. Mr. Stanton looked at him sharply. "I heard of the troubles," he said.

"No, Stanton, we're the last," said George.

The packs were removed and the mules were led away. George turned to some of the men. "Who's up to stand watch? It's time we let them boys on guard come in an' get supper."

"Mr. Stanton," I said, "we've got coffee here. Please help yourself. I'll fix some food for you and your men."

Stanton signaled his companions to take the coffee and the Indians squatted down in the shadows. Mr. Stanton sat down by the fire.

"Say, George, what's the story about Reed? Graves told me Reed killed Snyder in an argument and the company banished him."

"He told us it was a matter of defendin' himself. We don't know the whole story. But James did have some ugly head wounds from Snyder's whip handle. It's a troublin' thing. But you remember how it was 'fore you left? We were all kind'a crazed after fightin' our way through those terrible canyons an' crossin' the salt flats. If Reed can come back with supplies an' animals, it might help cool down some of the company who are still pretty sore."

George told Mr. Stanton about Mr. Hardcoop and Mr. Wolfinger and the accidental death of Mr. Pike.

"Well, it's over now. In a few days all will be behind us. What do you plan to do in California, George?"

"I'm gonna scout around, find some good horse land. I hope to get a good-sized piece. I hear they measure their holdin's in miles 'stead of acres. What'd the country look like there where you were?"

"It's good-looking country. There's timbered slopes up to these here high mountains, thick timber. Down further are gentle hills, looks like good livestock country. I was told it's not much good for farming, because rain is almost unknown in the summer."

"That so?" said Jacob. "We heard there're orchards, vineyards, an' crops growing almost wild."

"Yes, they say that close to a river or stream you can grow most anything with irrigation," replied Stanton. "I was told that over west of the valley of the Sacramento there's a range of mountains and on the other side there's beautiful land. That's where they have a lot of orchards and vineyards, but they're all irrigated. There was missions built there years ago and they tamed a lot of the Indians, made them kind of slaves. Then the mission people pulled out or were called back to Spain or somewhere. That's where the Pueblo of San Jose is located. Then there's Yerba Buena, big bay there, connects to the Pacific, I heard. I didn't get farther than Sutter's."

"*Yerba Buena,* it mean "good plant, good herb," said Juan Baptiste.

"These Indians are Sutter's *vaqueros,* work with the cattle," said Stanton. "The *vaqueros* have amazing ability with the rope."

Baptiste went over to the Indians. "*Hablan Español*?" he asked them. They nodded their heads and Baptiste sat down with them.

"Mr. Sutter's a true gentlemen," continued Mr. Stanton. "He lives like a king in a fiefdom, very civilized. I've heard his holdings are impressive, but the fort's not much to look at. The buildings are made of mud.

"Reed talked favorably of the Pueblo of San Jose," said George.

"I think Margaret's brother Caden wrote him of it. What's goin' on with the Mexican government?"

"Mr. Sutter had his fort taken over by federal forces. It looks like the country's going to be United States territory. It'll be a good country for business. The Mexicans have no mind for business, but with all the Americans that'll be coming in there'll be money to be made."

"Stanton, what kind of Injuns be those boys with you?" asked Jacob.

"These men are Miwoks. The bigger one's Luis, the other is called Salvador. Sutter's tamed them and they seem to be stalwart and loyal. I couldn't have come back without these men to guide me and work the mules. Mr. Sutter is a most kind and generous man."

George shifted around on the stump he was using for a seat, trying to get comfortable. "Charles, tell us a little about the country we're facin'. What's that pass like?"

"Actually, there's two passes, one at the end of a good-sized lake. The trail goes around the north side of that lake. There's another road opened by some of the last parties that went over. I suspect that with so many wagons trying to get over at one time, they had kind of a jam-up. The north pass has real steep rock face and the wagons have to be lifted in a couple of places. That takes time. The south way of going is higher, but has a lesser slope."

"Which do you recommend?"

"I think perhaps the south, since you don't have a lot of men to do that heavy work."

"Yeah, an' we're all about half a man. We're pretty much tuckered out."

"Now, it's going to take you three days, most likely, to get to that lake, an' two days to get to the top. Then you've got a hundred miles—"

"A hundred miles! Stanton, are you joshing with us?" exclaimed Jacob.

"No, sir. I wouldn't do that. There's all kinds of ridges and canyons before you find the foothills and ease of travel."

"I'm thinkin' that our animals ain't goin' to make it unless we let 'em recruit. They're in bad shape," said George.

Mr. Stanton nodded his head. "It's prudent to rest your animals here. Mr. Sutter assured me there's very little likelihood that the pass would close this early."

In the morning Mr. Stanton prepared to leave.

"Donner, we can travel much faster with the mules than you can with your wagons. We're goin' on to catch up with the others. We'll take Mrs. Reed and the children."

George shook Mr. Stanton's hand. "I can't thank you enough for everythin' you've done, Stanton. Once our animals are strong enough, we'll move on. We'll see you in California."

George and I went to help Mrs. Reed bundle up the things she would be taking with her.

"We still have goods in the Graves's wagon," Margaret informed us. "They've promised to take them on to Sutter's Fort. My husband will be meeting us on the trail with supplies and he'll be bringing horses for us. Goodbye, Tamsen, I hope that you will visit us in our new home."

I hugged Margaret. "Of course we will."

Mrs. Reed and Tommy were placed on one mule, Patty and James each behind one of the Indians and Virginia with Mr. Stanton.

We watched them make their way to the river and turn west. A moist wind whipped us and we looked up. Dark clouds hid the high spine of the mountain range and misty veils were flowing down the clefts into the canyons. I gathered my shawl tightly around my shoulders. A deep, deep sense of foreboding depressed my spirit.

"George, let's leave now. Look at the mountain, it's snowing up there."

"There's no point in moving out and then having our oxen give out before we even get to the pass," said George. "We've just got to give 'em time to recruit. While we're waiting some of us could get out and hunt while we're here. Fresh meat would be mighty fine."

Oct. 30

It makes me nervous to think we are the last people on this trail. I feel compelled to find and gather as much wild food as I can. Yesterday we dug cattail roots and spent most of the day cleaning and trimming our harvest. Today the girls and I (accompanied by Juan Baptiste and John Denton with their rifles) walked up a hill near camp where junipers are growing and gathered a basket of the berries and bark. On the way we discovered a patch of raspberries and we picked enough to make one pie. Shared around, it was only a few bites for each of us, but appreciated much. Tomorrow we commence to ascend the mountains. It rains on and off and every day the weather appears more ominous and threatening.

Again we faced west. We'd stayed in camp two days after Mr. Stanton and the Reed family left the camp. Although our oxen were still in bad shape, we could not with prudence delay any longer. Except for the small children, we were all walking as the oxen were barely able to pull our wagons. Light rain was falling as the men urged the poor creatures to move forward. It had been a pleasant respite for us, but we were anxious to get over this last hurdle and begin our new life. A week to get over the highest mountains, two weeks more of easy travel, and we would be there.

After leaving our camp we moved across a downslope and began following the river west. The ground was covered with coarse and sharp-edged gravel that cut and bruised the feet of the animals, adding greatly to their distress. To our left rose tall mountains, to our right across the river was a flat-topped hill. Ahead of us loomed the canyon of the river. I thought it was a grand and magnificent sight—the tumbling and sparkling water, the towering mountains with mists hanging on the slopes like thick white spider webs. The air was clean and I took deep breaths, feeling purified.

We crossed and re-crossed the river, the wagons lurching through gullies and side-slipping across slopes. The valley of the river was becoming narrower and the canyon sides steeper. The river rushed past us, cascading over rough areas and splitting around great boulders. There were many very large pine trees in the bottom of the river canyon. George measured one of the trees and found it was eighteen feet in circumference. The sky became gray and threatening and we wanted to hurry, to rush, but our oxen had no hurry in them. About mid-morning it began to rain. We crossed the river for the last time about eight miles from the meadow and climbed out of the river canyon onto a flat bench.

"George," asked Jacob, "was you counting? How many times in all did we cross that one river?"

"It was too many."

"It was near fifty times."

George rode up to the first wagon in line. "This is a good place to camp. There's a steep grade up ahead an' it's best to do it tomorrow. We need to rest the stock."

The next morning we followed the stream on an easy incline toward the mouth of a narrow, winding canyon. The forest began here and we relished the fresh clean smell of the pine trees, so agreeable after breathing desert sand and alkali dust for weeks. After entering the canyon the trail almost immediately went up a steep slope and we were above the canyon. As we stopped to rest we looked to the east from whence we had come and could see, far below, the beautiful valley we had left the morning before.

"You know, that there valley would be a good place to settle," said George. "Plenty of grass and water. It's good horse and cattle country."

"Oh, no. No pioneering in a wilderness for me," I said. "I was promised the land of milk and honey and forever sun and some semblance of civilization. There's nothing here but Indians that want to kill our stock."

"It won't always be that, Tamsen. In a few years there'll be people who'll come and settle. Always have, always will."

We ascended through a thick growth of pine, fir, and cedar, slowly snaking our way up, sometimes in a ravine, sometimes on the ridges above the canyon, only to jolt back down to avoid deep crevices and rocks. We stopped often to allow our animals and ourselves a rest. In the afternoon the wind began to pick up, but the clouds had disappeared. It was late in the day when we got to the top of the grade and debated where to make camp.

"George," said Jacob, "we can't camp here. There's no water an' no grass to speak of." He pointed. "The trail goes over the edge there. Come look. Down below there's water and grass."

We gathered at the edge of the canyon and looked down. Below us was an oval shaped valley surrounded entirely by high mountains. But to get down to the valley floor it was necessary to tackle a very steep slope. We could see that the descent was grooved into ruts from the locked wheels of previous wagons.

"Looks like most of the wagons before us skidded down all right, George."

"That's a mighty sharp descent. I wonder that some wagons haven't turned over," said George.

"Let's go on down tonight," said Jacob. "The stock'll be able to graze all night, recruit a little. That mountain we came up has plumb wore them down."

"All right, let's get started," said George. "Jacob, we'll take your wagons first. It'll be dark soon. We've got to move fast. Double-lock the wheels an' we'll ease 'em down with rope. What do you think? Six yoke up here on the rope?"

"That should do 'er."

"Hey you, Smith!" yelled George. "Get the poles in those wheels. Shoemaker, chain it up. The rest of you men, get the oxen hitched up."

There was a lot of confusion, the women and children gathering up to walk down, the men unhitching oxen to make up the six yoke needed for the counter pull to ease the wagons down. Jacob yelled at William. "Get the horses and start 'em down."

I called to George as he was walking away to help with the work. "George, Eliza and Georgeanna are in the wagon. Shouldn't I get them out before you start down with it?"

"Well, it's goin' to be hard for them to walk down, it's so steep an' it's slippery. I think they'll be better off in the wagon."

"I want to take them out."

"Tamsen, don't fuss. They'll be fine."

The men took the wagons down one by one. As our family wagon was being eased over the edge of the precipice, I started down with the other girls. We had to grab onto bushes to keep ourselves from tumbling down the slope. I was watching as our wagon passed us, the running gear creaking and groaning as it took the strain from being lowered. All of a sudden the wagon sprang forward as the ropes gave way, the wheel oxen scrambling as they tried to keep their footing. The front wheel grazed a large rock and the wagon began to tilt. There was a splitting and cracking sound and the wagon lurched and fell over on its side, pushing a thick slab of red mud before it as it settled at the bottom of the hill.

George and Jacob were quickly beside the wagon and I could see them pulling out Georgeanna. Where was Eliza? I scooted the rest of the way down the slope and ran to the wagon. The men were working frantically to remove everything and soon they found her and pulled her out. She was dazed, but all right. It was a good thing that the heavy boxes that had been in the wagon were buried in the cache back on the trail, as the girls would have been crushed beneath them.

"I shouldn't have left the girls in the wagon. You were right, Tamsen. I'm just a damned fool."

"She's all right, George. Don't fret yourself."

"Godamighty, what next?" asked George as the men examined the wagon.

"The axle's busted through, George."

"Nothin' we can do about it tonight. Let's get the last wagon down. We'll have to make camp right here."

"George," said Jacob, "leave the wagon. It's going to take us a day at least to make a new axle."

"Jacob," declared George, "I have two thousand dollars in goods that would have to be given up. Those goods are worth ten thousand in California. I can't abandon them."

"Uh-huh, an' if'n we don't get over the pass the goods're not going to mean anythin' no ways, George."

"No, one day ain't goin' to make a difference. An' it'll give our animals some time to rest."

"George, look." I pointed to the sky. A beautiful golden full moon was rising over the tree tops on the mountain.

"I sure don't like the looks of that ring around it. Back to home that would mean a storm comin'."

The next morning the men felled a tree and drug it to the broken wagon to fashion another axle. It was hard work and it took all day to do the rough shaping. As they were working the chisel slipped and George's hand was badly cut. I bound the wound up in cloth strips and he continued working.

"Don't fuss, Tamsen, it's nothing to worry about. We're almost finished with this shapin', but it's nigh to dark. We'll have to finish tomorrow."

The next morning Reinhardt and Charlie Burger came over to where George was working on the new axle.

"We are going to move ahead, Donner," said Charlie Burger. "We will try to catch up with those ahead."

"Ve take Frau Wolvinger's wagon, it haf our gear," said Reinhardt.

George looked up at the two men. "What does Mrs. Wolfinger say?"

"She vill go along ..."

George put down the tool he was holding. "Jake, I'll be back shortly." George walked over to Mrs. Wolfinger's wagon.

"I can speak a little German, but not enough to carry on a conversation. Ask her if she's in agreement with you men carrying her off."

"*Nein!*" Mrs. Wolfinger talked a steady stream of German language and within that monologue George could pick out certain words that led him to believe Mrs. Wolfinger did not want to go with them and she did not want them taking her wagon.

"Well, Reinhardt, it seems Mrs. Wolfinger is not in agreement on this. She wants to remain with the group. If you want to set out walkin', she'll carry your gear on for you."

"Ve cannot carry what ve need," said Reinhardt angrily. "That iss the same to tell us ve cannot go."

"I ain't tellin' you one way or t'other. I need to get back to the work. You men best leave Mrs. Wolfinger alone."

The two men turned away, but they didn't make any move to leave the camp. When George returned to the work, I went to speak with him.

"George, I think it would be a good idea to keep our horses close where we can watch them."

He looked at me for a moment, then called Solomon over to him. "Solomon, bring the horses up closer to camp an' stay with them."

"What for? Hey, Uncle George, there's two riders comin'." Solomon pointed up the valley.

"I see them. Do what I told you, Solomon."

It was Charles Stanton and one of the Indians.

"Hey, George. Jacob. Been worried about you. It looks like we aren't going to make it over. The top is snowed in with ten or twelve feet of snow. The others are building cabins to keep out of the weather until we can make another try."

"Where are they now?" asked George.

"About twenty miles ahead at the bottom of the pass. There's a cabin there. Breen took it."

"Is it a good camp site?"

"Well, there's water, but not much grass. But between here an' there there's a meadow with good grass, might be a better place to camp. Where they are, it's up against a high mountain to the west. That's the mountain we're going to have to cross."

"Where's the other Indian?"

"There's deer up there on that ridge and he's trying to get one. I heard a rifle shot as we were coming down so he'll be coming along shortly. Maybe your women folk will cook some of the meat up for supper."

"They'll do that gladly. We've got to finish this axle. Hope to move out tonight or first thing in the mornin'," replied George.

"We'll stay tonight and go on back in the morning," said Stanton. "We'll see if we can make more meat. We'll be back in time for supper, likely." The men mounted up, walking their horses off to the west where it was thickly forested. That evening at the campfire Mr. Stanton told us all that had happened.

"We tried to get over several times, different groups of us. The last time we tried, we packed some goods on oxen and mules and started out on foot, but no sooner did we get on the road than it commenced to storm and we had to go back. There's a cabin there that was built by that party that old Greenwood led out in '44. Breen took that and Mr. Keseberg built a kind of lean-to on the side of it. The Murphy woman's family built a cabin and there's a bunch in there. The Graveses made a double cabin, they're in one side and Mrs. Reed and some others in the other. It's going to be crowded. The two fellows and I will likely have to make something for ourselves."

The next morning the men prepared to leave us.

"Noah," said George, "go on with these men an' look the country over. Have 'em show you that meadow Stanton talked about for a camp. We'll meet up with you on the trail. Mrs. Donner will give you some provisions."

On we toiled, over low hills and rolling, heavily timbered country. There were numerous deer moving down toward the valley we had just left and our men killed several. We knew we had to make at least ten miles so we pushed on, walking close to the sides of the wagons for the small amount of respite from the pelting of rain and sleet and the cutting wind. We longed to be inside their sheltered interior, but we couldn't add our weight to the burden the oxen were almost too weak to pull. Chilled to the bone, we kept swinging our arms and chafing our hands to keep the blood circulating. In late afternoon we stopped in a small meadow that had good grass and water.

"Why are we stoppin'?" Jacob asked George. "We need to get on."

"We need to get some of this meat smoked," replied George. "We can't make it to the place those men told us of today anyways. This is a likely lookin' place to stop."

"George, the meat'll keep. We need to keep movin'. We got to get over them mountains."

"*Ja,* I think so, too," said Reinhardt, and Charlie Burger echoed the sentiment.

"You heard Stanton tell us they couldn't get over."

"We got to try, George. We have to get over. It'll melt an' we'll be ready."

"Well, you go ahead then. We'll stop here."

"Elizabeth, we're moving on." Jacob started toward his wagons.

"Jacob, you want to go, start walkin'. The wagons stay here," yelled Elizabeth. "You three men kin keep each other company. Solly, you git back there an' drive t'other wagon."

Elizabeth started the first wagon into the camping place with her oldest boy directing the second behind her. The other two men started to walk off after putting a few things in a sack.

"George," I said, "we may never see those men again and Mrs. Wolfinger believes Reinhardt has her money. We need to do something about it."

"Why do you think it's my business?"

"You're the leader."

"I'm the leader of this family. I ain't goin' to take responsibility for these other people. They're just with us, Tamsen, not *of* us."

"George, human decency still calls for—"

"Godamighty!" George walked over to the two men.

"Reinhardt, Mrs. Wolfinger believes you and Spitzer had somethin' to do with her husband's disappearance an' her missin' money. I don't hold no special feelin's, one way or t'other. Would you kindly let me look through your bundle?"

Reinhardt stared at George for a few moments, then dropped his bundle at George's feet. "You look and then you go back to your meddlesome woman."

George picked up Reinhardt's bag, looked through it, and then handed it to him. "You got a money belt?" Reinhardt stared sullenly at George and didn't answer.

"I'm askin' you, did you have anythin' to do with this? Look me in the eye, man, talk to me!"

Mr. Reinhardt looked at George for a moment, then turned and walked away. Charlie Burger seemed undecided, but then followed Reinhardt. George came back to me.

"He only showed his bundle," George said irritably. "I don't cotton to calling a man a thief when I have no proof. Why do we have to get involved in this mess?"

"Because that poor woman has been robbed and her husband murdered. There has to be some kind of justice for her."

"I'm not the sheriff nor the judge, woman!"

George began unhitching the oxen on our wagon and signaled the teamsters to start on the other wagons. The wind was beginning to blow with strength and rain, mixed with sleet, continued to pelt us.

"George, please see if you can't put up something to keep off the wind and rain and we'll need a windbreak behind the fire."

"Godamighty!" exclaimed George. He looked around and spotted Juan Baptiste. "Baptiste, take the ax an' cut some poles."

I found the girls huddling in our family wagon. "Girls, see if you can find some dry wood. We'll need a big fire, so bring as much as you can."

They moaned and whined, but jumped down and started dragging wood close to the wagon. Jacob was sitting on a log, arms crossed, face set, lips in a thin line. George went over to him and put his hand on his shoulder.

"Jake, I'm sorry. I would give anythin' if things were different, but they ain't."

Jacob sighed deeply. "Yeah."

"C'mon, it don't do no good to be in a pucker. Those men done told us there's no gettin' over now, so why get all worked up?"

Jacob threw up his hands in frustration and then stood up. "I ain't strong like you, George. You see the good side of everythin', but the bad's there fer me to worry about." He buried his hands in his pockets. "I done lost my gloves. Damn country's cold as a witch's heart."

"Let's go to my wagon. I'll get you a pair."

Jacob's manner was contrite as they walked over to the back of our supply wagon. "George, I don't know what's bitin' me. I just don't feel good about our chances of gettin' over an' I'm worried that we're all goin' to die here in the mountains."

George put his arm around Jacob's shoulders. "It's all right, Jake. Look, don't worry yourself about things until we see what we're facing. No point in cryin' wolf when you ain't seen one yet."

George searched around in the wagon, found the gloves, and handed them to Jacob. Then he took out a canvas. Noah was starting to unhook the oxen.

"Noah, wait. We got to get the wagons in a square here, so's we can stretch this canvas between 'em."

The wagons were placed in a "U" shape and canvas was stretched overhead. Baptiste made a framework of poles and brush for the open end of the space to block the wind and reflect some of the heat of the fire back into the enclosure.

While biscuits were baking I put the women and children to work cutting up the deer meat and hanging the strips on branches near the fire. Everyone cooked their own strip of meat by putting it on a stick over the fire, washing the meal down with lots of coffee and hot tea. Then we huddled in blankets, talking over our situation. We were bitterly disappointed knowing we were stopped, trapped here in the mountains, at least for the time being. But getting out of the constant pelting of rain and sleet and the battering of the wind cheered us somewhat.

"Folks, tomorrow will be a better day. We'll get to the meadow that Stanton told us of or if it looks like it's better to go where the other people are, we'll do that. We'll get out of the weather an' wait until we can get over. It's too early to have such deep snow, so likely it'll melt off. We'll find a place to stop an' build some shelters to wait out the snow."

Yes, surely it wouldn't keep on. It was much too early in the season. All the next day we were again lashed by a piercing wind and rain, snow, and sleet. The wind whipped particles of ice into us that rattled off the canvas covers of the wagons and our frozen clothing. It was late afternoon, almost dark, when we met Noah on the road. Reinhardt and Burger were with him. They looked miserable.

"The place is ahead 'bout three miles," said Noah. "We'll go on a mile or two, then head off to the right along a stream. There's plenty of wood, a clean stream, an' good grass. It's the best place I seen an' I went all the way to the other camps. You can't see it now, but the pass is over that ridge of mountain yonder."

"George," I said, "if it's three miles it'll be an hour or more and dark before we can get there. I want to stop here. The children are crying from the cold."

It was too wet to get a fire going. I put dry clothes on the children and they huddled close together in the wagon wrapped in a blanket.

"Warm your hands next to the lantern, girls. Make sure it stands upright. We don't want a fire. I'll bring some food."

"I'll hold it, Mother," said Leanna.

Charlie Burger came to me as I was handing out cold meat and biscuits.

"Why didn't you men stay on with the other people?" I asked him.

"We didn't get that far, ma'am. We came on Noah comin' back from there an' he tol' us how bad they were for provisions, nobody wantin' to share an' all, an' the pass blocked with snow. We figured we were better off with you. Ma'am, all our things are in Mrs. Wolfinger's wagon and she won't let us in it. We're freezing. We've got to get some dry clothes and some bedding."

"I'll give you some food to share with Mr. Reinhardt. I'll go with you now to get the things you need from Mrs. Wolfinger. When we make camp tomorrow, you take everything of yours out of Mrs. Wolfinger's wagon."

We spent a cold, miserable night in the wagons. By morning, it had cleared off and Juan Baptiste found some dry bark under a log and got a fire started. The only way he could get it tindered was by rubbing gun powder into a rag and firing his gun into it.

"Don't try to cook anything," said George. "Just make coffee to warm us up. We're gonna move out shortly."

The children clustered near the fire, their little faces pinched and red and their lips blue from the cold. I gave each a cup of hot tea and a biscuit and then I made coffee.

"Girls, get inside the wagon, the men are chaining up. We'll have a dry camp soon. It's only a little while longer and you'll have a cozy shelter and a warm fire."

George started the lead wagon and soon we were all on the road. As we rounded a bend in the stream, Noah pointed to some far-off mountains.

"Y'all see that there dip in the white line of them mountains? That be one'a the passes."

"Which is the one to take?" wondered Jacob.

"I don't know. Neither one offers any ease." Noah pointed. "See the yellow color there at the base of that ridge? That's grass. That's the place for the camp."

We were all straining to look, eager to stop. The site that Noah had chosen was about a mile or so off the road, but there was no place close to the road that offered firewood or grass. There was only a sage-covered plain with nothing to slow down the bitter winter wind.

November 7, 1846
Trapped at Alder Creek

We could tell as soon as we pulled our wagons into the glen that it had everything we needed. It was well stocked with pine trees, plenty of deadfall for firewood, a stream winding through, and stands of willow bushes. Behind the glen the ground sloped up until it became a low mountain. A short distance to the south was a tree-covered ridge.

"While the women are fixing food, let's look around," said George. When the men returned, they agreed that we had the best location in the area.

"It's higher than the marsh, but close to grass, an' these clumps of willows will shelter the stock some," said George.

They turned the animals to graze and after we prepared food and eaten, the men commenced to cut down trees. Soon a stock of pine boughs for beds was piled up and enough trees had been cut to make a cabin four logs high when darkness stopped the work. We built a huge fire and stretched a canvas overhead between two wagons and although we weren't comfortable, the fire blocked out the black night all around and the cover overhead kept the sleet and drizzle off our heads. The sky cleared before we retired to our beds and we could see a panorama of stars twinkling against the black night.

The next morning we awoke to find snow covering everything and still coming down. We heard muffled yelling and waded through the snow to Mrs. Wolfinger's wagon where Charlie was just helping her escape from under a load of snow.

"The snow's broke in the bows on one of our wagons too," said George. "If'n we don't get it cleared off, it'll break in the others. We've got to get some shelter made to keep us out of the weather 'til we can build somethin' better."

The men cleared the snow off the wagons and then started cutting down trees to make frameworks for temporary huts.

"I'll set up our tent and make a lean-to around it, against one of them big trees there," George said to me.

"Oh. Where? I mean which tree?"

"Do you have a preference, my lady?"

I pointed to a huge tree that was twisted and gnarled from the wind. "It's a grandfather tree and it seems friendly to me."

George gathered the men and told them what he wanted to do. John Denton looked doubtful. "Roit, but with what we 'ave for materials, loikly it will be a bloody poor house."

"We don't plan to have 'em for long. But we've got to get out of the weather," replied George.

For our shelter, the men built a framework of poles against the tree, similar to an Indian lodge, only ours wasn't a full circle. The doorway, on one flat side of the circle, faced southeast, so it would catch sun in the morning. On the other side we placed our tent, the opening facing into the main room. The frame of the hut was covered with limbs with willow branches and pine boughs woven in between. Over that we stretched quilts, ground covers, canvas, and hides.

"Elitha, you and Leanna gather up pine needles to carpet the floor. It will help keep us out of the mud."

A pit for our fire was placed next to the tree so the smoke from the fire would be drafted up and out along the trunk. A small opening was left at the top so the smoke could go out. We draped a canvas to provide privacy and a "necessary" place near the door. For the door, Baptiste stretched a buffalo skin over a frame and attached it to the doorframe with leather hinges. A similar shelter was fashioned of poles in the manner of an Indian lodge a short distance away for the single men. Jacob and Betsey went across to the other side of the stream and found a spot where there was a small open space surrounded by pine trees and willows.

"George, look." Jacob pointed across the stream. "See that big downed tree? That's a likely place for our camp. I'll back my two tents up to that an' build a roof over 'em. Keep some of the weather off'n the tents an' it'll kind'a shelter the cookin' fire. An' that log over there, you see it fallen over the stream? We kin cross over on that. We'll not be so close we'll step on each other's feelin's. The boys an' I'll start settin' up the tents."

"We'd best put another log across the stream. I don't think the women could cross without slippin'," said George. "We'll drag one over there. When we get time we'll level off the tops and fit 'em together. What will you do with your wagons?"

"I'll hitch 'em up after we get the shelter made an' take 'em across," replied Jacob.

We outfitted the shelters with beds by driving posts into the ground, with a web of branches and poles between and a layer of pine boughs on top. When the work was done, we furnished our new home with our camp table and chairs, our trunks, bedding, and the cooking things. With a fire burning brightly and food cooking, it was kind of cozy. I placed my rocking chair next to the fire.

Mrs. Wolfinger had a place with us, but the single men were assigned quarters in the men's hut. With our men, Noah James, Samuel Shoemaker and John Denton, were Charley Burger, Joseph Reinhardt, James Smith, John Baptiste, and Antonio.

It had been snowing and raining off and on lightly all day, but as the work was being finished dark clouds came from over the mountain and huge wet snowflakes began coming down, making a plopping sound that became faster and faster. Soon a curtain of white obscured the other huts from our view. The men hurriedly finished up, moved the livestock in closer to the huts, and secured the animals as best they could. We hoped the storm would quickly pass, but our hopes were in vain.

The storms raged for over a week. The wind buffeted our flimsy huts, rushing in with icy blasts, sending snow through places that weren't well covered. Each day we would awaken, clear off the accumulation of snow, and repair the area where the wind had torn the shelter apart. We would open our door covering in the morning to see if we would have to endure the storm yet another day and each day we were bitterly disappointed to see snow still coming down and the wind whipping and bending the trees. As the snow built up, it would melt and drip down on us. It became difficult to move about and impossible to keep dry. One dark and dreary morning I awoke to hear the children calling to me.

"Mother, we're cold. Our bed is all wet. There's no fire!"

"Yes, I know. We have no more wood to make a fire. Just stay in bed for the moment and I will do what I can."

I sat up and pulled my shawl around me. George got up, careful to keep from putting any pressure on the hand he had injured working on the broken axle.

"Honey, would you pull my boots on for me? God, I hate being a cripple."

We went in to the firepit and I poked around in the cold ashes hoping to resurrect a few coals.

"Baptiste's gone outside already," said Leanna, sitting up in the bed she shared with Elitha.

"You're pulling the covers off me," Elitha whined, yanking at their quilts. "It's so damn cold in here."

"Elitha, ladies don't use that word."

"Ladies who aren't trapped in a miserable cold hut freezing to death and wet to the bone and jammed in with twenty other people in the middle of a miserable cold storm—"

"Hush, Elitha, you'll upset the little ones."

"I'll roust the men out to cut wood," said George. "With all of us working at making a path an' digging out, we ought to be able to do somethin'. I'm worried about the stock."

I helped George put on his coat. He winced when the sleeve brushed against his hand.

"Tamsen, can you wrap something around my hand to keep it warm? I can't get a glove on."

I found a piece of wool and George held his hand out to me to wrap it. The wound was red and swollen and had an ugly blackish hue.

"Oh, George, your hand looks bad. You'll need help. I'll go with you. Let me get dressed."

"Mother! I'm so cold! Please, can I get in your bed?"

Eliza began to cry, and then Georgeanna, and then Frances. I felt sorry for them, but I could do little. Mrs. Wolfinger got up from her bed and went to the girls to see if she could comfort them. She gave them some biscuits to nibble on and sat down beside them, starting a lullaby.

"*Guten Abend, gute Nacht* ..." Although the words were German, the softness of her voice lulled them and stopped their crying. I tried to cajole them. "Girls, girls, listen, today it's going to stop snowing and the sun will shine and we'll all go outside and the sun will warm us."

"Are you sure, Mother?"

"I think so. I hope so. I don't hear the wind this morning, do you?"

"I don't hear the wind. The wind has stopped blowing! The snow-king is dead! Old man snow is gone!"

Oh, how could I get their hopes up only to find Mother told a fib and it's still snowing! Dear God, we've had enough! Please, please send the clouds away.

I pulled back the door and a cascade of snow fell on me and into the hut.

"Oh, George. We'll have to dig our way out again."

George handed me the shovel and I stood there looking at the wall of white. Baptiste had left a line of deep tracks up to the top of the snow.

"Oh, look, look! I see blue sky! It's stopped snowing!" I cried. I filled our big washtub and a kettle with snow and then started to push a path upwards toward the blue sky when Juan Baptiste's head appeared at the top of the snow.

"*Señora.* Me you give the shovel. I bring some wood."

He threw some pieces of wood to me and I handed the shovel up to him. I took the ax and chipped bark and splinters off the big tree that so stoically spread its arms over our shelter, standing so steadfast while the blasts of wind had toppled lesser trees all around.

"I am truly sorry, Grandfather," I said, "but I must have some dry kindling. My little girls are cold and hungry."

The girls began to chant as they sat up with their blankets wrapped around them. "The girls are cold and hungry! The girls are cold and hungry!"

"We'll have to start the fire with flint. The ashes are dead," I said.

George knelt before the firepit. "Tamsen, I can't do the flint with only one hand. You'll have to do it."

After several attempts a spark was thrown and a little flame curled amongst the chips and pine needles. Carefully, I blew on the flame and soon had a fire going and coffee boiling. It was quite a while before the men straggled over to our hut. They stood around hip deep in the snow, hunched over against the cold. I handed the coffeepot to Baptiste and followed with cups. Baptiste had made a small clearing in front of our doorway and I stood there looking at the men standing around, hands in their pockets.

"All right, men," said George, "we've got to find our animals an' dig out a stock of wood. I wish I could help more, but now my whole arm is sore an' I can't use it."

"Mr. Donner," said Charlie Burger, "I can't do nothing unless I get some shoes. Mine have come apart with all the wet. I would like a pair of your boots. What will they cost me?"

"Four dollars, Charlie."

"Me, I need boots," said Baptiste.

"You'll have them. Some of you get firewood enough so the women can make breakfast. The rest of you dig out the back of the wagon so I can get the boots. After we eat we're goin' to need to find our oxen."

When I had breakfast ready the men crammed themselves into the hut. I filled bowls with mush and topped each with a dollop of molasses and handed it out, along with more coffee. The girls kept calling to me from their bed.

"Mother, Mother, we're hungry."

"Yes, I know. Just as soon as the men finish I'll give you yours. Can you be patient for just a few more minutes?"

"I don't know. I'm very hungry and I'm cold," said Frances.

"Me too."

"Hush. Mother is doing all she can," said Leanna. "Mother, do you want me to help?"

"Yes, would you get the little ones dressed? There is hot water in the kettle. Take a basin and all of you wash up."

"C'mon, Elitha, you help," said Leanna. "I want to change too. I'm sick of these moldy clothes. Get up, you little girls, start moving! The sun is shining today!"

As the men finished their breakfast, George gave them instructions.

"When you find the oxen, move them into that patch of willow behind Jacob's tent. The ridges will keep them from goin' off that'a'ways an' when we get time we'll try some kind of fence to keep 'em from movin' off to the east side. If'n they're dead, mark the location so we can find them again."

"How many did we end up with?" asked Shoemaker.

"Twenty-four. No, twenty when we got here, if I recollect right," replied George. "An' two horses. The horses should be easy to find. They'd have put their tails to the wind an' found a clump of trees for shelter."

Before the men could start their work, they had to make pathways to the other shelters. They cleared to the bridge over the stream and found Jacob's boys digging their way to us. We were astonished at our appearances. In the huts it was dark and we hadn't realized how pale and sickly looking we had become. But in the bright sun, all was starkly revealed. We looked terrible. It came into my mind that death was hovering over us. *No! The sun is shining, the snow is melting, and even if we don't get over we'll survive until the snow clears off the mountain pass. We'll walk over if we have to.*

Later that day the men came in wet, cold, and exhausted.

"Mr. Donner, we didn't find but twelve of them ox, only six alive. There's a couple spots out there where the snow blowed off some. You could see where some of the oxen walked around an' around a tree digging a pit, but there was nothin' for 'em to eat. The six that're alive had gone into the willows an' they weren't snowed under. Looks like they commenced to eatin' willow. We marked the dead ones we found with poles. Those others ain't anywhere near. We've covered the country for a mile around."

"How about the horses?"

"No sign."

Betsey was there in our hut when the men came in and this bad news set her off into wailing. "Oh, Lord. What're we gonna do now? We have no way to git out'a here. We cain't walk an' we got no way to pull our wagons. We got no food. We're all just gonna die here an' the sooner the better, I'm thinkin'."

"Don't talk that way," I said. "We can walk, can't we? We walked most of the way here. We can come back for our wagons after we get settled in California. The snow melted a good bit today and tomorrow it will melt off more."

"Betsey," said Jacob, "stop yore complainin' an' git to cookin'."

"You're a fine one to tell me to stop hollering. That's all you do, complain an' moan and groan. If you was bein' hung you'd complain that it was with a new rope!"

"Men, get in some dry clothes," said George. "The women will give you somethin' to eat. We need to get one of those dead oxen dressed out an' divided up between the camps. If it's clear tomorrow we've got to find the horses an' the rest of the oxen."

As we worked to fix food, Betsey apologized for her outburst.

"I just get so down. Oh, lordy, I'm so afraid that we'll never get out."

"Betsey," I said. "Yesterday we were wet and cold and had no fire. It was still snowing. Today the sun is shining and we have fire and hot food. So isn't today better than yesterday? Look at the positive side and your worries will recede."

After we ate, we all sat around the fire. It felt so good to have a fire again.

"Men," I said, "I want a stock of wood cut and put up beside my door where I can get to it. There are many fallen trees. Two of those big ones would make a stock of wood to last quite awhile."

"Yes," said George, "I was about to get to that. Juan Baptiste, you an' Antonio, dig out some of them trees an' cut 'em up. At least, drag 'em over here close so's we can work on chopping the wood up when we can. We'll have it to hand."

Jacob got up and bent over the fire, tilting the kettle to pour coffee in his cup. "We sure as hell got our tails in a crack now. Looks likely we're gonna be trapped here for the winter. Should we think about goin' back to that big valley? Likely the snow's not as deep there. I mind we're at a high elevation here, much higher than that valley was."

"Which valley are you speaking of?" asked George.

"The big one where we started up the mountain. Where we camped on the river."

"Well, how far have we come from there?" George asked, but went on to answer his question. "Maybe thirty, forty miles. We came over two summits an' they were higher than this here. Am I right?"

Jacob nodded in agreement and George continued. "So even if it melts off here, it's likely to stay deep on those summits. Maybe not as deep as on those mountains yonder," George pointed west, "but if we go back we don't have a chance to make a run at the mountain when the weather breaks."

"Ya' know," said Jim, "I'm wonderin' if the oxen an' the horses didn't turn tail an' head back to that deep valley where we camped to fix the wagon. They'd remember all that green grass. They'd have no way a' knowin' it was gonna snow there too. I think I'll make a couple sets of snowshoes tonight an' if someone will go with me we'll strike back aways an' see if we can spot 'em."

"Ifn they weren't driven off by the Injuns."

"Most likely the Indians wouldn't've been out in the storms," said George. "Not to say they aren't out now like us, but they can't drive 'em unless it melts off good."

"It was 'bout twelve miles, warn't it, Jim? I don't see how you could go that far on snowshoes, it being uphill," said Jacob.

"We could track back a ways," replied Jim. "There's places where the snow's blown off an' we can use the snowshoes where it's deep. Ifn we find 'em dead, we kin butcher 'em and bring back some of the meat. We can take some dry kindling an' some food ifn we have to stay out."

"Look here, Jim, ifn it's clear in the morning, go on, but only as far as you can get back by night. Ifn a storm comes up again y'all might be stuck out there. Baptiste, I want you to try to get over to the other camps. Mebbe they're getting ready for another try."

Jim Smith and Charlie Burger went in search of the missing livestock and by evening they returned to report they hadn't found any.

"We went back three, four miles an' we found no sign. Not so much as a hair. They've plumb disappeared."

The next day Milt Elliot came with two other men from the camps at the lake. They were preparing to make an attempt to cross the mountains on foot and wanted to obtain some goods from us.

"What is it y'all need?" asked George.

"Coats, boots, gloves. Most of us don't got anything heavy enough for this weather an' our shoes're worn out."

"We need tobacco too, Milt," said one of the men.

"Yeah, an' tobacco. Do you have any meat to spare?"

"I wish we did, Milt. If we could find more of our oxen, we'd give you some. I can supply you with the goods you want."

"I'll have to pay you in California, George," said Milt. "Mr.

Reed didn't leave money with us. Miz Reed couldn't pay cash money for the oxen she bought from Graves an' Breen. They told her she'd have to pay two for one in California."

"How many did she get from them?"

"Four altogether."

"If you men can find any of our livestock under the snow, we'll give you some of the meat to take back," said George.

That afternoon Milt and Baptiste used poles with hooks on the end and searched deep into the snow but could not find any more of the oxen. Noah and the men made preparations to return to the lake camps and several of our men determined to go too. I made up a packet of food for them, enough to last a week. We had a dilemma in regards to our food supplies. We had a responsibility to maintain our family and employees as best we could, but what of the men who had attached themselves to us? They had been given a share of the provisions that Mr. Stanton had brought and now those provisions were exhausted. Should we share our dwindling supply of food with them?

"I fear that should we become trapped here until spring we will all be dead of starvation," I told George. "We must think of our own."

"I know. But we can't stand by and see others starve."

Nov. 8

Today we searched again for sign of our horses and the remaining oxen, but they are not to be found.

We talk of walking out, packing food on our two oxen that are still alive. Today Noah and Milt came with news from the lake camps. They are making preparations to make another attempt as soon as the weather allows. We hope to be able to follow them and are packing up to do so.

Nov. 19

Yesterday Milt and the other men left for the other camps. John Baptiste, James Smith, Charlie Burger, Noah James, and Antoine went with them. They're joining several in the other camps to try to get over the mountain. We wait for Noah and Juan Baptiste to return if it looks likely to get over. We're making preparations for the eventuality. Juan Baptiste has made two sleds that we can use to carry our supplies and the little ones.

Wood is hard to obtain. We don't have enough fire to warm us, barely enough to cook our meager fare. Everyone is becoming dispirited. I am also. I must not allow it to show.

I confess to you, my journal, fear is gathering. I feel it, but I force it back. I must remain strong for my husband and my children. Oh God, please deliver us from this tomb of snow.

That night I could not sleep. I was so restless I worried I would disturb George. Taking a blanket, I went to the fire. Only a few streaks of red showed under a gray mantle of ash. I added some wood, poked up the ashes to start the wood burning, and moved the kettle over to the flames. My stirring around woke Elitha and she got up and came to the fire, wrapping a blanket around herself.

"It's so cold in here, it's hard to sleep."

I gazed at the little flames that began curling around the wood and I thought that fire was the only comforting thing we had, except each other. When the fire had been going long enough to heat the water, I made tea.

"Would you like some?" I whispered.

Elitha nodded and took the cup I offered to her. We sipped our tea, staring into the flames. A wolf began a crooning howl and soon other wolf voices joined in a chilling chorus. *Only flimsy walls between us and the wolves.* I shivered. *I wonder how Jacob's family is doing. I must get over there.*

"No matter how big we make the fire it can't warm the hut. The cold comes through the walls," I said. "All we can do is bundle up."

"I can't stand this," cried Elitha. "I'm sick of being cold and wet and dirty, crowded together, everybody on top of each other. The hogs back home live better than we do. I hate Father for making us come here."

"Never say that!"

Elitha began to cry. "Oh, I didn't mean it. I'm sorry. I'm just so miserable—"

"Do you think you're the only one who's miserable?"

"No."

"We may be able to leave soon, but if not, we must think of when we can leave. We can't allow ourselves to wallow in despair. Think of things you can do to get your mind off the misery," I said. "I practically have to beat you to get you out of bed and moving around, but activity helps."

"I know, I know. But what's the use? We'll probably all die anyway."

I put my arms around her. "Honey, this will all pass. We'll get to California and have a wonderful life. We just have to grin and bear it for a while longer." Elitha took the hem of her night dress and wiped at her tears.

"I've started my monthly. Where did you put the cloths?"

"I'll get some for you. It was so hard to wash the things when we had no fire, I burned the old ones." I got the cloths for Elitha. "Wrap some of this cattail cotton inside the cloth. It absorbs well."

She returned to bed. As I sipped my tea I contemplated our situation. We had taken stock of our supplies and figured that if we didn't find the rest of our oxen, our supply of food would last a month if we rationed it carefully.

I put some more wood on the fire and sat down again, rocking slowly, soothed by the motion. *Surely we'll be able to get out before our food is gone. But what if we can't get over the mountain? What if James Reed can't get to us with supplies?*

• • •

The next day was fine and clear, so I determined to get everyone outside. After we'd cleaned and straightened up our quarters, I told the girls we would visit their cousins and take some meat to them. We tramped over a path that Juan Baptiste had made to the other hut. After every storm the path grew higher and higher and Baptiste would cut more steps in the snow. Then we slipped and slid down to the stream and gingerly teetered over the log bridge. The path from the stream to their camp was not as nicely cleared as ours was.

"Those boys need to get out here and do some clearing," said George.

We found Jacob's family crouched up in their beds, the little ones listless and sickly looking. Betsey got up and pointed to the cold firepit.

"There's so much water dripping down I cain't keep a fire. We're wet all the way through from the snow melt an' cold all the time. Can the Mexican boy get out an' get us some wood? I cain't even cook. Not that I've got anythin' much to cook."

She moved to a chair and sat down dejectedly, the little ones clustering around her.

"Yesterday we dug out an ox," said George. "We brought some meat for you. Baptiste's not back from the other camps an' we can't seem to get the men to do anythin'."

"We need to get a fire started for them," I told George.

"Elitha," said George, "you an' Leanna go fetch some kindlin' an' dry wood an' bring that ground sheet that's coverin' the wood pile."

The girls returned dragging a skin piled with wood and George put some pieces in the wet firepit and began to build a fire on top of them.

"It's hard to do this with only one hand. Solomon, break up

some of that wood into smaller pieces. We're gonna need some coals from our fire to start this," said George.

"I'll go get some," I said.

George went over to the opening in the tent that Jacob and Betsey used as a bedroom and stuck his head inside.

"Jacob, get up. This place is a mess. I've only got one good arm and I still do more than you."

Jacob's voice was weak. "George, don't get mad. I'm a'telling you, I'm sick. Cain't do nothin'."

"Well, I'll allow that you look sick. At least get up an' come in here an' sit. We're goin' to get you a fire goin'."

When the fire was going well, George had the two boys start clearing the snow off the roof of the shanty.

"Pull off all that stuff on there and spread this ground cover over. It's not big enough, but it'll keep some of the wet off. Godamighty, Solomon, you can't stand on it! You're breaking it down. We'll have to make a ladder."

George and the boys struggled for a while with the work and then George threw the materials he was holding in his good hand down. "We got to have more help to do this."

"George, let's have everyone go to our camp. I'm going back and I'll get a meal started."

"Good idea. I've got to get some of the men to help put this place in order. Elizabeth, take yer kids an' go on with Tamsen. Elitha, you an' Leanna help with the young'uns."

It was late in the day before the men came to supper. Melting snow dropped here and there, making a concert of plopping sounds accompanied by sizzles as drops would hit in the fire. The wind had come up and was howling and beating at our weak structure, the assortment of hides and covers flapping and flailing about. The flames of the fire whipped and sputtered as freezing drafts swirled around inside. Betsey stared dejectedly into the fire.

"Our camp is the coldest place I've ever been in my life. Half has done blown away in the wind."

"What we got done today will help," said George. "If it's clear tomorrow we'll try to get it closed more. The boys need to get you a stock of wood."

"You know," I said, "the layers of snow tend to provide shelter that the wind can't get through. Kind of like sod or dirt would. If you have the boys build walls of snow around your hut it would keep some of the wind out. You could cut bricks of snow, big bricks, like the Eskimos do. Have you ever seen a picture of an igloo?

"I never heard of any of it."

"Well, I will show you what to do," I said.

"Tamsen, the snow's already a wall aroun' the hut," said Jacob.

"Yes, but you need space and a barrier between you and the snow. If the snow is right up against the canvas of your tent, the cold transfers to the inside. If there's a barrier and an open space, it won't transfer to the inside as much."

"That don't make much sense to me," said Jacob.

"I assure you, if you try it, you will have more warmth for the same amount of fire."

"I cain't hardly lift my arm, much less a shovel of snow," whined Jacob. I looked at him. His eyes were sunken and circled with dark skin, his cheeks hollow. He had the look of death.

"Get those boys to do it," I said. "They need to work to stay strong. And so do you. If we don't keep moving and doing we'll lose strength. If we get the chance to walk out, we will need strength to do it."

"I'm gettin' out of here," said Solomon. "I'm goin' over to the other camps. The first good day I'm goin' over the mountain."

"No, you ain't," said Betsey. "You're stayin' right here. You'll get out there an' get lost, I know you. Noah's comin' back to tell us if anybody kin get over. Then we'll all go."

Jacob's chin was sunk into his chest and he slouched dejectedly against a cut-off stump we used for a stool. "I cain't walk half a mile," he said dejectedly, then he looked up and there was a little hope in his voice. "I might be able to go on a mule or horse if'n Reed got back with some."

"Jacob, you need to buck up," said George. "You got a family dependin' on you. There's no point to mopin' the day away feelin' sorry for yourself. Get out an' help get the wood, get some air. Move around."

"I'm movin' around. I'm here, ain't I? Me an' the boys try to get wood, but we just sink down in the snow, cain't even walk. All the dead wood is buried deep. Don't listen to Elizabeth. She thinks I shouldn't rest any. I ain't so spry in the mornin's. My bones hurt an' I cain't seem to find strength enough to get out'a bed. An' there ain't nothin' to get out'a bed for."

"I cain't get any a'them to do nothin'," said Betsey. "The place stinks worse than a skunk's nest an' no one will help clean it up. They won't even go outside to piss anymore."

Nov. 26

John Baptiste came back today with J. Smith, the rest stayed at the lake. It's very discouraging as it looks unlikely that we can get over. It began to snow again last evening, today rain and sleet. Our hope is that James Reed will arrive soon with supplies. But if we can't get out, can he get in?

"Some people, they try to get over, us too, but only two days an' we come back. The snow is deep," reported Baptiste. "The *Señor* Breen, he has meat because right away he kill all his *animales*. Some others they lose their stock, like us. Stanton, he come back with food an' supplies from the *Señor* Sutter an' those people there, they no share anything with him or the Indians. The food you give us is gone in five days an' from those people we get nothing."

"I reckon they're needin' to look out for their own," said George.

"There ain't no getting over 'less the storms stop an' the snow hardens up. Mebbe it will be possible fer some that're still strong to make it then," said Smith.

"Did you see any game at all?" asked George.

"No, sir, Mr. Donner. Nothin'," replied Jim. "Nobody's gonna make it out'a here. This here's a camp of death an' you might as well figure on it."

James Smith seemed beaten and we knew he had given up.

From that time, the men huddled in their shelter, making little effort to get wood or keep a fire going, even to cook the paltry provisions they had. Only Baptiste and John Denton moved about. Baptiste would take the little ones up to the top of the snow, sometimes making an overhead shelter of his old Navajo blanket, sometimes wrapping them in it. Often, when it was nice out, I would join them and I made George get out too, for I knew that living without the purifying effect of the sun was not a healthy thing.

Each time we had a clear sunny day we would drag out our wash tub and build a fire outside on the snow to melt and heat water so we could wash clothes and bathe. Over time the fire sank deeper and deeper into the snow until a large pit had formed. This gave me an idea.

"Baptiste, the fire has melted the snow so much I think that with a little more work we could clear it down to the ground. We could make a clearing if we remove the snow from here, where it's melted, over to the door. Then we'd be protected from the wind when we are out here."

Baptiste started the work and soon everyone was helping. When we'd cleared away enough snow to make a circle of about ten feet across, we were exhausted, but pleased by our accomplishment.

Baptiste continued working over the next few days, carving benches on one side and a new set of snow stairs to the top of the snow. Then he made snow canyons connecting the wagons to our clearing. Baptiste made a camp for himself under a wagon. The clearing became a favorite place for us to gather when the weather was nice. The little circle of Mother Earth under our feet was a pleasant respite from the glaring white snow that surrounded and enveloped us, depressing our spirits.

In mid-December Betsey came to us, much distressed. "Jacob's just laying there like he's dead, but he ain't dead. I don't know what to do. He's been like this fer two days."

Baptiste was squatting by the fireplace and looked up at Betsey. "He no want to live. He die when he get his body to give up."

"How would you know?" cried Betsey.

"I know some things, and this I know," said Baptiste.

George and I went to their camp. Jacob was lying in bed and was very weak. We helped him to a chair at the table. I tried to get him to drink the tea I'd made, but he would only take a sip. He laid his arms and head on the table.

"It ain't goin' to help."

Betsey shook Jacob's arm and tried to get him to hold his head up. "How do you know it ain't goin' to help? Oh, Jacob, what am I gonna do with you?"

Betsey sat down on one of the beds and slumped over with her head in her hands. Her voice was muffled.

"He don't want to live, that's all there is to it."

Jacob rolled his head to the side and looked up at George. "George, I seen our farm. In the new country."

"What was it like, Jake?"

"There was a big house, with pillars like to home in Carolina. There was green fields, all fenced purty like, an' yer horses, George. You 'member that black you had? He was in the field." Jacob lifted his head and cupped his chin in his hand to hold his head up. "I thought you sold that horse, but there he was—"

Betsey got up and stood behind Jacob, rubbing his back and shoulders. "He's been talking crazy like. He said he seen his Pa and Ma."

"I did, sure enough. Pa was mad as hell 'cause we left out of Illinois. He said we're never gonna see California an' we're all gonna die in these god-forsaken mountains. George, bury me deep. I cain't stand the thought of the wolves gettin' at me."

"Jake, the snow's gonna stop. Help is on the way from California. You need to keep goin'."

"Let me rest. I'm powerful tired." Jacob put his head down again on his crossed arms. His voice was weak, muffled. "We're paying now fer settin' our sights so high. I reckon the Almighty don't like a man to over aim. If'n he does, God sics somethin' on him."

The children were gathered around, the little ones with big eyes and their thumbs in their mouths, sensing the tension in the adults.

"Betsey," I said, "it might be best to have the children go over to our camp. Mrs. Wolfinger will fix some supper. They can stay the night there. Betsey—"

"What?"

"Take the children over to our camp. Solly, help your mother bring back some supper for us when Mrs. Wolfinger gets it ready."

George and I sat with Jacob most of the night. He wouldn't lie down, wanting to stay at the table. He drifted off into kind of a sleep, his breathing shallow and uneven. We couldn't rouse him. Toward morning he stopped breathing and his body gave up his soul. We laid him out on one of the beds and George sat beside him for a long time.

"We should never have left home. Jake would still be here—" George began to cry, deep sobs racking his body. I hugged him and then went back to our hut. Everyone was still asleep. I spoke softly to Solomon. "Solly, your mam needs you now."

"Huh? Oh, is Pa gone?"

"Yes. We'll need your help to dig a grave. You and William. Wake William up and take him with you."

I found Baptiste in his camp. He was making coffee over a little fire.

"Baptiste, we've got to dig a grave for Jacob. Solly and William can help, and the other men."

"*Señora,* those men in the hut, they all sick, they die soon. They no do nothing."

We walked solemnly to Jacob's final resting. Of the single men, only John Denton and Baptiste joined us. We'd chosen a spot at the foot of the ridge behind Jacob and Elizabeth's hut.

George's face was gray and haggard, his voice weak and raspy. Jacob's death and our situation rested heavily on him.

"We'll take him to California with us when we leave. We'll make a box for him."

The day had been cold and snowy, but as George began to read from the Bible a ray of sun pierced the clouds and we turned our faces to feel and savor the warmth. But in a moment it was gone and soft, wet flakes of snow began falling, melting on our faces and making a white frosty crust on our heads and on our clothes.

The snow fell on Jacob's face and soon it was covered with white. "Oh, Lord," wailed Betsey, "will it ever stop snowing in this god-forsaken place?" She sank to her knees beside Jacob and brushed the snow away. "He looks so peaceful. He's happy he don't have to worry no more, but what about me? What'm I goin' to do? He was always doin' that, gettin' out of things, not takin' responsibility."

She pulled the blanket in which we'd wrapped Jacob over his face and got up. "Cover him up. He's in a better place. I cain't abide to see him like this out here in this terr'ble lonely place, no box, no stone, no one to visit his grave."

"Elizabeth, we'll mark the place. We can take him up and carry him to California to a proper place. We're gonna have to come back for our wagons and such—" George's voice trailed off and he looked away.

I was very worried about George. The wound on his hand was very bad and all my efforts to heal it were failing. It was weakening him steadily. I thought back to the time of our marriage, back to the time when we'd first met. He was such a handsome man, tall, well-built, with a head of thick dark hair. Now, in just a short time, the physical vigor was gone. George looked old and sick.

"We're all gonna die here, George, an' it's yer doin's," moaned

Betsey. "You and your yondering. Jacob wouldn't have come, but you kept a yammering at him."

"Betsey," I said. "Jacob wanted to come as much as George did. It's not hopeless! We're not going to die here! There'll be people coming any day now to help us. Mr. Reed's spreading the word. He won't leave his family up here. Any day now, there'll be help coming."

"Well, it's too late fer Jacob, ain't it?" said Betsey.

Dec. 8

It's difficult to write these words. My tears are ruining the paper. Jacob died yesterday. There was nothing we could do. He was in poor health when we left Springfield, and the trials of the journey reduced his strength and exhausted his energy. I fear some of the men will also die soon. Seemingly, they have no desire to live.

Baptiste and I carried some food to the men's hut. Smith and Shoemaker had taken to their beds, unable, or unwilling, to move about. Reinhardt seldom arose from his seat by the fire.

"Why aren't you men stirring around? The inactivity will weaken you so you can't do anything," I told them. "This hut is a pigsty. It's unhealthy."

Reinhardt was staring into the fire, but turned his head to look at me. "Vat's the use? Ve all die here anyway. *Gott* iss punishing us."

"Mr. Reinhardt," I said, "why would God punish everyone in the camp, including the little innocent children?"

"God's fickle." Jim Smith sat up and swung his legs over the side of the bed. His voice was hoarse and he sucked in air after every few words. "He tempts men to be sinful just so's he can roast 'em later for doin' what he gives 'em a weakness for." He tried to stand, but his legs wobbled and he sank onto the bed.

"It don't make no sense to me," Shoemaker said from his bed. "Mebbe it keeps him from gettin' bored, looking down and seeing us squirm and suffer."

Baptiste squatted down by Jim's bed and looked at him earnestly. "It is *El Diablo* who asks the man to do the sin. If the man he say yes, is his mistake, not the fault of God. What sin you do that you must die?" asked Baptiste.

"Nothin' that I can think of. I'm God-fearin', but not a church goer."

"Well, then it is not for sure that you die, because God he say so. Perhaps you want to die, is so?"

"I think it's no good to fight. It's gonna happen."

"Then I think that nothing can be done for you. It is too bad. *Vaya con Dios.*"

• • •

I was surprised when one day Mr. Reinhardt came to our hut. He was weak and shaky, using a stick to steady himself. "I vant to talk to Donner," he said, his voice quavering. George sat up when we entered the little tent room we used for a bedroom. He put his hand out, but Mr. Reinhardt ignored it, pulling a leather bag from his coat pocket and handing it to George.

"I vant you give this to the lady after I pass on."

"Do you mean Mrs. Wolfinger?"

"*Ja.*"

"Is this—?"

Mr. Reinhardt turned abruptly, bumping into me and almost falling, but he steadied himself with the stick. "I say no more."

We left the room and I motioned him to a chair.

"Would you have some coffee, Mr. Reinhardt?" I asked.

"*Danke.*" He looked around the room, his head moving slowly and unsteadily. "Where your children?" he asked.

"They are with Juan Baptiste. They like to visit him in his camp. He keeps them entertained."

He nodded and then gazed into the fire, occasionally sipping the coffee I'd given him. Mrs. Wolfinger had retreated into the gloom and I could see her eyes glinting in the firelight now and again as she watched. The wind moaned and sighed in the trees. *I never again want to hear the sound of the wind as I hear it in this lonely and desolate place,* I thought. A piece of wood in the fire snapped and sizzled. The only other sound was the harsh uneven breathing of Mr. Reinhardt. He sighed deeply, raggedly, his body slumping, his cup falling to the floor. I looked at him, fearful that he'd passed on there in the chair, but he roused himself and with the help of the stick he got to his feet. Mumbling something I couldn't make out, he moved to the door and disappeared in the sudden white glare. Mrs. Wolfinger got up and pushed the door closed.

"Schmutztitel!" she exclaimed.

• • •

Milt Elliott and Noah James came from the other camps the second week in December. They reported that the situation was getting desperate there.

"The snow's eight to ten feet deep on the summit an' gettin' deeper," said Milt. Milt had a very bad cough and both men's eyes were red and swollen from the snow glare.

"Milford, I'm going to fix you men something to eat and then I will treat your eyes."

"I would appreciate it, ma'am. Noah had to lead me the last of the way, I was so blind."

After the men had eaten, George passed out tobacco and I made more coffee and tea. The girls asked about the other children.

"They's doin' all right, considerin'. Virginia an' Patty told me to tell you hello an' they wanted to know if'n you had any books you could send. They left everythin' of theirs back in the desert. It gets powerful boring with nothin' to do but sit and stare at the fire. There was some readin' stuff left in the cabin that the Breens took. We done read it all a hundred times. Mr. Graves an' some of the others are making snowshoes an' getting' ready to try to get over again. I think there's about twenty that'll go. We'll go with 'em if'n we get back before they leave."

"How's he makin' those snowshoes?" asked George.

"He uses ox bows. Cuts the ox bows in half an' weaves strips of hide in between."

"My snowshoes, they are better," spoke up Juan Baptiste.

"I like yours, John," said Noah, as he picked one up and looked it over. "How'd you make this?"

"It is the Indian way. The willow, it is strong and limber, it no break," replied Baptiste.

"You use a willow branch—"

"I put it to the fire for a time an' then I peel it an' bend it to the shape, you see, an' weave the willow back and forth. Like you make a basket, *sabes*? You know?"

"Yeah, these are much better. They're not as heavy."

Milt continued with his story of happenings at the lake camp. "They've recovered most of the dead animals by now, but it's poor meat an' we ain't got any salt. All the salt anybody had was in the wagons left up on the mountain. Do you have any you could share with us?"

"I have a little, Milt."

"I brung a note from Mr. Stanton. He wants to buy some goods. We're to carry them back with us."

"What does he want?" asked George.

Milt pulled a paper from his pocket and handed it to George. "He written a list. I mind tobacco is one thing."

"We have plenty of tea and coffee and tobacco. I'll send some with you, but we're short of provisions. We won't be able to share anything else," I told them.

"We'll appreciate whatever you can give us, ma'am," said Milt.

"What's the snow level there now?" asked George.

"When we left it was 'bout six or eight feet," answered Milt, starting to cough, "less under the trees an' where it's been blowed off. Seems like it's not ... as deep ... over here." His coughing grew worse and he took a swallow of coffee, but almost choked on it. I'd forgotten I had a cough remedy made up. I poured some into a cup.

"Try this, Milt, it might help."

Milt looked at the dark liquid, shrugged his shoulders, and downed it. The girls all looked at him in anticipation.

"She makes us take that stuff all the time. It tastes terrible!" said Frances.

"I guess I tasted worse, but I don't remember when," he said. When his coughing subsided, he continued with his report.

"Eddy killed a good-sized she bear. He pret' near came to an early end 'cause he wounded it, but didn't have time to reload 'fore it charged him. It chased him around a tree fer a spell 'fore it gave out. Scared the be*jesus* out of him. That meat helped, but with so many it didn't go that far. George, has anyone been out to hunt?"

"John Baptiste goes out when he can, but he hasn't seen anything. It's hard to get wood. Baptiste's been doin' his best, but we never have enough fire. With the snow so deep, we just don't have the strength to go far off."

"An' you have Miz Elizabeth and the children to look after too. Those men don't do much?"

"No, they ain't doin' anythin' but laying in bed. And I can't do much with this hand of mine the way it is."

"It looks bad, George. What're you doin' for it?"

"Tamsen pesters me with all the treatments she can think of."

"Well, we'll help get you in a stock of wood before we leave," said Milt.

Dec. 14

Jim Smith and Samuel Shoemaker died last night. Mr. Reinhardt is in a bad way. I think they gave in to malaise, a fugue, a disassociation with life. It is very difficult for me to be cheerful faced with a dwindling supply of food, constant wet and cold & the fear that grows inside of me. The sepsis has gone into George's shoulder and is very painful. Every day he is weaker. How can I keep my family in health until rescue comes?

"I cain't figure how they could just up and die. They weren't starvin', were they?" said Noah.

"No. They just gave up," I said. "I think they felt all was hopeless and they had no reason to live. It was a way to escape their misery."

"I tell you they will die. You don't fight to live, you die," said Baptiste. "Unless it is *El Destino*, then you die anyway."

"George," I said, "Noah and Milt are leaving as soon as the weather permits. We need to make up a note for the men to carry to Mr. Sutter. What should we ask for?"

George reflected for a minute. "Well, we've got to have animals to pack out on," he replied.

"He sent some fine-looking mules with Stanton," said Milt.

"Yeah," said Noah, "an' they're lost, likely driven off by those damned savages. Mules are best in snow, I suppose. I don't think Sutter'll have oxen, but mebbe he would," said Noah.

"Oxen are not gonna be any good in the snow," said George. "Let's ask for mules."

So we made our list. Five pack mules, two horses, and food supplies.

"Milt, when you leave, will you blaze a trail for us the best way back to your camp so we can follow it?" asked George.

"Well, the way it's snowing, any mark we make's goin' to be

covered up soon." He pointed to the west. "You can follow up this here stream a distance and you'll see a declivity going down to the left. Follow that down to the river and when the river goes off to the south like, keep goin' west and you'll find the camps on a stream right before a big lake."

"How far would you say it is?"

"I'd say 'bout seven miles or a mite less. John Baptiste knows the route, anyways."

"Yes," said Baptiste, "but I go 'round the ridge," he pointed to the south, "an' turn west. It take me along the river, same way. With *animales* an' women an' children, is the best way."

It was over a week before Noah and Milt could make their way back to the camps at the lake because of the storm. They left carrying the note from George authorizing Milt to be his agent and purchase at the settlements goods for our relief. We were fast using up our meager supplies.

Dec. 21

This morning we buried Mr. Reinhardt. Milt and Noah went back to the other camps today. John Denton went with them. It snowed all night with strong winds. We could hear trees crashing to the ground on the mountainside, a fearsome night. Today cloudy, windy, still snowing. George gave the leather bag to Mrs. Wolfinger and as we suspected, it was part of the money that had been stolen from her husband. We assume that the rest of the money is in the possession of Mr. Spitzer.

On the twenty-third of December, the weather cleared and I decided that we must make an effort to get some meat.

"Baptiste," I said, "I want you to go out on a hunt. In two days, we will celebrate the Lord's birthday and I hope, I wish, we could have a nice meal."

"The snow it is soft. I go to my knees even with the snowshoes. But I will try. Mr. Donner's rifle, perhaps I use it."

"George," I asked, "do you know where your rifles are?"

"They're under my bed," replied George. "Denton worked them over before he left. Baptiste, get that bundle out from under my bed. Yeah, that one."

Baptiste laid the bundle on the table and unwrapped it.

"Good thing he oiled 'em up good," said George. "Mr. Wolfinger, he had one that was better than these." He turned to Mrs. Wolfinger, standing by the fire. "Mrs. Wolfinger. *Gatte. Durchwuhlen?*" George held his arm out and sighted along it using his finger as if on a trigger.

"*Nein*. Keseberg." She made a motion as if taking something and moving away with it.

"Keseberg has it?" George turned back to the guns on the table. "I guess she has no use for it, but it's a valuable gun. Maybe she can get it back from him."

"*Nein, nein, geld, geld.*" Mrs. Wolfinger pointed to her open palm.

George shrugged. "She sold it to him, I guess."

Baptiste picked up one of the guns. "I use this one."

"Baptiste," said George, "the lead that you and Solomon been makin' ain't good enough, too rough. You need to use mine.That Hawkens is a good rifle. It'll give you distance, but best you practice a little. Tamsen, where'd we put the powder and ball?"

"It's probably still in the wagon, George."

"I know. I get it," said Baptiste.

"Baptiste, we will pray," I said. "We will ask God to show us his mercy and provide us with meat for our Lord's birthday."

"*Mi abuela,* when she has a need that is *especiale,* she go to the church an' she light a candle. Sometimes it work."

"Then we will do the same," I said.

I rummaged around in a trunk and found half a candle still in its holder. Kneeling down by the fire, I held the candle to an ember. The flame guttered and then held steady.

"Juan Baptiste, what does your grandmother do when she lights the candle?"

"She make the sign of the cross an' she think what she ask for. Sometimes the *padre* she tell him an' he ask *Dios* for it too."

"Baptiste, you do it the way of your grandmother and then I will do it my way."

I put the candle on the table and had everyone gather around. Juan Baptiste knelt in front of the candle, made the sign of the cross, and then whispered fervently. After a while he got up and I took his place.

"Our Father, God of us all, we ask you to be with Juan Baptiste as he goes out to hunt. Your will be done, Father, but our need is great. Bring an animal to Juan Baptiste so that we may nourish our bodies as we celebrate our Lord's birthday. Amen."

I got up and took Baptiste's hands in mine. "Juan Baptiste," I said, "you are a good hunter. You must tell yourself that you will not fail. If you are convinced you will find an animal to kill, it will be more likely to happen than if you do not. You must have every advantage if you are to be successful."

When he was ready to go, I gave him George's best gloves to wear and a hat that I had made from a soft fur. I handed him a little pack of food and followed him out of the hut. It had snowed during the night, but now it looked to be a fine day. *Perhaps we can wash some things today,* I thought.

"God will not let us down, Baptiste."

"*Espero que tienes razon.* I hope you are right."

I watched him until he disappeared in the dunes of snow and then went back into the hut and called to everyone to go outside.

"Everybody out. It's a fine day. It will be good to move about and get some sun. We must have a stock of wood. It can start snowing again at any moment."

I went to Betsey's camp and rousted out the two older boys. "It's Baptiste's job to get wood," complained Solomon. Solomon had been a little deranged and hard for Betsey to handle ever since he had insisted on going over to the lake camps one day by himself. He'd wandered in circles, finally making his way back exhausted and frozen.

"Baptiste's gone to hunt. I know it's hard, but wood we must have," I told him.

Juan Baptiste stayed out all day, coming back after dark empty-handed. The next morning he went out again. I gathered everyone around the fire, determined to have some semblance of our usual holiday. The children had all been moaning and crying, remembering the wonderful Christmas times we'd had back in Illinois. We never stopped thinking about food—roast duck, heaps of mashed potatoes, pies. Oh, it was agony. Mrs. Wolfinger went to the door of the hut and pulled open the door to look out. "*Achh, schnee, schnee.*"

"Yes, it's snowing again," I said. "Elitha, please, go over and ask Aunt Betsey to bring everyone here."

We gathered around the fire. I gave each one a share of the last little piece of dried deer meat and a square of hide boilings. One of Betsey's little ones began to cry. "I want bread." Then the other little ones began to cry and whimper too. I went to a kettle keeping hot on some coals and took out some flat cornbread-looking cakes that I had made.

"Here, I have one for each of you."

"What is it?"

"This is from the inner bark of a pine tree. It has life-sustaining properties and it's not bad tasting either."

"Is it bread, Auntie Tamsen?"

"A form of bread. And my other treat is Indian lemonade. You can have it cold as an iced drink or hot as a tea. It tastes good and it's good for you and because today is a special day, I have sweetened it."

"Mother! You always make us drink it without the sweet!"

"Well, I had only a little sugar left."

"What is Injun lemonade?" asked Betsey.

"It's made from sumac leaves. I gathered a basket of the plant when we were on the road."

"*Ja*. Sumac. *Goot*," said Mrs. Wolfinger.

I gave everyone a drink and a piece of the bread. Some found it agreeable, others did not, but they ate all of it anyway.

"Now we're going to play a game. We'll each picture a room in our new home in California and then describe it. After everyone has described their room, we'll decide who has the nicest. Eliza, you can go first."

"Ummm, I want lots of food in my room. I want yeast bread, an' corn an' apples an'—"

"Stop it, Eliza!" yelled Elitha. "Don't remind us! You're supposed to be telling us what you want in your room."

Eliza started to cry. "I'm sorry."

"It's all right, honey," I said.

We played our game, having a little fun for the first time in days and days. George participated too, insisting that a barn would qualify as a beautiful room.

"No, Father. A barn stinks. How can it be beautiful if it stinks?"

"To a farmer a barn never smells bad. Don't you remember the smell of the hay? Doesn't hay smell good?" asked George.

"Close your eyes and see if you can remember the smell of hay," I suggested.

"Mother, do you mean green hay from the field or old hay like straw?"

"Either one."

"I can remember the hay in the barn smell," said Frances. "I like it. I like to climb in the hay and play. But it's dusty and makes me sneeze."

"It would be so nice to have some of that straw and hay to put here on the floor, wouldn't it? But we do have pine needles. Perhaps today we can cut pine boughs to put down for our Christmas day tomorrow."

We played our games all afternoon, taking time to bring in some pine boughs. We put the fresh ones on the beds and the old ones down on the floor. The scent of the pine needles helped all of us breathe better.

All day in the back of my mind I worried about Baptiste. I

knew he'd be soaked through and frozen. Late in the day the girls and I went out, anxiously looking for sight of him. The rain had turned to snow. *Oh, why did I send him out?*

"Shhh, girls, listen. Do you hear something?"

Straining to see in the direction of the sound, I could see a dark form approaching, barely discernable in the white gloom of falling snow.

I called and waved my shawl. "Baptiste, Baptiste!" As he approached I could make out what the sound was—Baptiste was singing!

"Dans mon chemin j'ai recontre," he saw us and waved. *"Trois cavalieres bien montees—"* His clothing was covered with ice and he was wet all the way through, shivering and shaking with the cold. He was pulling a furry shape. The girls ran to him, dancing and jumping around, squealing with delight.

"Mother, Mother, Baptiste has killed something!"

I helped him drag the animal to the small clearing at the door to our hut. "I'll get you a blanket, Baptiste. Get those wet clothes off and come in to the fire. I'll fix you some coffee."

"I p-p-prayed many times to G-God to send an animal close an' he sent me a bear cub! But his m-m-mama no want me to have him an' me she almost kill."

"Your prayers and ours were answered, Juan Baptiste."

When Baptiste came inside George clapped him on the back. "Good work, son. Godamighty, you're frozen! Get over here by the fire an' get warmed up. Tamsen, you got coffee made?"

Baptiste told us of the struggle to kill the cub. He'd spied the bears, a mother with two cubs, from a distance. He wanted to kill the mother bear, as there would have been much more meat, but knew she would be hard to kill with one shot. He decided that he would try to kill one of the cubs.

Baptiste was shaking and stuttering from being cold, but was also so excited from the kill that he couldn't stop talking. "I see the b-b-bears are coming toward me, but I ask myself how I do this thing without the mother bear she attack me. I think they will p-p-pass this big tree, so I hide behind the tree and I wait.

I think they never come they are so slow! I am f-f-freezing from the rain an' s-snow. But after a time they come. I take the careful aim an' I k-kill the little one."

As soon as Baptiste had warmed himself and changed into dry clothes we began cutting up the bear. It was a good-sized second year cub.

"How did you manage to drag this animal so far? He must weigh well over a hundred and fifty pounds."

"Him I pull with my rope. I no think I can do it, but I no want to cut him in pieces. The wolves they will eat him before I can go back. So I pray for strength an' I do it, but many times I stop to rest."

Thank God! I thought. *We can live on this meat for several weeks if I stretch it with boiled hides. I must give Juan Baptiste extra portions to keep him strong.* I set the entrails to the side thinking I would make use of them later, but the dog was frantically whining and biting at the carcass, so I gave him some. As we worked cutting up the meat, Baptiste told me of something he had learned.

"*Señora,* I learn from an old man who was a trapper—I think he live most of his life with Indians—he say if you have a bad sore, you take the stomach of a bear an' you put it on the sore an' it will help to make it well. Maybe it can help the arm of the *Señor* Donner?"

"It won't hurt to try it. Cut the stomach out and set it aside, as soon as—"

Baptiste put his hand on my arm. "*Señora, mire, el lobo,*" he whispered.

I turned to see a huge wolf at the top of the snow peering over the edge at us. He'd planted himself with legs wide apart, his head bobbing up and down, tongue lolling, as he tried to decide if he could jump in and grab some of the meat. I picked up a piece of wood and hurled it at him, but he ducked away. In a moment he was back.

"I would kill him, but the meat it tastes like rot. I eat it one time, and it make me sick."

Baptiste had leaned his gun against the hut. I picked it up. "Is the gun charged? Shoot him. He's worrying me."

"Let us finish the work. Tomorrow I will think about killing the wolves," replied Baptiste.

I brought the barrel of the gun up. "Then I will do it," I said. Baptiste jumped to the side.

"Señora! Por favor, tome cuidado!"

"He's gone, but he'll be back and he'll come down here, right next to our door. You must kill him, Baptiste."

Baptiste took the gun from me and climbed up the steps.

"He is gone. Tomorrow is better. I will hide myself an' wait for him. For his dinner he will have the ball of lead."

That evening we were a much happier group as we sat around the fire, each roasting their own strip of bear meat. I supplemented the small pieces with a stew I'd made with a large bone, bear fat, the pine-tree inner bark, and cattail roots. I sent the older girls over to Betsey's camp with food for her family with an invitation to come to Christmas dinner the next day.

"Elitha, be sure to tell the boys to carry a rifle. That wolf worries me. He might attack one of the little ones, he's so bold."

Mrs. Wolfinger knew that I was talking about wolves. *"Die Wolfe, ich hasse das gerauch! Es nacht mir Wahnsinnig!"*

"I think she said something about the sound of the wolves making her crazy," said George.

"I hate it too. I want Baptiste to kill those that keep coming around. I am afraid of them."

When they came back Solomon and William were with them, eager to hear about the successful hunt.

"The mother bear, she no see me, but she hear the sound of my gun an' she see the smoke," said Baptiste. "She roar an' she come at me so I climb the tree fast. She almost reach me with her claws but I climb higher an' she start to shake the tree."

"Godamighty. I'll bet you peed your pants when she came after you," said Solomon.

"I was scared, but I no scared that much, Solomon," said Baptiste.

Dec. 24

Baptiste has returned with a fine bear cub. Our prayer for food has been answered. Each day I pray to God and ask Him to deliver us from this prison of snow. But even so, I wonder what God's will is in this horrible drama. This evening it has turned warmer and is beginning to rain and sleet. When I marked this day off on my calendar, a wave of sadness came over me. My first husband, Mr. Dozier, died on Christmas Eve, fourteen years ago.

The next morning Mrs. Wolfinger and I searched through our wagons for anything that had nutritional value. Most of my botanicals had long since disappeared into the kettle.

We found several cups of flour still remaining in a flour bag in the bottom of one of the lidded kegs, along with a pound or two of beans tucked in a tin container in a corner of the wagon. I also found some roots. The fragrance of the cooking drew everyone to our hut long before the meal was ready. I passed out an ample portion of the food to everyone.

George stood up. "Let's give thanks."

Everyone bowed their heads, some sitting, some standing. I peeked at the girls to see that they were behaving properly and they were, kind of. They had their heads down, but were nibbling at their food at the same time.

"Almighty good and gracious God, we thank you for providing this supply of food and we thank you for this fine young man, Juan Baptiste, who has brought in the food. Watch over and protect us as we wait out these terrible storms. Amen."

Everyone sat down wherever they could and began to eat.

"I know there must be a God, but mostly I think the God he sends the bad luck," said Juan Baptiste. "It is good that I kill the bear an' we have food, but why are we to starve in the first place? What we do that the God decide we must suffer?"

"I understand your point, Baptiste, but it's a matter of faith," replied George. "We are here for a purpose that we as mortals cannot see. We must have faith that in the end, whatever an' whenever that end is, it is for the best."

"I think there ain't no God," said William. "If there is, he don't leave civilization. He stays back to home doin' fer people that's smart enough not to journey to California. Aunty Tamsen, this is the most wonderful meal I have ever eaten in my life. I'm wondering what this potato-like stuff is?"

"Do you remember when those Indians visited our camp and gave us some roots? That's what it is, just a starchy vegetable."

"Oh no!" cried Solomon. "Thank God I haven't eaten mine yet!"

"Whatever is the matter with you? It's good. I'll eat yourn if'n you don't want it," said Betsey.

"You recollect when that Injun gave us some 'a those roots? He was eating the heads off'n grasshoppers an' chewin' on these roots. I didn't cotton to the grasshoppers, but I et a bunch of the roots. All night long I had terr'ble stomach pains an' had to run fer the bushes. That there Injun, he came back the next day an' offered more roots, expectin' to share beef an' biscuits with us again. He minded that I'd et the roots the evening before an' now I was refusin' 'em. I had a hard time of it to make 'em mind those roots made me sick."

Solomon stood up and demonstrated the "sign" language he used to convince the savage that the roots were a problem for him. "I pointed at them roots, then I bent over, holding my belly an' groanin'. Then I pointed to my rear an' made some sounds an' the Injun understood me perfect!" And so did we, and everybody laughed at the story. It was good to find something we could laugh about.

"I don't think this small quantity would have any effect," I said. "And even if so, it would be beneficial."

Everyone looked at the little lump of root on their plates thinking this over and I noticed George slip his off on the floor in front of the dog who promptly gulped it down.

I looked at George. "Maybe it's a good thing. He's eaten Frances's shoes and perhaps it'll help in the process of getting them through him."

"He was chewing on that bear skin all night," said Elitha. "If the shoes don't kill him, that fur will."

Betsey and I had made new mittens and stockings for everyone and for my three little ones I'd made dolls. The girls were thrilled with the little snowshoes Baptiste had made for them and they rushed outside right after we ate to try them out. I read stories, George read the Bible, and we told them that any day now we should see rescuers coming. It had been enough time for James Reed to gather supplies and horses. Yes, surely rescuers would arrive soon.

January 2, 1847
A New Year

We feel no joy or celebration. It was fair today, water dripping everywhere. The days drag on. Baptiste forages for wood and clears the snow. Each day I take the bear's stomach from George's arm and wash the arm and put the piece back. His arm looks a little better but he is very weak. I do not know what is sustaining him, as he insists I give the children most of his food.

The end of the first week in January, Milt Elliott and Eliza Williams, the Reed's hired girl, came to our camp. We welcomed the company, because we were anxious to hear news from the other camp. Any change in the daily routine relieved our boredom.

"Oh, Miz Donner," said Eliza, "it be the worse kind of fate we have. Miz Reed, Virginia an' Milt an' me, we tried to get over agin' a few days ago an' we like to froze to death. We couldn't find our way an' had to come back."

Eliza spoke in a strange flat voice that was hard to understand. I think it was because she was almost completely deaf, probably since early childhood. I tried to remember which childhood disease caused deafness, but it escaped me.

"Baylis died the middle of December," said Eliza. "Went into a delirium like an' was gone. Now I have nobody."

"We heard of it, Eliza. I'm sorry."

"Charlie Burger died a week or two back," said Milt. "Several are in a bad way, too weak to get around. Breen's been sufferin' from the gravels. His boys get wood an' help the others."

"We've had only hides to eat," said Eliza. "I jes' can't eat that gluey stuff, I throws it up. Miz Reed tol' me hides was all she had an' I'd have to live or die on 'em. The Graves's got meat still, but they ain't sharing it. Do you all have any food at all?"

"We have only a little bear meat. Soon we will have no meat at all, only hides. I still have some cattail roots. They make a tolerable stew with a little meat. We must look out for Jacob's family now and we must be very careful with our stores. But we have plenty of coffee and tea."

Although Eliza was almost deaf, if she could see a person's mouth when talking, she understood most of what they said. I handed her a cup of tea. "I've made you some tea. It's soothing to one's nerves and will help you forget about food. It has a little sustenance, too."

"Thank you kindly, missus, but there ain't nothin' that's goin' to keep me from thinkin' about food! I'll drink this an' some of yer coffee will taste good to me, too."

"I'll have some coffee, ma'am," said Milt.

"The coffee helps git us through the day," said George, "that'n tobacco. Smokin' my pipe is just about the only comforting thing left." George handed Milt a sack of tobacco. "You got a pipe with you, Milford?"

"Yessir. Thank you kindly." Milt filled his pipe and got it going. The smell of the burning tobacco was sharp and good. Milt took his knife out of his pocket, picked up one of the firewood sticks, and began whittling on it with the knife. He looked at me.

"Keeps my hands busy. I'll make some fire startin's fer you."

We were all quiet for a while, sipping our coffee and tea, the men puffing on their pipes. I watched Milt as he stripped off small yellow-white pieces of wood onto the ground in front of him. He cleared his throat. "I feel bad that I can't do nothin' to help Miz Reed an' the children. It's my fault that Mr. Reed had to leave them. If'n I hadn't got to arguin' with Snyder, if'n I'd just waited instead of tryin' to drive the wagon past—" His face twisted in anguish. "It's a hard burden to bear, thinkin' I'm responsible."

My heart went out to him. "Milt, it was not your fault. You were not responsible for Snyder's anger—he was. You were not responsible for James drawing a knife and plunging it into the man—James was. The whole matter could have been just a small annoyance, but something in James triggered a murderous impulse. He should have had the control to step back. If he had backed off and left Snyder alone, it would not have happened. You followed the correct path by stepping aside. He did not. You cannot blame yourself."

Milt nodded his head. "My pap always used to tell me that fightin's somethin' you do when you've tried everythin' else, an' I think I've followed that. But it eats at me." Milt puffed on his pipe for a while, then continued. "We've done gone through the four oxen Missus Reed bought from Breen an' Graves. The company agreed to look out for the family, but now none of 'em will help her, leastways they won't part with any food."

"That Miz Graves's mean as a stewed witch," said Eliza. "Miz Reed went to get the hides off'n her cabin an' Miz Graves wouldn't let her take 'em. Miz Graves told Miz Reed she has to pay fer the two oxen she got from her before she can have her goods."

"Hard times can make a person say things they don't really mean, Eliza," I said.

"I thought Mrs. Graves was nice," said Leanna.

"Well, you ain't had to live rubbing elbows with her like we have. Miz Reed, she ain't accustomed to have to make do or not get her way. An' you know, it's strange," said Eliza, "but Miz Reed, so weak an' frail like with those terr'ble headaches, she don't have 'em anymore, leastways that I notice."

"That's right, she don't," said Milt. "I guess God just up an' cured her, 'cause she has to look out fer the children an' all by herself."

"I no think *Dios* he cure her," said Baptiste. "I think she no has the husband to feel sorry for her, so it no good to have the headache."

Baptiste had no airs about him and always seemed to be able to peel away the layers of pretense or falseness that others maintained about themselves. I had often wondered whether Margaret's illnesses weren't caused by a desire to retreat or perhaps an inability to handle situations or pressures.

"We've still not found all of our oxen," said George. "We keep hopin' for a good thaw so's some of 'em will start showin'. We found twelve of the twenty we had left, but lost six of 'em in the snow again. They were poor, mostly skin and bones, but if we could find 'em we could share some with you. I cain't do a goldurned thing, I'm weak as a kitten. If it wasn't for Baptiste, we'd have a mighty hard time."

"Some of 'em's talkin' about usin' the dead fer food," said Milt. "They ain't come to it yet." Milt paused and cleared his throat. "I dunno. I think I'd rather pass on from starvation than—" His voice trailed away and he stared into the fire for a while, then continued whittling on his stick.

"Things are that bad then?" asked George.

"With some of 'em, it is. Graves still has some meat, an' Breen, but the rest of us is livin' on hides. I got the last of Missus Reed's meat from Breen two days before Christmas. We've eaten all the dogs that were still with us."

"The only dog we still had disappeared a few days after Christmas," said George. "He was such skin and bones, he wouldn't have made much of a meal anyway. I wish it would thaw off where we could find some of our stock. You could take some back, Milt, help the people out," said George. "They must be desperate to be talkin' like that."

Baptiste got up from where he was sitting cross-legged on the floor and began to work on the fire, poking and gathering the coals. The damp wood sizzled in defiance as he put more sticks on the fire. "You know the *Señor* Kit Carson? He tell me that one time he eat the man meat. He was in the camp of the Crow Indians an' he did not know this. They make the fool with him. He say the meat was *chungo*—" Baptiste paused and muttered to himself. "*Que es el Inglés*? Uh, rope. It was ... like rope." Baptiste shrugged. "Maybe it was an old one. He say the color was strange, kind of white. I do not know if he tell me the truth."

"Oh, please," said Elitha, "you're making me sick!"

Baptiste looked down at his feet, crestfallen. "I only say what someone tell me."

"Some will do it to live," I said. "Others won't. I cannot say what we would do. I hope we never have to make a choice."

"I would rather die!" exclaimed Elitha.

"You ate the mouse. How much is the difference?" asked Baptiste.

Tears welled up in Elitha's eyes. "I hate you, Baptiste," she murmured.

George frowned and raised his hand, signaling Baptiste not to say anything more. We became silent, the only sound for a few moments the fire murmuring at the wood and the scratch, scratch of a branch against the frozen hides on the top of our hut. *It is a terrible thing to contemplate,* I thought, *but if we should reach a point where we have no other food, what would we do?*

I wanted to change the mood that had descended upon us. "Elitha, Leanna, go over to Aunt Betsey's and ask them to come. They'll enjoy a change of scene and talking to our visitors." I caught Elitha in mid-whine. "No argument, Elitha. It will be good for all of you to get out."

"I go with them," said Baptiste. "I take the *Señora* Betsey some wood."

The girls bundled up and then helped Baptiste load some wood on a buffalo skin. I could hear their chatter fade away as they went off. "I don't know what we would do without Baptiste," said George. "He's not very big, but he's strong. From hardy stock, I guess."

I had taken my blue sprig dinnerware out of the wagon and arranged it on a shelf made from an empty wood supply box. It cheered me a little to see my things around me. I decided to serve the meal I prepared that evening in my dishes. I gave everyone a cup of soup, a small piece of pine-tree bread, and a small square of the tallow I had tried out from boiling the bones and scraps left from the bear. I felt that I should not be giving our food to our visitors, but how could I not?

"What is this stuff?" asked Eliza, holding up the square of pine bark.

"It is from the inner bark of the pine tree. Milt, tell your people over there about this. It is not easy to obtain and you can only get a small amount from each tree. It has sustenance. At least it can help keep one from starving if you can get enough of it."

"It don't taste bad, kind'a sweet," said Milt.

"Well, I used the last bit of my molasses in these, which makes it better. If you have any fat to mix with it, that helps."

"I hanker for salt powerful bad. We ain't had no salt at all since that you gave me last time I was here."

"I can give you a little more. We will share what food we have with you for a few days, but we won't be able to feed you longer. Surely the Graves family or the Breen family will give you something," I told them.

Eliza started crying. "The Breens have plenty of meat, but they won't share."

"They did take in Virginia," said Milt. "So at least maybe she's getting some food."

"That don't help us none." Eliza snuffled for a while, poking at the fire with a stick, raising sparks that blew upward in the dark.

"Listen, I think the wind's changed," said George, "it's coming from the northwest. Likely it's goin' to storm again."

"The goddamn storms never stop," growled Milt.

"I don't hate anythin' in this world as much as I hate snow," said Betsey.

Milt got up and pulled open the door. A blast of cold, moist air showered us with tiny sharp particles of ice. He quickly pushed the door shut.

"Well," said Eliza, "we cain't leave until it stops snowing anyways."

• • •

By mid-January the snow was twelve to fourteen feet deep in the drifts. One clear day we sent Baptiste to the other camps to see how they were faring. He took some tobacco and tea, of which we had plenty. He found they were in bad shape, same as we were. Several had died and several others were in such a pitiful condition that they would likely die soon. They were very short of food, living mostly on hides. The Breen family had taken in Mrs. Reed and her children when the hides that covered her shanty were needed for food. It was wet in our tents for days on end. Our beds and clothes were damp, even wet. Sometimes Baptiste could not get wood and we had no fire. The snow covered us so deep that little daylight could enter.

On days when the clouds cleared and the sun shone upon our world, our mood lifted, and we would warm ourselves outside and dry our things. We would look to the mountains hoping to see rescuers. Baptiste would climb a tree and spend many hours there looking for the men and listening for the halloos. Surely, we thought, they would come soon.

One day I was outside in my chair in a pensive mood, thinking of my childhood home. The warm sun reminded me of days I had spent in the garden and into my mind came a picture of a rosebush, my mother's, her favorite in all her garden. I could smell the fragrance of it so sharp that I looked around to see if there wasn't something nearby. Oh! How painful were the memories.

My precious Eliza came to me with her apron all bundled up holding something. "Mother, I have a surprise for you. Look." She held up her apron and unfolded it carefully. "Oh, it's gone!"

She had been fascinated by a sunbeam that for a brief time graced our doorway. She was enthralled with the bright little ray and sat down under it, holding it on her lap, then passing her hands through it, breaking it in two. It jumped and flitted playfully from one place to another. She caught it up in her apron and came to me. I explained to her what had happened and we went to the doorway just in time to see the last ray disappear.

"I hope it comes back again. Will it?" she asked.

"Oh, certainly, if there is sun tomorrow, it will visit you again. But you must watch carefully, for it comes for only a few minutes."

We tramped over to the other camp to see Betsey and the children. I was appalled at how weak and listless they all were. "Betsey," I said, "the sun is wonderful today. Bring the children out for a while. They need the light. Solomon, you and William get out and get your mother some wood."

Pushing and prodding, I finally got them outside for a little while. The two older boys listlessly poked around and found a few limbs sticking out of the snow, but as soon as they'd drug them close to the hut, they disappeared inside. I admonished them.

"Solomon, that is not enough wood. You boys go right back out there until you have a supply for a week or two."

"Aw, get Baptiste to do it."

Picking up one of the limbs I swung it at Solomon and then William. "Get out there. Right now. Get your mother some wood." They ducked away from me and grudgingly began searching for wood.

On good days we would take our clothes and bedding outside and drape the things over a line to dry and I would clean and renew our hut as best I could. I would put the girls to tasks, too.

"Mother, why do we have to work when we're so tired?" asked Georgeanna.

"I'm dizzy when I get up," said Leanna.

"You must keep active or you will not be strong enough to walk when the rescuers come to take us out."

"It hurts me," whined Frances.

"Yes, and it hurts me too, but I want to stay strong so I move about as much as I can and you must also. Look, it's so pretty today, we don't want to spoil it by moping around. Let's finish the work and then we'll have a tea party. Tonight I will plan a special time and I have a surprise, a treat."

"Is it something to eat? I'm so hungry," said Leanna.

"What will we do?" asked Frances.

"Wait and see."

I managed to get the girls up and busy with the cleaning and although they protested, they began to feel better and became more cheerful.

"When it is dark Baptiste will build a fire and we will have our party outside," I said.

"Mother, it's freezing. Why can't we have our party inside?"

"We'll bundle up. Believe me, it will be all right."

Baptiste built the fire early and by dark the fire had enough coals to heat a kettle of water. There was much grumbling, but after I told the girls that only the ones who were outside would participate in the surprise, they all trooped out and sat down. Opening the lid of the kettle I had brought out, I took out a jar.

"Yesterday when I was going through a trunk I found this." I showed them the jar. "Do you remember back home in the winter, we would all gather and play games and have music, and make popcorn in the fireplace?"

"Yes. Mother, is that popcorn?"

"Yes, there will be enough for everyone."

I placed the kettle over the fire and when it was hot a little piece of fat went in to melt and then the popcorn.

"We have just enough to make two kettles, one for us and Baptiste will take one to Aunt Betsey and your cousins. I couldn't get them to come over."

When all the corn had popped, Baptiste took the kettle from the fire and placed it on some sticks of wood before us. I gave a bowl of popcorn to each one. "Eat very, very slowly and drink lots of tea. We don't want to have stomachaches."

"Mother," said George, "give the girls my share."

I looked at George and nodded my head. It would do no good for me to argue. Frances and Georgeanna took the kernels one by one and chewed slowly around the edges, popping the last bit in their mouth before taking another. Little Eliza ate hers as fast as she could. I sighed as I looked over at the three girls, so happy with this small bonanza of food. *I must keep them strong. I must keep them alive!*

"Baptiste, I'll make the other kettle and then you can take it to Betsey." Eliza held out her bowl to me. "Mother, please, may I have some more?"

"I'll share mine with you, Eliza."

When Baptiste came back, I told everybody to look up at the sky and I would teach them to read the stars and how to recognize the North Star. I gazed up. It seemed one could almost touch the star clusters that were suspended above us like chandeliers against the deep blue black of the heavens.

"First you must be able to find the Little Dipper. You know the Big Dipper already. Then you find two stars that make up the Little Dipper's handle. These two stars are called the pointer stars. The North Star lies above these two stars in a straight line about five times the distance between the pointer stars. Has anyone found the Little Dipper?"

"I see it, I see it," exclaimed Frances. "But I don't see the North Star."

"The North Star stays in one place all the time and always to the north of you. So that way you can tell which way is generally north. It's a very large and bright star. I will tell you a story about this star, an Indian legend explaining why the North Star stands still. There was a brave Indian named Na-Gah who tried to impress his father by climbing the tallest cliff he could find. He climbed and climbed until one day he found himself at the top of a very high mountain. The mountain was so tall that Na-Gah looked down on all the other mountains. Unfortunately, there was no way down. When his father came looking for him, he found Na-Gah stuck high above. He didn't want his son to suffer because of his bravery, so he turned Na-Gah into a star that everyone can see and that star honors all living things. The star's real name is Polaris. I have found it. Does anyone else see it?"

"Why does it have two names?"

"It is called the Pole Star, or Polaris, because the earth's axis always points to it in the northern sky. That's a little hard for you to comprehend, but you will understand that it is always in the north."

"I know of this," said Baptiste. "I learn this by an old man I travel with. If you can tell the stars, it helps you to know where you are or which way to go."

"It's called celestial navigation," I said.

"Mother, how did you know about the stars?"

"I was taught by my father, your grandfather. I learned the art of navigation and surveying from him."

"What is that?"

"That is when you learn how to find direction and how to mark off boundaries. For instance, a new town needs to make boundaries for each farm so that they can keep everything straight and property can be sold or transferred."

"Can I learn?"

"Well, yes, of course, after you have had more schooling. It is rather complicated, but for now we will learn about the stars."

Jan. 31

It froze very hard last night, and today is cloudy, no sun to cheer us. Another dreary month has passed and I worry constantly that we will not survive to see another unless help comes over the mountain. Surely the party that left in December has reached the settlements. Help must be on the way, it is past time. Oh, God, have mercy on us.

February 19, 1847
Alder Creek

"*Señora! Veo a los hombres! Señora* Tamsen, there are men coming. It is men from California. Three men are coming!"

Juan Baptiste began yelling and jumping up and down. I was tending my fire outside, preparing to melt some snow for washing, when Baptiste came to the top of the snow steps. I grabbed his hand and we started toward the men, waving and yelling, but were stopped by the deep soft snow. I took off my shawl and waved it in the air and Baptiste shouted.

"We are here ... we are here. Men, men ..."

"Oh God, do they see us? Do they see us?"

"*Si, Señora.* They come."

We stood there in such excitement and anticipation that it seemed hours before the men came close. Walking in the lead was a man who, with all his winter clothing on, looked to be about as broad as he was tall, his face red and chapped, his lips cracked and sore from exposure.

"Miz Donner? I'm John Rhodes. We sure been worried about you people, and it seems, rightly so."

"Yes, I am Mrs. George Donner. We are very glad to see you. You weren't able to bring mules?"

"No, ma'am. No way can mules, or any livestock, get over the snow. We brung what food we could carry in. Most of it we cached back along the trail to use on the way out."

"Well, we're very glad to have what you have brought. Please come in and talk to my husband. He's suffering from weakness caused by an injury to his hand."

Mr. Rhodes turned and pointed to the other men.

"Miz Donner, this is Sep Moultrie an' the man coming up is Reason Tucker. His foot's been frostbit. He's needin' some doctorin' on it. Men, this is Miz Donner, George's wife."

The men nodded their heads in my direction. "Ma'am."

"You've got another family here?" asked Mr. Rhodes.

"Yes, Jacob's family, George's brother." I pointed in the direction of the other camp. "Their camp is just over there."

"I take the men there," said Juan Baptiste. Mr. Rhodes instructed Mr. Moultrie and Mr. Tucker to proceed on to Betsey's camp and give her some of the food they had brought and then he and I went inside our hut. George was unhappy when he learned that the men hadn't been able to bring horses.

"We couldn't bring 'em up further than the snow line, Mr. Donner. Sure wish we could've. It would have been easier on us."

Mr. Rhodes went on to explain to us that only those who were strong enough to walk could be taken back with them. We were bitterly disappointed, but understood the situation.

"There's several from the lake camps that aren't strong enough to go," said Mr. Rhodes. "We're gonna try to carry out some of the children. We haven't enough men to carry more, but another rescue party will be along in a short while. That is, if it quits storming. If it don't quit, well, it'll take 'em longer. We'll leave what we can spare in the way of provisions."

Betsey came to our tent, crying and wringing her hands. I was shocked at how bad she looked. Her face was gray and gaunt, her body nothing but angular bones. Betsey, the kindest-hearted, the most generous of all of us, was falling apart, mentally and physically.

"I would go, but they won't take my little ones an' I cain't leave them. I won't leave them. William and George can go. What did they tell you?"

"They can't take our three little ones either, Betsey, but Leanna and Elitha are strong enough, and Noah and Mrs. Wolfinger. We'll just have to wait for the next relief party."

"I don't know why those men cain't each carry a child."

"It might weaken them to the point that they couldn't make it and both would die," I said. "We don't want that."

"What have we done to deserve this?" cried Betsey. "If God loves us like the preachers say, why ain't he watching out fer us? What kind of a God would allow this to happen?" Betsey collapsed on the floor, wailing.

"Elizabeth. Elizabeth, listen," said George. "There's always a picture that we, as mortals, can't see. Dyin's not that bad. We're all goin' to end that way anyway. We'll all be together again in the afterlife."

"That's supposed to make me feel better, watching my children suffer an' starve?" she asked between sobs. "Nothin' to give but hide boilin's, their little hands beggin' for somethin', anythin' ... oh, God." She stopped sobbing and was quiet for a few moments, then looked at me. "They ain't leavin' enough food to keep us alive fer more'n a day or two. I told that Mr. Tucker that if'n we didn't find our animals under the snow by then, we'd have to start diggin' up the dead bodies for food." Betsey put her hands over her face and began sobbing again. "Oh God, what have I come to?"

"We still have hides, Betsey," I said.

"My babies have got to have food or they're going to die. I see nothing else I can do. They cain't eat that glue, Tamsen. They're weak an' sick, look like death. I got to do it."

"Betsey, the teas that I make do help sustain—"

"I don't like them teas. I drink the coffee an' I give it to the young'uns, they like it better." Betsey was pensive for a long moment. "Tamsen, do you recollect, just after we left home, that swarm of gnats that got into our bread dough an' turned it black?"

"Yes, we threw it away."

"I was thinkin' of it all day yesterday. I'd eat it now an' be glad. I'd give everything I have for that pan of bread dough. I'd be happy to just have the crumbs we swept off the table at home." Betsey sighed deeply and fidgeted with the edge of a blanket. "Did you talk to Juan Baptiste? He's wantin' to go, he tol' me."

"George promised him if he would stay that he would always have a home with us in California and be taken care of. He's reluctant, but he's agreed not to leave. I feel badly for him. He has no obligation to us."

We were heartsick to part with Elitha and Leanna, but knew it was best to get them out of the mountains. I dressed them in as many layers of clothing as they could wear and provided each with a blanket to use as a shawl in the day and a blanket at night. When they were ready to go, they went to George to say goodbye.

"Girls," said George, "I know it's hard, but think about how wonderful it will be to be in California. We'll be along as soon as we can." George looked up at me. "Did you give them money?"

"Yes, I sewed it in their cloaks. They each have ten quarter-eagles and some silver. I would rather give them all of it in silver, but fifty dollars would be too heavy. Elitha, don't show the money. Take only a little out at a time. Do not let people know you have money or they might take it from you. Perhaps you could leave the money with Mr. Sutter to handle for you. Yes, that would be a good idea. It is enough to keep you until we can join you. I know it's hard, but you must be brave."

"Honey, that's not enough," said George. "What if we don't get out before spring?"

"I don't know what kind of people they might encounter. I am sure Mr. Sutter will see that they are cared for and we can repay him when we arrive there."

I gave Elitha a letter to give to Mr. Sutter, asking if he would serve as a guardian to look after the girls until such time as we could join them.

Leanna began to cry again. "We want to wait until we can all go together. We don't want to go with strangers."

"Noah will be with you, and Mrs. Wolfinger, and William and George, and the Reed family. You'll be with people you know."

"Girls, come here, sit down," said George. They sat beside George on the bed clutching their reticules, tears streaming down their faces.

"You'll just be gettin' to California before the rest of us. There's more rescuers comin' an' spring will be here before long. They'll bring mules to carry us out. It's just a temporary thing. You're both old enough to be alone for a little while, aren't you?"

They nodded their heads and rubbed the tears out of their eyes.

"Yes, Father, we'll try."

"Come along, girls," I said, "I think the men are anxious to be off."

As we left the hut, Mr. Rhodes stood, bending over as he tried to shift his pack higher on his back. "Miz Donner, I tol' that Mex that he needs to stay 'cause you ain't got anybody to get yer wood an' such—he got some surly with me."

"He's agreed to stay, Mr. Rhodes. Please take care of our girls. Will you deliver them to Mr. Sutter?"

"Ma'am, I will do my best. Another relief should be here in a few days if the storms will hold off."

"Elitha, look out for Leanna, she's not as strong as you are."

"I know. I'll help her."

The three little girls and I watched them move off, the strongest in the lead and each thereafter stretching to step in the footsteps of the one before. They kept turning to look back, waving again and again, until they disappeared from view. Heavy of heart, I took my rocking chair outside to our patio. Baptiste placed the three little ones all in a row on his blanket atop the snow.

"Now, be little *ángelitas* an' I will tell you a story an' also I will teach you some more words in the *español, está bien?*"

"Si!" They all chorused.

"*Mi Papá,* he was a trapper an' hunter an' so I was too. *Un hombre muy fuerte,* as men must be who go to the mountains. *Hombre muy fuerte.* Very strong man. *Comprenden?*"

Another chorus of "*si, si*".

"That is very good. *Muy bien! Mi papá,* he went deep into the lands of the Indians an' took the furs. Sometimes the Indians, they find the trappers an' many they kill in ways that were terrible."

"Did they kill your papa?"

"Yes, I think it was so. *Mi pápa,* he go on the fur hunt an' he never come back."

"When your papa didn't come back, what did you do?"

"This was when I was very young an' I was raised by *mi abuela,* my grandmother. She is a Spanish lady, a lady of worth. I hope to return to see her before she die, but first I must go to California an' see for myself what it is that is there. Since I have nine years I work. I work here an' there, I hunt the furs, I work on the freight wagons. One day a great company of men came to our village. The leader was the Captain Frémont. I hear that his expedition is going to the Pacific Ocean an' I say to *mi abuela,* I will go to him an' offer myself an' I will travel to far-off places. I will tell him that I speak the language of the Utah an' I know the language of signs."

"What is that?" asked Frances.

"The language of signs is when you talk with your hands instead of your mouth. This language is known by all Indians an' many white men. You remember that I show you?"

"Can you teach us some of that language?" asked Frances. "I would like to talk that way instead of this way. Leanna says that I am too loud." Frances burst into tears. "But Leanna's gone—"

"I don't want 'Litha an' 'Anna to go," said Eliza and she started crying too.

"Little ones, you must not cry. They are going to California where there is no snow an' the sun shines an' there is food to eat. You miss them, but they are going to be happy! Now, stop crying an' I will tell you more of the story."

The girls sniffled a little more, but began to listen to Baptiste's story.

"This man Frémont, he had a very large company of men an' horses. When they came to my village, they wanted to buy food, but there no was food to sell. So they camped an' men went to the fort of the *Señor* Bent to buy supplies. That is when I talk to the *Señor* Carson. He ask me if I know the work of horses."

Baptiste stood up and pounded his chest. *"Por supuesto! Soy el mejor*! I say I am the best! I no need to speak the *Inglés* because the *Señor* Carson, he know the *español muy bien."* Baptiste sat down again.

"They employ me to care for the horses, but I hunt too. Sometimes I trap for furs. One time when I was out with my traps, Indians they come by the stream where I am. They no see me, but they saw where I walk. They were the Utah."

"I don't like Indians, they scare me," said Georgeanna.

"They don't scare me!"

"Then why did you cry when those Indians came to camp?"

Eliza put her thumb in her mouth, a habit I thought she'd given up. "I did *not* cry!"

"Shhh! Let Baptiste tell his story!" said Frances.

"I know they will find me, so I go in the water. My traps they are upstream so I go downstream. When I leave the water I was almost frozen, but I find a bear cave. Can you guess what was in the cave?"

"A bear?"

"Yes! A big mama bear and a cub."

"Did they growl at you and eat you up?" asked Eliza.

"I am here, so how the bear eat me up? No, the bears were in their winter sleep. My wet clothes, I take them off an' I lay near that mama bear, I am a little warm. I stay there for two days an' then I think the Indians they are gone an' I go out of the cave. But the Indians they steal my traps so I no could hunt the furs anymore. I go back to the *Señor* Frémont's party. They no let me in camp."

"Why not?"

"They say I stink. They make me go in the stream an' wash an' they throw my clothes away. What they give me was old an' it no fit me. But I have Old Navajo. He patted the blanket on which the girls sat. "I trade my furs for this blanket when I was at the fort of the *Señor* Bent."

"We like Old Navajo. We're glad you still have it," said Frances.

"I decide that it no good with Frémont. The work it was hard an' the food, *no buena*. I decide I go to California by myself. That is how I meet your *papá y mamá* at the Fort Bridger. I go there and I wait for the wagons. I know that me someone will employ."

I left the girls enjoying Baptiste's story. George turned his head as I entered the pitiful little tent we called a bedroom.

"They've gone?"

"Yes."

"Do you have any willow bark left?"

"Yes, I'll make you some tea."

Although the suppuration in his arm had abated, the withering away of flesh had continued and was very painful. He had become very weak and had begun refusing most of his food, begging me to give his share to the children.

I took some stones that I had placed by the fire to warm and put them around George on top of his blanket. Then I went out and gathered some snow which had turned to ice, wrapped it in a cloth, and placed it under George's hand and lower arm. He yelped when I lifted his arm and placed the ice around it.

"Oh, honey, I'm sorry. If you can stand it for a minute or two it should start to numb the pain."

"Yeah. It helps. I'm just a cry-baby."

"I think you have every right to flinch. I just wish I could do something that would help."

"You've done everythin' you can. It's just not gonna get better. You've got to face up to it. We've got to talk about you an' the children goin' over to the other camp, to be ready for the next relief. I ain't gonna make it, Tamsen, we both know it."

"I'll get your tea. I think the water's hot enough—"

"Tamsen, listen to me—"

"George, you might as well hush up about it. I will not leave you here alone. That is all there is to it."

"Godamighty, you are a stubborn woman."

I made the tea and sat on the edge of the bed while he sipped it.

"This stuff is god-awful," he complained.

"It's worth it to feel better, George."

"I'm not sure about that."

I had some laudanum, but I was saving it to use later if his pain became unbearable. I could hear the girls talking and laughing at something Juan Baptiste was doing. It was bright and beautiful outside, but in the tent it was cold and dank. I laid down beside George, pulling a quilt over both of us, curling my body into his.

"George, tomorrow I want you to move to the bed beside the fire. It will be warmer and more cheerful."

He stroked my face. "And I want you to take the girls to the other camp, ready for the next relief."

"Hush. You need to rest. Is the ice helping any?"

• • •

And so we waited. I tried to make George comfortable and I tried to entertain everyone to make the days go faster. Juan Baptiste was a great help. Not only did he gather wood and do all the heavy chores, he entertained the girls, taking them outside often. He would sit with them and tell them stories. Sometimes I sat outside with them, writing in my journal, sketching, or just enjoying the opportunity to get out of our dark and depressing quarters. At night I would knit as I could do that by the firelight. I would tell the girls stories and we would talk of our family back in the States.

"Mother, where is your mother and father?"

"They lived in Newburyport, Massachusetts. That was where I was born. But both my mother and father are gone now. My father, William Eustis, passed on—well, I guess it's now four years. My mother died when I was Frances's age, but I was very lucky, because my father married a very kind and generous woman and I loved her like I did my own mother. She taught me many things and helped me to understand life. I had a good education. I was always a good student and I loved to learn new things that would stretch my mind. That's what I want for you, to have a good education, to use your minds and be independent. I always loved to learn, so it was natural for me to become a teacher."

"Mother, tell us the story again about those grouchy men at your school," asked Frances.

"Well, let's see. That was my first teaching job in Illinois. I came to Illinois from my home in Newburyport to help your Uncle William."

"Why?" asked Frances.

"His wife had died and your cousins needed someone to care for them. Well, then I decided to take a teaching position nearby. I had a wonderful class of students, but a problem developed. The men who were in charge of the school did not like it that I would knit while the lessons were progressing. They wanted to dismiss me, because they felt I couldn't apply myself to teaching if I was distracted by knitting. So I invited them all to come in and observe the class and then pronounce whether or not the lessons proceeded in good fashion. They did so and afterwards they agreed that the children were receiving a full measure of my teaching skills. You see, I stood up for what I believed was right. I want you to always keep in mind that you must *do* what is right and always stand up for what you believe. And if someone is not being fair to you, you must let them know you will not tolerate it."

"Mama, you'll make people be fair to us."

"Well, it might come to pass that you will be leaving the mountains before your father and I can. If so, you will be among strangers for a while."

"Mother, we don't want to go without you and Father. Why can't we go together?"

"Because your father is too weak to walk and we must wait

for horses so that he can ride. I must stay to help him. But spring will come, the snow will melt and we'll be able to leave. Elitha and Leanna will be in California and will have made a place for all of you to stay until we can come to you. But remember, when anyone asks you who you are, always answer that you are the children of Mr. and Mrs. George Donner. And you must always be polite and mannerly, no matter what, because strangers might not have a lot of patience with little children."

Feb. 24

We talked today of my home in Massachusetts and my family. It made me very sad. The days drag on and on, gray, monotonous, cold. Only the wild, sad wind has life. Now and again we are relieved by days when the sun shines, but they are bittersweet days, because the snow melts and the water drips down on us and wets everything. Yesterday it was so nice it seemed like early spring, but today it became cloudy and the wind commenced to blow hard from the west. I fear another storm.

By that time we had no food left except the boilings from hides and some tallow that I had congealed out of the beef jerky that the first rescuers had given us. I supplemented this with the bread that I made from the scrapings of pine bark when we could obtain it.

One day not long after the rescue party left, I visited Betsey and learned something that horrified me and yet released a worry that I had been fighting for days. Betsey and her children were barely clinging to life and in order to save her children, Betsey and Juan Baptiste had resorted to the unthinkable.

"Baptiste, Elizabeth tells me that you have dug up the body of Mr. Shoemaker."

Apprehension was on his face as he looked at me, then he

began to cry. "P*or favor, yo no quiero—Señora,* I no wish to hurt you or make you feel bad. I no keep strong to do the work eating only the hide."

"Yes."

"One day, when I climb the tree to cut off the branches, I see the wolves. They are digging in the snow an' already a leg of Shoemaker is out of the snow. I think that we have no food an' meat is meat. The man that was there, he is gone, only the dead body is left. Like the deer, the buffalo. Is there difference?"

"I don't know," I murmured.

"I have to fight the wolves for the bodies. I am much afraid, but I hit at them with a heavy stick an' they move away, but not far. I dig out Shoemaker an' I drag him to the hut. There is no one there anyway. The *Señora* Betsey, she ask me to do this thing, so I give some to her, then I go back for the others. She say, please, not Jacob, cover him so the wolves they no can get him, an' I try to do that. I don't know if it was enough. *Señora,* there is no other way to survive."

"Baptiste, you can get more of the pine bark."

"*Señora,* only a little can I get this way. I have taken from all the trees around here. It is much work an' I am getting weak. It is all my strength to get the wood for the fires."

"Yes, I know, Baptiste."

"The *niñas,* they must have more than the glue you make of the hides or they will sicken soon. You want that I bring some to you?"

A sob caught in my throat and I turned away. "Not yet, Baptiste, not yet."

• • •

It was perhaps two weeks after the last rescue party had left that the next party of rescuers came to our camp, but to us it seemed like years. I was outside when I saw three men approaching. I struggled through the snow to greet them.

"Are there more men coming?" I panted.

"Yes'm, Mr. Reed and some others'll be comin' on shortly. They're at the other camp helpin' the poor people. I'm Cady, this here's Stone. The man comin' up is Clark. He seen some bear sign. Soon's he leaves his pack he's goin' after the bear. Big one, looked like."

The men shrugged off their packs, took out some packages of provisions, and handed them to me.

"This is all that you have brought?"

"Yes'm, we done cached most up on the mountain to use on the way out."

"Then you must take part of this to Jacob's family."

I pointed in the direction of Betsey's hut where only a wisp of smoke identified the location. "Follow this path and be careful going over the stream. The logs are slippery."

Juan Baptiste had been gathering wood when he'd heard the men's voices. He rushed back to camp as the men were making their way to Betsey's hut.

"Three men *solamente*?"

"They say more are coming. But Baptiste, they have no mules, no horses. That means Mr. Donner cannot go."

"Is not he too weak, even so?"

I turned away. *He's right. George is too weak even to ride.*

Mr. Clark immediately left to hunt the bear. Later in the day, James Reed, with several in company, came to our camp. It had been months since I had last seen James. It was when he'd left the group, in company with Hiram Miller, to go ahead to California. He looked so well, so fit that it was a shock to me to compare our physical situation to that of his. Perhaps I was a little embarrassed because of the condition we were in and of the way we must look. It is hard to put into words the feelings that flooded through me in those first moments before I gathered myself and greeted James in a proper manner.

"James. How good it is to see you."

"How are you? How is George?"

"George is not well. Please, come in. Would you like coffee?"

"That would be wonderful. Thank you."

James followed me inside, pausing while his eyes adjusted to the gloom. I went to George and gently touched his shoulder.

"George, James is here."

George turned his head and found James with his eyes. "Oh, James, it's good to see you. Have you brought mules?"

"No, we couldn't get through with horses or mules. The snow up above is twenty to thirty feet deep. I apologize for the lateness of my arrival here in the mountains. It was most difficult to get over."

I brought a mug of coffee and handed it to him.

"Do you have news of my daughters?" asked George. "They went out with the first party to come here."

"Yes, yes, they are safe. I met that party as we were coming up; my wife and children also. They are all on their way to Sutter's Fort now."

"Your family? Are they all right?" I asked.

"Yes, thank God, my family is safe. Mrs. Reed and two of the children are now on their way out and the other two, Patty and Thomas, they're still at the lake but all right. I cannot tell you how distressed I am for what has happened. It is a most terrible situation."

James stopped, fighting emotion. I brought a chair for him and he set it close to George. It was several moments before he could talk again.

"It was very difficult to move over the snow and fight the constant storms. Even now we are worried whether or not we will be able to get the people out. It is a good distance to an elevation where there is no snow."

"James, please, take my wife and children with you."

"George, my group is too small to take children that cannot walk. It is extremely arduous—"

"James," I exclaimed, "the other men promised us the next party would take our children out! The men who came this morning brought little food. We cannot survive much longer!"

"There is another much larger party following me and they will be able to take them. I will leave as much food as I can.

Hopefully it will last you until they arrive."

"A few days?"

"A week at the most. Of course, that depends on the weather. This has been a most unusual course of storms, or so they tell me at Sutter's."

James got up from his chair. "I must see to the people in the other tent. I can't express how sorry I am about Jacob. I'll come again before we leave, but we must make haste. I am leaving men here to care for you until the next relief party arrives."

"We are grateful for that. Thank you," said George.

James and I left George and went outside, squinting against the white glare from the snow.

"We're all suffering greatly from the effects of the snow glare on our eyes," said James. "Tamsen, I want you to know that as soon as I arrived in California—and it was a hellacious journey—I worked diligently to form up a relief party. I could not obtain men as the rebellions and wars took most of the able men away from the area. Mr. McCutcheon and I made an attempt in November, but the deep snow prevented us from ascending and we had to turn back. As God is my witness, I have done everything I could do." His voice trembled. "It seemed everything was against the effort."

We began walking toward the other camp, James ahead of me on the narrow path carved in the snow.

"I know you've done everything you could, James. Elizabeth and her little ones are in a bad way. I've done what I can, but I'm afraid that it's too late. I fear they will not survive."

I heard the crunching of boots on the snow coming toward us and recognized Hiram Miller. *It was in ... July? Yes, about the time we celebrated the glorious Fourth when Hiram left with Mr. Bryant's group. We were so happy then.* I forced my thoughts back to the present.

Hiram began talking excitedly as soon as he came up to James. "Things are bad over at the other camp. They's been eatin' the dead. Did you go in that teepee-like hut? The empty one? God have mercy—"

James raised his hand signaling Hiram to stop talking. "Yes, I did. Go ahead and get started on resetting the tents. We'll wash the children and give them a little more food." James turned half-way around to me. "Mrs. Donner, here's your man, Hiram."

Hiram looked past James with a surprised look on his face. "Miz Donner, how you be?"

"As well as can be expected, Hiram. So you made it to California?"

"Yes'm, but hardly had a chance to collect myself before we started on this expedition."

"Would you go in and visit with George? He'll be so glad to see you—"

James interrupted. "When we get this work done we'll do that, but we must make haste."

Hiram turned around and we continued on to Betsey's camp and the men began the work of moving the tents.

"They're taking Mary, Isaac, and Solly but they won't take my little boys," Betsey cried as soon as she saw me. "Oh, God, Tamsen, what am I to do?" She collapsed on the ground, crying pitifully. I knelt down and put my arms around her.

"James says another relief party will be here in a few days. It's a larger party and they'll be able to carry them out. We just need to keep on until they get here."

"I ain't got no strength to keep on. I ain't goin' to make it to California," she sobbed. "I'm gonna be joining Jacob in the hereafter, there's no use a' thinkin' different. But what will happen to my little ones?"

"Betsey, you need to get the children ready to go. They're going to leave as soon as they get your tent moved."

"Yes," she said wearily. We got up and got the two older boys and Mary ready for their trek and Hiram Miller conducted the selling of Jacob's store of goods. When it was finished, I noticed that some of the men were putting together bundles of the goods they had purchased.

"Do they mean to carry goods and not help get a child out?" I asked James.

"Tamsen, these men are volunteers. I have no authority over them. They do as they wish. But I can tell you they have suffered great hardship to get here."

"In other words, they have suffered greatly in order to purchase goods that will make them a lot of money in California. How has that helped relieve us?"

"All of the men have carried in heavy packs of food. Most of it we cached along the way in order to feed the people as we go out. The labor was extremely hard; some now feel their task has ended. I wish it were different."

The girls and I and Juan Baptiste stood on a bank of snow and watched the group of rescuers and rescued until they disappeared around the spur of the ridge.

"Those men, *Señora,* I no like them. They treat me bad. Reed, he say I must stay. I stay because you need me, because the *niñas,* they need me. Not because he tell me. I think he is the ass of a donkey."

"Baptiste, I sympathize with your feelings, but I am very grateful that you will stay. Mr. Reed says another party is coming soon."

Baptiste shrugged. "For you, I do it. For them, *nunca.*"

We went back to Betsey's tent. My girls sat on one of the beds, feet dangling, watching as I fed their little cousins more of the soup I had made. *They aren't going to survive,* I thought. It was all I could do to keep from breaking down. *I must not show my desperation.*

Betsey began crying again. "Tamsen, promise me you'll take care of my babies after—"

"Hush such talk, Betsey. I will do everything I can to help you and the children, but you must not give up. I've got to go back now." I motioned to the girls to come along.

"Betsey, Mr. Cady will keep your fire up."

"I heard them men talking. They's leaving."

Betsey was right. Mr. Cady and Mr. Stone were growing apprehensive that they were going to be forced to join us in our starved camp.

"Miz Donner, we gotta' leave. We need to catch up with Mr. Reed's party. Our provisions is near gone an' we're a'feared'a bein' trapped here fer days, mebbe weeks 'fore another party kin get o'er the mountain."

"You were charged with our care and you are being paid to do so."

"We ain't bein' paid to risk our lives becomin' trapped our ownselves. There be a storm a'coming."

"Then take our girls out with you. Please."

"We'd have to carry 'em an' we cain't."

"I believe they can walk. If you break the snow for them they'll walk in your tracks."

"No. I'm sorry, we cain't take 'em. We'll need to move fast to find Reed."

"Mr. Cady, would you do it for money? For five hundred dollars?"

He looked at me for a moment. "Well, I dunno. I'll talk to Stone, see what he says."

In a few minutes he was back. "Ma'am, we'll take 'em if you'll give five hundred apiece. That's five hundred fer me, five hundred fer Stone. They'll have ta' walk. We'll leave as soon as they're ready to go. We cain't wait fer Clark to git back. Ma'am, you should go with us. Your husband an' the other woman an' young 'uns, they ain't gonna last much more'n a few days."

What sorrow, what pain. I thought my heart would burst from grief. I readied the girls, putting on their traveling outfits and their cloaks. I made a bundle of a few treasures and asked Mr. Cady to carry it. They said their good-byes to George and then we went up the steps of packed snow.

"We will come as soon as we can. God will take care of you until we do," I said, but I had fear in every fiber of my body. I watched as the rescuers made their way out from our camp, the little girls stretching their legs to put their feet into the depression made by the footprints of the men. I could see it was going to be hard for them. I returned to our dungeon and sat down beside George.

"They'll be better off, gettin' out, Tamsen. It's for the best. I wish you'd gone with them."

• • •

Mr. Clark returned late in the day, empty-handed. He came into the hut stomping the snow off his boots.

"I tracked a she-bear, but only wounded her. She took off an' I lost her."

"The other men have left, Mr. Clark."

"They're gone? How long?"

"Mid-afternoon."

"The bastards!"

"They were concerned that another storm is coming. I begged them to stay. When they would not, I asked them to take our three girls and they agreed to it. I pray that I did the right thing."

"Most likely they're right about a storm. I felt it when I was out." Mr. Clark pulled off his hat and gloves and slapped them against his leg in vexation. He muttered to himself crossly as he pulled off his heavy coat and then sat down, staring morosely into the fire.

Shortly thereafter a storm struck with terrible fury and lasted for several days. It was impossible to get firewood and some of that time we had no fire. Melting snow dripped on us and ran through the floor of our tent, keeping us in a constant wetness. We had only cold boiled hide to eat. Sometime during the storm Betsey's little boy, Lewis, died. When the storm subsided, Betsey came to our hut with the dead child in her arms. She laid him on my lap and sank to the floor, too dispirited and numb to cry.

Mr. Clark, now an inmate of our prison, went out to collect some wood for our fires and after dumping the wood near our door, he came into the hut and picked up his rifle.

"I seen tracks. It's probably the cub I seen before with the mother. I'd guess she went down from the wound an' the cub is out searchin' for her. I'm gonna go back an' foller them tracks."

"I go with you," said Juan Baptiste.

"No, you need to stay with Miz Elizabeth, keep her fire goin'."

When Mr. Clark returned many hours later he was dragging a large bear cub. He'd followed the tracks for a distance when he saw the cub snuffling here and there and then making a beeline for an opening at the foot of a ridge. He pondered what to do, reluctant to follow the cub into the cave, but desperate to return with meat. Finally, he took his rifle and shot into the cave thinking to scare the cub out, but it didn't appear. After waiting for a time, he summoned great courage and with determination made strong by impending starvation, he crawled into the cave. He partly fell, partly slid to the bottom and as his hand went out to steady himself, he recoiled as he touched something furry.

"It knocked the breath out of me," he told us later. "Oh Jesus, I was in a state of shock."

But he heard nothing. No breathing, no stirring. He'd touched the bear cub and it was dead. When he pulled the cub from the den he saw that the shot had entered its brain.

We had food in our camp, but it came too late to save Betsey and our little nephew Samuel. Now there was only Juan Baptiste, George and I, and Mr. Clark. I was fretful and worried about the girls. Had the men started over the mountains and got caught in the storm? Sick with fear, I implored Mr. Clark to go to the lake camps to see if the men had started over with the girls or had been stopped by the storm.

"Mr. Clark, take some of the meat with you. If they're still there they'll need food. And take some to the others."

I was beside myself with nervousness as we waited for Mr. Clark to return.

"Maybe he'll just go on. Won't come back," said George.

"He come back," said Baptiste. "He want the goods he buy of Jacob's. The goods, they are still here."

Clark returned the next day. Baptiste and I were watching and waiting on the top of a snowbank.

"They didn't take them," he told us. "They left your daughters with Miz Murphy. You best go over there. That Dutchman, Keseberg, he's there livin' in the cabin an' the children are skeered 'a him. Miz Murphy, she's weak an' blind an' cain't hardly move about. Only one child there besides yourn. No tellin' what that man might do. It's lookin' likely to storm again. I'm leavin'."

"I go with him," said Baptiste.

"I must go to the other camp to see about the girls. Please, Baptiste, stay with George until I get back."

"I stay too long already. I no want to die in these mountains. You must go too."

I knew they would need most of the bear meat to survive the trek over the mountains. I bundled it up and put it in Baptiste's pack. I took his hands in mine. It was so painful, this business of parting.

"Baptiste, I hope that I will survive, but if not I want you to know that we truly appreciate what you have done and we love you for it." I put a handkerchief with some money tied in it into his hand. "This will help you as you find a new life."

Tears were streaming down his face. *"Gracias, muchísimas gracias. Te espero ver otra vez. Adios, Señora. Vaya con Dios."*

"And you also, Baptiste. God be with you."

I watched them move off. Mr. Clark was carrying a large pack of items he had bought in the sale of Jacob's things. I felt the sun touch my body, but I was cold through every tissue of my being. I went in to George.

"Baptiste left with Clark?" George asked.

"Yes. I cannot fault him, George. Clark tells me that the girls were left at the lake in the cabin of Mrs. Murphy and that the conditions there are horrible. Those men didn't take them out as they promised and after we paid them! I must go to the other camp and bring them back."

I was more distraught than I had ever been in my life. I was torn between the need to stay by George's side and concern for the safety of the children.

"You must go to see about them. Stay there at the other camp. Don't concern yourself with me. I can't last more'n a few hours or days."

"It's too late for me to go now, but I will go in the morning."

That night I was so fearful for the children that I could not sleep. The wind had strengthened again and I could hear it wailing through the trees. Through the wailing was the sound of the stream rushing free from its deep covering of snow. *The snow is melting fast,* I thought. When dawn came I gave George some laudanum and hot tea and did what I could to make him comfortable, smoothing his covers, tucking in the edges, and placing warm stones around him.

"I hope we can make it back this evening, but it may be tomorrow. I hate leaving you alone."

He spoke without opening his eyes, so weak that I almost couldn't make out what he was saying.

"Tamsen. Save yourself and the girls. Don't come back."

I made my way to the lake camps, sometimes walking on crusted snow, sometimes floundering in the deep drifts, and occasionally finding solid ground in places where the wind and sun had dissipated the snow. When I got to the other camps, I found the girls in the cabin of Mrs. Murphy, huddled together next to the door. I could barely make out their little white faces in the gloom of the cabin. I reached out to hug them and they cried out and tried to scramble away before they realized it was I who touched them. They all began to cry. A form stirred and a harsh voice grated across the room.

"Be still, you brats, or I'll add you to the fire."

I recognized the voice. Mr. Keseberg.

"Hush, hush," I whispered to the girls. "It's all right. I'm here."

"Who is it there?" quavered a weak voice. "Is it men from California?"

The girls were clinging to me so tight I had trouble getting to my feet. I moved over to where I had heard the voice of Mrs. Murphy, the girls pulling on my arms and dress. My eyes were adjusting to the darkness, aided by a few flickers of flame from a hearth against a huge rock. I realized that the rock served as a wall for one side of the cabin.

"It's Tamsen Donner, Mrs. Murphy."

"Oh, Tamsen," said Mrs. Murphy. "Thank God you're here. I cain't do anythin' for the little ones. I cain't hardly move about." A child sat on the floor next to her bed. "Simon helps me all he can, poor thing. I tried to keep the babies alive, but now Simon's the only one left."

I heard Mr. Keseberg shuffling toward us. He bent over and peered at me. "Ah. Mrs. Donner. Those men they leave the *kinder* here."

I moved back toward the door with the children still clinging to me. I thought I would faint from the dankness and stench of the cabin.

"Mr. Keseberg, we will go to the other cabin."

"That cabin is empty. The Breen's have gone."

"Yes. Do you have something I can carry some coals in? I will need to build a fire."

"*Ja*. I think so."

Mrs. Murphy held a trembling hand out to me. "Don't go away."

"I will be close by, just to the other cabin. I'll come back." *Oh God, I cannot come in here again. I'm going to retch if I don't leave immediately.*

The snow was still high, but there was a path through the mounds that was not as deep. I had a hard time pulling the door of the cabin open as snow had drifted against it. It was dim and damp inside. *At least there are no dead bodies.* There was a pile of firewood near the fireplace and with the coals Mr. Keseberg had put in a kettle I had a fire going in short order. I stripped the girls of their wet clothes and bundled them up all together by the fire in a quilt I found on one of the beds. I'd brought some tea and what was left of the bear meat. I melted snow to make the tea and gave each girl a piece of meat. All that night I lay with the girls curled around me, worrying and fretting about what I should do. I had to stay with them or take them back to our camp. I worried about George. *The fire will be out. He'll be cold.* By morning I had resolved that I would take the children back to our camp, but I needed to get their clothes dry enough to wear before leaving.

"Mother, I'm hungry. Do you have any more food?" asked Georgeanna.

"No, I'm sorry."

"Can you go to the other cabin and get some? Simon gets meat from the dead bodies and cooks it for us," said Frances.

"Didn't Mr. Clark give you meat?"

"Yes, we shared it with those people. It's all gone."

I was spared from going to Mrs. Murphy's cabin to find food by the arrival of a rescue party.

"Halloo, the cabin!" I heard shouted outside.

I pushed open the door and went outside. I was surprised to see a group of men, including Juan Baptiste.

"Baptiste! Why are you here?"

"Me and Clark, we go the other side of this lake to the foot of the mountain pass, but Clark he is very tired because of the pack of things he carry. We camp there last night. This morning I see these men an' I come with them." Baptiste waved in the direction of four men. I knew William Eddy and William Foster, Mrs. Murphy's son-in-law. They had left the cabins in December to go over the mountain on snowshoes. Both were very thin and haggard looking. And there was Hiram Miller again, back over the mountain from the Reed relief.

"We met these men as they were coming up," said Hiram, "an' I decided to come back to help. This here's Thompson," he said, pointing to the fourth man.

"Mrs. Donner," said Eddy, "we must hurry on. My son, and Will's son, were left in the care of Mrs. Murphy. We were told they were still alive."

I looked at him, tears welling in my eyes. "They're all dead, Mr. Eddy, except Mrs. Murphy, Simon, and Mr. Keseberg."

"Oh, God." Mr. Eddy sank to the ground, his face in his hands.

"Did ... did you say my son is dead?" Mr. Foster asked me.

I nodded. "Yes."

The men hurried off toward the Murphy cabin. Shortly they came back with Simon, helping him struggle through the snow.

Mr. Foster was pale and looked sick. "I saw the body of my wife, my child—" He gagged, turned away, and retched.

"I can't blame them." Mr. Eddy was drawing in deep breaths. "We also—" He turned away from me and his body shook. Then he seemed to pull himself together.

"We can do nothing for Mrs. Murphy. I fear she will die shortly. Keseberg is too weak and lame to walk. We will have to leave them here. Baptiste has told me that George will not live much longer."

My voice quavered as I tried to say the terrible words. Mr. Eddy nodded to let me know he understood. "I've left what food we can spare. We will take you and your girls and Simon. We must leave soon. It looks like a storm is coming."

We went inside the cabin and he gave the girls some biscuits and a little dried beef. I whispered to him that I must return to George. I begged him to stay long enough for me to return to our camp and if George had already passed, I would return to the lake and go over.

"Mrs. Donner, it does not seem reasonable for you to return to your camp." I put my finger to my lips and he dropped his voice. "If you know that George cannot survive, you must go with us."

"I cannot."

I dressed the girls. Their cloaks were still a little damp, but their underclothes were dry. "Let's go outside and sit in the sun," I suggested. "It's so much nicer."

I searched about looking for paper and pencil and found both in a trunk. We went outside and sat down on a log and I began a note to Elitha.

Elitha, look after the little ones. You must keep everyone together no matter what happens. I have given Mr. Eddy money for you to get a place where you can all stay together. Have courage.

All our love, Mother

My pencil wavered over the paper. My tears were erasing some of the words. *What more can I say? You might never see us again?*

"Girls, Mr. Eddy and the other men are going to carry you over the mountain to California, and Simon too. You'll be safe with them. Be good girls and do what they tell you."

"Aren't you going too?"

"I must return to take care of Father. We will come as soon as we can."

All three of the girls began to cry and cling to me.

"Everything will be all right. Think about how nice it will be in the new country. It will be green and warm and there'll be plenty of good food. Think of that."

Mr. Eddy came to where we were. My heart went out to him. He had lost his wife *and* his children. *My children will survive.*

"Mrs. Donner, we are ready to leave. I implore you to leave with us."

"Mr. Eddy, I have money and a letter for our daughter, Elitha. Would you see that she gets it? She and Leanna will be at Sutter's Fort. Will you promise me that you will watch over my little ones and get them safely to Mr. Sutter? I will give you money."

"I will do my best. All that is within my power, but I will take no money. If we delay any longer, the storm that is coming may take us all." He looked away from me as tears began running down his cheeks. "I could have saved my children. We could have gotten help earlier if only we had not been lost in the mountains." His voice broke. "It was a *month* we struggled in the snow."

"You mean the group that went out on showshoes?"

"Fifteen of us and only seven are now alive. There are no words to describe my suffering and anguish, the terrible agony to leave my wife and children, and now to return to find them all dead—" He cried then, deep sobs racking his body. It took awhile before he could compose himself again.

"My wife saved my life."

"Eleanor saved your life?"

"Before we left, the fifteen of us, she hid a piece of bear meat in my pack. She deprived herself of this food! I found it in a moment of greatest need."

Mr. Eddy pulled a slip of paper from his pocket. "She wrote me this note. I found it with the meat."

I took it from his trembling fingers.

"She hopes the meat will save your life," I read.

"It did save my life. The strength I got from that little piece of meat kept me alive and I kept at the others to not give up."

"Who survived of the fifteen?"

"Myself, and William," he pointed at Mr. Foster, "and his wife, Sarah, Mary Graves, Sarah Fosdick ..." He thought for a moment. "Mrs. McCutcheon, and Harriet Pike."

He related to me how they had struggled through deep drifts, falling into pits and chasms, cold, starving, desperate, exhausted, and suffering from snow blindness. They made only a few miles each day, once having to retreat to the previous night's camp because the soft snow clung to their feet in such huge clumps they were too weak to lift the added weight.

"The wind and snow tore at us, knocking us around, driving at us. To breathe, we had to turn our heads and suck the air in gasps. Stanton became blind from the brightness of the snow and was the first to give up. He strived to keep up with us and we helped him as much as we could, but finally he couldn't go on. We left him sitting by a tree smoking his pipe. He never came up."

I gasped. "Mr. Stanton is dead?"

"What could we do? He could not go on."

At one time, in a blinding snowstorm, they lost their fire and would have all perished but for Eddy.

"I made them lie together and we covered ourselves with blankets. The snow covered us, but the warmth of our bodies kept us from freezing. Dolan became delirious. We couldn't keep him under the covering. You can't know, no one can know how we suffered."

The desperate group discussed who would give up their life in order that the others might use their body to survive. They chose by slips of paper which was to die. No one could do the terrible deed. It became unnecessary as Patrick Dolan, the one who had been chosen, became the second of the party to die. The storm raged for more than two days. They had been four days without any food and two and a half without fire. The ordeal began on Christmas Day and they remained in the same place, huddled together for four days. During this time Franklin Graves, Antoine, and Lemuel Murphy died. They finally managed to kindle a fire and then they began to consume the flesh of their dead companions.

"We struggled on, floundering, crawling. We would slide down the sides of canyons and ravines, only to have to climb the other side. I managed to kill a deer, but it was small, gone in a day or so. Jay died and we ..." He paused and then went on. "By this time we were all demented to some extent. The Indians, Stanton's Indians, had gone off. They were supposed to guide us, find the way, but they became lost. They were afraid of us, I think. They had cause."

Mr. Eddy related how they came across the footprints of the two Indian men and followed them.

"They were almost dead. It was only a matter of minutes, hours at the most." Mr. Eddy lowered his voice as he looked over at William who was sitting with the other men, eating some of the dried beef they had brought. "William was wild, crazed. He shot the Indians and we used them for food. We had to if we wanted to survive!" he exclaimed. He stopped talking for a moment, then looked at me with a haunted look in his eyes. "No one can know what we suffered or understand the pain."

On they went, feet swollen, cut and bleeding, their foot coverings, even the rags they had wrapped around their feet, gone. Finally they came to the foothills where there was no snow. Stumbling into an Indian village they were given acorn meal to eat and finally made their way into a settlement.

"If only we hadn't got lost," he groaned. "If only we hadn't got lost! All of us could have made it. We could have told of the desperate condition of our company."

He sighed dejectedly and began to tie up his pack. "We were

dogged by misfortune and bad luck. If there is a God, he surely deserted our company."

"Is there another party coming soon?" I asked.

"I can't say. It will be at least June before the snow melts enough so horses can get over the mountain. Some of the others will be coming back to get the things they have cached." He stood up and hefted his pack onto his back. "We must go."

Sick of heart, I kissed and hugged my girls again and then I hurried away, not daring to turn to look for fear I would weaken and go with them. I hastened back to camp, stopping for a moment to watch some geese overhead. *It is the middle of March and the snow is melting away. Spring must be near.* As I neared our hut, I saw a mound in the snow, the leg of an ox sticking out. The melting had exposed one of our oxen. I hastened into the tent. *Oh! How miserable it is in here!* I knelt beside the bed where George lay and placed my hand on his throat. *He's still alive.*

"George, honey, I'm back."

He stirred and opened his eyes, only little slits, his voice a faltering whisper. "Were the children all right?"

"Yes. Another relief party came while I was there. Everyone has been taken out except for Mrs. Murphy and Mr. Keseberg. They were both too feeble to walk."

"You shouldn't have come back."

"There's one of our oxen showing in the snow. I'll make a fire and then I will make you some soup. It will make you feel better."

After I saw to making George as comfortable as I could, I pulled my rocking chair next to him and sat holding his hand, going over and over in my mind what I should do, what I could do, about my situation. I was sure that George would die, and Mrs. Murphy. That would leave only myself and Mr. Keseberg in the mountains.

Night came. I heard coyotes yipping up on the mountain. I liked to hear the voices of the coyotes, but hated the howling of the wolves. The wolves were constantly prowling about the camps and loping across the meadow. They didn't come close to our hut now, since Juan Baptiste had killed two of them and nailed their carcasses to trees on each side of the hut. They hung there, heads moving back and forth in the wind, mouths frozen in fanged snarls.

I hadn't had much practice with firearms, but I knew how to load and fire. I looked for George's guns, but couldn't find them. *I remember, Juan Baptiste told me that Mr. Clark took them. But what about Jacob's? Betsey kept his rifle. She wouldn't sell it in the auction. It might still be in the other camp.*

I thought about it for two days. I didn't want to go to the other camp, but I wanted the comfort of having a gun in case the Indians should come around the camp. They knew we were here; Baptiste had seen them a time or two, crossing the meadow.

Finally, I steeled myself and crossed the stream to the other camp. The water was very high, crashing against the log bridge, overflowing the banks and flooding through the camp. I found a heavy stick with which to steady myself and crossed over. We had managed to bury Betsey and the two boys in the snow, but it had melted and the wild creatures had gotten at the bodies. Bones, skulls, hair, all were scattered about. A dull aching sadness came over me. *Poor Betsey, poor little ones.* I found the rifle, but it had lain in water and was ruined. I pulled one of Betsey's chairs out into a patch of sunlight and sat down, the stick across my knees. I looked up at the mountain behind the camp, squinting my eyes against the brightness. A soft moaning wind flowed across the trees, then flowed again, reminding me of waves on a gentle ocean.

Then, from a sky that hadn't had a bird in it, three crows came flapping. One alighted in the top of a tree that towered over me, the other two dropped down in front of me and stepped back and forth, pecking here and there and twisting their heads to look at me.

"Oh, so it is you again, following me," I said to them. "Here for another funeral? Yes, join me. We have no other mourners, you see. Everyone is gone. Now it's only you and I to mourn my husband. But this time you will not have my children." I jumped up, hitting at the crows with my stick, yelling. "I have sent them away!"

The crows squawked in surprise and flapped clumsily away. I watched them circle into the sky. Then I crumpled on the chair and the deep grief that I had been holding in for so long burst forth and I cried and shook in agony until I was spent and weak and could cry no more.

In the next few days, I set about organizing our things. I counted the coin money we had left, almost six hundred dollars. It would be too heavy for me to carry, at least all of it. I kept some of the gold coins and put the rest in the bottom of one of my trunks in the wagon. Then I repacked everything that was still good into our family wagon. *I can hire men to come back to get the wagons and carry George and Jacob back to be buried. Everything will be ready.*

George's pain seemed to leave him and most of the time he drifted in and out of a deep sleep. One morning I awoke to find that George had passed on. I sat in my chair for several hours, not moving, not seeing, numb with grief and cold. I had known that George was going to die, but now the actuality left me adrift. Then gradually, memories of my girls began coming into my mind. I realized I was now free. *My daughters! I must go to my daughters!*

I wanted to bury George, but had not the strength to dig a grave, much less move his body to it. So I wrapped him up tightly in a sheet. *I will come back and if I cannot, I will send someone. I will keep your promise to take Jacob to California, and you will go too.*

I tied the bag of coins to my waist and took the quilt that contained all our paper money from a trunk. The memory of sewing the quilt flitted through my mind. I closed the hut up as tightly as I could, then wrapped the quilt around me for a cloak and began walking toward the lake camps. Toward California.

We'd had another storm during the last two weeks and new snow covered the ground. Part of the way to the cabins I stepped onto a thin covering of ice and snow over a creek channel and fell into the icy water. I thrashed about, gulping and gasping, the weight of my wet clothing and the quilt heavy on my body. I struggled to crawl out of the creek, finally pulling myself up the bank by holding on to willow bushes. I wrung some of the water out of my clothes and the quilt, but I was thoroughly soaked. Frozen to my core, I struggled on. It must have taken two hours after I had fallen into the creek before I came to the cabins. I could smell smoke and I followed the scent to the Breen cabin. I was so stiff I could barely walk and crawled the last few feet to the door. I tried to call out, but my voice was too weak to be heard. I hit the door with my fist. Nothing. My hands found a stick and I hit the door with it until Mr. Keseberg heard the noise and came to help me inside. He made me a drink of coffee and offered me food, but I could not eat it.

"Mrs. Donner, would you deny yourself the sustenance which you need to survive? Put the source from your mind and look at it as food, food you must have if you want to live. The rescuers left only a day or so of provisions for me. It was a long time before I could bring myself to—"

My lips were so stiff it was difficult to speak. "No. I m-must rest. I will go at first light. Can you make more fire?"

"You must get out of your wet clothes. I will find you a blanket."

The man rose from his seat by the fire and brought some blankets to me, taking off the soggy frozen quilt and throwing it into a corner. Stooping before the fire he pulled a few sticks of wood off a pile to the side of the fireplace and put them on the fire, blowing on the embers. The flames flared, sparks shot up, and then died down. I moved closer to the warmth, gathering the blankets around me. I sipped the hot coffee. Mr. Keseberg fidgeted with a stick of wood, poking at the fire.

"I moved to this cabin a few days ago. It has a better fireplace, but it is not easy for me to gather wood. It takes me three or four hours to find a day's supply." His voice trailed off and then he spoke again. "Mrs. Donner, you are not strong enough to withstand the travel. You must not attempt it."

I was shivering so much I could barely speak. I only wanted to rest, sleep. "I m-m-must go to my ch-children."

He stared at me with wild, haunted eyes. "Yes, and I want to see my child, my Ada. Ada's sister, her twin, is dead before we start this journey. My baby boy is dead. You are fortunate. Your children—" He stopped and gazed into the fire poking at the wood. "I know not whether Ada and my wife are alive or dead."

My body felt disengaged from my mind. His voice came to me from a far distance.

"Several times I have seen geese flying. If we could obtain some fresh meat we could restore our bodies and then we can walk over the mountain. You see the heel of my foot? It is so damaged from a slip of the ax it is difficult for me to walk. There should be another party coming to help us. It's likely we would meet them on the way."

He put another stick of wood on the fire, stirring the coals. Orange flames licked around the wood and the light flickered on his gaunt face. He stared into the fire for a while, then turned to look at me.

"The misfortune that has overtaken us was predestined. There is nothing we can do but finish our roles in this horrible tragedy. It began the moment we took that cut-off. If there is a God, and many times I have wondered if there is, why would this suffering be allowed to happen? Perhaps God has kept me alive to make me suffer, to punish me. Many times I have put my gun to my head wanting to end my misery, but each time I thought of my wife and little daughter and I could not do it. I am conversant in four languages and I speak and write them with equal fluency, but in all four I cannot find words that express the horror I have experienced."

I should have removed my wet frozen clothing, but I was weak and I did not want to disrobe in the presence of this man. I wrapped the blankets around my body and lay down close to the fire, quaking and shivering, hurting from the icy cold that had penetrated deep to the organs in my body. I gazed for a few moments at the fire licking against the wood, drawing comfort from the flames, but not warmth. *So pretty, fire.* Then my eyes closed. Sometime before the dawn, my soul passed from my body.

April 1, 1847
A Different Dimension

Now I was without physical form. I was a field of awareness everywhere at all times. I was no longer attached to the physical world, but still I did not leave. Much later, when the cords that bound me to my daughters loosened, I found my way. As a field of awareness, I saw Mr. Keseberg try to wake me.

For several hours, perhaps days—I cannot track time in this dimension—he sat dejectedly by the fire. Only when the cold became unbearable to him did he stir, to gather wood and make the fire again. He didn't cause my death, but he did use the body I left for food. Perhaps you recoil in horror, but it is not my purpose to help you understand, to massage your sensibilities.

One day I saw Mr. Keseberg make his way to our camp and I followed him. He went to Jacob's tent and then ours. I watched as he searched through the shelters and the wagons, taking a thing here and a thing there and then he found the gold and silver in the bottom of my trunk. I had not thought to hide it. Gold and silver meant nothing, only life had meaning. He buried part of the money and left our camp. I wondered, would he now start over the mountains? Would he take to my daughters the money and the things he had taken from our camp? Did he intend to tell my daughters where he had buried the money?

I remained in the camp, sitting in my rocking chair, trying to puzzle out my situation. The wind blew, but I did not feel it. Clouds passed in front of the sun, but I was not aware of it. Night fell and the stars moved across the heavens and then a pale dawn edged above the mountains. I had no sense of it.

Then voices and movement made me aware there were men there, four men. They were led by a huge blue-jowled man with bushy black hair. He was clothed in the manner of a mountain man. It entered into my frame of consciousness that the man, whom the others called O'Fallon, was of the pirate genre. I got up from my chair and greeted them, but they did not answer.

"Are you rescuers?" I asked. "You are too late, don't you see?"

They did not hear me. They searched our camp like Mr. Keseberg had. They found the remains of Elizabeth, Samuel, Lewis, and the others. They entered our hut and I followed them. They looked through everything. They saw George's body, but I would not permit them to touch him. I held them with my thoughts and they felt cold and morbid and they went out.

"Did you look in there where Donner was? Did you find his money belt?"

"I seen nothin' but his body, all wrapped up. I guess it was him, who else would it be? Looks like this place was gone through. Ever'thin's been torn apart. An' where's the money? You suppose they lied to us about Donner havin' thousands of dollars?"

"I dunno, but several told of it."

"Mebbe some a' them took it, makin' out like it's still here so's nobody would know."

They were disturbed and angry, for they had expected to find a large amount of gold. They ransacked the wagons, pulling out the most precious of the goods and making up large packs. In the morning they departed the camp and I followed them, wanting to see what they would do.

"I'm wonderin' about Miz Donner. Suppose that's her bones o'er to the other camp?"

"Could be."

"Look here, O'Fallon, here's them tracks again. Suppose it be an Injun? They's headin' off to the east."

"It's not a foot or moccasin track, you'd see some toes in the print, wouldn't yer? An' here, you see this one in the mud, that's from a shoe, er boot. No, this ain't no Injun."

"Suppose it's her, Donner's wife?"

"That's a fair-sized mark, big, a man's track."

They followed the tracks, but lost them. They were puzzled, but gave up and went on to the cabins at the lake.

"O'Fallon, look, there's smoke comin' up from that cabin yonder. Someone's still alive here."

They entered the cabin and there they found Mr. Keseberg. They had no time for courtesies as they were bent on finding treasure.

"We saw footprints goin' over to the other camp. Was they yourn?" they asked, but not nicely.

"No. I have not left this place."

"Where is Miz Donner?"

"She is dead."

"We didn't see her body at the other camp an' we didn't find the money they had. We think you've been over there an' stole the money that belongs to the Donners. You killed Mrs. Donner to get her money."

They began to search and they found the gold money and the other things Mr. Keseberg had taken. They besieged the man, offering no pity, no human kindnesses. They told him they would kill him if he did not divulge all he knew. They placed a rope around his neck and choked him, frightening him so much he divulged that he had indeed taken the money. Then they forced from him the confession of where he'd buried the remainder. The men were very cruel to Mr. Keseberg, angry because they found only a small portion of what they believed we had in treasure. Although they searched diligently, they could find no more.

As Mr. Keseberg prepared to leave the cabin where so much had happened, I realized that there in the corner, dirty and looking like a pile of rags, was my quilt. The quilt with all our American dollars tucked inside. Later it would burn in that cabin along with the remains of those who died beside the gray waters of the lake that would one day have the name of Donner.

I followed the men as they made their way over the mountains, Mr. Keseberg trailing behind, the men offering no assistance. Small wonder, as each man of the four carried packs of booty of a hundred pounds or more.

So strong was my desire to go to my daughters that although my soul was no longer in my body, I could not pass to the other side. They longed for me, and I for them, and then I was with them. I return to that day that I had to leave them in the care of the men of the relief party—Mr. Foster, Mr. Eddy, Mr. Thompson, and Hiram Miller. Mr. Eddy carried Georgeanna and Mr. Miller carried Eliza. Frances was able to walk, but sometimes one of the men would help her along. They spent the first night at the head of the lake on the mountain-side. The girls were very hungry as the food they were given was in small amounts so that their bodies could adjust to the increase without getting sick.

The next morning the men struggled to climb the mountain while carrying their burdens. Baptiste and Clark were a short distance ahead. Toward the end of the day, Mr. Miller, who was carrying Eliza, put her down.

"I am very tired of carrying you. You see that big black rock up ahead there? If you will walk that far, you shall have a nice lump of sugar with your supper," he said.

Eliza was sore from being carried all cramped in a blanket and wanted the sugar so much that she agreed to walk. Mr. Miller held her hand and pulled her onward. She stumbled and sank to her knees many times, but pressed doggedly on, thinking of the reward she would have. After they had their supper, Eliza asked for her sugar.

"Little girl, we don't have any sugar. I just tol' you that so's you'd walk. Now hush yerself 'bout it."

The disappointment was bitter. Eliza, huddled together with her sisters, cried until she fell asleep exhausted. The next day, when Mr. Miller told Eliza she must walk again, she refused to go forward and cried to go back.

"Look, little girl, you're gonna haf' to walk. If'n you don't want to, you can stay here on the snow an' cry. There was a big bear snuffling 'roun' the camp last night an' he might come an' eat you up."

Frances and Georgeanna went to Eliza and tried to get her up. "We can't go back. Come on, we'll help you."

Eliza cried all the harder. "I don't like that man. He's mean."

Frances and Georgeanna began to cry too, fearing that the men would leave Eliza behind. After the other men intervened and spoke sternly to Mr. Miller, he grudgingly wrapped Eliza in a blanket and put her on his back. As they proceeded they saw other people, rescuers and rescued, moving down from the mountains. They were stragglers from the Reed rescue party. The Reed party had made it over the summit, only to be struck by a savage storm. They were trapped for days, their provisions exhausted. When the storm abated, Mr. Reed and the other five rescuers left the camp, taking with them Patty and Thomas Reed and Betsey's boy, Solomon, leaving Mr. Breen and his family, Mrs. Graves, her children, and Betsey's girl, Mary. They were left with three days fuel, but no food. Their fire melted the snow and formed a deep pit in which they took refuge. Mrs. Graves and her son Franklin died the first night after the rescue party left. The flesh from the dead bodies kept them alive. After seven days, Margaret Breen looked up to see three men peering at them over the top of the pit.

Rescue! Her family would be saved. Two of the men, Mr. Stone and Mr. Oakley, knowing they would be given a bonus for bringing out a child, took up Mary Donner and the baby Graves and prepared to leave. Mr. Stark, the third man, protested the abandonment of the seven members of the Breen family and the two Graves children, Nancy and Jonathan. Left alone, with nine people to save, the heroic Stark carried the provisions on his back, along with most of the blankets and most of the time the weaker children too.

My three girls, Simon Murphy, their rescuers, and the other stragglers haltingly made it to the rescue camp. Eventually, they were taken to Johnson's Ranch and then on to Mr. Sutter's fort.

Elitha and Leanna had prepared as best they could for the time when we would all be brought down from the mountains. They welcomed their three little sisters with tears of joy. Each day they watched the road that they might at last see George and me brought down from the mountains. Then O'Fallon's group, the fourth to make it to the camps in the mountains, came back with only Mr. Keseberg limping behind.

The children of George and Tamsen Donner were now poor orphans and others controlled their destinies. Of the five girls, only Eliza and Georgeanna remained together. But they all survived, grew to womanhood, raised families, and the cycle of life continued. Of the eighty-seven people of the Donner Party, forty-one lived and eventually returned to a normal life, but each was forever damaged in some way by the experience.

The snow comes every year to those mountains. Never since our ordeal has the snow been quite as deep nor quite as terrible as it was the winter of 1846.

Within the domain of existence sometimes referred to as "earthly" we choose our destiny. We are the writer, the director, and the producer of our role in the play of life in that dimension. Each experience is random chance, each life an individual destiny, a flicker in the Ultimate Reality. I cannot tell you or show you what the Ultimate Reality is; only a very few in your domain can divine a glimmer of it. I will tell you something you can understand. What you have in your physical domain, the earthly domain, is not all there is. Prepare yourself.

List of Characters

Bold type signifies those in the Donner Party who survived the ordeal.

Characters Who Were Real

George Donner, 62
Tamsen Eustis Donner, 45
Elitha Donner, 14
Leanna Donner, 12
Frances Donner, 6
Georgeanna Donner, 4
Eliza Donner, 3

Jacob Donner, 59
Elizabeth Donner, 45
Solomon Hook, 14
William Hook, 12
George Donner Jr., 9
Mary Donner, 7
Isaac Donner, 5
Samuel Donner, 4
Lewis Donner, 3

Employees/Traveling with the Donner families
Noah James, 20
Samuel Shoemaker, 25
John Denton, 28

James Reed, 45
Margaret Reed, 32
Virginia Backenstoe Reed, 13, Margaret's daughter
Martha (Patty) Reed, 9
James Reed Jr. 5
Thomas Reed, 3
Sarah Keyes, 73, Margaret's mother

Employees of the Reed Family
Eliza Williams, 31
Baylis Williams, 24
Milford Elliott, 28
Walter Herron, 25
James Smith, 25

Joining the Donner and Reed Families to form the "Donner Party"
Luke Halloran, 25
Charles Stanton, 35

Patrick Breen, 51
Margaret Breen, 40
John Breen, 14
Edward Breen, 13
Patrick Breen Jr., 11
Simon Breen, 9
Peter Breen, 7
James Breen, 5
Isabella Breen, infant

Traveling with the Breen Family
Patrick Dolan, 30

William Eddy, 28
Eleanor Eddy, 25
James Eddy, 3
Margaret Eddy, 1

Lavina (Levina) Murphy, 36, Widow of Jeremiah B. Murphy
Landrum Murphy, 16
Mary Murphy, 14

Lemuel Murphy, 12
William G. Murphy, 10
Simon P. Murphy, 8

Sarah Murphy Foster, 19, Lavina's daughter
William M. Foster, 30, Sarah's husband
George Foster, 4

Harriet Murphy Pike, 18, Lavina's daughter
William M. Pike, 25, Harriet's husband
Naomi Pike, 3
Catherine Pike, 1

Lewis Keseberg, 32
Philippine Keseberg, 23
Ada Keseberg, 3
Lewis Keseberg Jr., infant born on trail

Jacob Wolfinger, 26
Doris Wolfinger, 19

Karl Burger, 30 (Dutch Charley)
Augustus Spitzer, 30
Joseph Reinhardt, 30
Mr. Hardcoop, 60

William McCutcheon, 30
Amanda McCutcheon, 30
Harriet McCutcheon, infant

Franklin Ward Graves, 57
Elizabeth Cooper Graves, 45
Mary Ann Graves, 19
William C. Graves, 17
Eleanor Graves, 14
Lovina Graves, 12
Nancy Graves, 8
Jonathan B. Graves, 7
Franklin Ward Graves Jr., 5
Elizabeth Graves, infant

Sarah Fosdick Graves, 21, daughter
Jay Fosdick, 23, husband of Sarah

Employee/Traveling with Graves family
John Snyder, 25

John Baptiste Trudeau, 16
Antoine, 23

Miwok Indians
Luis, 19
Salvador, 28

Rescuers Mentioned
Charles L. Cady
Nicholas Clark
William O. Fallon
Charles Stone
John Stark
Reason Tucker
William Thompson

Others on the trail in 1846
Edwin Bryant
Lilburn Boggs
Jim Bridger
James Clyman
Reverend Cornwall
Reverend and Mrs. Dunleavy
Charles Frémont
Miles Goodyear
Jacob Harlan
Lansford Hastings
Mr. and Mrs. Hoppe
Lucinda
John Rhodes
Colonel "Owl" Russell
Captain John Sutter
William Sublette
Nancy and J. Quinn Thornton

Luis Vasquez
Joseph Walker
Old Bill Williams

Other Characters Who Were Fictional

Zeb, the old mountain man
Mr. New, mountain man.
Blue Whirlwind, Indian healer.
Little Elk
Mr. Tibbets, owner of the mule. The story of the mule is true.

Jim, the mountain man sent out from Ft. Bridger to doctor Edward Breen's leg. The story of a mountain man coming out from the fort is true.

List of Sources

Acuff, Marilyn. Keseberg family history.

Angier, Bradford. Stackpole Books, 1978. *Field Guide to Medicinal Wild Plants.*

Askenasy, Hans. *Cannibalism, From Sacrifice to Survival.* Prometheum Books, New York, 1994.

Bancroft, Hubert. *History of California, Vol. Five, 1846-1848.*

Bornali, Halder. Article: *Lakota Sioux Plant and Stone Symbolism.* LakotaArchives.com.

Breen, Patrick, *Diary*. Manuscript in Bancroft Library, University of California.

Brown, Dee. *The Gentle Tamers.* University of Nebraska Press, 1958.

Bryant, Edwin. *What I Saw in California.* University of Nebraska Press, 1985.

Clyman, James. *Journal of a Mountain Man*. Tamarack Books, Boise, Idaho.

Curran, Harold. *Fearful Crossing. The Central Overland Trail Through Nevada.* Nevada Publications, originally published in 1982.

Davis, William C. *Frontier Skills, The Tactics and Weapons that Won the American West.* The Lyons Press, Guilford, Conn., 2003.

Devoto, Bernard. *The Year of Decision 1846*. Little, Brown and Company, 1943.

Donner, Tamsen. *Letter,* May 11, 1846, manuscript in Huntington Library.

Donner, Tamsen. *Letter,* June 16, 1846. *Springfield Journal,* July 30, 1846.

Donovan, Lewis. *Pioneers of California, True Stories of Early Settlers in the Golden State.* Scottwall Associates, 1993.

Durham, Michael S. *Desert Between the Mountains,* Henry Holt & Company.

Egan, Ferol. *Fremont, Explorer For A Restless Nation.* University of Nevada Press, Reno, Nevada. Originally published by Doubleday, 1977.

Farnham, Eliza. *Narrative of the Emigration of the Donner Party to California in 1846. California Indoors and Out.* New York, 1856.

Graves, William C. "Crossing the Plains in '46," *The Russian River Flag* (Healdsburg).

Graydon, Charles K. *Trail of the First Wagons Over the Sierra Nevada.* The Patrice Press, Tucson, Arizona, 1986.

Hardesty, Donald L. *The Archaeology of the Donner Party.* University of Nevada Press, Reno, Nevada, 1997.

Harlan, Jacob Wright. *California, '36 to '48.* The Bancroft Company, 1888.

Hassrick, Royal B. *The Sioux, Life and Customs of a Warrior Society.* University of Oklahoma Press, 1964.

Houghton, Eliza P. Donner. *The Expedition of the Donner Party and Its Tragic Fate.* A.C. McClurg & Co., 1911

Johnson, Kristin. *"Unfortunate Emigrants" Narratives of the Donner Party.* Utah State University Press, Logan, Utah, 1996.

Johnson, Kristin. *Article: Tamsen's Other Children.* Donner Party Bulletin, September/October 1997.

Kelly, Charles. *Salt Desert Trails.* Western Epics, Inc., Salt Lake City, Utah.

King, Joseph A. *A New Look at the Donner Party,* K & K Publications, 1992.

Korns, J. Roderic & Morgan, Dale, Ed. Revised and Updated by Will Bagley and Harold Schindler. *West From For Bridger, The Pioneering of Immigrant Trails Across Utah, 1846-1850.* Utah State University Press, Logan, Utah, 1994.

Laycock, George. *The Mountain Men.* The Lyons Press, Guilford, Conn., 1988.

Lockley, Fred. *Conversations with Pioneer Women.* Rainy Day Press, Eugene, Oregon, 1981.

Lavender, David. *Bent's Fort.* University of Nebraska Press, 1954.

Luchetti, Cathy and Olwell, Carol. *Women of the West.* The Library of the American West. Orion Books.

Marcy, Randolph B. *The Prairie Traveler.* Applewood Books, originally published 1859.

McGlashan, C.F. *History of the Donner Party.* A.L. Bancroft Company, 1880.

Morgan, Dale Ed. *Overland in 1846: Diaries and Letters of the California-Oregon Trail.* University of Nebraska Press.

Mullen, Frank Jr. *The Donner Party Chronicles.* Nevada Humanities Committee, 1997.

Munkres, Robert L. *People & Places on the Road West.* New Concord Press, 2003.

Murphy, Virginia Reed. *Across the Plains in the Donner Party.* Outbooks, 1980.

Myres, Sandra L. *Westering Women and the Frontier Experience, 1800-1915.* University of New Mexico Press.

Peterson, Lee Allen. *A Field Guide to Edible Wild Plants.* Houghton Mifflin Company, New York, 1977.

Pringle, Lawrence. *Wild Foods,* Four Winds Press.

Reed, James Frazier. "From a California Emigrant, *Sangamo Journal* (Springfield). November 5, 1846.

Reed, James Frazier. "Narrative of the Sufferings of a Company of Emigrants in the Mountains of California, in the Winter of '46 & '47." *Illinois Journal* (Springfield).

Reed, James Frazier. "The Snow-Bound, Starved Emigrants of 1846." *Pacific Rural Press.*

Reed, James Frazier. *Letter, May 20, 1846.* Transcribed by Kristin Johnson, published by the Utah Crossroads Chapter of the Oregon-California Trails Association.

Schlissel, Lillian. *Women's Diaries of the Westward Journey.* Schoken Books, 1982.

Schmidt, Jo Ann. Donner family genealogy.

Stewart, George. *Ordeal By Hunger.* Henry Holt & Co., 1936.

The Gaps Index, *Listing of Old Disease Names and their Modern Definitions.* Genetic Information and Patient Services, Inc. (GAPS).

Thornton, Jessie Quinn. *Camp of Death: The Donner Party Mountain Camp 1846-47.* Harper & Brothers, New York, 1849.

Tilford, Gregory L. *Edible and Medicinal Plants of the West.* Mountain Press Publishing Co., 1997.

Whitman, Narcissa Prentiss. *My Journal, 1836.* Ye Galleon Press, Fairfield, Washington, 2002.

About the Author

Frankye Craig became interested in the Donner Party saga while developing a sesquicentennial event at Donner Memorial State Park in 1996. Since then she has become one of a number of people active in Donner Party history and has been interviewed several times for television programs. She has also put together a series of Donner Party events, including three cross-country tours. She lives in Reno, Nevada.

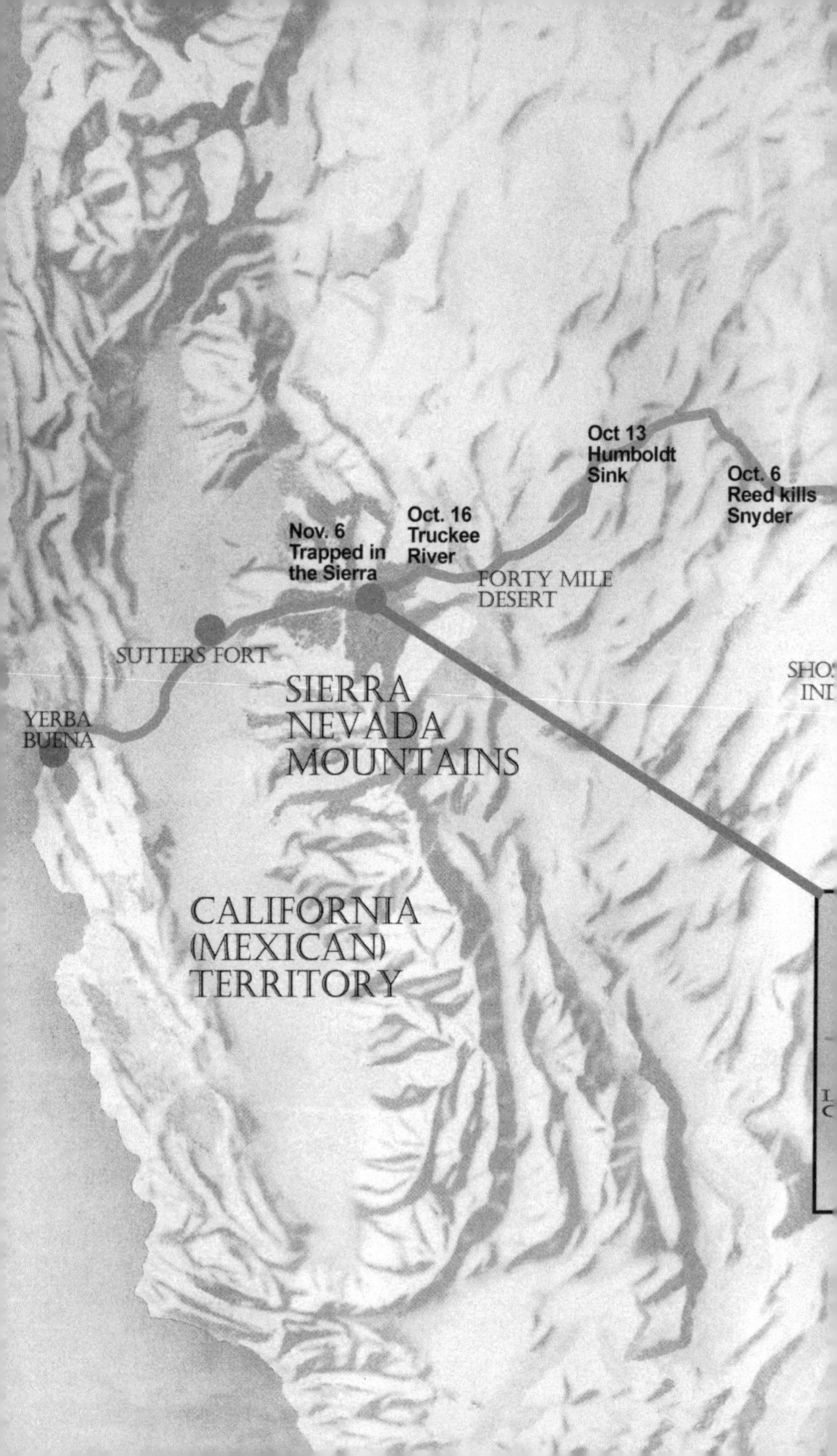
Oct 13
Humboldt
Sink
Oct. 6
Reed kills
Snyder
Oct. 16
Truckee
River
Nov. 6
Trapped in
the Sierra
FORTY MILE
DESERT
SUTTERS FORT
SIERRA
NEVADA
MOUNTAINS
YERBA
BUENA
CALIFORNIA
(MEXICAN)
TERRITORY

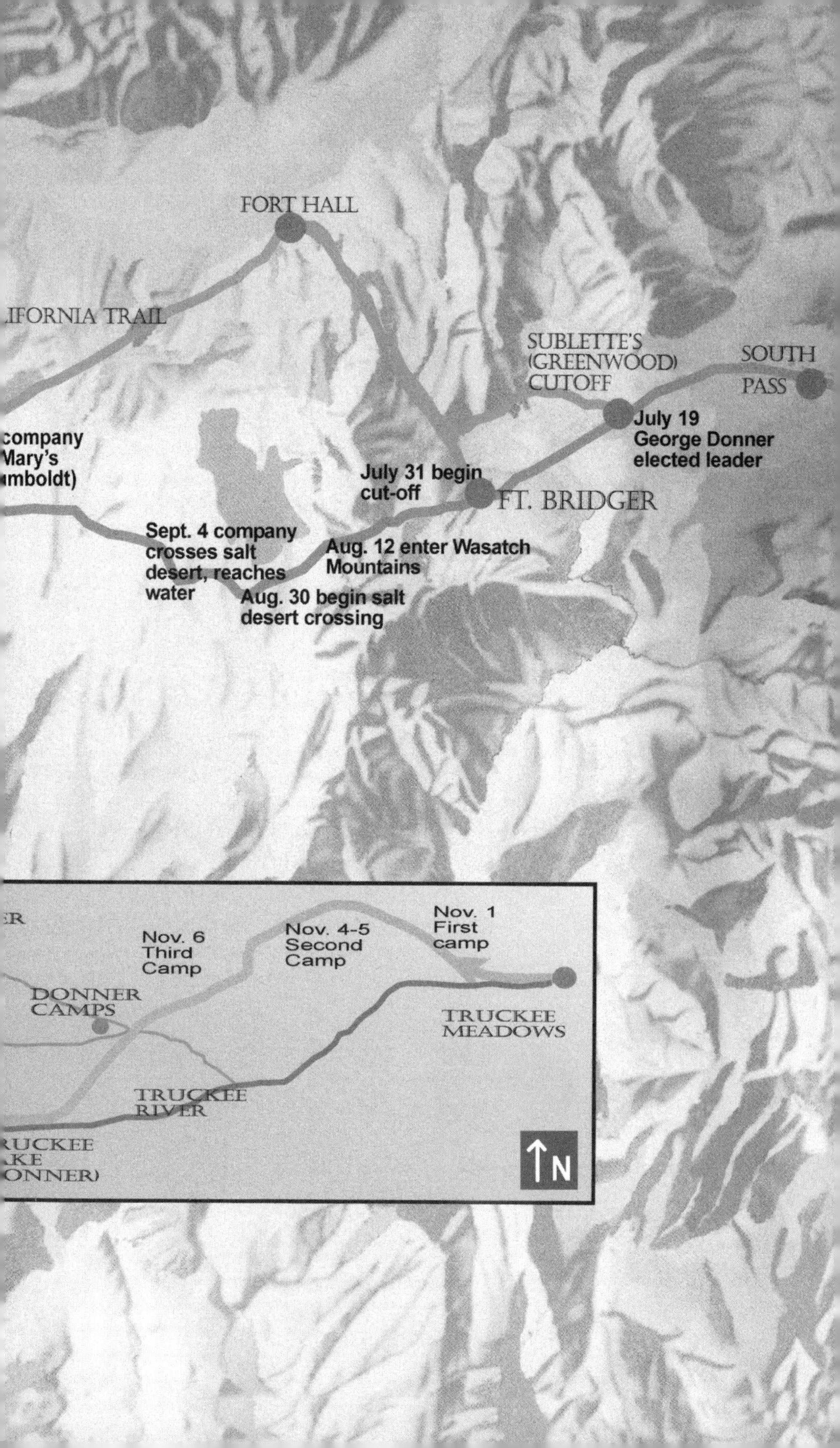

FORT HALL
IFORNIA TRAIL
SUBLETTE'S (GREENWOOD) CUTOFF
SOUTH PASS
July 19 George Donner elected leader
company Mary's mboldt)
July 31 begin cut-off
FT. BRIDGER
Sept. 4 company crosses salt desert, reaches water
Aug. 12 enter Wasatch Mountains
Aug. 30 begin salt desert crossing
Nov. 6 Third Camp
Nov. 4-5 Second Camp
Nov. 1 First camp
DONNER CAMPS
TRUCKEE MEADOWS
TRUCKEE RIVER
N